THE CRIMSHAW MEMORANDUM

- - - - -

HIJACK

- - - - -

Lionel White

Introduction by Rick Ollerman

Stark House Press • Eureka California

THE CRIMSHAW MEMORANDUM / HIJACK

Published by Stark House Press
1315 H Street
Eureka, CA 95501, USA
griffinskye3@sbcglobal.net
www.starkhousepress.com

THE CRIMSHAW MEMORANDUM
Originally published by E. P. Dutton & Co, Inc., New York, and
copyright © 1967 by Lionel White.

HIJACK
Originally published by Macfadden-Bartell, New York, and copyright ©
1969 by Lionel White.

Reprinted by permission of the Estate of Lionel White. All rights
reserved under International and Pan-American Copyright
Conventions.

"Crime à la White" copyright © 2017 by Rick Ollerman; revised version
copyright © 2025 by Rick Ollerman.

ISBN: 979-8-88601-141-8

Book design by Mark Shepard, shepgraphics.com
Proofreading by Bill Kelly
Cover art by James Heimer, jamesheimer.com.

First Stark House Press Edition: May 2025

THE CRIMSHAW MEMORANDUM

Harry Crimshaw, who seems to have fallen from his boat, is presumed drowned. Lt. Richard Martingale is assigned to help an insurance investigator confirm the missing man. It seems simple enough, except that Martingale senses something wrong about the situation. Crimshaw's wife, Marguerite, is set in receive $150,000 from his insurance policy, but seems curiously unconcerned about her husband. Crimshaw's boss is outright hostile, more concerned for Marguerite than the missing Harry. Martingale's casual assistance turns serious when the insurance man is severely beaten. Then it becomes personal when he himself is also attacked. But who could be behind these attacks… and why?

HIJACK

It's a hell of a plan. The four of them will kidnap the Boeing 707 that transports the old bills from L.A. to Denver for shredding. The easy part is taking over the plane. Scar, Handle, Sis and Dude—are enough to manage the small number of passengers, with Red waiting for them at the landing. Dude, the Captain, flew in Vietnam, and has no problem piloting the plane to their desert rendezvous. The problem is the passengers. One of them is an alcoholic with an attaché case full of booze. One is a defecting scientist, another his CIA keeper. One of them has just robbed the bank where he is a teller. And one is a jet-setter with a bottle full of pills. What could possibly go wrong?

LIONEL WHITE BIBLIOGRAPHY (1905-1985)

Fiction

Seven Hungry Men (1952; revised as *Run, Killer, Run!,* 1959)

The Snatchers (1953)

To Find a Killer (1954; reprinted as *Before I Die,* 1964)

Clean Break (1955; reprinted as *The Killing,* 1956)

Flight Into Terror (1955)

Love Trap (1955; reprinted in UK as *Right for Murder,* 1957)

The Big Caper (1955)

Operation—Murder (1956)

The House Next Door (1956; first published in *Cosmopolitan,* Aug 1956)

Hostage for a Hood (1957)

Death Takes the Bus (1957)

Invitation to Violence (1958)

Too Young to Die (1958)

Coffin for a Hood (1958)

Rafferty (1959)

Run, Killer, Run! (1959; re-write of *Seven Hungry Men,* 1952)

The Merriweather File (1959)

Lament for a Virgin (1960)

Marilyn K. (1960)

Steal Big (1960)

The Time of Terror (1960)

A Death at Sea (1961)

A Grave Undertaking (1961)

Obsession (1962) [screenplay published as *Pierrot le Fou: A Film,* 1969]

The Money Trap (1963)

The Ransomed Madonna (1964)

The House on K Street (1965)

A Party to Murder (1966)

The Mind Poisoners (1966; as Nick Carter, written with Valerie Moolman)

The Crimshaw Memorandum (1967)

The Night of the Rape (1967; reprinted as *Death of a City,* 1970)

Hijack (1969)

A Rich and Dangerous Game (1974)

Mexico Run (1974)

Jailbreak (1976; reprinted as *The Walled Yard,* 1978)

As L. W. Blanco

Spykill (1966)

Short Stories

Purely Personal (*Bluebook,* May 1953)

"Sorry—Your Party Doesn't Answer" (*Bluebook,* July 1954)

The Picture Window Murder (*Cosmopolitan,* Aug 1956; condensed version of *The House Next Door*)

To Kill a Wife (*Murder,* Sept 1956)

Invitation to Violence (*Alfred Hitchcock's Mystery Magazine,* May 1957; condensed version of novel)

Death of a City (*Argosy,* Jan 1971; condensed version of novel)

CRIME À LA WHITE

by Rick Ollerman

Lionel White was one of the most prolific and consistent writers of noir (French for "black" as most crime fiction readers are no doubt aware—ironically the opposite of his own surname). His characters were not always the most original but he imbued every one of them with the sort of depth usually found in works by authors working the literary genre. Only in White's case he needed to use only a tiny fraction of the words to do it. And his plots….

I have to say this: no one has ever been better at plotting a crime story than Lionel White. Either before him or after him. Almost every book reads like a master class in how to craft a story, be they written in first person or third.

Even better known and less forgotten names like Harry Whittington and Gil Brewer couldn't match the meticulousness of the straight-ahead, relentless style of storytelling in which White excelled. He was equally adept at writing from the first-person perspective as he was in the third. He could deliver a linear, sequential narrative, or carefully interlace his complex stories by alternating the close third-party points of view of his myriad characters.

Considered from a structural standpoint, his books cut like a sharpened scalpel with their precise details; not a hair is out of place. Even when he came close to something resembling a "happy" ending, the stories still ended up on a noirish note—it was not a happy time for everyone, especially the main character (with just a few exceptions).

There's always been that endless conversation of what kind of work constitutes the genre of "noir," what that word really means to the literary world. If readers want to figure it out for themselves, I tell people to read James M. Cain's *The Postman Always Rings Twice* (1934). Not only is that book a classic in its own right, it masterfully gives the reader all the elements most people think of when they consider noir. There's the *femme fatale*, the first-person protagonist who makes one bad choice followed by others as he tries to shortcut his way to a better life, the eventual betrayal, dirty deeds compounded with crime, and ultimately, the punishment, once so avoidable yet at the same time always so inevitable.

But still, they think, if things had just broken a different way, if only one lucky break could have come their way in this miserable life....

The shorter definition I like to use is much less prone to debate and I think crystallizes the noir concept more succinctly than analyzing a particular book: a noir story is one where the protagonist starts out screwed—and ends up screwe*der*.

The question of *femme fatales* or bad choices or anything other element always leads us to the inescapable fact that in noir, the protagonist has to be in worse shape at the end of the book than he was at the beginning. This is one of the reasons noir sequels are so rare and difficult to pull off—the protagonist has most likely already taken his last seat in an electric chair. Dan Marlowe pulled it off with *The Name of the Game Is Death* (1962) and its sequel, *One Endless Hour* (1969) by effectively rejuvenating his lost protagonist. In the first book "Earl Drake" is critically injured and left for dead after but he actually recovers at the start of the second book—and promptly does it all again.

In any case, this is why books like Dashiell Hammett's *The Maltese Falcon* (1930) or Raymond Chandler's *The Big Sleep* (1939) aren't noir. Physically, at least, Sam Spade and Philip Marlowe actually end up in pretty good shape when all is said and done. Where *Postman* is about as good an example of noir that's ever been written, most of Hammett's and Chandler's novels are examples of hard-boiled writing. Tough, unforgiving lean prose that hits hard and doesn't waste time on a lot of the touchy-feely things that might be missing on the underside of life.

As for White, he usually wrote in the same sort of pared down, simple sentence structure designed more to stab a point home rather than paint a pretty word picture in the reader's mind. Indeed, his deceptively simplistic style belies the intricate plotting as well as the emotional feel he has for each of his characters. Not only was White unquestionably an author of noir, his prose itself was mostly in the hard-boiled vein, especially when he approached such distasteful subjects as dangerous lust and even—in *Death of a City* (1970), where a racially split town is carefully engineered to implode thus clearing the way for the actual caper—the taboo of cannibalism (*!*). When it came to the actions of the criminal world, White's depictions were raw and cut as deep as he needed them to.

Much of this may have come from his time as an editor and publisher of "true confession" and "true detective" type magazines with names like *World Detective* and *Homicide Detective*. Born in Buffalo, New York on July 9th, 1905, White later died in Asheville, North Carolina, on the day after Christmas in 1985. In between he served in World War II, married twice, had a son, became a police reporter in in Ohio, and moved up the magazine publishing chain in New York City.

What we know him for today is, of course, his fiction, nearly forty novels of some of the hardest-boiled noir stories from the PBO, or paperback original, era. Starting in 1952 with a book in digest format from Rainbow Books (*Seven Hungry Men!;* it would see a somewhat altered version in paperback a few years later as *Run, Killer, Run!*), White's "first" book was a mass market paperback called *The Snatchers* for Gold Medal. He stamped out the model he would stay close to for most of his literary career. As the title boldly announces, *The Snatchers* is a book about a kidnapping. More importantly, though, it announces White to the world as a plotter second to no one—yes, even in that first book.

While the prose itself lacks all self-consciousness—a great trick for a beginning novelist, one that usually takes many, many words to achieve and was likely aided by his time with the newspapers—it may best be described as a reporting style applied to creative fiction.

Over time and more books, White's prose improves in style and quality but it never becomes his focus as a writer. For White, the stories always come first, with the characters coming in a close second. The writing was always up to the job but it was delivered with the blunt side of the blade, hard hitting and clear. Rainbows, sunsets and flower scents could only be distractions—there was no purple prose here.

Noir stories are ultimately stories of failure. What else could they be? There may be a failure of circumstance or of character but noir stories always end up with the main character in a far worse place than where they started. So what keeps reading them from being an exercise in depression and pity? If the characters are truly bad people, why is there such an audience for noir in both literature and in film?

It is far easier for an author to give his or her readers characters that are likeable, people that can be thought about in a good, positive way. But how to do that in the case of noir, where the characters are criminals, often living on the edge of society and picking at the scabs of the social underclass?

They may not start out as such but there's always that first step, that first wrong step, taken by someone who knows it's a bad move but takes it anyway, either through diffidence or a criminal nature. Or it could be greed. Lust for the wrong woman. A desire for the better life they never earned on their own.

On the other hand, sometimes the characters can be good people who have made so many wrong turns it seems as though fate has turned them into criminals or immoral degenerates because nature, in a way, has turned its back on them. It's not really their fault. Destiny has tagged them and it won't let go, at least not without the kind of fight the characters aren't willing or aren't able to win.

The key is that the reader doesn't necessarily have to care about the characters—after all, they're engaged in reprehensible things like murder and kidnapping—but readers do have to care what happens to them. We want their crimes to fail and for them to get the punishment they deserve, but we have to be *engaged* in the manner in which they fail and in which they are punished.

Otherwise we may as well be reading police reports while our stomachs are turning. Just as well we may be hoping against hope that they can rise above their circumstances and somewhere along the line finally make a right choice—it really doesn't matter. Everyone who commits a crime or is led astray in not always a *bad* guy.

This is a very narrow path for the author to walk but it is precisely that quality of making us care about characters we may despise that is the true magic and appeal of noir. It is what makes a compulsively readable book out of what otherwise would likely be a throw-it-across-the-room experience for the non-depraved. Without this quality the book could still be noir but would likely fail to garner much of an audience let alone become such an important and pervasive popular culture genre.

Very little of White's characters is described through dialogue, a departure not only from his PBO contemporaries but also from much of the crime fiction being produced today, where the name of the game is often a speedy yet engaging read through extensive use of dialogue. A thick book with lots of white space often fits the needs of the busy commuter.

White defines his characters mostly through exposition. He relates their back stories, their dreams, their past failures, almost solely through his succinct yet detailed and poignant portraits and description. It's this style or technique from White that allows us to get to know his characters and subtly obscure the lack of perceived lyricism or grace in his work. His stories are a series of gut punches, starting at the beginning where the crimes or capers are already laid out all the way through until the end, the often very bitter end. In a very short period of time, we know what White is delivering and most importantly, it *works*.

As a master of the caper novel—or better, the *failed* caper novel—this served White's unsurpassed plotting powers well.

If we name "literary fiction" merely another genre like "romance fiction" or "crime fiction," it's probably fair to say that character is more often paramount while plot itself is downplayed. It's like the silly question of asking which is more important, characterization or plot. That's really more of a reader's question—most established authors probably feel it takes strong usage of both elements to make a really good book. If an author gives you characters you don't like, you may not care what they do. On the other hand, if the plot is one that keeps you glued to your chair reading pages, you may be more inclined to forgive a somewhat dull or unoriginal character.

White strikes an elusive balance in his novels, giving us characters with enough emotional depth that readers can find ways to empathize with them, which is more than good enough to entrance us with his dazzling ability to chart a course through a story, even with a prose style that is other than pyrotechnic. His plot pulls us in but his characters make it matter and this is what makes White such a deceptively good writer.

In *Death Rides the Bus* (1957), he gives us a story that is made up of a string of interconnected character backgrounds, where almost no one is "good" though there is a wide variance of "bad." Though it has a far subtler plot than a book like *The Snatchers*, the hard-boiled prose carries us through to the end where the reader doesn't know until the very final sentences if the book is simply callow and sharp or if it's a true noir. Even up to the last paragraph, White reserves the ability to turn the book on its head by his character's actions and yet still manages to remain a noir novel without cheating anyone.

With 1970's *Death of a City*, White again uses the third-person technique where he jumps from character to character but also from situation to situation. What stands out in this book is how White gives us a bleak and narrow social commentary, namely race relations in a small city and how easily they can be manipulated by an outside agency for their own purposes (in other words, a really big series of crimes). In many ways it is a daring if unflattering book and in this day and age of political correctness where it's all too important not to risk offending anyone of any ethnic stripe, White is unsparing in his portrayal of income inequality in a city that boils over with the just right combination of violence and rumor. It is an absolutely unsparing picture of mob mentality at its most dangerous. If White's books are blueprints, this is one we don't want the bad guys to read…

.

Filmmakers have also found use of White's brilliant plotting skills although some have been quite ironic in their approach. French "new wave" pioneer Jean-Luc Godard adapted—or perhaps more accurately was inspired by—White's 1962 novel, *Obsession*. Although it stars beautiful people like Jean-Paul Belmondo and the stunning Anna Karina, Godard's wife, the cinematic style of *Pierrot le Fou* ("Pierrot the Crazy") having no script and coming up with dialogue the morning of each day's shooting could not be more opposed to White's meticulous approach to plotting. The result may be a standout example of the *Nouvelle Vague* movement but as an illustration of White's strengths of deep characters and intricate plots, the movie comes off as anything but. Still, Godard liked noir as source material and even made a film version of Donald Westlake's/Richard Stark's *The Hunter*, starring his Karina as a female version of Parker in the movie, *Made In the U.S.A.* (1966). Once again, though, the effect of the film is far different from that of the source book.

A better use of White's work as the basis of film work is made in an episode of the overlooked television anthology series *Thriller*, hosted by Boris Karloff. Season one, episode 21 is named after White's 1959 novel, *The Merriweather File*.

Although it is impossible to film everything in a novel for even a two-hour movie (and not likely desirable), it is obviously even more difficult to capture the essence in a one-hour (minus commercials) television script. Even so, the show does a wonderful job of capturing the essence of the story at that length, giving the viewer more than just the gist of the plot.

Oddly enough, in the book version, White shows perhaps an unexpected versatility with his prose by not only telling the story in the first person from a non-criminal's point of view, but also writing in a decidedly gothic tone. It combines crime, romance, sorrow and suspense in a tightly woven plot that keeps the reader guessing despite how many times White appears to give the simple and obvious answer to the book's puzzle. You can almost smell the after-dinner brandy coming off the dusty old narrator's top lip as the oaken logs burn in the fireplace.

An even more faithful rendition of book to movie was given to us with White's book, *The Money Trap* (1963). The book doesn't start out with a ready-made cast of criminals implementing their version of the "can't fail" caper but rather with two policemen who stumble into something they find too tempting to pass up. One of the cops is motivated mostly by greed while the other, a no-nonsense salt of the earth grinder who had the misfortune to marry over his head, makes the noir-requisite bad decisions.

In 1965 Burt Kennedy, a director known mostly for his television work (mostly in westerns), worked with one-time blacklisted writer Walter Bernstein to bring us the big screen version of this book. It was one of five movies underrated actor Glenn Ford made with one-time pinup Rita Hayworth, and also starred Elke Sommer, Ricardo Montalban and Joseph Cotten.

The black and white movie is a faithful adaptation of the mood of White's book and the entire cast gives a nearly pitch perfect performance as the story focuses on how one man especially rises to his level of incompetency. And yes, the ending is a quintessentially noir one—no one wins.

The Money Trap is certainly one of the two best films made from Lionel White's books although it is far from the most famous and well-known. That award has to go to a movie made from the 1955 novel *Clean Break*. In fact, the film version eventually became so successful that subsequent editions of the novel were published under the title given to the movie. It became known as *The Killing*.

The film became a critical darling but only turned out to be a mediocre box office draw. Time, as it has done for many works of art initially overlooked, has increased *The Killing*'s—and director Stanley Kubrick's, whom many regard as one of the most brilliant filmmakers America has ever produced—reputation and status. The movie, though shot in only twenty-some days (twenty to twenty-four, depending on who's doing the telling), has come to be known as a film noir classic.

The Killing still stands as a classic of film noir and despite Kubrick's lower regard for writers, it follows Lionel White's plotting about as well as it can, adding touches of voiceover narration to smooth over some of the viewpoint jumps in the book.

Another notable adaptation of a Lionel White book is the Herbert Cornfield directed version of *The Snatchers*. Cornfield only helmed a handful of films and probably peaked with the 1962 release of *Pressure Point* which starred Bobby Darin and Sidney Poitier. Cornfield found trouble with his next film, *The Night of the Following Day* (1968), that included a Marlon Brando who was magnetic as ever on screen but who lived up to every bit of his difficult reputation both on and off it. Richard Boone also starred in an eerily watchable portrayal of a sexually sadistic member of *The Snatcher*'s kidnapping mob and for a while, the performances of these two, plus that of the criminally underrated and underappreciated Rita Moreno, almost make this film rise above the tepid filmmaking style.

We also have Robert Steven's version of *The Big Caper* (1957) starring Rory Calhoun and the beautiful Mary Costa (who went on to have a bigger career singing opera than she did acting in movies, where her biggest highlight is the voicing of Aurora in Walt Disney's animated *Sleeping Beauty* (1959)). Here screenwriter Martin Berkeley takes just enough from White's book to keep the story roughly the same—the biggest differences are in the natures of some of the main characters.

Where the movie falls flat is at the climax, an overwrought fight scene between Calhoun and James Gregory. The entire film seems to build up to the one dramatic confrontation that attempts to show a knock-down, drag-out, no-holds-barred fight between the two principals, but it suffers from a major problem: it looks for all the world as though the scene had neither been properly choreographed or rehearsed.

Two other oddities emerge from the world of filmmaking and Lionel

White's work. First, his 1959 novel *Rafferty* was made into a three-and-a-half-hour television movie in the former Soviet Union. Secondly, *Obsession*, the same White novel that was used as the basis for Godard's *Pierotte le Fou*, also served as the inspiration for a Finnish movie called *Karvat* (1974), or in English, *The Hair*. Like Godard's film, Seppo Huunonen's version also leaned more to the comedic than to something resembling actual film noir.

White did try his hand at a few stories outside of actual noir. As previously mentioned, his first book appeared as a Rainbow Books digest magazine called *Seven Hungry Men!* The cover featured several taboos of the time, including a shirtless black man playing with a knife, a nasty expression on his face, alone in a cabin with a haughty white women wearing a high-slitted skirt and tipping a bottle of booze.

The back cover is almost equally scandalous—it shows a black and white photograph of a woman resembling the one from the front cover wearing nothing but a matching set of underwear and a wide-open lacy peignoir. Shocking stuff for 1952's America.

Unusually for White, the ending of the book has something of a happy ending, at least for the surviving characters. But when the book was reprinted in mass market by Avon in 1959, the title had not only been changed to *Run, Killer, Run!* but it had a more typical White ending. It was both romantic and noir and delivered with a subtle and bittersweet touch.

In 1966 White published a novel called *Spykill* with Lancer Books that featured "freelance counterspy" Tom Marco under the name "L. W. Blanco" ("blanco" is the Spanish word for "white"). The name and the book may have been an attempt by White to jump into the burgeoning post-pulp men's adventure genre but regardless, the book necessarily has a more successful ending for Tom Marco's first and apparently last appearance.

That same year, an entry in the long-running men's adventure series featuring Nick Carter, Killmaster, an agent of a government agency known as AXE, was issued by Award Books. Carter was a character who had first appeared in a serialized story in 1886 and was the subject of a series of attempted revivals as he evolved throughout the pulp years, finally culminating in the Killmaster series of over two hundred and sixty novels, all written under the house name, "Nick Carter."

White's entry, *The Mind Poisoners*, was the eighteenth in the series and was begun under a pseudonym and then finished by a woman named Valerie Moolman, the author, co-author, or reviser of a number of other Killmaster titles. Could the pseudonym White used have been "L.W. Blanco," and could the book originally have been intended as another Tom Marco book? Those answers may have been lost to time, but once again, as a series book, it once again ends with a happy ending—in more ways than one—for both Nick Carter and the woman he's with at the time, Chelsea Chase.

White certainly fell prey to the prejudices that affected so many Caucasians of his era. His portrayal of minorities can be painful to read in the light of not only what should be a more socially enlightened society but one that's also afflicted with the vapid insipidness of "political correctness." Like most of his contemporaries, White's use of stereotypes in light of today's sensibilities don't hold up any more than you'd expect.

White treats his female characters with a bit more complexity. They can be good and they can be bad. They could be dumb or they could be razor sharp, brave or cowardly, virtuous or loose. One thing they almost always are is powerful. Rarely as powerful as a man, they usually have the power to undo any of them.

White's men can be made by a woman or broken by one. There is often a contest going on between which man gets a particular woman, or how a woman can reverse their role and bring down a man. What we don't see are women who are ineffective or casual observers. Women are often critical to the success or failure of any given caper and they're just as often the impetus when the perfect crime begins to unravel.

Critics of White's work often point to what they see as misogynistic tendencies or too many times invoking rape, or the threat of rape in his books. White treats rape as an awful, unforgivable act—it may be fair to say he treats it as the worst thing that can happen to a woman; it certainly carries more weight than even a casual murder— and he never uses it as titillation for the reader, ever.

What he does do is show is the act as a characteristic, the worst sort of characteristic, of some of most despicable characters he's created. He writes it as a horror, as a terrible threat or even experience, and in some ways it makes his stories more starkly realistic, at least in his eyes. Women who live among criminals, who take their money and their booze, can find themselves misused in the worst of ways. A virtuous woman can experience the threat of rape as the ultimate demise, even worse than death.

To White there was no such thing as a casual rape. The fact that he wrote about it as often as he did can, I think, be seen as repugnant to White, a consequence to and for the sort of people he wrote about. These were bad people. To him, rape was the ultimate ravage, the one thing he couldn't condone, so he used it in the books where he wrote about his most hardcore and depraved criminals.

While it can make for uncomfortable reading, the threat of rape is also an effective though politically incorrect (by today's standards, at the very least) device. One has to wonder if he would be "allowed" to write those scenes today. Likewise, would a major publishing house like Dutton put out a hardcover titled *The Night of the Rape* in 1967? Certainly not. (Though its effects are devastating, which is a theme of the novel, the event itself takes place well offscreen.)

Ultimately, no matter how we break down or analyze an author's body of work, especially in fiction, the thing most of us want to know more than anything else is simply, "Is this writer any good?" Lionel White's books are very good, some rather excellent, and like Hammett's or Chandler's and countless others, are very much of the times in which they were written.

His three dozen or so books are all meticulously plotted and planned, with nary a scene out of place. White never gives us the sense that he is winging it or is lost or is putting words on paper just to put words on paper. He is not an improviser. Every chapter or page marks a cog in the larger machine of his story. His characters have depth though they often give a sense of being trapped in their own bodies, as if their lives have a fey quality and their failures preordained. Success (usually in the form of money) is the butterfly they will never stop chasing even as it flies further and further from their grasp, sometimes by mere inches.

White's work has inspired other crime writers, most notably Donald Westlake, and given inspiration to a dozen screen works, of both the large and small variety. He sold millions of books, starting with the digests and moving to mass market paperbacks with Gold Medal, Avon and others. When Dutton started publishing hardcover crime fiction, White published with them, a hallmark many other PBO authors never achieved.

There are only so many places to rob or steal from and indeed some of White's settings sometimes seem to overlap. He uses a few of the same techniques in a few books, including methods of laundering bills with noted serial numbers into more anonymous lots of cash. Undeniably clever stuff but like with many if not most writers of non-series books at the time, it's probably a better idea not to read too many of one author's books in a row. Styles become too familiar, for one thing, and a unique stylist like White are best appreciated with a little space left between.

The certainty here is that what White did best, no one else did better. The plots for his crime fiction could be used as blueprints for actual crimes as well as scene layouts for feature films. He did this with characters who if sometimes not quite inspired were at least easily understood, their weighty motives giving them more heft than they'd have in lesser hands.

The quality of his prose grew with each book, and it is pleasantly surprising when he turns his considerable skills to a new voice or style. He was that rare writer that could offset any weakness with even greater strengths.

And it bears repeating that no one could plot a crime novel like Lionel White. If you don't know what this means, just pick up one of his books and you'll see it from the first page. Perhaps the rough portrayals of some of his female characters holds him back in the eyes of today's literary climate, but perhaps not. It could be that the dearth of information about Lionel White the man makes it easier for the work to simmer just below the public eye and is keeping him from being rediscovered as handily as his work deserves. This certainly wasn't the case while he was alive and at his peak, and for fans of hard-boiled writing, of true noir writing, White should not be missed.

If you happen to be a crook looking for a better way to pull a heist without getting caught, well, I'm sure you could do worse, though with tools like DNA testing and ever-increasing video surveillance, you'd be better off just reading a book. Remember, these books are prime examples of noir.

Better to pick up *The Snatchers* or *The Merriweather File* and see how someone else did it, or how they failed to do it, at least in the imagination of one of the all-time PBO greats. The more attention you pay to what he's doing the more it can only add to your pleasure and appreciation of the magic behind the curtain.

Just do yourself a favor and don't get any ideas. Banks and racetracks aren't what they once were, you know.

—January, 2017
Littleton, NH

[Originally published in an unabridged version as the introduction to *The Snatchers / Clean Break*, March 2017, Stark House Press.]

....

Sources:
Crider, Bill, entry from *Twentieth Century Crime and Mystery Writers, 2nd Ed.*, ed. by John Reilly, St. Martin's Press, 1985
Haut, Woody, *Heartbreak and Vine,* Serpent's Tail, 2002

THE CRIMSHAW MEMORANDUM

- - - - -

Lionel White

Chapter 1

1.

It's going to be another scorching, humid, July day. The perspiration is already forming beads on my forehead and staining my shirt, but I'll still have time to shower and change before leaving for the church in St. Michaels. I'm not due until two o'clock, which should give me a fair amount of time to complete my report on the Crimshaw Case.

Our plans called for a quiet, private wedding, not only because we had both been married before but also because of the unfortunate notoriety surrounding the events of the last few months. It is because of these plans that I'll be driving over to the small, out-of-the-way village on the Eastern Shore.

It's difficult for me to take my mind off the events that will take place in a few hours, but I must put all personal thoughts aside and finish what I have to do. I must make out the last of my official memorandums on the Crimshaw Case, and close it forever.

In a sense, it is only proper that I should be ending this case in the very room where, so far as I am concerned, it all started. I'm sitting in a private office on the second floor of the Maryland State Police Headquarters in Pikesville. The gilt sign on the pebbled-glass door reads DETECTIVE DIVISION, Lt. RICHARD MARTINGALE. It has been my office for three years now, since the time I was promoted from the rank of sergeant in the State Troopers to that of lieutenant, and assigned to plainclothes duty in the Criminal Investigation Division.

The public image of a State Trooper is that of a rather tall, well-built, clean-cut chap who wears a neat, well-tailored uniform, drives around in a high-powered sedan with a spotlight and siren combination on the roof, and hands out tickets for speeding and other traffic offenses.

The public fails to realize that very frequently the State Police do a great deal more than merely handle traffic problems. In Maryland, for instance, as in many other states, the State Police has its own detective division, which handles all major crimes—and many minor ones—in all areas with the exception of the very largest towns and cities.

I happen to be one of those who became a trooper because I wanted a career as a law officer. I chose the State Police because I didn't want to be connected with a purely local law enforcement agency, which all too often is politically oriented. I wanted to do detective work and I took a law degree at night, as I believed it would aid my career.

I believe I fit the pattern most of the other ways. I'm reasonably clean-cut, stand six feet two, weigh a hundred and seventy-five pounds, have sandy blond hair and blue eyes. I'm thirty-four years old, spent four years in the Air Force and was mustered out as a captain. I've been married and divorced, drink only moderately, smoke too much, keep in good physical condition. I don't care for spectator sports, prefer sailing to fishing, do a certain amount of gunning during the season.

My work takes me all over the state. For the past year I've been on a sort of troubleshooting assignment that takes me wherever my immediate boss, Captain Carey Rhinelander, decides to send me. I keep an apartment in Baltimore, but spend more nights in strange beds than I do in my own. I have a private, unmarked car assigned to me, but use my own two-year-old Ford station wagon when I'm off duty.

I don't make a great deal of money and, unfortunately, I spend what I make just about as fast as I make it.

I like to bet on the horses and play poker. I don't play around with women, but I guess that's because, after my three years of marriage with Pat, whom I divorced, I was pretty well fed up so far as women were concerned.

That will have to do as a thumbnail sketch; I must get on with the Crimshaw Case.

I shall never forget the first time I met Marguerite Crimshaw.

Almost exactly one year ago, a humid day toward the end of July, late in the afternoon, and Captain Rhinelander on the intercom, asking me to stop by his office for a moment if I wasn't tied up. I was tied up trying to get a report out on that rumble down at Cambridge, on the Eastern Shore, where trouble had broken out again between some Freedom Riders and the local merchants, and someone had set off an incendiary bomb. We try not to take sides, but when some hothead starts tossing around dynamite or committing arson, we step in fast. It was tricky and complicated because local feelings were running pretty high.

I was looking forward to twenty-four hours off—and a weekend over at Rehobeth for a little swimming and lying in the sun—but I should have known better. The Captain has a positive genius for finding some matter particularly urgent at just about the time I'm ready for leave.

This one didn't sound so urgent, but because it was a personal friend of the Captain's who'd called in about it, it might as well have been.

"Dick," Captain Rhinelander said, when I walked into his office, "Dick, I just had Lloyd Wilson on the wire. Friend of mine; don't know whether you know him, but he's a great chap. Investigator for the Missouri and Texas Indemnity Company."

"I've heard you mention him," I said. I hadn't of course, but the Captain, who is really a great guy, likes to think that you never fail to remember anything he might ever have said in your presence.

The Captain nodded as though I could have said nothing else. "Lloyd tells me his firm is carrying a hundred-and-fifty-thousand-dollar life policy on Harry Crimshaw."

I nodded, trying to look intelligent.

"You remember reading about the Crimshaw business of course," the Captain said.

I didn't. In a vague way the name sort of rang a bell, but just what bell failed to register.

"Crimshaw?"

The Captain was too fair to be annoyed, but he was disappointed.

"The fellow over on the Eastern Shore. You know, about a week or so ago. Fell off a damned boat or something. Anyway, Lloyd called me all in a heat and said that his company has this hundred-and-fifty-thousand-dollar policy on him."

"And he was drowned?" I asked.

The Captain shrugged.

"They usually are," he said. "I haven't checked, but as I remember, his body didn't turn up, just the outboard. He'd gone out fishing alone, around dusk, and they found the empty boat the following day.

"Lloyd just got the notice from his office about the policy and has been assigned to make a routine investigation. So the first thing he did was call me and ask if we had anything on it."

"It would be too early for anyone to file a claim," I began, but he quickly interrupted me.

"Damn it, I know that. But that isn't the problem. I didn't want to plead stupid, so I told Lloyd I'd make a check and see just what we might have. I called the barracks over in Easton—it's in their jurisdiction—but all they have is a routine missing-persons. Guy went fishing; apparently a squall hit him and he went overboard. Body has not turned up. Nothing particularly unusual about it. Except now it turns out he was insured for a hundred and fifty thousand dollars."

I shrugged. I couldn't get too excited. "After all," I said, "that's why they take out insurance. So in case of an accident—"

"Don't read me any lines," Captain Rhinelander said. "I feel the same way you do, but in this case there is one slightly unusual angle. The Crimshaw character was a used-car salesman, worked in Baltimore. He and his wife rented a summer place over on the Shore where they spent weekends. Probably makes about a hundred and fifty a week. The hundred-and-fifty-thousand policy doesn't exactly fit."

I had to agree with that.

"So Lloyd is naturally concerned."

He would be. Under the best of conditions, insurance companies suffer when they get hit in the teeth for a hundred and fifty grand. But if they think there's a little fraud involved along the line, they really start screaming.

"We haven't been asked to investigate or anything like that—yet," the Captain said. "But Lloyd is a friend, and anyway it's always nice to have our hand in in advance. So . . ."

"So you want me to—"

"I want you to check the Easton report, check with the Coast Guard and Maryland Fisheries Commission, which would naturally have made an inquiry into anything involving an accident on the Chesapeake, and then take a ride out to Severna Park."

Severna Park was about forty-five miles of heavy traffic away, and I could see my Rehobeth Beach plans shot sky-high for the weekend.

"The Crimshaws rented a house there. I had my girl make a call, and she set up an appointment for you to see Mrs. Crimshaw, the wife, this evening. Now, don't try to grill her or anything; just talk to her. I just want you to try and get a feeling about it. You know, if anything smells a little fishy or anything . . ."

Captain Rhinelander and his damned friends. I would be doing this Lloyd Wilson's job for him, and the Captain knew it, but he asked anyway. Of course in one sense he was right about it. If a crime had been committed—and fraud against an insurance company is considered a crime—it was our duty to investigate even if the insurance people do have their own private staff of snoopers.

"If you get anything," the Captain said, "give me a buzz. I'll be around most of the night. Don't bother to call Lloyd directly; he's going to be over at the beach with his family for the weekend."

I was about to say, Fine, I hope he drowns, but considered it a little indiscreet, so I merely said I'd follow it up, and went back to finish the report on Cambridge before canceling my weekend reservation.

2.

I left headquarters a little after seven. A few phone calls had filled me in with certain incidental information that might or might not come in handy. A newspaper editor over in Easton gave me the brief outline of the tragedy that had taken place the previous weekend.

Harry Crimshaw and his wife, Marguerite, had a rented cottage near Bellevue, and they had driven down from Severna Park on Friday night.

Crimshaw was thirty-eight years old; his wife was twenty-five, and they were childless. They had been married for two years. On Saturday afternoon, around six o'clock, Crimshaw had loaded his fishing gear into a sixteen-foot outboard motorboat and taken off from the dock in front of his place on the Choptank River so as to be out on the fishing grounds off Sharps Island in the Chesapeake Bay for the turn of the tide at about dusk.

They had had a party the night before, and neighbors had complained about the noise. My friend the editor said that it was very likely that Crimshaw had a classic hangover on Saturday. His wife denied that he'd had anything but a single Bloody Mary to drink before he left to go fishing, but she did say he'd taken along an ice chest with a couple of six-packs of beer. He may or may not also have taken a bottle of booze. An empty gin bottle was found on the drifting boat the next day, but it could have been left over from a previous trip. The icebox still held four cans of beer.

Crimshaw had told his wife he might be late getting back. He had running lights, a set of charts and a good compass, and the usual lifesaving jackets, and so on aboard. He often stayed out half the night when he went fishing, particularly if he was having any luck.

Thunderstorms and squalls hit the area around nine o'clock, and according to weather reports, winds up to thirty knots were blowing late in the evening off the Chesapeake. Because Crimshaw was pretty familiar with the water, Mrs. Crimshaw hadn't been too worried; but she should have been. No sixteen-foot boat, and especially no outboard with a low stern, is safe on the shallow water of the bay in that kind of weather.

Mrs. Crimshaw had gone to bed around midnight. She didn't realize that her husband had failed to return until she awakened next morning to find herself alone in the room. At eight o'clock on Sunday morning she called the Tidewater Fisheries and reported him missing, as she knew that their boats patrolled the nearby waters. They in turn notified the Coast Guard.

Mrs. Crimshaw believed it quite possible that her husband, realizing the weather was getting rough, might have cut in for one of the offshore islands and decided to sit it out until the seas calmed down. He had done so on several previous occasions, and, not carrying a ship-to-shore radio, would have no way of notifying her.

The Coast Guard felt the same way about it, although they were a little more concerned. A man with a hangover in a small boat with beer and booze on board always worries them.

At three fifteen on Sunday afternoon, two college boys sailing a Rhodes Thirty, out of Annapolis, sighted a drifting outboard boat some two miles off Chesapeake City, on the west coast of the Bay and a few miles to the south of a point across from Sharps Island. When they saw the boat was unoccupied, they drew abreast and made it fast.

They at once noticed that the cover of the outboard motor had been removed and that there were tools lying on the back seat. The boat was half full of water, and they at once assumed that the owner had had engine trouble, had tried to make repairs, and been washed overboard. An anchor and line were in the boat, and the boys knew that if whoever had been in it had been taken off by another craft, he would have either had it towed or tossed out his anchor.

They raised the Coast Guard on their ship's radio and were met halfway back to Annapolis. There were neither clothes nor personal effects on the drifting, half-sunk craft, but a quick check of the marine number on her bow established that it was registered in the name of Harry Crimshaw of Severna Park, Maryland.

Mrs. Crimshaw was notified by the State Police. A search for the missing man or his remains was at once instituted. The fact that the body had not turned up by the end of the week was not too unusual. The Chesapeake is a big body of water. Drowned bodies, contrary to general opinion, do not always come floating to the top; the tides and currents and rips can carry them for miles and snag them on the bottom for weeks or months or forever.

That is what I got from my friend the weekly-newspaper editor.

The Police Barracks at Easton didn't have a great deal to add.

The Crimshaws had been renting the summer place for only a few weeks. They had rented the same place the previous summer. They didn't mix with the natives but had a few friends among the other summer people. The friendships were pretty limited as there are very few strictly summer people on the Eastern Shore. They threw parties now and then, but mostly for out-of-town visitors. Mrs. Crimshaw was considered a nice, pleasant little woman, and the shopkeepers spoke well of her. Her husband was considered pretty wild. Apparently he'd been a vaudeville actor or an entertainer at one time or another, and he was supposed to have a good voice. In any case, the neighbors said that they'd had to complain a couple of times because of his singing late at night and playing his hi-fi stereo set at all hours at the top of its capacity.

Crimshaw had no police record and so far as was known had never been in trouble. He was considered a bad credit risk, and owed money both on the Shore and in Severna Park. Weekends he spent a good deal of time on the water. Mrs. Crimshaw did not like the water and rarely went out with him. He usually fished alone, and the few people who knew him or had seen him around thought he knew how to handle small boats.

So far as anyone knew, he and his wife got on well enough together. No investigation in depth had been made, of course. It was generally assumed that the man had merely been the victim of a small-boat accident and his own stupidity. It happens all the time.

Mrs. Crimshaw had left for Severna Park on the Tuesday following the accident and had not returned to the Eastern Shore.

The Coast Guard were still holding the outboard and the equipment that had been found aboard.

A telephone call established one other fact.

The outboard motor undoubtedly had conked out. A loose connection between the distributor and the coils was discovered, and it was safe to assume that Harry Crimshaw had attempted to make repairs sometime during the dark of the night and in the heavy seas. He would of necessity have had to take considerable risk, leaning far over the stern, to have accomplished anything. Even sober, it would have been damned risky.

3.

It was just after eight o'clock on Saturday evening, with almost an hour of sunlight still to go, when I turned off Ritchie Highway into Severna Park. Severna Park is actually more of a suburb of Baltimore than a town in itself, a pleasant collection of well-designed modern homes on well-proportioned, nicely landscaped plots. I would guess that they cost somewhere between twenty-five and fifty thousand dollars for the most part, and they are inhabited by families who like to surround themselves with pleasant modern conveniences, if not actual luxuries.

I found Randolf Avenue without difficulty, and when I drove up and parked in front of Number 72, I was at once struck by the charm of the rather large, sprawling one-story home set well back on the tree-shaded green lawn. It occurred to me that either Crimshaw must have a private income to augment that hundred and fifty a week he made as a car salesman or else had been living just a bit beyond his means.

The shades in the house were drawn, which could have been because of the heat, and it had a vacant, deserted look about it. But a white convertible was parked in the driveway, facing the closed doors of the double garage, so I got out and walked up the flagstone path to the front door.

I put my finger on the doorbell and heard the sound of chimes inside. While I waited I took a cigarette from the pack in my jacket and lighted it—and then, after a little wait, again punched the bell. I didn't hear the sound of approaching footsteps and was about to give it up as a lost cause when the door suddenly opened.

"Yes?"

The small, slender girl gazing up at me with wide-spaced, deep brown-flecked eyes had a pert, slightly turned-up nose above a generous mouth. She looked like a child fresh out of high school.

"I'm looking for Mrs. Crimshaw," I said, and smiled down at her. There was an odd quality in that small upturned face—innocence, naïveté, whatever it might be—that made me smile.

She said, "Come in," and turned, holding the door open. Crossing the deep-piled pale-blue wall-to-wall carpet that covered the entrance hallway, I followed her into the beamed-ceiling living room, a room some twenty by thirty-two feet, with a huge fireplace, lined by bookshelves, at the far end.

I didn't sit down in the great red-leather couch that she indicated with a nod of her head, but stood in the center of the room and took the card out of my case and handed it to her.

"If you would just give this to Mrs. Crimshaw ..." I began.

She took the card from my hand—it merely carried my name and rank and the insignia of the State Police—and glancing at it, again looked up into my face, without expression.

"I'm Mrs. Crimshaw," she said. "Won't you please sit down? I suppose it's about Harry."

She walked past me and sat in a small, green upholstered chair a few feet from the couch I dropped into. She still held my card in her hand, and her eyes again went to it.

"They haven't—they haven't found him, have they, Lieutenant?"

"No—I'm sorry. I hate to bother you at this time," I began, "but I am anxious to verify certain details...."

"I've told the authorities everything I knew several times," she said. "I want to do anything I can, but it is rather hopeless after this length of time, isn't it?"

You usually tell them that it is never hopeless, but for some reason I found it impossible. I knew that if her husband hadn't turned up within a week, there was almost no possibility that he would be found. Of course, there was every likelihood that the body would come to the surface sooner or later, but that would be small compensation.

"I'm afraid there is little chance your husband is still alive, Mrs. Crimshaw," I said. "I'd like to be optimistic, but ..."

She gave an odd little toss of her head and interrupted me.

"My husband is dead, Lieutenant," she said in a voice that was little more than a whisper. "I am quite sure that Harry was drowned. I don't believe there is anything—"

"One can never be sure," I said quickly. "There is always a chance a passing streamer, outward bound from Baltimore ..."

She shook her head.

"Steamers have radios—ship-to-shore sets—on board," she interposed. "No, I'm afraid there is no point in fooling myself. But exactly what is it, Lieutenant, that you wish to talk about?"

She suddenly stood up, this time pushing that vagrant lock of honey straw hair back with her right hand.

"I was just making coffee," she said. "Won't you let me bring you a cup? Or perhaps you would rather have a drink. I believe Harry has some Scotch. I don't often take a drink myself, but I'll be glad to get you—"

"Coffee will be fine for me," I said.

"I'll only be a moment."

She was gone for several minutes, and while she was out of the room my mind was busy trying to organize my thoughts and reactions.

For a newly made widow, Mrs. Crimshaw was showing an amazing amount of control. It wasn't just that she didn't show grief; there was an almost total absence of any emotion in her voice and manner. And yet in this first impression of her, I couldn't help sensing that this woman was certainly neither cold nor unemotional.

I didn't say anything as she handed me the thin china cup that held the coffee and then extended the tray with the sugar bowl and cream pitcher.

She spoke as she stirred her own cup.

"Why are the police interested, Lieutenant?" she asked. "Is it because you suspect foul play, if that is the correct expression?"

"Not exactly," I said. "I understand that your husband was not carrying anything but a little change with him. That there were no known enemies . . ."

"Oh, Harry had a few enemies all right," she said suddenly. "Customers who thought he'd cheated them. People he owed money to, but I don't believe there was anyone who cared enough, or hated him enough, to have done anything to him. Harry had a lot of charm, and there were some very nice things about him. I guess most people felt about him the way I felt—and still feel."

I looked up quickly at her then, and this time she smiled. It was a small little smile, almost whimsical.

"Please don't be shocked, Lieutenant," she said. "There is really no point in my faking something I simply do not feel. I've been married for two years now, but for more than a year my husband has meant very little to me. I certainly never wished him dead; but it has been a long time since I loved him, and very frequently, during this last year, I didn't like him very much either."

I took a sip of the coffee, more to stall for a second than because I wanted it.

"Perhaps you would like to tell me about it," I said at last

"About what?"

"About your relations with your husband."

Again she sort of half shook her head.

"There is nothing to tell," she said finally. "I was in love with my husband when I married him. I stopped being in love with him. There was no other woman, or man, involved or anything like that. I just stopped."

"And your husband? Did he stop being in love with you?"

She was thoughtful for several moments.

"No," she said at last. "He didn't. He was in love with me when he married me, and I believe he was still in love with me on the day he was drowned."

"And did he know that you were no longer in love with him?"

She looked at me curiously for a full minute.

"If you are thinking that he might have committed suicide," she said, "you couldn't be more wrong. Harry was far too selfish, far too satisfied with himself and confident in himself ever to have taken his own life. But to answer your question: It would never have occurred to Harry that anyone could not love him. Harry Crimshaw was probably one of the world's most conceited men. He didn't need anyone to love him. He was far too much in love with himself."

I could sense her freezing up then and I knew that she would say nothing more about her personal feelings. So I changed the subject and got around to discussing what I had really come to talk about.

"I understand," I said, "that Mr. Crimshaw carried a hundred-and-fifty-thousand-dollar insurance policy on his life."

She nodded.

"Yes, he did. It was a gift to me on our wedding day."

"Wasn't it just a little unusual?" I suggested. "After all, I believe that your husband earned something in the neighborhood of seventy-five-hundred dollars a year. The premiums alone would have . . ."

"The policy was typical of Harry," she said. "He liked to make expensive gestures. As I say, he gave me the policy as a wedding present. I was named the beneficiary, and he had paid up two years' premiums in advance. Later on, he wanted to borrow against the policy when we needed money, but I refused to give the necessary permission. Harry always needed money, and of course when he took out the policy he was quite positive that in no time at all one of his wild schemes would pay off and he would be able to afford it."

"Of course you realize that unless his body does turn up, there may be certain difficulties in collecting...."

She nodded quickly.

"I really couldn't care less," she said. "I have no great desire to capitalize on my husband's death."

For the first time her voice showed a trace of anger, and I felt a slight embarrassment.

Damn it, why had Captain Rhinelander involved me in this thing in the first place? What right did he have asking me to do Lloyd Wilson's dirty work for him? I was beginning to feel like a bastard, sitting there harassing this girl with the sweet face and the tired, unhappy voice. No matter how she might speak of her dead husband, she was going through a bad time.

I wanted to change the subject, so I said, "Do you plan to return to the Eastern Shore or will you close the place?"

For a moment she looked as though she didn't quite understand me, and then her face took on a lost, helpless expression.

"I really don't know what I'm going to do," she said. "This whole thing has happened so suddenly...."

She seemed to sink down in her chair, and once more gave that odd little shake of her head. I started to stand up, but stopped halfway, interrupted by the front-door chimes.

For a moment she looked startled and then quickly got to her feet. She didn't excuse herself but quickly left the room.

I heard their voices in a moment and I waited. A moment later a tall, rather heavy-set man with a bald head and baby-blue eyes stepped into the living room. He was immaculately dressed and he held a half-smoked cigar in a highly manicured right hand. There was a large sapphire ring on the middle finger.

"Lieutenant Martingale?"

I nodded.

"My name's Compton. Loring Compton. Harry Crimshaw worked for me."

I held out my hand, which he studiously avoided seeing.

"Alice, my wife, and I just dropped by to see how Marguerite was doing. She says you've been questioning her."

"That's right," I said.

"Well, the poor kid's tired and upset, and I think the least the police could do would be to leave her in peace," Compton said. "God knows she's had enough to go through these last few days without having to face—"

"I'm sorry, Mr. Compton," I interrupted, "but we were merely checking up and—"

"Checking up what? What the hell's to check up? Harry went out on his boat and was drowned. It's as simple as that. God knows this little girl has had to go through enough without the police coming around and giving her some sort of third degree."

"I have not been giving any sort of third degree," I said, "and we haven't wanted to make any extra trouble for Mrs. Crimshaw, but there are a few questions—"

"You come see me and I'll answer any question you got," Compton said. "I've sent Alice in to take Marguerite to bed. The kid is dead on her feet and needs rest. You want to ask her any more questions, I'll get her a lawyer and you can—"

"Oh, I hardly think a lawyer will be necessary," I said.

"Okay, then." He whipped a card out of his inner breast pocket. "You come around to my office Monday morning. I know more about Harry Crimshaw than anyone else does. I'll tell you any damned thing you want to know. That's my address and phone number, and I suggest you call before you come by."

"I will," I said

"Good. Now if you will just leave, I'll go back inside and see that the girls are all right and if they want anything. Someone has to look after them. But you come by and see me Monday morning."

I hesitated for just a second in the doorway.

"Tell me one thing now, Mr. Compton," I said. "Do you think Harry Crimshaw is still alive?"

The blue eyes suddenly hardened and he flicked an ash angrily from the end of the cigar to the carpet. He didn't answer for several seconds and I didn't think he was going to, but at last he spoke, and his voice was bitter.

"That son of a bitch," he said. "Anybody would have asked me that question a week ago, I'd have said he was too selfish to ever die. But he's dead all right. You can be sure of that. Harry Crimshaw is dead, and it's probably the only decent break he's ever given that little sweetheart he married."

Chapter 2

1.

I could have still gone on to Rehobeth Beach for the weekend. I could have gone on back to my apartment in Baltimore. I could have called Captain Rhinelander and let him know what I had found out. I did none of these three things.

I went to a bar and sat in a booth by myself and ordered a double bourbon and water without ice. I wanted to do a little thinking.

As a policeman I didn't like it. I didn't like it at all. Going over in my mind the few facts I had at hand, I began to consider the various possibilities.

Harry Crimshaw could have drowned. Every bit of evidence pointed to the fact that he was dead. Accepting this premise, there were two possibilities:

It was an accident.

It could have happened exactly as all evidence seemed to indicate. A man had foolishly ignored weather reports: his motor had conked out; he'd been washed overboard and drowned when he attempted to make repairs. What little I had learned of Crimshaw, combined with the physical evidence in the case, certainly upheld this theory.

Or—it was not an accident.

Crimshaw could purposely have taken his own life so that his wife might collect insurance. Crimshaw could have been murdered.

Murder. A hundred-and-fifty-thousand-dollar insurance policy is always a possible motive. And Harry Crimshaw, from the little I knew of him, was the type of man who may very well have inspired homicide.

One thing was certain. Loring Compton had no particular love for the man who had been his employee.

Compton had rubbed me the wrong way. It wasn't only his manner, his brusqueness, his appearance. I began to realize that what I had resented was his proprietary attitude toward Mrs. Crimshaw.

It suddenly occurred to me that I was being a bit unfair. Why in the hell should I care if he had a proprietary manner? What was Mrs. Crimshaw to me?

And that was when I ordered another double bourbon and began to think about Harry Crimshaw's wife.

Policeman are, contrary to the opinion of a good many people, human beings. And no man is capable of completely desensitizing himself. A good police officer tries to avoid any personal relationship with the people who may be involved in an investigation he is making. He wants no emotional strings that might in any way prejudice his judgment. He wants to be under no obligations, financial or emotional or any other.

But it isn't always possible.

From the few moments I had spent talking with Mrs. Crimshaw, I liked her. I liked her a great deal. I'll be completely honest. I not only liked her as a person; I found her extremely attractive as a woman. She aroused a sexual desire in me. This is something I had felt for no woman since the day I had made the discovery that the woman I loved and to whom I was married was sleeping around with other men.

Perhaps my year of celibacy had suddenly made me vulnerable. I quickly finished the bourbon and went to the phone booth in the lobby. I put in a call for Captain Rhinelander.

The desk sergeant who took the call told me that the Captain had left for the night, and I was about to hang up when he said, "By the way, Lieutenant, I have a message for you."

"Yes."

"A man named . . ." he hesitated for a moment, apparently checking his sheet . . . "named Lloyd Wilson left a number and asked if you'd give him a ring when you called in." He gave me the number and hung up. Lloyd Wilson must have talked with the Captain after I had left, and apparently the Captain had told him he'd asked me to make an investigation.

I left the phone booth and went to the desk and changed a five-dollar bill into change. Mrs. Rhinelander answered my call and told me the Captain had been home but had just left. She didn't tell me where he'd gone, and I knew that Captain Rhinelander would not have told her.

A good policeman with a properly trained wife never does tell her where he goes if he's called out on a case. Cops don't like their wives worrying. He'd left no message for me.

The operator rang Lloyd Wilson's number at least a dozen times before I gave up.

I went back to the table and called for a check. I suddenly decided that I would take a run over to Talbot County on the Eastern Shore. There was a motel on the outskirts of town where I could spend the night and get a few hours' sleep. In the morning I would locate the Shore cottage the Crimshaws had rented. I wanted to look the place over and talk to some of their neighbors.

Actually, I was not on the case officially, and I was probably about to do a little more than the Captain had really asked me to do. But I was on my own time and I was curious. Not necessarily curious about the disappearance of Harry Crimshaw so much as I was curious about that very pretty, very attractive widow he had left behind when he had taken the outboard out to go fishing in stormy weather.

2.

The desk sergeant at the Easton Barracks of the State Police gave me the information I wanted when I stopped by at ten o'clock on Sunday morning.

"Crimshaw," he said, when I asked my question. "Yeah, I know the place he rented. He's that guy got drowned a week ago when his outboard conked out, right?"

"Right."

"Well, he rented a sort of fishing and hunting cabin on the old Fletcher place. That's out on Benoni Point, where the Tred Avon converges with the Choptank River. You familiar with the area?"

I told him that I wasn't particularly, so he dug out a county map.

"You drive through Easton and out the St. Michaels Road," he said. "Turn off and go through Royal Oak and head for Bellevue. About a half mile before you reach the village you turn right." He traced it out on the map with a red pencil.

"Horace Fletcher lives in the main house, which you have to pass to reach the cottage. It's a pretty big estate. I'd say probably three, four hundred acres. Some of the best damned gunning on the Shore. The old man lives alone in the place. His wife died a couple of years back, and the kids have all left. Has a couple or three in help and he's pretty much a recluse. If you're going out there you best stop by and see him first. Place will probably be locked up."

I told him I would, and he got on the phone. He talked for several minutes and then hung up.

"The old boy says to come on out. Don't stop at the main house. He won't be there. He was just about to go down to the cabin himself. Seems that yesterday the Coast Guard returned the outboard Crimshaw was drowned from. The boat belongs to Fletcher; he had let Crimshaw use it when he came down for weekends. The old boy probably wants to check it for damage. Anyway, he'll be down at the cottage. It's about a quarter of a mile past the manor house. You can't miss it. You'll see a big duck blind a couple of hundred feet offshore, and just as it comes into view the road turns right and there's the cottage. He'll either be there or at the dock."

"You seem to know the layout pretty well, Sergeant," I said.

"I should. Used to gun that spot when I was a kid. That was before Horace Fletcher inherited it. He don't let anyone gun there now but himself."

"Did you know the Crimshaws?" I asked.

He shook his head. "Heard of 'em, that's all. We had Crimshaw in here at least twice on a drunk test. Passed. He used to collect tickets like they were going out of style. Drove an XKE. But I never personally met him. Understand he was pretty wild. But I know old Horace Fletcher. Think he's related to the Du Ponts or some of that crowd. Filthy rich. But a pretty nice old guy, even if he won't let anyone shoot his property."

I thanked the sergeant for his help, rolled up the map he'd marked for me, and got back into my car. I stopped at the inn at the center of town and had a breakfast of creamed dried beef, toast and coffee. I picked up a *Baltimore Sun* and a *New York Times* and started out for the Fletcher place.

I found it with no trouble. A long, tree-lined drive led to the main house, a beautiful old colonial that must have contained at least twenty-four rooms. A colored man wearing a short apron was in the driveway, polishing a ten-year-old Rolls-Royce town car; he looked at me curiously as I drove past him and on toward the waterfront.

The duck blind came into view, and I made the turn and there was the cabin. The sergeant had described it as a hunting and fishing shack, but it was actually a handsome cottage, with old brick and a wide screen porch. It faced the water. I parked in the driveway and got out and walked toward the dock.

A very tall thin man, wearing only a pair of faded canvas shorts, with bare feet and a face almost burned black, was leaning over a sixteen-foot outboard skiff that had been pulled up on the shore and turned over. He looked at me with sharp blue eyes under a wide brow and a thatch of uncombed white hair, straightening as I approached.

He didn't smile or speak.

I introduced myself.

"I'm Fletcher," he said. "Glad to see you. Now, just what can I do for you?"

I told him that I was investigating the Crimshaw drowning, and asked if I might take a look at both the boat and the cottage.

"The man drowned," he said. "Why are the police interested?"

"Well, when there appears to be a death and there is no body—which means no autopsy—we always make at least a superficial investigation," I said, not strictly sticking to the truth. But it sounded fairly logical.

He looked thoughtful for a moment, and then nodded. "Well, here's the boat," he said. "Coast Guard returned it last night but they still have the outboard motor, if they salvaged it. Boat belongs to me but the motor was Crimshaw's. Boat doesn't seem to be damaged, but it certainly was swamped all right. Cushions, Crimshaw's tackle box and equipment and stuff were in it, and I had one of my boys take it all up to the cottage. Damn fool. He should have known better than to take it out in that kind of weather."

"Were you well acquainted with the Crimshaws?" I asked.

He shook his head.

"Yes and no. They rented the cottage here for the summer for the last couple of years. Didn't know Crimshaw to speak of. Didn't like him either. But Betty—that's my youngest; she's married now and lives out in Arizona with her husband—Betty went to school with Marguerite Braintree. That's Mrs. Crimshaw. Never would have rented them the cottage if it weren't for Betty."

"You say the boat belongs to you?"

He nodded.

"Crimshaw bought it but never paid me for it," he said. "I know just how the fool drowned himself." He walked over toward the skiff.

"She's turned over now so you can't see," Fletcher explained, "but this boat has mahogany decks. Crimshaw waxed the decks down. I told him it was dangerous. Makes them too damned slippery. When his engine failed, he must have laid out on the deck surrounding the cockpit where the outboard goes in. It was the only way he would be able to work on it. Even in a relatively calm sea, with no one to hold his feet, it would have been foolish. Guess he just slid right off. Damn fool. Had to make it look shiny and flashy with his wax and all. He was a great one for appearances. Well, it cost him his life. You want to look the boat over? I can have the boys turn her up on the keel."

"I don't think it will be necessary," I said. "But I would like to take a look at the house they occupied."

"It's okay with me," Fletcher said. "Although I don't see what that has to do with it."

He led the way and we went to the cottage. The door was open, and I followed him in. I was surprised by the luxuriousness of the furnishings. It was a lot more than a simple hunting and fishing lodge. It looked like a very expensive guest house.

"Take a seat," he said. I did.

"I understand they had the place last year as well as this summer?" Fletcher nodded.

"Through no fault of mine," he said. "Betty, that's my daughter I mentioned, rented it to Marguerite. And then early this summer Crimshaw showed up and wanted a summer rental. Said he just wanted it for weekends and a two-week vacation. Normally I don't even want to rent the place, but because I knew that they really couldn't afford a summer place, I told him he could have it. I could get a couple of thousand for a summer rental—there's a pool and it's pretty comfortable. But I told him right out I knew he was running on short money so I'd let him have it for two hundred and fifty. Well, you know what the phony did? He said he wouldn't dream of taking advantage of me—that he'd pay me fifteen hundred. So he owed me the fifteen hundred. He was the kind would rather owe fifteen hundred than pay two fifty in cash. I had his number last summer when the finance company man showed up several times threatening to pick up that fancy foreign car he was driving around in. A red Jaguar. I tell you, if it wasn't for my daughter's friendship with his wife, I wouldn't have put up with him for a minute."

"You say he was a phony, Mr. Fletcher...."

"Just a personal opinion. He wasn't my type. One of those handsome, happy-go-lucky guys. All charm and no guts. And a really fast talker. Tried to sell me a car and was always trying to get me interested in backing him in some wild venture or another. Must have been crazy. I wouldn't have backed him in a peanut stand."

"He was carrying a hundred-and-fifty-thousand-dollar life insurance policy," I said. "Seems a little odd for a man who you say was rather irresponsible."

Fletcher looked up at me sharply. He nodded, and I could see the way his mind was working. I could also see that the information surprised him.

"Well, I'll be damned," he said. "Last fellow in the world I would have thought would have made any provision for his wife. At least he's worth a lot more to her dead than he was alive."

"How did they seem to get on together, Mr. Fletcher?"

His eyes narrowed. He grunted.

"I was wondering why a policeman would be down here asking questions," he said. "So that's it, eh? The insurance policy. Well, let me get you straight on a couple of things. If you think there was anything wrong—that is to say, if you think there was anything funny going on about that accident—you're dead mistaken. It was an accident, pure and simple. Harry Crimshaw wasn't the man to kill himself so his wife could collect an insurance policy. Not by a long shot."

He had been leaning against the mantelpiece over the fireplace and now he crossed over and stood looking out the window toward the water. He spoke with his back turned to me.

"I'll tell you right out," he said, "that I think Marguerite was getting a little fed up with her husband. I knew that she was embarrassed about his debts and his chiseling and a lot of other things. He was one of those charm boys who had to take over at parties. Liked to sing and play a guitar, and I must admit he was good at it. Told funny, or at least dirty, stories. It would embarrass her."

He swung around then and stared at me, almost defensively.

"The night he was lost"—he hesitated, thinking for a minute—"that would be a week ago last night; Marguerite Crimshaw spent the evening over at my house. I had guests, the Printemps from Washington. She came over to make a fourth at bridge. We played until after midnight, and I walked her back here myself. Saturday morning I sent Howard—he's my farmer—down here with a couple of quarts of milk. We keep a few cows on the place. Mrs. Crimshaw was still sleeping, but she got up when he knocked on the door, to take the milk and put it in the refrigerator. So if the police have any idea that there was something wrong . . ."

I quickly shook my head.

"Quite the contrary," I said quickly. "As I explained, we always make a routine investigation in cases of this kind. I was merely curious because of a few things I'd heard about Crimshaw."

Fletcher reached over and picked up a framed photograph from an end table and held it out.

"Here's a picture of him," he said. "You'll find photos of him all over the place. That's the kind of fellow he was. In love with himself."

I reached for the photograph.

It was a studio shot and it showed only the head and shoulders. The photographer had not only caught Harry Crimshaw's dark, good looks, but also caught the intrinsic vanity in the man. It looked like the publicity picture of a Hollywood actor. A lean, rectangular face, high forehead, and dark curly hair with an attractive streak of gray dramatically cutting through the center. It was in semi-profile and showed to best advantage the fine, deep-set eyes under rather shaggy brows, small ears, a good nose over a generous though slightly petulant mouth. A square, masculine chin.

In the lower, right-hand corner was an inscription in a flowing, theatrical hand:

From Harry to the girl he adores, on her twenty-fifth birthday— Harry.

"That's Crimshaw," Fletcher said sourly. "The kind of man who gives his wife a picture of himself on her birthday. You want to look around you'll find several more just like it around the place."

3.

Fletcher had things to do and he left shortly, telling me to take my time in looking around. There wasn't much to see.

He was right about the photos of Crimshaw. They were all over the place: Harry Crimshaw playing a guitar, Harry Crimshaw sitting on a piano bench and singing, Harry Crimshaw . . . No point in enumerating. The odd thing was that there were no pictures of Harry Crimshaw and his wife. In fact, there were no photos of Marguerite Crimshaw at all.

They had obviously taken the cottage furnished. I was surprised in checking through the living room, the small dining alcove, the library, to find almost no personal possessions. There were two bedrooms, each with its private tiled bath. The first bedroom held twin beds, made up, but when I lifted the bedspread, I saw there were neither sheets nor blankets. Its bathroom was completely bare, and so I assumed this was used only as a guest room.

There was a king-sized bed in the second room and it too was made up, but it had sheets and blankets and pillows. An oversized double closet held both men's and women's clothes; two bureaus also contained clothes. The bathroom was one of those modern affairs with both shower and tub and twin sinks. Above each sink was a medicine cabinet, and the first one must have been used by Mrs. Crimshaw. It held the usual compliment of aspirins and minor medicinal bottles, as well as a collection of cosmetics. The other cabinet contained nothing but an electric razor and a bottle of hair tonic. There was an electric toothbrush on a sideboard.

I was a little surprised. From what I had learned of Harry Crimshaw, I would have expected him to have had more beauty aids than his wife.

Nowhere in the place were any letters, bills, or personal papers. I realized of course that Mrs. Crimshaw might have taken things home with her when she'd returned to Severna Park. But the almost complete lack of any personal possessions, aside from the clothes and those photos of Harry Crimshaw, seemed unusual.

4.

Horace Fletcher was checking the polishing job his man had done on the Rolls when I drove past on my way out. I stopped to thank him for his cooperation.

"Will Mrs. Crimshaw be coming back or has she given up the cottage?" I asked.

"Didn't say," he said. "She's welcome to its use as long as she wants it, and I told her so when she left earlier in the week. She knew that her husband hadn't paid the rent, but I told her it didn't matter. She was still pretty upset of course, and probably wasn't even hearing what I said. Her car was piled with stuff, so I don't really know if she plans to come back or not."

I turned in at the driveway leading to the nearest neighbor, but there was no one home, so I went on into Easton and stopped at the inn. I put in a call for Captain Rhinelander; his wife said he'd been called down to his office a half hour ago. When I finally got him on the phone, he sounded excited, which is a little unusual for the Captain.

"Where in hell are you?" he asked at once.

I told him I was over on the Eastern Shore.

"Well, get back here as fast as you can," he said. "Did you see Mrs.

Crimshaw last night?"

I said I had.

"What time?"

"I talked to her between eight and eight thirty. Why? Has something—"

"Plenty. Lloyd Wilson was found in the back of his car, badly beaten and unconscious, a couple of hours ago. The car was parked in front of the Crimshaw place out there in Severna Park. He's in emergency at Johns Hopkins. You get here as soon as you can."

He hung up before I had a chance to ask a question.

Chapter 3

1.

By the time I got back to Pikesville and had walked into Captain Rhinelander's office, it was almost four thirty. I wanted to know what had happened to Wilson, but the Captain didn't even let me get in a question. He was anxious to know about my interview with Mrs. Crimshaw. I gave him a detailed report of my conversation with her, and told him about meeting Loring Compton, Crimshaw's employer. When I mentioned going to the Eastern Shore to make a further check, he looked at me quizzically.

"How did you happen to go over there?" he asked at once. "I just wanted you to talk to the widow. After all, we aren't officially on this case. I was just trying to do Lloyd a favor."

"Well, I became interested and I—"

"You mean something about Mrs. Crimshaw led you to suspect . . ."

I shook my head.

"No—nothing about Mrs. Crimshaw. I can't explain it, but I began to have the feeling there might be a little more to it than a simple drowning or accident." I told him what I had learned on the Shore and then I asked about Lloyd Wilson.

"I can't understand it," the Captain said. "I talked with Lloyd Saturday morning, and he told me he was headed for the beach with his family for the weekend. He has a couple of teenage kids, I understand. Anyway, at twelve o'clock this noon, a report came in that he'd been found unconscious in the back of his car in Severna Park.

"Lloyd is still in emergency, unconscious, so no one has any real information as yet. I'm waiting for a call from the hospital right now. Somebody beat the living hell out of him. From the doctor's first report, it would appear that he was gone over with a blackjack. Concussion with a possible fractured skull, mouth and teeth smashed in, his face a mess. Whoever did it may or may not have been trying to kill him, but they certainly wanted to punish him.

"We checked as much as we could. His car was found parked in front of the Crimshaw place. He was crouched down in the back, more or less out of sight. We checked with Mrs. Crimshaw first, and she denies knowing anything about it at all. Told us she saw the car outside early this morning but had no idea it was Lloyd's. The officer who talked with her had the impression she was telling the truth.

"We checked the neighbors. No one heard a thing, but it would appear that Lloyd was beaten up outside his car and tossed back into it when he was unconscious. A woman across the street swears that the car was not there when she and her husband got home shortly after midnight. No one else remembers seeing it either. But around seven thirty this morning, a guy down the street was walking his dog, and he says the car was parked there at that time. A couple of other neighbors also remember seeing it early this morning.

"Around eleven thirty a patrol car happened to be driving by, and the officer noticed that the parking lights were on. He got out to cut off the switch. That's when he saw Lloyd crumpled up in the back. And that is every blessed thing we have."

"Has anyone been in contact with Mrs. Wilson?"

"We don't even know where she is. All we know is that they were due to go to the beach. Of course, we've called his home in Baltimore, but there is no one there. I have a man trying to get hold of someone from his firm in an attempt to find out where they might have been planning to go. But so far—"

The telephone interrupted him and he picked up the receiver. He listened for a moment or two, grunted, and hung up.

I started to get up.

"By the way," the Captain said, "one other thing. When Lloyd was found, his wallet and a platinum wristwatch were still on him. There were around seventy-eight dollars in his wallet. It would sort of rule out robbery. And so far as mistaken identity or anything like that is concerned, well, it's just a little bit too much of a coincidence. An insurance investigator found beaten half to death in front of the beneficiary of a pretty big policy who happens to have been—"

He didn't finish.

"I'll try to talk to him," I said. I hesitated as I reached the door. "By the way, Captain, am I now officially on the Crimshaw Case?"

"Hell," the Captain grumbled, "there is no Crimshaw Case, at least as yet. But we do happen to have laws in this state against trying to kill guys driving around in cars—even if they do happen to be insurance-company investigators. And as far as the Crimshaw thing goes, I can tell you one thing: Something smells. Something smells to high heaven."

2.

The resident doctor's name was Milton Bornstein. He wasn't at all enthusiastic about letting me talk with Lloyd Wilson. Dr. Bornstein was a short, fat, youngish man with thyroid eyes, a bulbous nose, and a deceptively slow way of speaking that might lead you to think he was a bit stupid. He wasn't; he was as bright as they come, and nobody was kidding him.

"Yes, he's conscious and he's going to be all right," Dr. Bornstein said. "I'll have him out of here within a week or ten days. But whoever went to work on him meant business. They made a mess of his face and they kicked his testicles up into his guts. Hit him around the kidneys, and they didn't use fists. They had either a piece of iron pipe or a leaded blackjack. You should see the guy's sides and groin."

"Can he talk?"

"Yeah, he can talk but just barely. Lost a few teeth of course. They got him in the throat a couple of times, but he was lucky. They missed the larynx. He can't see. Both eyes puffed closed. For a man in his late forties—his driving license says he's forty-eight—he took one hell of a beating. You come on back in a couple of days and maybe—"

"Look, Doctor," I said, "I'd really like to just ask him a couple of questions now and—"

"He isn't going anywhere. Why not wait and—"

"But you say he's out of danger."

"I didn't say that. I said I hope to have him out of here in a week or so. Anybody who's absorbed the beating this guy took can always be in danger. We don't think there's a skull fracture, but—"

"Well, if I were to spend just a minute or so with him, and you could be with me and I'd stop any time . . ."

"Oh, hell, all right. But just for a minute or so. He isn't going to get any pleasure out of talking, I can tell you that. I have him half doped up with morphine, but I guess he'll be able to understand you. Come on."

He led the way to a private room down the hallway and nodded to the nurse on duty, who left the room. I said hello to the trooper who was standing outside in the hallway when I entered, and I carefully closed the door after the nurse left.

He looked like a mummy. Bandages completely covered the upper part of his face and most of his head. Only the tip of his nose and a bruised pair of lips showed, and he was completely motionless. I thought he must be asleep.

"Mr. Wilson," Dr. Bornstein said, "I have Lieutenant Martingale of the State Police here with me. He says Captain Rhinelander sent him. He wants to ask you a few questions. If it bothers you too much to talk, you don't have to. I don't want you to strain yourself or tire yourself. Do you understand?"

The bruised mouth opened and emitted a sound.

I stepped closer.

It was only with the greatest difficulty that I was able to make sense of the words that came through his broken teeth. But Wilson seemed anxious to communicate with me, and the doctor didn't interfere as I persisted with my questions.

He remembered nothing of what had happened. At first he seemed concerned only that his wife and family not be told about it, but after the doctor had explained that he would be in the hospital for at least a week or more, he informed us that his wife would be home from the beach that evening. He didn't want her to see him in his present condition.

He said that he had worried about the Crimshaw Case after he'd been assigned to it and that after he'd taken his family to Ocean City, he'd decided to make the trip back to Severna Park Saturday evening to talk with Mrs. Crimshaw. He'd arrived, he thought, somewhere around eleven o'clock. He remembered parking in front of the house and getting out of the car. And that is the very last thing he did remember. He didn't know who had attacked him, whether it had been a single man or several. He didn't know a thing from the time he'd stopped in front of the place until he came to in the hospital. He wasn't much help.

I asked him if he'd talked to Mrs. Crimshaw previously, and he shook his head. With a great deal of difficulty, he told me that at the time Crimshaw had taken out the policy, he, Lloyd Wilson, had been the salesman who had handled the transaction. It was some six months later that he'd transferred from the sales force to the investigative division.

He explained it was because he had been the salesman in the case, and was the one assigned to investigate it after Crimshaw's death, he'd taken a particular interest. He'd felt personally responsible. That was why he had suddenly decided to interrupt his weekend vacation to see Mrs. Crimshaw.

I was about to ask him how he'd happened to meet Crimshaw in the first place when Dr. Bornstein interrupted and put a stop to my questions.

He reached over and felt Wilson's pulse, then called the nurse and gave her instructions about a hypo. "I want him to rest now," he said. "He's had enough for the time being. Any more questions, you can come back tomorrow or the day after."

I thanked him for his courtesy, and left.

It was just possible someone not connected with the case could have had a grudge against Wilson. He could have been followed and attacked when he parked his car. But I didn't believe it for a moment. It was, however, a loose end that I would like to clear up. I decided to call the office to see if Mrs. Wilson had been found and notified. If not, I would suggest I go out to her house that evening and see her when she returned from the beach.

3.

It was around eight o'clock when I started to drive out to the Wilson house in North Baltimore. I had contacted the office and been told that Mrs. Wilson had not as yet been informed of her husband's accident, as no one had been able to ferret her out over at the beach. The Captain had had a man waiting at the house to tell her the news when she returned, but he recalled him when I volunteered to take on the task.

I thought it rather strange that she had made no missing-persons report. After all, Lloyd Wilson had told his wife early Saturday evening that he had some work to do on a case and would be back sometime that same night. He had not returned or tried to get in touch with her. It would have seemed only natural that she might have become worried.

Perhaps he was the sort of man whose wife was used to having him disappear for a day or so at a time without letting her hear from him. But I doubted it. He was a personal friend of the Captain, and Captain Rhinelander has pretty conservative friends.

The moment I pulled up and parked in front of the modest ranch house, I knew that the family must have returned. It wasn't quite dark, but every light in the place was on. As I got out of my car, I vaguely wondered how they'd managed to get back. Wilson had been found in his car earlier in the day in Severna Park, and even had the family had two cars—there was none in the driveway at the side of the house—I doubted if they would have taken them both for a weekend at the beach.

I shrugged and walked up to the front door.

They had returned all right, and with a bang. The windows in the front of the house were open, and the crash of someone playing the drums almost shattered my ears. Above the din, I could hear a female voice yelling something as I pushed my finger on the doorbell. I had to ring several times.

Whoever was playing the drums suddenly stopped, and for a second there was a dead silence. A girl's high-pitched voice cut the air then with a shriek of profanity. I heard the words, and so too, probably, did most of the neighborhood:

". . . an' if I wanna go out with my boyfriend there ain't nobody going to stop me. You may not like motorcycles, but until this goddamned family can afford to have more than one shitty little car . . ."

There was a lot more to it.

". . . and I'll be back when I damned well please. I may be fourteen but I can still take care of myself, and Howie—"

The door suddenly crashed open and a slim blond girl wearing a short skirt and a sweater, her hair hanging loose and stringy around her pointed, petulant face, banged past me, almost spinning me off my feet.

"Out of the way, buster," she said, not bothering to apologize or so much as look at me. She called back over her shoulder as she started down the street, "And tell Dad anything you want. Who cares?"

She climbed onto the rear of a motorcycle that was parked several houses down. The driver probably lost three dollars' worth of rubber as he spun away from the curb. A couple of real nice kids.

A thin, tired-looking woman with gray-streaked hair, a faded sallow face and wearing dowdy, wrinkled clothes, stood in front of me across the threshold.

"Yes?"

"Mrs. Wilson?"

She nodded and sort of half stepped back. She didn't seem in the slightest bit curious.

I followed her through the hallway into the living room. She spoke in a wavering, complaining voice as she indicated a chair.

"Just can't seem to do anything with that girl," she said. "These kids today . . ."

I thought, Well there's one thing you could do. You could turn her over your knee and whack her little round bottom. I tried to look sympathetic and was just opening my mouth when the room suddenly seemed to explode. He must have hit the bass drum, the cymbal, and about six other instruments at the same second. For a moment or two the sound was deafening and it apparently came from the next room.

Mrs. Wilson was either stone deaf or so used to it that she was no longer able to react. She merely sighed and shrugged and went into the next room; a moment later the drums stopped. A boy's rasping voice said:

"By God, Ma, nobody can do anything around this lousy place. The hell with it. I'm going out."

A moment later an overweight, pimply-faced lad of around seventeen, with long, uncombed hair cut Beatle's style, walked through the living room carrying an open can of beer and slammed through the front door

Mrs. Wilson came back into the living room.

"I hate to disturb Georgie," she said, "but I just can't hear a thing above that racket. He gets so upset when anyone interferes with his music...."

He'd get a damn sight more disturbed, I reflected, if he were my kid. I began to think that maybe Lloyd Wilson wasn't so bad off after all, having to spend a week or so in a hospital.

I waited until she had sat down and then I said, "Mrs. Wilson, I'm Lieutenant Martingale, of the State Police, and I have come out to—"

"I suppose you came out to tell me about Lloyd," she interrupted in that half-complaining, half-whining voice. She couldn't have sounded less interested.

I looked at her curiously for a moment or so.

"Why, yes," I began, "but—"

Again she interrupted.

"Some doctor, Borman or Borngold or something, called just before you got here. He already told me. Said Lloyd had an accident and was in Hopkins. He said Lloyd would be all right."

I don't know what possessed me to say it, but I asked, "Do the children know?"

She nodded, without expression. "Yes, I told them."

Again I thought, Nice kids. Real nice.

"Exactly what did Dr. Bornstein tell you, Mrs. Wilson?"

"He just said Lloyd had an accident. Somebody attacked him or mugged him or something. That he was all right and I wasn't to worry but that it would be better that I didn't try to see him until tomorrow."

"When did you return from the beach, Mrs. Wilson?"

She thought for a moment. "I guess about a half hour or so ago. We had to come back by bus. Lloyd had the car and so we had to take a bus...."

"Weren't you worried when Mr. Wilson failed to return after leaving you last night?" I asked.

She looked up at me and sort of half sighed.

"I always worry about Lloyd," she said. "Ever since he stopped selling and started this investigating business, I have worried. It keeps him out all crazy hours; I never know where he is or what he's doing and . . ."

She went on complaining for several minutes. Finally I interrupted her.

"Is it usual for Mr. Wilson to just disappear without calling or . . ."

She shook her head.

"He has crazy hours. I expected him back sometime this morning, but when he didn't show up I just figured he must'a got involved. The kids have to get to school tomorrow—that is, Georgie does as he's making up in summer school 'cause he failed math and English. So we just took a bus and came home."

"Did Mr. Wilson explain to you where he was going when he left Saturday night?" I asked.

She shook her head

"He said he had business. I never ask him about his business. But I wish he was back selling again. It isn't only the money. He made good money selling, even if it didn't come in regular. Of course it was bad enough his always making bosom—and boozin'—friends out of his customers."

She looked up at me almost slyly, and her tired face broke into a sort of caricature of a smile at her sad little joke.

"Yes, Lloyd made money selling, but at least he had some kind of regular hours. But since he's been in this investigating thing I just never know when he will be home. Kids, growing kids, they need a father's steady hand...."

Her particular growing kids needed not only a steady hand but a heavy one. But I just nodded sympathetically.

"You wouldn't know of any particular enemies your husband may have?" I asked. "Someone who may have made threats, may have . . ."

She shook her head.

"Lloyd's trouble isn't enemies," she said. "Lloyd's trouble is too many friends. Lloyd isn't a drinker or a chaser or anything like that. It's just that everyone likes him and he likes everybody and he just can't say no. So people use him. He's just too good to people. Nobody would hurt Lloyd."

I felt like reminding her that somebody very definitely had hurt Lloyd. In fact, I rather suspected that this family of his also probably hurt him a great deal in their own particular way.

"Did you know the Crimshaws?" I asked. "Mr. and Mrs. Harry Crimshaw?"

She was thoughtful for several seconds, looking blank. Then she shook her head. "No—I don't think so. I seem to have heard the name, but I don't remember where. Are they friends of Lloyd's?"

"Clients," I said.

We talked for a few more minutes, and then I left. It was a pretty fruitless conversation, and about the only thing I really learned was that Lloyd Wilson had just about as dismal a family as you could find in a long day's journey. I might even have felt a little sorry for Mrs. Wilson if it hadn't been for that whining, complaining voice. And even a woman in her late forties, no matter how plain she might be, could make an effort to wear clothes that are clean and pressed, and do something about her face and complexion.

4.

The telephone on my desk was ringing when I entered my office just after eight thirty the following morning. It was Loring Compton.

"Lieutenant Martingale?"

"Yes."

"Compton. Loring Compton. I want to see you. I just heard a news broadcast and I want to see you."

"To tell you the truth, Mr. Compton," I said, "I want to see you. I was just about to call and—"

"You come on out here. I'm at my Charles Street lot."

"I'll be out in half an hour," I said. "You're at—"

"The Charles Street lot. Always hit this place first on Monday to see what my boys did over the weekend. Four damned lots and the biggest independent agency in the metropolitan area, but I always hit the Charles Street—"

"A half hour," I said, and hung up.

Captain Rhinelander wasn't in when I left, so I dropped off a message as to where I would be. The drive into town, with the early Monday morning traffic congestion, took me a good twenty-five minutes, but because I decided to stop off for coffee and orange juice I was about eight minutes late. Compton was as annoyed at the delay as though I had failed to make the countdown on a moon shot. He was standing in the doorway of his office, his watch in his hand when I came up.

"Public servants," he said. "You guys have it made. All the time in the world. If I ran my business like they run city hall, I'd be broke in a month."

I let it pass.

He talked as I followed him into his private office.

"I heard that broadcast this morning about that fellow Wilson who was mugged in front of the Crimshaw place. I suppose you know he was a friend of the Crimshaws?"

I said I did. I started to ask him a question, but he didn't give me a chance.

"Can't imagine where the police are when things like that are happening," he said. "Marguerite Crimshaw has enough to worry about, it would seem to me, without something like that happening to upset her. Don't suppose you got the thugs who did it. Police never do seem to solve these things. It's getting so a decent, tax-paying citizen . . ."

He took the cigar out of his mouth with his left hand, and for the first time I saw that his right hand was bandaged.

"What time did you leave Mrs. Crimshaw Saturday night?" I asked.

He looked at me sharply. He didn't like the question.

"We were trying to set the time of the attack," I quickly added. "We've talked with Wilson, and he isn't quite sure what time he stopped in front of the place."

"I left early, right after you did. Alice, that's Mrs. Compton, stayed on with Marguerite, and I returned a little before twelve o'clock and picked her up."

"You say he was a friend of the Crimshaws," I said. "Would you think it a little unusual for him to be visiting that late?"

Again he looked at me sharply.

"Don't you go getting any funny ideas about Marguerite Crimshaw," he said. "She's as straight as a die. No, I wouldn't know what he could be doing coming by after midnight, if he actually was planning to stop in. It could have been about the insurance. Wilson was the Crimshaws' insurance man. Matter of fact, Harry introduced him to me—that's how I knew him—about a year ago in the hopes I'd take out a policy with him. I didn't. I figured Harry was out to make a split commission on the deal. That was Harry Crimshaw all over. Always an angle."

I nodded. "I get the picture. What is your impression of Wilson?"

"He's a sort of nothing. Not a bad little guy, actually, but he struck me as one of those quiet, mousy little types who lets everyone run over him. Don't know his wife, but I'll bet she runs the show. You can always tell."

"Just how close was he to the Crimshaws?"

"Well, he was around a lot. Always did think it was a little strange, his friendship with Harry. Both salesmen, but different as day and night. Harry made the hard sell. Come to think of it, it seems to me that someone told me Wilson was no longer peddling insurance. That he was working out of the main office as a clerk or something like that."

"What sort of man was Crimshaw, actually?" I asked, to change the subject. "Was he a pretty good salesman?"

Compton took a long puff of the cigar and seemed to inhale the smoke. He thought for several moments, staring over my head at the ceiling, before answering.

"Yes and no," he said at last. "He had one weakness you often find in this business. He always seemed to take the attitude he was putting something over on the customer. And he'd get a bigger kick out of selling a lemon for a hundred and fifty bucks than he would in selling a cream puff for a couple of thousand. That's the kind of guy he was. I had more trouble with his sales than with the whole rest of my boys put together."

He turned suddenly and looked directly at me.

"I'll tell you something frankly," he said. "I would have fired him a long time ago if it hadn't been for his wife. Both Alice and I felt sorry for her."

"Why? Did Harry Crimshaw abuse her?"

Compton shook his head. "No, in all fairness I can't say that. In his own way, he was really nuts about her. But he was just no damned good. Always in hot water. And I'll tell you something else. He was nuts about her, but he also went for anything in skirts. He just couldn't keep away from a good-looking broad. Or any broad, far as that goes. My God, I'll never forget that Jaguar deal."

He shook his head and sucked in his lips.

"And what was that?"

"I gave Harry a hundred and seventy a week drawing account, and he usually made it all right. Some weeks he made a hell of a lot more when things were going good, but he was always broke. Wouldn't matter what he'd make, he was the kind who would always live beyond his means. So a little more than a year ago, he goes out and buys himself an XKE Jaguar. For almost seven thousand dollars, for God's sake! He got it new from a dealer, and it had everything but the kitchen sink on it. Loaded. Damn fool. I could have got him a deal if I'd of known what was in his mind."

"And . . ."

"And naturally he financed it to the hilt. He was always late with his payments, and every month they threatened to come and get it. Well, about a month ago a girl comes in. Out on the very lot here. She was looking for a small, secondhand sports car. Harry of course shows her what we got around, which wasn't much at the time, and then he takes her for a spin in that Jag of his. As I say, she was a doll. And don't you know that he talks her into buying the Jag?"

"Maybe it was just as well that he unloaded it if he was having trouble with the payments."

"You don't get the point," Compton said. "Sure, if he'd have really sold the car it would have been the smartest thing he could do. But he didn't sell it—he gave it away."

"Gave it away?"

"Yeah, gave it away. Sold it to her for three thousand bucks cash. Christ, the blue-book value is forty-five hundred, and that car was a little gem. A little gem, and loaded."

"She must have been a doll," I said.

"Not only that, but he phonies up the bill of sale and everything else. Hell, he still owed a lot more than a grand on the car when he dumped it. Got into all sorts of trouble when the finance people and I personally had to go to bat and get it straightened out. Had to loan him the dough on his future salary so he wouldn't have landed in serious trouble."

"From what I've learned of Crimshaw, it hardly seems creditable that he would sell a car worth several thousand dollars for a mere—"

"You would have had to know him," Compton said. "He was a guy who liked to make big gestures. Another thing, he was a real sucker for a pretty girl, and this one happened to be in show business. I think she was a TV singer or something like that. Harry used to be an actor or a singer himself, or so he said, and he was still stagestruck. I guess the combination was too much for him—a sexy-looking broad in show business, and there's no doubt he was trying to make her. That's the funny thing about Harry. He was nuts about his wife. In fact he was about the most jealous bastard I ever ran into. And yet he still went for other dames on the side."

"Why was he jealous? Did his wife give him—"

Compton shook his head.

He suddenly stood up and tossed the cigar into an ashtray. "But the hell with Harry Crimshaw. I want to talk to you about this business with Wilson. I talked to Marguerite Crimshaw after I read that story in the paper, and she's damned upset about it. She's living out there alone and she—"

"We're investigating the Wilson thing," I said. "I don't quite see how it can tie in with Mrs. Crimshaw, but until we can really talk with Wilson we won't know too much. In the meantime, there are a couple of things I'd be interested in finding out. Did Crimshaw leave any money? Did he have any—"

"Not a goddam dime. His bank account was overdrawn and he's overdrawn here. He owed dough all over the lot. Hell, Alice and I had to see that Marguerite had enough groceries in the house to keep living on. I don't want it to get around, but I actually had to force a small loan on her until she can get on her feet."

"Would you mind a great deal if I looked through Crimshaw's desk while I'm here?" I asked. "I'd just like to see—"

"You won't find much but bills—and some photos from *Playboy* of naked girls," Compton said. "But go ahead, be my guest. I have to be running along now anyway."

As he reached the door, I asked, "How did you hurt your hand, Mr. Compton?"

He turned and glared at me.

"None of your damned business."

Chapter 4

1.

I returned to the office around noontime. Captain Rhinelander was waiting for me impatiently. He had just returned from Johns Hopkins Hospital after spending more than an hour with Lloyd Wilson.

"Dick," the Captain said, "I am assigning you officially to the Crimshaw Case. I'm convinced that the attack on Wilson is directly tied in with the Crimshaw matter. He's a lot better today, but I got the impression he was being evasive."

"In what way?"

"Well, I can't honestly say. Just an impression I got from talking with him. But that's only part of it. The people at Missouri and Texas Indemnity have also been in touch with me. They strongly suspect there was fraud involved in the Crimshaw matter. You can be sure of one thing; they are not going to simply pay off and forget it. They want a body."

I shook my head.

"They may never get one, especially if the man did drown. The Chesapeake is a damned big body of water to begin with, and if for any reason Crimshaw's body was snagged and failed to come to the top the crabs would make short work of the remains."

"If Crimshaw was murdered," Captain Rhinelander said, "whoever killed him could have made sure that the body wouldn't come to the top. Have you thought about that?"

"I have," I said. "It has also occurred to me that if the man wasn't drowned, and also wasn't murdered, if he merely disappeared, his body also wouldn't float to the top."

"The insurance people are a little more inclined to go for the possibility of murder," the Captain said. "They don't like that hundred-and-fifty-thousand-dollar double-indemnity clause. Not one little bit. And then when their investigator starts to work on the case, he is beaten up just as he's about to question the woman who is the beneficiary. Now, doesn't that sort of raise a few questions in your mind?"

As a cop it raised a lot of questions in my mind. On the other hand, I had talked with Marguerite Crimshaw. I simply couldn't believe that she was involved in either the murder of her husband or his possible voluntary disappearance. But it would be pretty difficult to explain that to Captain Rhinelander. Cops are not supposed to go on impressions or hunches. They are supposed to go on facts.

The Captain must have been reading my mind.

"The very first thing I want you to do," he said, "is check out the Crimshaw woman. I want you to learn everything about her there is to learn. Her background, her finances, her personal life. Was there a man in her life before Crimshaw? Has she been fooling around with anyone since she was married? Has she ever been in trouble before? Has she collected on previous insurance policies? Everything about her is important. We're not essentially interested in protecting the insurance company—they have their own people for that—but we are interested in knowing what crimes have been committed. The fact that we don't have Lloyd Wilson's murder on our hands is purely a matter of luck. He could have been killed as easily as not."

The Captain reached for the interoffice phone.

"I'm going to let you have Sergeant Barnes," he said. "He's a little inexperienced, but he's young and bright and from what I hear around, he's also pretty much of a lady-killer. It might be a good idea for you to have him ingratiate himself with the Crimshaw woman. I understand the girls find him irresistible. So long as he keeps his identity a secret, he shouldn't have any trouble in gaining her confidence. But use him any way you want to. He's done a damned good job in a couple of cases recently doing undercover work in digging out information. I'll have him sent to your office, and you can consider him on the case as long as you need him. Just so you get results."

I was thinking about Jim Barnes as I left to return to my own office a couple of minutes later.

I had known him almost from the time he had become a State Trooper some four years ago. Jim Barnes is bright and he's a good, conscientious cop. He made the plainclothes divisions and obtained his sergeantcy in amazingly quick time. I didn't for a moment doubt but what he deserved it. Everything the Captain had said about him was true. But at the same time, I didn't particularly like him and I didn't like the methods he frequently, although I must admit, successfully, used.

Jim is one of those boys who is just too damned good-looking, and knew it. A little too arrogant, a little too inclined to skip ethics in seeking success.

He would have been the very last person I would have selected to contact Marguerite Crimshaw. I just couldn't believe that she would go for his type.

Or was I being completely honest? Was it just possible I was afraid she would go for his type?

That's the trouble with a police officer becoming too interested in the people involved in the cases on which he works.

In any event, the Captain had told me to use Sergeant Barnes in any way I thought best. I thought it best that I see Marguerite Crimshaw and set Jim to checking other angles in the case. Have him do a little digging on Lloyd Wilson's background. Determine once and for all if the attack on Wilson was really tied in with his work in the Crimshaw matter.

So when I talked with Jim a few minutes later, I briefed him on the little I knew about the Wilson attack, and told him to take it from there. I suggested he find out just what was the relationship between Wilson and the Crimshaws, how long and how intimately they had known each other. But also to see if he could find any other possible motive for the attack.

When Jim finally left my office I reached for the telephone and put a call in to the house out in Severna Park.

Marguerite Crimshaw said she would be there until around four o'clock and would be glad to see me if I wanted to stop by.

I arrived at three thirty.

The white convertible was standing in the driveway, and the trunk lid was open. Mrs. Crimshaw was putting the last of several suitcases in the car.

2.

She slammed the lid down on the trunk as I pulled to a stop, and I guess she heard me because she suddenly turned and for a moment stood poised and motionless as she stared at me. I somehow obtained the impression that she was frightened; it was almost as though she were on the verge of sudden flight.

She was wearing a pair of orange stretch pants, and had thrust her bare feet into sandals. A cashmere sweater that matched the trousers did nothing to conceal the soft pear-shaped contours of her small, beautifully formed breasts. She still looked like a schoolgirl as she tossed a lock of blond hair out of her eye.

And then she recognized me and started toward my car. I got out from behind the wheel.

"Lieutenant Martingale," she said, and she actually sounded happy to see me. She held out a small hand, naked of rings.

She went on speaking, almost breathlessly, as we shook hands with odd formality.

"I'm so glad you were able to make it early," she said. "I was hoping you would." She gestured toward the car. "I'm going over to the Shore for the night. This place makes me nervous—being here alone—especially after what happened to poor Lloyd."

I was a little surprised at her use of Wilson's given name.

"I'm probably very foolish," she said, "but I just don't want to stay here any longer."

And then, rather wistfully: "In any case, I'm giving up the place. I simply can't afford it and I'm going over to the Shore for the rest of the summer until I can make plans. Mr. Fletcher has told me I can use the summer place as long as I want to, and it will be a lot more practical untll I can become a little more adjusted."

"Will you be giving up this place permanently?" I asked. I was wondering about a lease, wondering just how she was going to manage it.

"Yes—yes; it's far too expensive. And I have already arranged about the furniture. I'm turning it back to the finance company. I'm taking only a few things with me now; I'll come back and clean out the rest of my possessions in a few days."

She stopped then and looked up at me almost shyly.

"Is Mr. Fletcher expecting you?" I asked, for no particular reason. I just wanted to keep the conversation going.

She shook her head.

"Well, yes and no. I did call him a couple of days ago, and he himself suggested I stay at the cottage. I told him I thought I would. But I telephoned him this morning, when it suddenly seemed I simply couldn't bear to spend another night here, and I got no answer. I tried a couple of more times, but I still couldn't reach him. However, I'm sure he won't mind if I move in. It's only about an hour's drive, and I'll be there well before dark."

We had walked up the drive while we were talking, and she opened the front door. For a moment she hesitated.

"I don't know why," she said, "but empty houses always depress me, frighten me just a little."

I suddenly thought of the empty house on Benoni Point over on the Eastern Shore. I thought of the telephone calls to Horace Fletcher that had not been answered. And then I heard myself saying about the very last thing in the world I had planned to say.

"I have to make a stopover at the State Police Barracks in Easton. Why don't I drive over with you and help you get settled? Perhaps we might have dinner together. Then, if you're coming back tomorrow, you might give me a lift. I'll plan to spend the night at the barracks dormitory."

She instinctively reached for my hand with both of hers and pressed it, looking up at me with complete guilelessness.

"You are kind," she said. "But I'd hate to put you out. You really don't have to take me to dinner, but if you are going over anyway, I would feel a lot happier about it if you did come out to the cottage with me until I can see if Mr. Fletcher is going to be there. When I move in permanently, I'm going to try to get a girl to stay with me; but in the meantime I must admit the thought of being there alone is upsetting. Although not quite as upsetting as spending another night here."

Later, driving her white convertible out Ritchie Highway and across the Chesapeake Bridge and down Route 50, I was very glad I had decided to see Marguerite Crimshaw myself rather than turn her over to Sergeant Jim Barnes. Barnes would have been far too aware of the undeniable sexuality of her slender, beautiful body to let her childlike quality interfere with his thinking. Or his actions.

There was something completely vulnerable about her as she sat beside me and chatted away, once she was secure in the knowledge that she wouldn't have to be alone.

We stopped off in Easton and had dinner before we went on out to the cottage. She had a dry martini before dinner, and I had a double bourbon and soda. She said that the drink relaxed her. In fact, she was feeling so good that when I suggested a bottle of sparkling wine with the dinner, she readily agreed. She turned down my suggestion of a B&B with our coffee, but smiled and told me she had a bottle of brandy in one of her suitcases and suggested we wait until we got to the cottage. She would make a pot of coffee, and we could have the brandy then.

It sounded like a great suggestion.

It was a little after eight thirty when at last we turned into the drive leading past Horace Fletcher's mansion house. There were no lights on in the house, but a car was approaching and I slowed down as the white convertible came even with it.

A colored man was at the wheel and he apparently recognized Mrs. Crimshaw at once.

"Mr. Fletcher is in New York," he said, "and I was just leaving. He told me I could take the night off 'cause he won't be back until tomorrow sometime. But is there anything I can do for you, Mrs. Crimshaw?"

She told him that she would be spending the night at the cottage and moving in within the next day or two but that there was nothing she would need him for. He thanked her and said good night.

3.

I still can't quite understand what happened to me, but during that next six hours, from around nine o'clock in the evening until three the next morning, I didn't once remember that I was a policeman. It was, in many ways, one of the best evenings I had ever spent in my life. And it wasn't because I had planned it that way. It just happened.

Marguerite had brought several bags and suitcases with her, and a couple of them held some canned goods and assorted foodstuffs. I carried her luggage in from the car, and while she was arranging her clothes and personal possessions in the closet of her bedroom, I insisted on going into the small kitchen and getting the coffee ready. Later we took our cups, along with two small crystal glasses and the brandy bottle, out to the screen porch overlooking the waters of the

Choptank and sat in the semidarkness.

She said that the electric lights attracted tiny bugs that came through the screen, and so she had lighted a pair of candles. For a long time we just sat and sipped the coffee and brandy, and then at last we began to talk.

She ended the silence when she suddenly said: "You will probably think it very strange, but do you know, this is probably the first time I have ever been really at peace in this house. The first time I have ever completely relaxed."

"You mean that you, you and your husband . . ."

"Oh, it wasn't that Harry . . . I really don't quite know how to explain it. I'm not saying that we didn't get along, that he was hard to live with or that he abused me or anything like that. It was just that with Harry there was no such thing as peace. I know I'm not really making myself clear. But have you ever known anyone, well, been intimate with anyone or married to anyone whose very presence just seemed to upset you? As I say, I'm not making very good sense. It was just that with Harry, even when I thought I was very much in love with him, I never could feel at ease."

I knew what she meant. I knew all too well. It was a feeling I'd had with my own wife. Long before I discovered her adultery and the relationship developed into a bitter and continuing cat-and-dog fight.

"I've been married," I said. "I no longer am. I obtained the divorce after I discovered my wife felt that one man in her life wasn't enough. I think I know what you mean."

"It wasn't quite like that with Harry and myself," she said. "Not that I think Harry was completely faithful to me. In fact, I feel sure he wasn't. It was something a little more complex. Harry was a restless man. A man who could never stay still for a moment. Without doing anything, he seemed to create a sense of tension. It is really very hard to explain. It wasn't that he didn't love me. I'm sure that he did. In fact, he was one of the most jealous men alive. Maybe that was a part of it. In any case, I was never at ease. And never really happy."

"Are you happy now?"

"If you mean this minute, yes. I believe that I am. If you mean since Harry is gone, I don't honestly know. It has all happened too quickly. I haven't really had a chance to think, to try and adjust myself."

"It takes time," I said. "After my divorce—well, it's taken me more than a year to reach the point where I even wanted to do anything but bury myself in work, and forget. Have even wanted to spend as much as an hour with another woman."

"You are an unusual man," she said, and turned and smiled slowly at me. "Most men who are unhappily married can't wait to find some woman's shoulder to cry on."

"I don't think I would have trusted another woman enough to do any crying," I said. "I'm afraid I was bitter about women for quite a time."

"I didn't cry at first when I heard about Harry's drowning," Marguerite said. "Maybe I was too shocked. But then later I did. I'll confess something to you. I don't know for sure whether I cried because my husband was dead and I loved him, or whether I cried only because I was lost and lonely and upset. I don't honestly know."

I got up and poured two more ponies of brandy, and she suddenly looked at me and giggled.

"Lieutenant Martingale," she said, almost coyly, "if you keep this up I shall be drunk."

"Sometimes it might be a good thing to get drunk," I said. "It's an escape I can rarely afford myself, but one I can understand."

I lifted my glass and we drained them together.

She leaned back then, and without quite understanding how it happened I found that my arm was behind her. She turned her head and looked up at me, her eyes very wide. But not surprised. Almost questioning.

I moved and bent my head and then I kissed her.

For the briefest of moments we held the kiss, and then I felt her body tense. She took her lips away and she sighed. Her arms reached up and her hands went around my neck and she pulled me to her, and then I found her lips again and this time we held the kiss. Her lips parted, and as I pressed harder against her my hand moved and came up under the fullness of her breast and she turned toward me and her mouth opened wide as she came to me.

There was no coyness about her then, no false modesty. She was a woman, young, vital, and alive. A woman who had been married and knew about love, knew how to make love.

We did it without words.

I carried her into the bedroom; she was as light as a child. But there was nothing childish about that small, exquisitely formed body when I took her clothes off and put her on the bed. Nothing childish about the passionate response with which she met the surging urgency of my own long-pent-up physical needs.

It was utterly natural. It contained nothing of aggression but everything of passion. It was very, very beautiful; utterly and completely fulfilling.

She whispered to me just before she fell into a gentle sleep.

"Please don't leave me tonight," she said.

4.

But I did leave. I left just before five o'clock. I wanted to take no chances on being there should Horace Fletcher be around in the morning.

She was still sleeping as I slipped into my clothes. I checked to see that the telephone was still working and then left a note for her propped up on the washbasin in the bathroom. I told her that I was taking her back but that I would call her later and that she should tell Fletcher I had driven her down to the bungalow. And that I would pick her up around noontime.

Driving back into Easton, where I planned to pay a quick stop at the Police Barracks, I should have felt some trace of guilt. It had been the first time since I had been on the force that I had had an intimate relationship with anyone involved in a case on which I was working. But I had no regrets. I had done something that I considered the most natural thing in the world at the time. And I was utterly sure in my own mind that it would make not the slightest possible difference in any investigation I was about to make.

Even then, in that early period of our relationship, I tried to analyze my feelings. Was I suddenly in love with this woman who hardly a week ago had lost her husband? Was it merely a physical infatuation? Was it only the result of the fact that my own life for a long time had been unsatisfactory and unfulfilled?

I wasn't sure. But I suspected that I had very suddenly, and without warning, fallen deeply in love.

I managed to get in some three and a half hours' sleep at the barracks dormitory and at nine o'clock put in a call to headquarters in Pikesville. I avoided asking for Captain Rhinelander and merely requested any messages that might be waiting for me.

Sergeant Barnes had been in my office but had already left. There was a message in which he said that he had a little information but that it wasn't too important and could wait until I returned. Nothing else.

I telephoned Marguerite a little after ten. She'd talked with Fletcher and made arrangements to return to the cottage for the rest of the summer and the fall. She wanted me to pick her up sometime shortly after noon.

She sounded cool; we might merely have been the most casual of friends.

At two that afternoon we were once again pulling up in front of the house in Severna Park. She was going to pick up the rest of her personal possessions, and I was planning to return to headquarters. But it didn't work out that way.

The minute I twisted her key in the front door and opened it, I knew something was wrong. She was standing just behind me, and I could hear the slight gasp as she looked past me and into the living room. It wasn't that the place was a shambles or anything like that, but the opened drawers pulled out of the desk, the papers scattered about the floor, told the story clearly enough. The place had been systematically searched and ransacked.

Whoever had done it had made an entrance through the back door. She had left the screen locked from the inside, and they had carefully cut through the wire netting before jimmying the door itself. Nothing was disturbed in the kitchen, but whoever had entered the place had done a very complete job in the bedroom.

I thought that when she discovered her jewelry box missing, she was going to cry.

"It isn't the value," she explained to me after we had made the discovery, "but the few trinkets I had were mostly things from my mother and grandmother. I don't suppose they could have been worth more than a couple of thousand dollars at the most, and I believe that a floating insurance policy I have will cover that. But they were things that meant a great deal to me. My mother's wedding ring, my own engagement ring, which never did fit very well and is why I don't wear it; a string of pearls my grandmother gave me when I graduated from high school and which she had been given by her grandmother. Things like that."

A camera worth a couple of hundred dollars, a transistor radio that had belonged to her husband, a small television set, some of the fishing tackle she had brought back from the Shore—all these were taken. Though the thieves hadn't stolen any of her clothes, they had cleaned out the closet that contained Harry Crimshaw's garments. Two guns, a .30-.30 Winchester and a twelve-gauge shotgun, which she had given him on his birthday, were also missing. Whoever had entered the place had made a very thorough search and had missed very little of value.

After we had made a quick inventory, she sat on the bed and shook her head, looking bewildered and unhappy.

"I guess maybe you had better call the police," she said. For the moment she'd forgotten that I was the police.

I tried to cheer her up then. The thieves had taken things that had a pawnshop value, and there was every chance they would turn up sooner or later.

She looked up at me forlornly.

"I can't wait to get out of this place," she said. "Dear God, it seems it will never end. First Harry and then the other night Lloyd Wilson. And now this. What's happening, anyway? Why me? Why . . ."

Looking down at her I had an almost overwhelming desire to hold her and to comfort her, but I overcame it. I knew that I would have to phone in a report immediately and get fingerprint men and someone from the local burglary detail out to the house. Another thing—I wanted a clear mind. I was beginning to wonder just a little myself. Why her? What, if any, was the connection between this latest thing that had happened and the things that had preceded it? Or could the robbery be merely another coincidence? Could someone have learned that she would not be home last night? Could they have watched her leave and realized that they could burglarize the place without hindrance?

It took a little longer than I had expected. She didn't want to be left alone, and I didn't want to leave her alone, so I stayed on while the local police came and made their inspection. And then she insisted on making out a complete list of missing articles so that she could report it to her insurance company, which, incidentally, was not the Missouri and Texas Indemnity, but another firm. Later, I helped her carry the few remaining possessions she owned out to her car and then returned to the house with her while she called up and notified the telephone company to disconnect the service and did a few other things preparatory to departing for the Shore.

Because it was well after six before we were through, I suggested she have dinner with me before driving over to the summer place, and she agreed. In the meantime, I again called my office, and this time talked with Barnes. He said he had come across several interesting things and wanted to talk with me. I told him I would meet him in my office that evening at nine o'clock. Barnes told me that he'd talked with the boss and that Captain Rhinelander was anxious to know what progress was being made on the case.

At six fifteen we left the house, and Marguerite followed my car in hers. I went to a small cocktail lounge and restaurant out on the Ritchie Highway.

It was still a little early for the dinner hour when we arrived, and I was surprised to find that the parking lot was almost completely filled. I had to park at the furthest end, and she pulled in behind me. The bar itself was jammed, but we found a small table for two at one side of the dining room.

I don't suppose there is a man alive who doesn't feel a certain sense of pride when he accompanies a really beautiful woman into a restaurant and realizes that several dozen eyes are on him. I know that as I followed Marguerite Crimshaw past those crowded tables and was conscious not only of the envy of the males present but also of the glances of the women, I couldn't resist a sense of satisfaction.

It was a feeling I had often had during the first months of my marriage, and it was only later, when I realized that my wife was playing around with other men, that the feeling changed.

But following Marguerite to the small table for two, I again had that sense of pride. The waiter pulled her chair out, and I smiled and leaned forward, starting to say something; then I saw her face suddenly pale and her eyes take on an odd, sick look.

"What is it?" I asked quickly. "Are you all right? Do you want—"

"I'm sorry," she said. "It's really nothing—nothing at all. Just that I suddenly remembered. Harry and I used to come here at one time. A long time ago, right after we were married."

Women are strange, and I daresay I shall never completely understand them. I couldn't see why the restaurant should bother her, even if she and her husband had used to come to it. After all, she and her husband used to go to the Eastern Shore, used to spend their nights in the house out on Benoni Point, used to sleep in the same bed....

But I didn't want to think about that. I merely started to stand up and tell her we could go somewhere else. But she quickly shook her head. No, she insisted we stay. It really didn't matter at all. It was just, she said as we walked over to the table, she had thought she'd seen someone she used to know, and then had realized that this was a place she used to come to and for just a moment it had upset her.

We stayed, and she ordered a drink and only half finished it, and barely touched the seafood dinner I had the waiter bring. She said she was a little too tired to eat, and I could see that she was still nervous. Her eyes kept wandering around the room, and she only half listened to me when I talked.

She understood that I had to return to my office, and she said that she would skip the coffee as she was anxious to get started herself. But she insisted that I wait and have my coffee, and so at last I agreed with her and stood up as she herself got up to leave.

"Please call me soon," she said. "And thanks—thanks for everything."

And then she was gone.

I finished my coffee and ordered a brandy and looked at my watch. It was only a little after seven, so I took my time with my coffee and smoked a cigarette and then called the waiter for the check. It was just beginning to get dark when I finally walked out of the place and started across the parking lot to get my car.

5.

I was suddenly feeling very let down and depressed. I was also having a rather belated sense of guilt. There had been any number of questions I had been planning to ask Marguerite Crimshaw, and I had asked none of them.

I had wanted to find out about Loring Compton.

I wanted to find out just how close a relationship she and her husband had had with the Comptons. There had been something about the man that had disturbed me. Something about his attitude toward both Harry Crimshaw and Marguerite Crimshaw that I hadn't understood. Or at least wanted clarified. Also, I wanted to know just how well he had known Lloyd Wilson. Someone had administered that beating to Wilson, and the following day Compton had turned up with a bandaged hand and had become angry when I'd asked him about it.

I had wanted to go much deeper into Marguerite's own relations with her husband, but because of what had happened between us out at the cottage, I had not. It just hadn't seemed the proper time.

Perhaps Captain Rhinelander had been right after all. Perhaps it would have been best if I had assigned Sergeant Barnes to Marguerite

Crimshaw and devoted my own efforts to other facets of the case.

I rounded the rear fender of my station wagon, my mind preoccupied with my thoughts, and that is probably why I didn't see the figure standing next to the car by the driver's side until I was almost upon him. Until he spoke.

He said, "Got a light, buddy?"

I jerked to a stop and started to look up, and that's when he hit me. He didn't hit me with his fist; he hit me with the sawed-off handle of a billiard cue. I know. I found it on the ground some time later.

The only reason I found it was that when the cue stick hit my head, it cracked and broke. If it hadn't, it would have caved in my skull and I wouldn't have been around to find it at all.

As it was, the blow landed with sufficient force not only to stun me but also to knock me to the ground.

The cue stick broke and I fell, and when I hit the pavement at the side of the car I was only about half conscious; and so when I rolled, it must have been sheer instinct that propelled me. But whatever it was, it probably saved my life.

He must have held on to the end of the broken cue stick, because even as I rolled under the station wagon it came down again, and this time it cracked across my leg. I think the sudden agonizing pain of the blow brought me fully conscious.

I lifted one hand and jerked and hauled myself farther under the car, and at the same time I pulled my service revolver from the shoulder holster. It was tight quarters, and I wasn't able to turn over because of the lack of space, but I got the gun out to one side and fired at random. If I had seen his legs in the dark I would have shot at them, but I wasn't able to see anything. And then, before I could get off a second shot, I heard the sound of running footsteps. Before I could haul myself from under the car and get on my feet, I heard the roar of a powerful engine and then the screech of tires as a car made a sharp turn and a fast getaway.

I found the broken cue stick before I pulled myself behind the wheel of my station wagon. My head was splitting. But I stopped long enough to question the attendant.

He said that only two cars had left the lot during the last five minutes. One was a Volkswagen driven by an elderly couple, and the other was a red Jaguar. He hadn't noticed the driver or whether there was more than one person in the car. The Jags, especially the XKEs, are so low it's almost impossible to see inside one unless you make a special effort.

I didn't go directly to my office at Headquarters. I stopped at the emergency ward at Johns Hopkins Hospital and had four stitches taken in my head. By a sheer coincidence, I received the services of Dr. Milton Bornstein, who had attended Lloyd Wilson. It was quite a coincidence.

I wondered if it was equally a coincidence that I had been murderously attacked after spending a certain period of time with Marguerite Crimshaw, while investigating the disappearance of her husband.

Chapter 5

1.

The Irish—that is, the male Irish—come out of two very distinct molds. There are the tall, black-haired, black-eyed, blue-jowled handsome ones with glittering white teeth who go to prove that the Spanish did pretty well when they invaded the Emerald Island. And there are the rather short, stocky ones, with red hair and blue eyes and fair skin. Both have charm. It's part of their stock in trade.

Jim Barnes belonged to the latter type and had plenty of charm but was slightly lacking in modesty.

He was grinning like a Cheshire cat as he sat across the desk from me, one eye cocked and his mouth twisted sarcastically.

"I remember seeing her picture in the newspapers right after her husband was drowned," he said. "I suppose the only reason they used it was because she is a real doll. So naturally I figured you were giving me the short end of the stick when you decided that you'd be the one to talk to her and I could just play around in the second-string squad. But, Lieutenant, here you are, back home with a broken head, and I—well, boy did I have a day."

"Maybe you'd like to tell me about it, Sergeant," I said.

"I started out as you suggested, checking into Harry Crimshaw's background. It didn't take long to learn that his credit rating was lousy, that he had a reputation as a deadbeat and a bad financial risk. He used to be a small-time entertainer, playing club dates and now and then a spot on a radio or TV show. But he wasn't good enough to really make the grade."

"We knew that," I said.

"Until he got married, he had one hell of a reputation as a ladies' man. After he got married a couple of years back, he settled down a little bit and took a job as a used-car salesman. That led me to his boss, Loring Compton."

"I've already talked with Compton," I said.

"I haven't. But I've talked with Alice, his wife."

He looked up at me out of the corner of his eye.

"So?"

"I gather that she is about twenty years younger than her husband," Jim said. "In fact, she and the Crimshaw woman went to school together."

"That so?"

"Yeah. That's how Crimshaw happened to land up working for Compton. What Compton didn't know, and may still not know, is that Harry Crimshaw was laying Alice Compton before Crimshaw himself got married, before Alice Compton married her husband. And very likely afterward."

"And just how did you find that out?" I asked, trying to keep the sarcasm out of my voice.

Jim smiled evilly.

"Well, I'm a good cop," he said smugly. "And of course the fact that Alice happens to be a lush—as well as a nymphomaniac—was a certain amount of help."

"You are quite sure about it?"

"Just about as sure as a guy can be who has spent one hell of an afternoon with a dame who just loves to talk."

"How come you don't think Compton knows about it?" I asked.

"I don't know one way or the other," Jim said. "It was the one time she clammed up, when I asked her if her hubby suspected."

"And how about Marguerite—Mrs. Crimshaw? Did she know her husband was having an affair with her friend?"

Jim shook his head.

"I don't think so. Alice swore to me that Mrs. Crimshaw never suspected anything. I think she was telling the truth. Another thing: The two of them, Alice Compton and Mrs. Crimshaw, are still great friends. I don't think they would be if Mrs. Crimshaw knew."

"What else did this combination drunk and sexpot have to confide?" I asked.

"Well, I'll tell you," Jim said. "She, Alice, really seems to like Mrs.

Crimshaw. But she said a funny thing. She said the reason she has always liked Marguerite Crimshaw is because she admires her. Admires her because she is the toughest, most self-sufficient woman she has ever known."

This time I laughed.

"That dame must really be a lush," I said. "I've seen Mrs. Crimshaw under rather severe pressure. The last thing in the world I would call her would be either tough or self-sufficient."

"Well, of course you could be right," Jim said. "This Alice Compton broad is like most lady drunks. Sentimental as all hell. What might be tough to her could be just normal to anyone else."

"It sounds as though you spent considerable time with the woman."

"You're right," Barnes said. "I met her while I was waiting for her husband at his office. He didn't show up, so after a while we went out to a cocktail bar and had a couple. We ended up at a motel on the edge of town."

"When you do a research job, you do it up right," I said. "Did it ever occur to you that Captain Rhinelander might not quite approve—"

"I get results," Barnes said a little shortly. "When a woman gets drunk and wants to talk—well, then, if going to bed with her is one of the conditions, I do my duty and go to bed. My job is to learn the facts."

"So just what do you make of the facts?"

"I might make plenty," Jim said. "A guy named Crimshaw disappears. Turns out he's been having an affair with a young broad named Mrs. Compton. Mrs. Compton has a husband, a husband considerably older than she is and one who has every reason to be a jealous bird. Maybe he had something to do with Crimshaw's disappearance. This same Crimshaw has a good-looking wife. The wife stands to make a hundred and fifty grand on his death. Maybe she knew about the affair—which would give her a double motive.

"I got a little something else as a sort of bonus. Loring Compton was a good friend of Mrs. Crimshaw. He fell in love with and married Mrs. Crimshaw's girlhood friend. Just maybe, he also fell in love with Mrs. Crimshaw. Which would have given him a double motive. And I have one additional little tidbit which may or may not be something."

"You seem just loaded with goodies, Jim," I said.

"Maybe I am. In any case, Alice Compton told me that Marguerite Crimshaw has known Lloyd Wilson for a number of years. That the guy was almost like a father to her. It strikes me that it is just barely possible that if an older man, like say our friend Compton, had fallen for her, maybe Wilson also flipped. And maybe that was why he got himself beaten up. Maybe Compton didn't like the idea of Wilson's stopping by to see her around midnight while she was alone in the house. Possible?"

I thought about it for several minutes.

"Yes," I said at last. "It is possible. I don't know Lloyd Wilson and only talked to him for a moment while he was half unconscious in the hospital, but having met his wife and family, I could see how it would be very easy for him to fall for almost any woman. But I'll tell you one thing. If Wilson or Compton, either one of them, was in love with Marguerite Crimshaw, you can bet it was a one-sided affair."

"You speak with a certain amount of authority, mine Lieutenant," Jim Barnes said. "By the way, have you any idea of who laid that cue stick over the side of your noggin? Couldn't be that someone might have objected to your spending a little time with the lady, could it?"

"I have given the matter a bit of thought," I said. "You might do a little checking tomorrow. Find out just where Loring Compton spent the evening on the night Harry Crimshaw was drowned. Find out what his alibi is for the time when Lloyd Wilson was attacked. And find out where the bastard was from approximately seven thirty to eight thirty tonight."

"Will do," Jim said, and stood up and reached for his hat. "And you might do yourself a favor, Lieutenant. Have a talk with our little alcoholic friend Alice Compton. See if you get the same impression of her that I got. Talk to her about her dear old schoolgirl friend. It might give you a slightly different slant on the Crimshaw dame."

"I'll do that little thing," I said. "And by the way, one more thing you might check on tomorrow if you have the chance. Harry Compton sold a red XKE Jaguar to some television and nightclub singer a couple of months or so back. His own personal car. I'd like to get her name—Loring Compton has it—and find out just where she is working and living now. I'd also like to know just where that car was tonight, at the same time. Between seven thirty and eight thirty. Okay?"

"Your slightest wish is my command," Barnes said, and waved good night.

2.

Police work, especially the work a detective does, can be, and often is, excruciatingly dull. During the ensuing week, a period in which I suffered almost continuously from severe headaches as a result of the blow from the cue stick, I spent most of my time running down a series of inane facts all of which related in some way to the Crimshaw Case but none of which seemed to lead anywhere.

One thing we determined almost at once, mostly as a result of legwork on Jim Barnes's part.

Loring Compton had an absolutely airtight alibi for the night of Harry Crimshaw's disappearance. He had been tied up in a long-distance stud poker game with half dozen cronies in a hotel room in Washington from nine o'clock in the evening to noon the following day.

On the night when Wilson was attacked, Loring was with his wife, and she swore that he had picked her up at Marguerite Crimshaw's before midnight and that they had driven directly home and gone to bed.

Alice Compton had been almost obscenely insistent that her husband had not left that bed until some time early the following morning.

On the evening when I was struck down, Compton explained his whereabouts by saying he had been driving from Washington to Baltimore. He had left Washington around seven o'clock and had arrived at one of his parking lots around eight fifteen. He explained the apparently extra-long time the forty-odd-mile trip had taken by saying that traffic was heavy, which it undoubtedly was. The manager of the lot backed him up, but the man could have been lying. After all, his job depended on Loring Compton, and Compton wasn't the man to fail to let an employee know where his interests lay.

It may have been a bit of a coincidence that Compton happened to have a pool table in his game room at home. But what the hell, that didn't mean he had an option on every billiard cue in town.

The one thing that I had hoped might turn up during that week didn't. That was the body of Harry Crimshaw.

Another thing that failed to turn up was one—any one—of the various items that had been taken from the Crimshaw place; under normal circumstances something would have floated to the top in one of the pawnshops around town.

It was, in fact, a week of things not showing up.

Jim Barnes had no trouble at all in finding out the name of the girl who'd taken over Crimshaw's XKE. She was Gale Everts, and the address on her driving license was a number out on Falls Church Road. I drove there myself.

It was a slightly rundown apartment house in what at one time had been a rather good neighborhood. Half of the names were missing under the doorbells and from the mailboxes. Among those that remained was nothing that even vaguely resembled "Everts."

I pushed the button that said "Superintendent."

A blousy woman in her late fifties, wearing too much makeup and dyed blue hair, came to the door. She didn't bother to take the half-smoked cigarette from the corner of her mouth, and she sounded like every madam in the world when she said, "Well, darling, what can I do for you?"

I told her I was looking for Miss Gale Everts. She laughed, if you can call it a laugh.

"Ha," she said, "who isn't? What are you, some kind of a collector?"

I told her no, I was some kind of a cop, and I showed her my identification card.

She stopped looking friendly but she held the door open and waved me inside.

"Come on in," she said. "Don't stand out here. Gawd knows I got enough problems without cops coming around and giving me a hard time."

I told her I didn't want to give her a hard time; I just wanted to talk to one of her tenants, a girl named Gale Everts.

She didn't say anything until we had walked down a long, dirty hallway, and she'd pushed open the door at the end and waved me inside. We entered what I took to be her living room.

There was a couch across one wall, and it was piled with Kewpie dolls. Two small, yellowish toy pugs with thyroid eyes lay on the seat of an upholstered chair and glared at me. Opposite them was one of the largest television sets I had ever seen, and on top of that was a smaller set, so I gathered she watched two programs at the same time. Both had pictures moving on their screens, but no sound came from them. In each of three corners were triangular hanging shelves loaded with toys, dolls, and stuffed animals. And everywhere were plants. The place actually reeked with vegetation.

She pushed a straight-backed chair my way and then moved over and lifted the top of a Styrofoam icebox and took out two beers. She flipped off the caps and handed me one.

"What would you want with Miss Everts, officer?" she asked.

"Now you know better than that, Mother," I said. "Just tell me which is her apartment and I'll thank you for the beer and be on my way."

She lifted the bottle to her lips and slowly shook her head. Wiping her mouth with the back of her hand, she said, "She's gone. Doesn't live here anymore."

"When did she leave?"

"Oh, I'd say about two, three weeks ago."

"And where did she go?"

She took another slug of beer, and shrugged.

"Who knows? She just up one day and took off. Packed her suitcases in that fancy red hot rod of hers and just left."

"How about her mail?"

"She didn't get much. Mostly circulars and bills. I saved it for a week or so and then gave it back to the postman and told him she'd moved. So now he just sends it back."

"Do you know where she works?"

She let out a snort.

"That type don't work. She said she was a singer. But mostly she slept until around noon and then would get up and go out. Sometimes she'd come home at night; other times it would be the next day or maybe two days before she'd be back."

"How about her friends? She have many visitors?"

She looked up at me sharply for a moment, cocking her head to one side.

"Say," she said, "has something happened to that girl? Don't tell me . . ."

I shook my head.

"No—no, nothing has happened to her so far as we know. Except she seems to have disappeared. That is to say, we can't seem to find her at the moment. But why did you ask? Was she the kind you would expect something to happen to?"

Again she shrugged.

"With those kind anything can happen. But about visitors. No, she didn't have very many. Once in a while some guy would bring her home and might stay over. A lot of guys picked her up here to take her out. I can't remember any girlfriends, though."

I took a copy of a photo of Harry Crimshaw out of my pocket and showed it to her. She studied it for several minutes and then nodded.

"Yeah, he was one of them. Main reason I remember him was because about the only time I had a complaint was one of the nights he stayed over with her. They were having a fight and making all kinds of racket and keeping other people up."

"Drunk?" I asked.

"Well, they were drinking, all right. But I think it was more than that from the way they were fighting."

"When would you say was the last time this man was around?"

She thought for several seconds, and shrugged.

"Couldn't tell you exactly. Maybe a week or so before she left. Fact is, I don't remember anyone else visiting her after the last time he was here but I couldn't really be sure. I don't pay much attention to the tenants, just so long as they pay their rent and we don't have to have the police in."

She offered me another beer, but I declined. I got up, ready to go, and then I said: "Tell me something, Mother. You've been around and seen all kinds. Just what was your impression of this Gale Everts? How did she stack up in your mind?"

She took her time answering, and I knew that she was trying to give me a fair picture.

"Well, she probably was a singer. She certainly practiced a lot, accompanying herself with a phonograph record. She had a lot of music in her place, sheet music and stuff like that. Used to read *Variety* regularly, and I do seem to remember letters now and then from talent agencies and a couple or so from radio and television stations.

"I'd say she was one of these dames with a small talent, not really quite enough to support herself by. She wasn't a lush and she was no full-time pro, but she must have been kept by someone. She dressed very well and had expensive clothes. Still, she wasn't a whore. They never fool me no matter how hard they try. No, I remember thinking when she checked in that she probably wouldn't be here long. She was the kind some man was sure to put in a fancy place sooner or later."

"We have an idea of what she looked like," I said, "but maybe you can describe her to me. I imagine you have a pretty good eye."

"Well, she was about five six or seven, weighed in at around one twenty-two or so. But she wasn't skinny. She had a real million-dollar figure. She was a natural brunette and had enough sense to stay that way. The most striking thing about her was her eyes. She has those same eyes Elizabeth Taylor has; same sort of dusky complexion. Good-looking girl, but her mouth was little too large. Pert nose and she didn't need to use rouge. Her cheeks had a sort of natural healthy glow."

"Sounds pretty glamorous," I said.

"She was. There was only one thing, and I can't quite explain it. There was something a little cheap looking about her. Hard to figure, because she dressed well, didn't use too much makeup, and she spoke well. But somehow or other she gave that impression. Maybe it was because of her expression. She always looked as though she were on the make. Not like a whore, if you know what I mean. Just a sort of shrewd, calculating something about her. You see the same thing very often in showgirls. Maybe it's just a concealed toughness."

We talked for a few more minutes, and then I thanked her and left. Later on, I checked the post office and the license bureau to see if there were any change of addresses, but I knew it would be a waste of time, and it was.

3.

The week's labors in the vineyards of research did turn up some interesting facts about Harry Crimshaw, but I couldn't see where they were going to help us a great deal. He was thirty-eight years old, which we already knew; had been born in a small town in Alabama, and had three years of high school. He'd done four years in the Navy and been honorably discharged as a gunner's mate.

He had drifted around a lot, working at all sorts of unskilled jobs until he started taking singing and guitar lessons. He had had one rather brief and fairly successful career with his own program on a small radio station in Louisiana: it had lasted for about six months. He was billed as Harry Crimshaw, the Singing Cowboy. He had used "Tumbling Tumble Weed" as his theme song and put on a program of Western and Country songs, accompanying himself on the guitar.

As far as we could find out, that career ended abruptly when he was found shacking up with the separated wife of the used-furniture dealer who sponsored his program. The wife went back to her husband, and Crimshaw beat him up in a jealous rage. No charges were brought against him, but he lost his job and must have been blackballed, because it was the last job he had in radio or television.

It was then he started selling used cars. There were a series of girls he lived with for longer or shorter periods, and he had a reputation for being excessively jealous.

A little over three years ago he'd moved to Baltimore and he'd run into Lloyd Wilson—he'd sold him a car—and it had been Wilson who'd introduced him to Marguerite Braintree. He courted her for several months and then they were married.

Marguerite, through her friendship with Alice Compton, had managed to get him his job with Loring Compton.

All in all, it was a dull, routine, completely uninspired biography of a man who had led an undistinguished and slightly seedy existence. There was only one thing about Harry Crimshaw and his background that utterly baffled me. What in the world had Marguerite seen in him to inspire her to marry him?

The two of them appeared to have almost nothing in common. Crimshaw was a fairly heavy drinker; he liked fishing and hunting; he was something of a gambler. Until the time he was married, he spent a good deal of time hanging around pool halls and was supposed to be a pretty good pool player. He was a snappy dresser, a fast talker, and apparently had a certain amount of charm.

Marguerite Crimshaw was an only child. She was born twenty-five years ago in Canton, Ohio, the daughter of a general practitioner named Dr. Caldwell Braintree and his wife, Mildred. Dr. Braintree died when Marguerite was sixteen, the year she was graduated from high school, and his wife died two years later.

The doctor had left an estate of some two hundred and forty thousand dollars after taxes, but his wife, through bad investments and the advice of hopelessly incompetent friends, had managed to diminish the estate so that there was barely thirty-five thousand dollars left when she herself died two years later.

Against the advice of her guardian, an aunt living in Chicago, Marguerite used up some fifteen of the thirty-five thousand dollars putting herself through college. She spent four years taking a general arts course at Ohio State, and after she got her B.A., she went to a business school for a year.

Alice Compton, with whom she had gone to school, had been responsible for her moving to Baltimore. Alice knew one of the executives of Adler and Adler, an advertising agency, and had been instrumental in getting Marguerite a job with the firm. It had been her only job: she worked for them until she and Harry Crimshaw were married.

Lloyd Wilson had at one time lived in Canton and had been a friend of her father's. He had known her slightly as a child, and when she moved to Baltimore she had learned through a friend that he was also living there. Knowing no one in the city aside from Alice Compton, she'd looked him up.

Some of this information we got from Marguerite herself, some of it from Wilson, who toward the end of the week was rapidly recovering.

So far as I had been able to determine, Harry Crimshaw had been the first man in her life, aside from a few temporary adolescent romances during her school years.

The slightly more than fifteen thousand dollars that Marguerite had left at the time of her marriage had been placed in a mutual fund, yielding her something like eight or nine hundred dollars annually.

And that was the sum total of what we learned after a week's investigation.

It wasn't much.

We still didn't know whether or not Harry Crimshaw had been drowned in a small boating accident. We didn't know if he had been murdered. We didn't know if he had purposely arranged to disappear.

4.

Eight days after Lloyd Wilson was taken to the hospital, he was released. He still wasn't in the greatest shape, but he was able to get about and he was going to be all right.

I had lunch with him the following day. Captain Rhinelander arranged it.

During the previous week I had not seen Marguerite Crimshaw. I thought it best to stick strictly to the job for the time being. I wanted my mind completely free.

I met Lloyd at the Chesapeake House in Baltimore, and he looked like hell. He was walking with a cane and he still had bandages on his head. He was very pale and he'd lost considerable weight.

We ordered a drink, and he smiled thinly and said something about being pretty much on a liquid diet until he managed to get a few teeth replaced.

I didn't waste time with preliminaries.

"Mr. Wilson," I said, "do you think this attack on you is in any way connected with the Crimshaw matter?"

He shook his head. He had a little difficulty in talking, but I was able to follow him all right.

"I don't see how it is possible," he said. "I am, of course, investigating the matter of Harry Crimshaw's accident, but I can't see how there could be anything I could turn up which might lead to an attack on me, either to keep me from passing on information or for any other reason."

I looked at him curiously.

"How do you know?" I asked. "How do you know what you might turn up?"

"It's open and shut," he said. "The man took a small boat out in bad weather. He was drowned. The fact that he was carrying a rather large insurance policy is beside the point. Everyone who is insured dies sooner or later. It is true we don't happen to have a body, but that in itself is not so unusual. Frequently in cases of accidents at sea, we don't get bodies. No, I don't think the attack on me had anything at all to do with Harry Crimshaw's death."

I nodded, and decided to pursue it no further. His mind was made up.

"In that case," I said, "is it possible the attack had anything to do with Mrs. Crimshaw? With the fact that you were about to pay her a visit rather late at night?"

He looked at me sharply.

"Just what do you mean by that, Lieutenant?"

"I mean is it possible someone who has an interest in Mrs. Crimshaw may have resented your—"

He looked suddenly annoyed and spoke in a harsh voice.

"Are you hinting that there was anything about my relationship with Marguerite Crimshaw which—"

I was quick to interrupt him.

"Not in the slightest," I said. "I have talked with Mrs. Crimshaw on several occasions, and I am quite confident that she has the utmost integrity. But she is an extremely attractive woman and, like all handsome women, she undoubtedly attracts a certain amount of attention, welcome and otherwise. What I am getting at, is it possible some secret admirer of hers may have resented your visiting her late at night?"

"Secret admirer, Lieutenant? What secret admirer?"

"Well, let us say someone like Loring Compton. I understand that Mr. Compton is quite an admirer of Mrs. Crimshaw."

Wilson shook his head.

"Mr. Compton is quite aware of the fact that my interest in Marguerite Crimshaw is purely paternal. Her parents were both friends of mine years ago in Ohio. Dr. Braintree was a particularly close friend. No, I am afraid you will have to look a little further than that. I know Compton and I am quite sure that he understands my relationship with her. Furthermore, I don't believe that Compton has any interest in Marguerite."

"In that case, can you think of any reason for the attack on you?"

"I cannot. But I will tell you one thing. I'm damned glad that she is out of that house. I've worried about her."

"Because of the attack on you?" I asked.

"Well, not exactly. I just worry, that's all. She's alone now, a young, attractive, unprotected girl. I feel a certain responsibility for her, which I think is only quite natural."

"I understand how you feel," I said. "Well, we'll pass over the attack on you for the time being. It would appear to be a complete mystery, unless you have enemies you know nothing about. But I do want to discuss the Crimshaws. Just how well did you know Harry Crimshaw?"

"Fairly well. Not, of course, as well as I knew Marguerite. I don't know whether you know it or not, but I introduced them to each other. I have regretted doing so several times since."

"And just why have you regretted it?"

"You would have had to have known Harry to understand," Wilson said. "When I first had Marguerite meet him, it was only because she was alone in Baltimore and knew almost no one. Harry is, or was, fairly young and quite attractive. I thought it would be nice if she had someone to take her out now and then. It never occurred to me that she would fall in love with him and marry him."

"Did you disapprove of him as a husband?"

Wilson nodded his head emphatically.

"I certainly did. I knew Harry's weakness for women, and realized that even if he was married to a girl he was crazy about, he'd still play around. Also, I realized exactly how careless Harry was about money. No basic sense of responsibility. That was one reason I more or less talked him into taking out that insurance policy. I wanted to see to it that Marguerite was protected, once she'd decided to marry him."

"Wasn't it a bit risky selling a man you considered a bad financial risk a hundred-and-fifty-thousand-dollar insurance policy? How did you expect him to keep up what must have been very heavy premiums?"

"In a way, of course it was. But on the other hand, I happened to know that Harry had made a big killing at the track a few weeks before he was to get married. Had enough money in hand to pay a couple of years' premiums in advance. And I thought marriage would settle him down."

The waiter was at my elbow, and I took time out to order another round of drinks, and lunch. When he left, I said, "If Harry Crimshaw hadn't had his accident when he did, do you think he would have picked up the next premium payment?"

Wilson shrugged.

"I have no way of knowing. The payments were to be made quarterly, and in the business he was in I feel sure that sometime during every ninety days Harry would come into a fairly good piece of money."

"And he would have been willing to put it out on insurance?"

Wilson thought a moment before answering.

"I really think he would," he said at last. "You see, you would have to know Harry to understand him. He was absolutely nuts about Marguerite. I know it sounds funny, but even though he couldn't pass up any dame who as much as looked at him twice, he was still in love with his wife and would do anything for her."

"Would he commit suicide so that she could collect double indemnity on that hundred-and-fifty-thousand-dollar insurance policy you sold him?"

Wilson looked at me and slowly shook his head.

"Don't think I haven't given that considerable thought," he said. "And don't think that my company hasn't. The fact is, on the basis of the double-indemnity clause my firm will very likely try to settle the case whether or not the body turns up. There is a suicide clause canceling the entire policy if a suicide takes place within the first year. The double-indemnity clause is void if the suicide occurs after the first year."

He sipped his drink, and continued:

"On the other hand, Marguerite has a very good case if she refuses to settle. Nothing, absolutely nothing in Harry Crimshaw's past would indicate that he was the suicide type. I, personally, will never believe that Harry would take his own life. He got far too much of a kick out of living. If I have to, and even if it should cost me my job, I would so testify in court."

"Granted that he wasn't the suicide type," I said, "how do you feel about his being the candidate for a murder?"

"You policemen do have suspicious minds," Wilson said. "Who could possibly want to murder Harry Crimshaw?"

"Who could have wanted to beat you half to death?" I asked in return. "Who could have wanted to try and brain me with a billiard cue?"

Wilson looked at me a little sadly.

"The only person who can possibly benefit from Harry's death is his widow," he said in measured words. "Can you think of any conceivable reason she might have to beat me half to death, assuming she would be physically able to do so, which I certainly doubt. Can you think of any possible reason she would try and brain you with a billiard cue or anything else?"

I had to admit that I couldn't.

"And she certainly wasn't out on that boat with Harry—and I doubt if she could have pushed him overboard by remote control."

"Someone else might have," I said.

For the first time Lloyd Wilson laughed.

"You're barking up the wrong tree, Lieutenant," he said. "Nobody pushed Harry Crimshaw overboard. No one murdered him. He was drowned in a boating accident, pure and simple. He didn't commit suicide and he wasn't murdered. He was drowned because he foolishly went out in stormy, uncertain weather, and his motor broke down and he tried to fix it in heavy seas. It's as simple as that. If you knew Harry and you knew Marguerite, you would realize it."

Chapter 6

1.

At the end of ten days, Captain Rhinelander pulled Jim Barnes off the Crimshaw Case. It was just as well that he did, because I was finding it difficult to manufacture something for him to do. In fact, it began to appear very much as though we didn't even have a Crimshaw Case to begin with. The Missouri and Texas Indemnity Company certainly had a case, and it looked as though they would have to pay off sooner or later. But that was their affair. So far as a crime was concerned, I was beginning to wonder if one had taken place at all—except of course for the attacks on Lloyd Wilson and me. We had not been able to tie those in with Crimshaw's accident, and I was getting ready to go in and say as much to the Captain when I was pulled off the case myself.

A teenaged girl had accepted a lift from a stranger over near Elkton, around dusk. Her young brother had seen her get in the car. The next morning they found her violated nude body in a ditch beside the road. So for the next six days I was up to my neck on that one. We got the guy who did it within forty-eight hours—he was a respected businessman and churchgoer from Philadelphia with a wife and four kids of his own—but it took us several days to wrap it up and get a confession.

During those six days I thought of Marguerite a number of times and once or twice I was tempted to call her on the phone, but I didn't. I knew that if I talked with her I would want to see her and I also knew that I was not going to be paying any social calls so long as our good churchgoer held out. But we finally managed to get the evidence we needed without beating a confession out of him, as his attorneys later accused us of doing in court. Actually it was pretty simple. We had him take a lie detector test; it was inconclusive, but it gave us just enough to go on so that he melted under continual questioning and finally cracked when we confronted him with his own teenaged daughter. She had told us of a sexual attack her father had made on her less than a month before he selected his final victim.

We figured a man who would commit incest, with the use of force, would be quite capable of murder, and we were right. Fortunately, we had enough material evidence so that when the case did ultimately come up, we didn't even need the confession.

It was one of those clean-cut cases that a detective takes a certain satisfaction in solving, for any time you get a rape-killer you very likely have saved one or more women from the same sort of fate. So I was feeling pretty good about things when I finally returned to my office in Pikesville. I had all but forgotten the Crimshaw thing during the week's intense work, but I had not forgotten Marguerite

Crimshaw.

I was surprised, however, to find a message from her waiting for me on Tuesday noon when I returned. She had telephoned that morning and asked that I call her back when I came in.

There was also a memo on my desk from Captain Rhinelander. The note was marked *Confidential: Crimshaw*. It read:

"Had a talk this week with Lloyd Wilson while you were away. He tells me he is satisfied there is nothing suspicious about the Crimshaw accident and that so far as his own private investigation is concerned he has been able to turn up no evidence which would justify further suspicion of fraud or criminal activity. Immediately following this conversation I received an urgent message from the Colonel (he was referring to the head of the Maryland State Police), who in turn had had a phone call from the Governor. It appears one of the top executives of the Missouri and Texas Indemnity Company is a friend of the Governor's, and we have been asked to turn over to the company all reports of our investigation into the matter. It would also appear that the insurance people and their own investigator are at odds concerning the case. The Colonel feels we should not become involved unless we have very tangible evidence upon which to proceed. His feelings are, and I agree with him, that the insurance company should pull their own chestnuts out of the fire. Please advise me as to your own opinions in this matter."

Two minutes later I had the Captain on the interoffice phone.

"We have found no evidence at all which would lead to a concrete theory of murder," I said. "So far as suicide is concerned, even if we had a body I doubt if anyone could say whether it was suicide or an accident."

"Let's just suppose it was neither murder, suicide nor accident," the Captain said. "Suppose the man just simply disappeared."

"We might have a case of conspiracy to commit fraud," I said.

"We couldn't even act then until the insurance people brought charges," the Captain said. "So the hell with it. The Colonel is out of town for a few days, but I'll get hold of the Governor directly and let him know just what the situation is."

I was about to hang up when he said, "By the way, Dick, that was a nice job you did over in Elkton. You must be a little pooped. Why don't you take a couple of days off?"

I thanked him and said I guessed I would. And then I put in the call to Marguerite Crimshaw, over on the Shore.

2.

She recognized my voice at once, and she sounded a little breathless. I was just a little breathless myself. I hadn't realized quite how much I wanted to hear her voice, talk to her.

"Dick," she said. "Dick—I'm so glad you called. I've been very worried and—"

"Is something wrong? Are you all right? Has—" She cut me off with a small laugh.

"Oh, it isn't me," she said. "It's Alice."

"Alice?"

"Alice Compton. She and her husband, Loring Compton, have had some sort of wild fight, and he took her car keys away from her, and she phoned to tell me he threw her out of the house. She's holed up in the Lord Baltimore and she called and said she's scared stiff of what he might do if he finds her. She wants to come over and spend a few days with me while things cool off."

"I'd like to spend a few days with you myself," I said.

"Oh, Dick. Dick, could you? Could you come over for a few days? It would be marvelous. And if Alice were to be here, then everything would look all right. I've been terribly lonely and . . ."

"It just so happens that I have a few days off," I said. "But I would a lot rather spend them with you alone than . . ."

"I'm afraid that if I were to entertain a single man alone, old Mr. Fletcher would run me right off the place," Marguerite said, and laughed. "But it would be marvelous if you could pick up Alice and bring her over. In any case, when she phoned and sounded so worried, I told her I would talk to you about it and that you would see that nothing—"

"You're probably right about old Fletcher," I interrupted. "Maybe Alice Compton's rumpus with her husband is a good thing after all. Suppose I call her and ask her to ride over with me. Are you sure you can put both of us up?"

"Alice was going to come anyway, and you know I want you here," Marguerite said.

"I'll get hold of that Compton woman and drag her over by the heels if I have to. If I don't call you back, expect us sometime late this afternoon."

Ten minutes later and I had Alice Compton on the other end of the wire. She was checked into the Lord Baltimore under an assumed name, and I had asked for the room number Marguerite had given me. The minute she started talking, I realized that Marguerite hadn't exaggerated. I could almost smell the fear in her voice as she answered the phone. In spite of what Jim Barnes had told me about her, she sounded completely sober and she seemed terribly relieved the moment I identified myself.

She was only too willing to have me drive her over to the Eastern Shore, but refused to let me pick her up at the hotel. She said that she would meet me at the main entrance of Hutzler's department store and that if I would drive by in three quarters of an hour she'd be on the curb waiting.

It gave me time to stop at my apartment and pack a Gladstone with a couple of changes of linen, some sports shirts and slacks, and get together some fishing gear. It was a little early for rock or blues, but I would give it a try anyway.

I was about to close the bag when I came across a little .25 caliber automatic I had taken away from a slightly misguided teen-ager some time back so as to keep him out of trouble, and I tossed it in the bag with a box of shells. It happens to be a rather nice little gun, and I liked to use it for target practice. A .25 doesn't look particularly lethal and in most cases it isn't. But that's only because people don't know how to shoot them. You have to be dead accurate. If you are, they can do just as much damage as their bigger brothers.

She was waiting just where she said she would be, and I recognized her at once from the description Jim Barnes had once given me.

A blond. Big, bosomy, curvaceous, and SEX written all over her in capital letters. Peaches-and-cream complexion. Tremendous baby-blue eyes and long dark lashes. She could have stopped traffic if she'd half tried.

But she wasn't trying when I picked her up. She was trying to make herself as inconspicuous as possible. Pulling to a stop in front of her and seeing the way she kept looking over her shoulder, I knew at once that she wasn't faking the fear I'd heard in her voice over the telephone.

I opened the car door. "Mrs. Compton?"

She gave me a frightened look, hesitated a fraction of a minute, and then quickly climbed in beside me without a word. She was carrying nothing but a small airline bag.

She didn't talk until we were well out on the Ritchie Highway.

Then she pulled a cigarette from a crumpled pack and lighted it with an unsteady hand and turned toward me.

"God—but do I need a drink!"

I would have thought that it was a tremendous hangover had I not recognized the fear.

There was a cocktail lounge up the road on the right, and I pulled into the parking lot.

She didn't speak again until she'd downed the double gin on the rocks I'd ordered for her. I'd remembered that Jim Barnes had told me she was a glutton for gin.

She suddenly looked up at me and gave me the full treatment with the eyes. Whatever she was, I had to say one thing for her. She had sex appeal. It fairly oozed out of her.

"Your husband didn't strike me as such a frightening man, Mrs. Compton," I said. "I met him, and he seemed mostly bluff."

"You don't know what that son of a bitch is capable of," she said. "Why he . . ." she hesitated, and her eyes focused on mine. "What did you say about my husband?"

"I said he didn't strike me as such a frightening man."

"Loring—frightening? Good God!" She suddenly laughed, and about half the people in the room turned and stared at us. "What ever gave you the idea that Loring could scare a fly?"

"Well, it did seem to me that you were a trifle upset over the telephone, and when I picked you up—"

She snorted.

"Loring doesn't begin to scare me," she said. "It's just, well just . . ." She hesitated, seemed to stop to collect her thoughts. Then she continued, but her voice was calm now and it was as though she were explaining something to a child.

"I wasn't really afraid of Loring," she said. "But we had a real nasty fight and we had words and I left. I don't want him to think he has any evidence that he could use against me in court. You just don't know how cheap—how miserably small he can be. I just don't want him thinking he has any grounds . . ."

Her voice dwindled off, and I ordered another round of drinks. For some reason she was lying through her teeth. When I'd picked her up in front of the department store, she'd been frightened stiff. Maybe it wasn't her husband who'd inspired that fear; I wouldn't know. But certainly someone or something had.

She wouldn't eat anything, but she insisted on a third drink. I never should have started her off with the doubles; she seemed to think that's the only way they came. It was during the third one that she became coy. She suddenly reached across the small table and took my face between her hands.

"So you are Marguerite's policeman," she said. "Well, I must admit the girl has taste. You are a good-looking brute, you know."

I gave a weak imitation of a smile.

"Hardly handsome," I said. "And I don't think I'm really anyone's policeman. I just happened to be on the Crimshaw Case, and Mrs. Crimshaw seemed to me to be a very nice—"

That raucous laugh cut me short, and this time more than half the people in the room turned around to stare.

"Haw! The man is shy. And don't you try to kid me about Marguerite. I know her like a book. She always did have a way with really big, good-looking men. Why, when Harry Crimshaw first saw her I knew that he was a dead duck before he'd finished saying 'How are you.' Yes, you big handsome ones always go for her. But Margie is the best. The very best friend I have in the world. I wouldn't trade her little finger . . ."

I could see that she was on the verge of getting maudlin.

"Don't you think we'd better be getting along? I know that Mrs. Crimshaw—"

She cut me short. It was a habit of hers.

"I just hope to God you're good enough for her," she said. "She's sweet—that's what she is. Sweet. Waiter! Hey, waiter!"

The waiter came running.

I didn't argue with her. I let her order another double. It would make a total of eight normal shots of straight gin, and I figured that it would be easier to let her drink it and probably pass out than to have a scene.

Little did I know.

Alice Compton wasn't just a simple drunk. She was a human sewer. The fantastic thing was—and I don't know why it occurred to me at the time—but she never seemed to get rid of the stuff. Before we left that cocktail bar she'd had four more doubles and she still managed to get out under her own power.

It was during the last drink that she really got out of line. Her hand had found my leg earlier and it had gradually worked its way up, caressing as it went along. Twice she had leaned across the table and planted moist kisses on my startled mouth. She was telling me by then that her trouble was she was married to an old man and that she was a girl who needed love. Needed a lot of love.

She managed to keep from spilling that last drink she ordered, but in reaching across the table, possibly to pinch my cheek—God only knows—she did tip my glass over in my lap. The waiter came with napkins, and I stood up to wipe myself off. I was conscious of the fact that by now everyone in the room was watching us. She chose that moment to reach out and take my hand and put it against one of those rather fabulous breasts of hers.

I'm tough, but that did it. I felt like a man who is dreaming he is getting laid in Macy's window at high noon—and suddenly wakes up and realizes that it isn't a dream at all.

I took a twenty and a ten and put them on the table and told the waiter to keep the change, and I took her by the arm and propelled her to the door.

She sulked for a while in the car, and a few miles farther on told me that she was tired and wanted to go to bed. She suggested we check in at one of the motels we were passing.

I reminded her that her dearest friend was expecting us.

"I shared Harry with her, why shouldn't I share you?" she muttered.

"Did she know you shared Harry?" I asked.

She snapped up then, and her voice sounded almost sober.

"Don't be a complete damned fool," she said. "Of course not. Do you think I'd tell my dearest and best friend that I was sleeping with her husband? What kind of a person do you think I am, anyway?"

I was tempted to tell her. But it wasn't worth the effort; anyway, my mind was occupied with something else. I was wondering just how much Marguerite had told her about herself and me. I decided that Alice Compton was merely guessing at a relationship between us.

She probably assumed that all women approached sex with the same tasteless abandon that characterized her own behavior.

But I was more than ever surprised and confounded by the friendship between two such completely different persons.

3.

We arrived at the cottage out on Benoni Point just before dark, and Marguerite was waiting on the porch when we drove up.

Walking down to the car, she looked utterly lovely. She was wearing a terry cloth bathrobe over a minute bathing suit, and her slender, beautiful body had taken on a golden tan during the last week or ten days. She wore a Turkish towel twisted around her still wet hair; her face was without makeup. She looked like a cross between a pixie and an angel, and my heart turned over as I watched her approach.

Alice half fell out of the car, and grabbed Marguerite in her arms and hugged her, and Marguerite looked over Alice's shoulder at me, quizzically. And then suddenly she winked, and I knew that she got the picture. Alice was mumbling sweet nothings as the two of them turned and went into the house. I started to unpack the car.

Five minutes later Marguerite came out to the porch where I stood smoking and looking at the early-evening shadows on the river.

"You didn't by any chance bring a bottle of brandy, did you?" she asked.

"It just so happens I did," I said, "but I was going to save it for after dinner." I was thinking of that other evening when we had sat and sipped small ponies of brandy, and talked.

"I need it for a worthier cause," Marguerite said. So I dug it out of my bag and, a bit petulantly, handed it to her.

She was gone almost a half hour this time and when she finally returned she was alone and had changed into a cotton dress.

Without a word she came to me and lifted her face. I kissed her long and hard.

At last I released her and nodded toward the inside of the house. "Our chaperone?"

"Out like a light. On my bed, fast asleep. I poured her some of the brandy."

I shook my head in mild disbelief.

"Nothing—but nothing, darling, could make that one pass out. I know. I have been trying to do it most of the afternoon."

Marguerite smiled wisely.

"I just kept pouring—in a water glass," she said.

"Honey," I said, "you're a Borgia. And I love you."

This time when I kissed her, I did it for real. My arms were around her, and she was standing on tiptoe, her own arms around my waist, under my sports jacket. Our half-opened mouths were glued together, and she was moaning just under her breath and I picked her up and started to carry her inside.

And then I froze.

The cough came from just behind me.

I put her gently back on her feet, and her eyes opened and she gave an odd gasp. I swung around.

Horace Fletcher was standing directly behind me, and his eyes were like ice. He never took them from my face all the time he spoke.

"Thought you told me you were a policeman," he said. He didn't wait for an answer. "I've just had a phone call at the house," he continued, still staring at me but speaking to Marguerite. "Some fellow from Baltimore. Wanted to know if his wife was here. Said he tried to call you but they told him your number is unlisted. Fellow said his name was Compton or Comely or something like that. Wanted to know if his wife was here, and he was damned unpleasant. Seemed to think I was running some sort of house of ill repute or something the way he acted over the telephone. I just thought I would let you know, Mrs. Crimshaw."

The way he pronounced "Mrs. Crimshaw," you would have thought it was some sort of curse. He turned on his heel and stalked back toward the manor house.

Marguerite said, "Oh, dear!"

I said, "Damn!"

We started inside then, and she said: "You know, he's terribly straitlaced. Betty—that's Mr. Fletcher's daughter—and we were in school together. Betty always said her father was just about as hard-nosed when it came to morals and manners as they come. I think she was even afraid of him just a little bit herself. In fact, I was surprised that Mr. Fletcher let Harry and me have the place again this year. He didn't approve of Harry at all."

"What was there about Harry—"

"I guess Harry just wasn't his type. Harry always gave an impression of being a lot wilder than he really was. It wasn't that Harry drank, although he certainly did. Mr. Fletcher isn't against drinking as such. But getting drunk . . ."

"It's just as well he didn't see our little playmate in the bedroom," I said.

Marguerite suddenly looked alarmed.

"Oh, Lord," she said. "He said that Loring telephoned him. Alice must have told him where I was staying, and of course Loring knew about Mr. Fletcher. Do you suppose—"

She stopped, her hand to her mouth.

"Do I suppose that Compton will drive out here?"

"Yes. You know he's terribly jealous. I think that's what they were fighting about. He probably found out about some man that Alice has been fooling around with. And if he thinks for a second that she might have come out here with someone, why . . ."

"Well, she did," I said. "She came out with me."

Marguerite giggled.

"I have got you into a nice little jam, haven't I?"

"I can always leave," I said. "But I'll be damned if I will unless you tell me to."

"I'm not going to tell you to leave," she said, suddenly serious. "And I can't ask Alice to leave. I know—after what he saw just now—that Mr. Fletcher would never put up with your staying if he thought the two of us would be here alone."

"It looks like we're damned either way," I said. "If Alice stays, her husband shows up and probably shoots me. If she leaves, I have to leave also. Of course I can leave alone, but I don't feel quite comfortable taking off and leaving the two of you here. Compton probably will show up, and I understand he can be a rather nasty customer."

"He wouldn't be nasty with me," Marguerite said, almost primly, I thought. "But I don't want you to leave in any case."

The bellow from the bedroom interrupted her. "Oh, Gawd, where's a drink?"

I shuddered.

"Better get out the brandy bottle again," I said.

Marguerite twisted her head and smiled up at me.

"This time she gets the house gin," she said. "I'm saving the rest of the brandy for just the two of us—for later."

As she turned to go back to the bedroom, she said over her shoulder: "I'll just go in and quiet her down for a while. Why don't you mess around in the kitchen? There's a steak and some salad and some charcoal and . . ."

I went into the kitchen to mess around. I roundly damned Alice Compton and her husband. I also damned Horace Fletcher, who had a very bad habit of sneaking up on people in rubber-soled shoes.

4.

I had the charcoal down where it showed a nice gray and red glow and was getting the steak ready to put on when Marguerite came back into the kitchen. I could see at once that she was upset.

"Alice is leaving," she said. "I told her about her husband calling Mr. Fletcher, and she sobered up so fast that it was unbelievable. She's afraid he's going to show up here, and she won't stay. I don't honestly understand what is the matter with her. She and Loring have had plenty of fights before, but this is the first time I have seen her really panic. She seems frightened to death of something."

"I doubt if it's her husband," I said. "Not from the way she talked this afternoon."

"I had the same feeling, but apparently he is a part of it. I tried to argue with her, but it didn't do any good. She's getting ready to leave now. I told her I would lend her my car. She wants to check into a motel somewhere until she sees what Loring is up to. There's something Alice isn't telling me, and I can't understand it. If Alice has one weakness, it's blurting out everything she knows. Especially when she's been drinking."

Marguerite left the kitchen, and a couple of minutes later she was carrying a flashlight and had thrown a light coat over her shoulders.

"I'm going up and talk with Mr. Fletcher," she said. "I simply have to try and explain to him, after his coming on us the way he did. I want you to stay here tonight. I just hate to be alone, especially without a car, and if you leave I won't have one, as Alice is all ready to go with mine. I don't know how I can explain things to him, but I'll try. I think maybe the simple truth will be best. We discovered we are in love with each other. I think he knows me well enough to realize that I wouldn't be kissing someone unless it really meant a lot to me."

"Would you like me to come with you?"

She shook her head, and I must admit I was a little relieved.

"No, I think I can handle him better alone. You get that steak ready to put on. No matter what happens, we'll at least be able to have something to eat."

So I went back to my cooking, and she went to beard old Fletcher in his den. I didn't envy her the job.

She'd been gone almost a half hour when I heard the car drive up and park outside. My first thought was that Alice Compton had changed her mind and decided to return. I said, "Goddamn it" under my breath, shrugged my shoulders, and took the steak off. I then turned and went toward the front door.

It opened with a bang that almost tore it from its hinges.

It wasn't Alice Compton. But I had been half right. It was a Compton—Loring, Alice's husband.

He stood in the doorway, wild-eyed, staring at me; gradually his face became more flushed as he started to stutter something. I thought that at any second he was going to have a stroke. He finally got it out.

"Where the hell is my wife? And what are you doing here?"

"Take it easy, Mr. Compton," I said. "I haven't the faintest idea where your wife is. And I am here visiting Mrs. Crimshaw."

His eyes began to half close and his thin lips drew in, and I could see his body tense. He opened his mouth to say something but he didn't get it out. Instead, he suddenly lunged forward and swung a haymaker that, had it connected, would have knocked my head clean off my shoulders. I dodged, tripped him as he went past me, and he collapsed on the floor. I had his arm twisted behind him as he struggled to his feet.

"Now, just take it easy, Mr. Compton," I said. "Calm down and behave yourself and perhaps I can tell you something about where your wife is. To begin with, she's not here."

"You dirty bastard." He growled the words, but I could feel him begin to relax. He didn't like the pressure on his arm. "You louse. She was here. I know she was here."

"Yes, she was here," I said. "And the reason she came here was that she wanted protection. She's afraid of you, and when she heard that you'd called Fletcher she took off again."

"Afraid of me?" He seemed genuinely shocked for a second, and I released his arm and he slumped into a chair. "Why the hell should she be afraid of me?"

"You'd know that better than I would," I said. "All I know is that she called Mrs. Crimshaw and asked if she could stay with her for a few days."

"Well, what the hell are you doing here, then?"

"I have already told you. I am visiting Mrs. Crimshaw, and it has nothing to do with either you or your wife."

"Well, if you're visiting Marguerite, then where the hell is she? That's what I'd like to know. Where is Marguerite?"

Marguerite Crimshaw spoke from the doorway.

"I am right here, Mr. Compton." She entered the living room and dropped her coat on a chair. "I suppose you're looking for Alice," she said.

It took the best part of an hour before we finally managed to get rid of Compton, and we managed it then only because Marguerite finally convinced him there was no chance his wife would return. He wasn't happy when he left, and he was mumbling under his breath. But he did leave and he seemed a lot calmer.

As his car pulled out of the yard, Marguerite turned to me and gave a long-drawn-out sigh.

"I guess our dinner is about shot," she said, "but let's try and salvage something of it anyway. I'm about two-thirds starved."

"I am too," I said. "I can't take these emotional scenes. But tell me how you made out with Fletcher. I've been dying to know...."

She never had a chance to answer me. The phone rang at that moment and she picked up the receiver, listened for a moment, and beckoned to me, holding out the receiver.

I couldn't imagine who it could be. I took the instrument and said, "Yes?" in a resigned voice.

"Dick?"

It was Captain Rhinelander and he wasted no time at all in giving me the answer to the question I had just asked Marguerite as to how she had made out with Fletcher.

"What in the name of all that's holy are you doing over there with the Crimshaw woman?" the Captain asked, not waiting for me to get in a word.

I fumbled around for a second, trying to get my bearings. "Why I— I am just here paying a—"

"Listen," the Captain said. "I just got a phone call, at my house, goddamn it, from a man named Horace Fletcher. You may not know who he is, but he's a damned big shot in this state and he throws a lot of weight over at the State House. Anyway, he finally ran me down at home and told me that one of my men was over at his place and that he had come on him in a compromising position with a young woman that he has been more or less looking out for and who is living on his estate. He named Mrs. Crimshaw."

"Why, the damned old goat!" I said. "What the hell does he mean calling you and saying—"

"Listen to me, Dick," the Captain interrupted. "I don't want to hear about it over the phone. You don't have to explain your actions to me, boy. But I don't care if this guy Fletcher is a nut or not; he has influence. He told me to get you off the place, and I want you to get the hell out of there right now. And for God's sake, don't take the woman with you."

He didn't wait for me to say anything, but hung up. Marguerite listened until I was through explaining to her, staring at me and shaking her head with a bewildered expression on her face. When I finished, she said: "I don't understand it. I simply don't understand it at all. Why, Mr. Fletcher told me, when I explained things to him, that he understood completely. He said that he knew I was a good woman and wouldn't do anything wrong. He even said that one reason he'd always liked me is that I was young and innocent and reminded him so much of his daughter Betty."

"I'm glad he didn't tell you what I probably remind him of," I said. "Anyway, I just have no option. The Captain said I was to leave and leave right now. And that, as they say in Hollywood war films, is an order, sir."

In spite of what the Captain had said, I still wanted her to come with me, but she refused. She said that if she did she was afraid it would get me in even more trouble.

So, after I kissed her good night, I left, and I left alone. But I did one thing before I left. I took out the little .25 caliber automatic and gave it to her. I showed her how to use it, how to set the safety catch and all. And I told her if anything should happen, anything at all, not to hesitate. Shoot first and ask questions afterward.

But I was pretty darn sure nothing would happen.

When I drove my station wagon past Horace Fletcher's manor house a few minutes later, on my way to the main road, I noticed a lot of lights in what I took to be the living room.

I gave the horn a couple of loud blasts.

I hope it shook him a little. He undoubtedly had saved Marguerite's virtue for that night at least, but he sure as hell spoiled something I had been looking forward to for the last three weeks.

Chapter 7

1.

Detectives in fiction stories always seem to have two rather unusual characteristics. They never seem to have to go to the toilet and they never seem to get any sleep. One is true and one is not, so far as real-life detectives are concerned. Real-life detectives do have to go to the toilet. But they get damned little sleep, especially while they are working on a case.

It was almost two thirty in the morning when I got back to my apartment, and I was dead on my feet. But I did something I always do when I get home. I called Headquarters to let them know where I might be found in an emergency and to pick up any messages that might be waiting for me.

The trooper on the night desk had a message. He had about ten messages, and they were all from the same person. He explained it to me in a slightly bored voice.

"Her first call came about an hour ago," he said. "At first I thought she was drunk. But along about the third call, I sort of got the idea that she wasn't drunk so much as just plain scared stiff. She wouldn't leave a name, wouldn't talk to anyone else, wouldn't even tell me what it was all about. Just said that she had to get in touch with you. Said it was a matter of life and death."

"So what did you tell her?"

"I said we'd let you know as soon as you called in. Anyway, after about six calls, during all of which she left the same telephone number, I got a little curious and ran a check on the number. Turns out it's a motel out on Route 1, about five miles south of the city line. I should have guessed."

"Why should you have guessed?"

"Well, she left an extension number also."

"I see. And when did the last call come in?"

"Not more than ten minutes ago. I tell you, Lieutenant, this dame really sounded as though she meant what she was saying."

I sighed. "All right, let's have the number," I said. "And the extension."

I had a pretty strong hunch who was making the calls, but I dialed the number anyway. Not one person in ten thousand who uses the phrase "a matter of life and death" really means it, but I would hate to be the cop who got the message that ten thousand and first time and paid no attention to it.

After about twelve rings a sleepy voice finally came on the wire and yawned:

"Oasis Manor Motel."

"Let me have Extension 56," I said.

"This the State Police?"

"Yes, the State Police. How'd you know, buddy?"

"My Gawd, that dame in 56 has been keeping me awake for two

hours putting in calls to you people. I just hope you got the answer she's been looking for. I need my sleep."

"Just put her on, son," I said. "And stay off the wire. We can tell if anyone is listening in." It wasn't true of course.

"Who the hell wants to listen in? All I want is a little sleep."

I felt like telling him that's all I wanted too. There was a buzz over the wire, and a moment later a voice whispered, "Yes?"

"Lieutenant Martingale," I said. "I understand you've been trying to reach me."

"Oh, thank God! I called you out at Marguerite's but you had already left. I have to see you. Right away. I—"

"Could you tell me what it's all about, Mrs. Compton?" I said. She didn't have to explain who she was. I knew.

"I can't explain over the phone. But I have to see you right away. It's about Harry. Harry Crimshaw and what happened to him."

"Couldn't I see you in the morning, Mrs. Compton? I just got in and I'm dead on my feet."

"For God's sake, Lieutenant, don't you understand? This is important."

"Well, could you possibly get a cab or drive into town? I could meet you...."

"I wouldn't unlock this door or leave this room for all the money in the world. I tell you I'm frightened to death. I don't know what I would have done if you hadn't called...."

"Now, Mrs. Compton," I said, "please don't become hysterical. I'm sure—"

"You're sure of nothing, damn it," she said, and her voice reached a new pitch of hysteria. "Don't you understand? I'm frightened half to death. I'm sure I have been followed here. You have to come at once. Dear God, please promise me...."

"All right," I said. "All right, just take it easy and stay calm. No one is going to hurt you. I'll be out as soon as I can get there. Just keep your door locked if you're nervous."

"Nervous!" She almost screamed the word. "Oh, God, please hurry!"

"As soon as I can make it," I said. I hung up and reached for my coat.

I climbed into my station wagon and headed for the outskirts of the city.

I didn't have any trouble at all in finding the Oasis Manor Motel. About a mile after I passed the city line, a pair of headlights showed up in my rear-vision mirror, bearing down fast, and a moment later I heard the sound of the siren. It was a State Trooper's patrol car and it passed me doing about seventy-five or eighty, the red light on its roof turning in quick orbits and the siren blasting a warning ahead.

I stepped on the gas and followed as close behind as I could.

The driver made those next four miles in a lot less than four minutes, and I was falling behind when he started putting on his brakes. I saw the neon Oasis Manor sign up ahead and to the right.

He skidded into the driveway on two wheels and was already getting out of the car when I braked to a stop behind him. He moved over next to me with his hand on his holster.

"Just where the hell do you think you—"

I already had my identification card in my hand. "What's the call, Trooper?"

"Night clerk, Lieutenant," he said hurriedly. "Phoned in an alarm about fifteen minutes ago. Said someone slugged him."

We reached the lobby of the motel abreast and shoved the door open. A pimply-faced youth of around nineteen or twenty was sitting on one of the leather chairs, holding his head in his hands. He was holding a wet rag against the side of his head, and he looked up with blank eyes as we crowded in.

"What's the trouble, son?" the trooper asked. "You the one who called in?"

The boy nodded.

"Yeah. Someone came in and slugged me. Knocked me cold. I got a bump like an egg on my head, and think maybe they broke my skull or something."

I took his hand gently away, and he winced.

"They steal anything?" the trooper began, but I cut in.

"Get on the phone and get an ambulance out here," I said. "I don't think this is too serious, but you never can tell about a fracture."

I turned back to the boy.

"Now, son," I said, "just take it real easy. Try and tell me exactly what happened. You're going to be all right, so just relax and tell us about it."

He groaned, shook his head, and gave a sort of weak smile.

"About half an hour ago," he said, "I was sleeping and someone came in."

"You leave the door open when you go to sleep?"

He shook his head, and again winced.

"I'm not supposed to sleep," he said. "But I go to school daytimes and I get pretty tired. The damned phone was going most of the night, but finally it stopped and I was over at the desk trying to study and I guess I dozed off. Anyway, next thing I know I thought I heard the door open and footsteps and I started to sort of raise my head and come to. And then the whole damned ceiling seemed to fall on me."

I nodded sympathetically.

"And then?"

"I guess I was out for several minutes. Then I slowly came to and I saw that Coke bottle laying on the floor and I realized that someone had sneaked in and hit me over the head with it. I called the State Police."

"Did you check to see if anything was taken?"

"Just looked in the cashbox, and it hadn't been disturbed."

"Anything else you can remember?"

"Well, while I was coming to I heard a car start up with a hell of a roar. I looked out of the window, and a red sports car was tearing out of the parking place. It made so much noise that I thought my head would come off. That's when I called the police."

I had walked over to the desk and was looking at the rack that held the keys while he was talking.

"You have an extra key for Room 56?" I asked.

"There's one on the board."

"No," I said. "There isn't one on the board."

"Well, there was one...."

I turned to the trooper, who was hanging up the phone.

"Get back on the phone," I said. "Or use the radio in your car. Get hold of the homicide detail and hold them until I get back. I'll only be a minute or two."

I turned again to the night clerk.

"Which is Number 56?" I asked.

"Outside and to the left. Last one on the end."

2.

They hadn't bothered to lock the door behind them nor had they taken the time to turn off the electric lights. I stopped at the threshold. There was no need of going any farther.

Alice Compton lay on one of the twin beds. She'd kicked off her shoes, and her skirt was hitched up so that it showed her leg and her thigh almost up to her pelvis. You could tell that she must have heard the door open and had thrown one foot over so as to try and sit up. But she hadn't made it.

Whoever had done it must have reached her in a couple of steps and had grabbed the front of the thin silk shirt she was wearing and pulled it down so that her large, pear-shaped left breast had fallen out. And then they had plunged the knife in, and they must have twisted it, because of the tremendous amount of blood.

They hadn't withdrawn the knife. The bone handle still extended from the wound. She had fallen back on the bed, her neck twisted at an odd angle. Her baby-blue eyes were wide, and her mouth was half opened as though a scream had been interrupted by death.

She should have looked a little obscene lying there with her leg and breast exposed, but for some reason she didn't. She merely looked pathetic.

I carefully closed the door and locked it with the key, which was still on the outside, using my handkerchief on the key. I wrapped the key in the handkerchief and put it in my pocket and then went back to the office of the motel, where the trooper was still holding the telephone receiver.

I nodded to him shortly.

"Bring them in," I said. "And get another ambulance. The one with the basket."

I didn't waste any time while we were waiting for the Homicide Squad to show up; the cameraman, the fingerprint expert, technical people. I got on the radio in the trooper's car and contacted headquarters in Pikesville. I had them put out a pickup order on Loring Compton. I gave them specific instructions that if he was found he was to be told nothing about his wife but was to be brought out to the motel immediately.

I next had a pickup put out for a red sports car. The only way I could describe it was by asking that every red XKE Jaguar be stopped and the driver made to identify himself thoroughly. Any suspicious person was to be brought in. It was awfully vague but it might just possibly catch a fish.

Then I had them transfer me to the barracks over in Easton. I told the sergeant on the desk to send a trooper out to the guest cottage on the Horace Fletcher estate on Benoni Point. The trooper was to pick up Mrs. Marguerite Crimshaw and drive her over to Pikesville and take her up to my office and see that she was comfortable until I got there. I got them to transfer me back to Pikesville and I told the operator to get Captain Rhinelander on the telephone at his home. He was to tell the Captain where I was and what had happened out at the Oasis.

Then I went inside again and called Marguerite from the telephone booth in the lobby.

There was no point explaining over the phone, and in any case I was still a good enough policeman not to give information to someone involved in a case, no matter what my personal relations with them might be. Once I was sure she was awake and able to understand me, I merely told her that a State Trooper would be by to pick her up within the next few minutes and that she would be taken to my office and was to wait for me. I told her to open the door to absolutely no one until that trooper showed up. Not to worry, not to be upset. Just be ready to leave.

I hung up while she was still asking questions.

I heard the sound of the distant sirens as I reached Sergeant Jim Barnes at his apartment.

"Jim," I said, "I'm at the Oasis Manor Motel some five miles south of the city line on Route 1. I believe Captain Rhinelander is on his way out here now. The Crimshaw thing has suddenly busted wide open, and I'm sure he's going to want you back on the case, so if you want to jump the gun, come a-running."

By the time I stepped out of the phone booth, the boys had begun to arrive and I heard the ambulance driving up. I knew that all hell was going to be breaking loose and that for the rest of the night and probably all of the next day as well as the following night, I wouldn't be getting any sleep.

I decided I had better take time out to go to the toilet. At least I could get that in before the circus started.

3.

I got back to my office over in Pikesville at ten o'clock the following morning. When I opened the door I heard a soft sound of breathing. I looked across the room, and there was Marguerite, hunched up in my big leather desk chair, her knees under her and her small, exquisite head lying on her shoulder and her arms tight around her breasts. She was sleeping.

I closed the door, tossed my hat on the desk, and fell into the other chair. I had reached the point of physical exhaustion where I was too tired even to want to sleep, too keyed up to be able to. But I would just sit back and relax for a few minutes—and let her get a few minutes more of the sleep she needed.

The toughest part had been when they had brought Loring Compton into the office of the motel.

Compton had been picked up at his home. He'd been in bed, in his pajamas, and was madder than hell when he'd had to get up and answer the insistent ringing of the bell. The trooper was sure he hadn't been faking. That he'd been sound asleep.

He'd blustered a lot at first, but as the police car had approached the motel he'd suddenly quieted down. It was almost as though he'd sensed an impending tragedy, according to the trooper.

I walked down the line of units, making sure that the guests, all of whom had been awakened, were staying in their rooms, and then went into Number 56. I had everyone clear out of the place, left the lights all on, and closed the door.

Then I went back and got Compton. He walked between Captain Rhinelander, who'd shown up sometime previously, and myself, as we approached the last unit. He was trying to question us, but he got no answer.

I had him by the arm as the Captain opened the door, and together we stepped into the room.

It was cruel—a hell of a thing to do to a man. But police work is never nice. It can't be if you want to get results.

We had to rearrange things, but she lay exactly as she had been when I found her.

It took him just a second or two to adjust his eyes to the light, and then he took one step forward and stopped as though someone had hit him.

His mouth opened and emitted a series of soft little sounds.

He said, "Oh—oh—oh—oh—"

And then he screamed.

The following twenty minutes was one of those times when I wonder why in the hell I don't hand in my badge and get into some kind of work that's fit for a human being.

I don't like Loring Compton. He's an arrogant, egotistical, unpleasant man. A rather ugly man. But watching him as he slumped in the chair, his head in his arms and the sobs shaking his great frame, sort of tore me up.

We didn't book him, didn't even hold him for questioning. We had the trooper drive him back to his place after he'd given a statement about his activities from the time he had left the place out on Benoni Point on the Eastern Shore.

We instructed the trooper to stay with him and bring him into headquarters in the morning for a formal statement.

I butted out the cigarette I had lighted, stood up and crossed the room and looked down at Marguerite. I hated to wake her up, hated to have to tell her what I was going to have to tell her.

Her eyes suddenly opened as I watched her. She yawned, looked up at me, and smiled.

"Marguerite," I said, "I think your husband—your husband—Harry Crimshaw—is alive. I think either he or a girl I believe he is living with murdered Alice Compton sometime during the early hours of this morning. Alice is dead, Marguerite."

For several moments she just stared at me, as though she didn't understand a word I was saying. I repeated it.

"I think your husband murdered Alice Compton last night," I said.

Her hand slowly went to her mouth, and she moved and her feet came out from under her and reached the floor. She started to stand up.

She didn't scream.

I caught her as she started to fall.

4.

It was late, almost midnight, two days after Alice Compton had been murdered. I hadn't had my clothes off in almost sixty hours and I was beginning to smell. But I had managed to get in an hour or two of sleep, periodically, sitting in an office chair.

Four of us were in Captain Rhinelander's office: Captain Rhinelander, Jim Barnes, Lloyd Wilson, and myself. I was doing the talking. It was, officially, my case.

"Loring Compton is out of it," I said. "We can't write him off officially, of course. We can't write anyone off until the thing is all wrapped up. But for the time being, I am satisfied that he didn't murder his wife.

"Five things have happened. Let me review them. Harry Crimshaw ostensibly loses his life in a boat accident. Lloyd Wilson is attacked and almost murdered. Mrs. Crimshaw's home is robbed. I am attacked soon after leaving Mrs. Crimshaw. And Alice Compton is murdered. I believe that these five things are all a part of a whole."

Captain Rhinelander grunted. "It could be, but I don't see it that way. Maybe you have some theory which would tie them all in together. If you do, let's hear it."

"I was just coming to it, Captain," I said.

I stopped long enough to take a drink of water and get another cigarette going.

"First, let us assume that Harry Crimshaw was not drowned. That he arranged a fake drowning. He could have had one of two possible motives. We can assume he was shacking up with this singer Gale Everts. Maybe he only wanted to cut out and take off with her. On the other hand, perhaps the thing hinges around a plot to collect on that insurance policy."

Lloyd Wilson spoke up, and his voice was angry. "Are you suggesting, Lieutenant, that Mrs. Crimshaw is involved in the plot? After all, the insurance was made out in her favor."

"Take it easy," I said. "At this moment I am ruling no one out. But to answer your question, I, personally, do not believe that she is involved. But that doesn't rule out the insurance as a motive.

"I think it is quite possible that Harry Crimshaw planned an insurance swindle. Perhaps he hoped that after his wife collected, he would be able to blackmail her. Or perhaps he had some vague thought in the back of his mind of substituting the new girlfriend for his wife in collecting on the policy. I wouldn't know. However, let me get on with it. Let's assume that Harry Crimshaw, for some unknown reason, arranged a fake drowning and then took off with the girlfriend. After all, she did disappear at the same time he did, and he had transferred a valuable car over to her shortly before they both disappeared."

"How does the attack on me tie in?" Wilson asked.

"Harry could have made that attack for one of three reasons. But let's cover the robbery of the Crimshaw house in Severna Park first. Two things struck me as very odd about that robbery. First, aside from some jewelry, only Harry Crimshaw's clothes and personal possessions were taken. Second, none of the stuff, such as cameras and radios and so on, has showed up in pawnshops. So it looks very much like Harry could have pulled the job himself to get his stuff back.

"Now, as to the attack on Wilson here, Crimshaw could have been on the scene, planning the robbery, the night Wilson showed up to question Mrs. Crimshaw. Harry might have thought that Wilson saw him. He would have to kill Wilson under the circumstances to protect himself. Besides, we know that Harry was almost pathologically jealous, whether he was playing around with someone else or not. Isn't it possible that when he saw Wilson drive up to his house after midnight, he might have suspected—"

Again Lloyd interrupted.

"Good God, man," he said, "I've known that girl since she was in her teens. Why . . ."

I held up my hand to stop the tirade.

"From your point of view he had no reason to be jealous," I said. "But think of it from his angle. Why the hell would you be visiting her at that hour? When she was alone in the house. Why would you . . ."

Wilson was on his feet now, his face red, and he was starting to yell. Captain Rhinelander interrupted.

"All right, everyone calm down," he said. "We can assume two things. First, that Lloyd's visit was perfectly innocent, which I am sure it was. Second, that if Harry was around and saw him, he could have put the wrong interpretation on it, lost his head, and beaten the hell out of him. So let's get on with it."

"Right. That brings us up to the attack on me when someone tried to brain me with a billiard cue."

I hesitated for a moment, and I knew I was beginning to blush, but I swallowed a couple of times and plunged in.

"The night previous to the attack on me I spent alone with Mrs. Crimshaw at her house over on the Eastern Shore."

I could feel their eyes on me and I knew that if Jim Barnes made just one crack, I would smash his face in.

"It is quite possible that Harry Crimshaw could have known about it. If he did, he could have made the attack on me for the same reason he could have made that attack on Lloyd here."

There was silence for a moment, and then Captain Rhinelander said, "Quite possible, Dick."

"Which takes us to the murder of Alice Compton," I hurried on. "We know several things about Alice. First, she had been having an affair with Harry. He could have taken her into his confidence. Or she might still have been seeing him. As we know, he couldn't resist any dame who was available. She could have known about or suspected the fake drowning. The other thing we know about Alice is that she was a drunk and that when she drank she talked. Harry could have become worried about that. Or Alice could have discovered about Harry's living with the Everts girl, and threatened him. In any case, to play it safe, he would have to shut her up. I, for one, am convinced he did. Either alone or with the help of Gale Everts."

There was silence for several moments, and Captain Rhinelander got up to pace the room. At last he turned to me.

"I'm not going to fault your theory," he said. "But I want to ask you one thing, assuming it is correct. Just why couldn't Mrs. Crimshaw be involved? Why couldn't she be a part of the entire conspiracy?"

Wilson started to protest, but I cut him short.

"She could be," I said. "There is no reason, logically, that she couldn't have been in on it from the first. But I don't believe it."

"Nor do I," Wilson said.

For the first time Barnes spoke.

"We-e-ll ..."

"I don't think," I said, "that Marguerite Crimshaw would have tolerated an attack on Wilson. And I don't think she would have stood by and let someone murder her friend Alice Compton. If my theory happens to be right, if Harry Crimshaw is alive and has done the things I think he has done, I feel that Marguerite Crimshaw's life is in jeopardy. For that reason I convinced her to take an apartment in Baltimore."

"That should make it convenient," Barnes said.

I swung to him.

"Just what the hell do you mean by that crack?"

"Oh," he said, "I mean it will make it convenient to keep an eye on her in case she is involved—or, if she isn't, convenient so far as her own protection is concerned."

"All right, boys, let's keep it on an impersonal basis," the Captain said. "So it comes down to this. If you are right, Dick, there is only one way to solve this thing. Find Harry Crimshaw. What are you doing about it?"

"Tomorrow morning," I said, "Jim here is going to start looking for that red Jaguar. If they used it in the killing of Alice Compton, they are bound to dump it quick. Fortunately, we do have the registration number. I don't doubt that they are using phony plates.

"Next, we are going to make one hell of an effort to trace Gale Everts. She has to be somewhere. And Mrs. Crimshaw told me that after her husband disappeared, she had a lot of his personal possessions—papers, photographs, things of that sort—packed in a trunk and stored. Tomorrow I'm going to get that trunk out and go through it."

I turned to Wilson.

"Since you are the insurance company investigator involved in this thing, I'm going to expect cooperation on your part. I want you to really start trying to find Crimshaw. Up to now, I know that you believed he drowned and didn't make much of an effort. But . . ."

"You can count on me from now on," Wilson said. "I know I can't compete with the police, but insurance companies do have a certain expertise in tracing...."

"Good," the Captain said. "As for me, goddamn it, I'm going home and try to get some sleep. I suggest the rest of you do the same. And in the morning—well, get cracking."

5.

I got back to my apartment at a little after 2:00 A.M.

The shaded floor lamp over the big overstuffed chair I like to sit in when I read was on. She was in the chair.

She'd taken off her clothes and climbed into my pajamas, and she sat there, her arms around her knees, her head forward. She had fallen asleep waiting for me.

I stopped for a moment and watched her, and my heart suddenly ached. She was so utterly lovely.

I slipped out of my shoes and crept past her and went through the bedroom and into the bathroom. It took me only a couple of minutes to get out of my clothes and into the stall shower. I scrubbed myself down and got out and toweled myself and tied a bath towel around my waist and opened the bathroom door.

She must have heard me. She was in bed now, the covers pulled up to her chin and her soft hair spread around her beautiful face. Her eyes were closed, and she was breathing gently.

I went into the living room and turned off the light and then came back and crawled into the bed beside her. I reached up and clicked the switch on the light beside the bed. I turned toward her. She'd taken off the pajamas.

She moaned softly as I put my arms around her, bringing her small body close to mine.

Her arms came up around my neck, and I fell asleep still holding her gently. Not waking her up.

Chapter 8

1.

Jim Barnes is a bit of a bastard, but he's going to make a really first-class detective. I don't know of any young cop on the force who is better at straight legwork. By three o'clock on Friday afternoon he had located the red XKE Jaguar. As he explained it, it was simply a "matter of using this fine brain of mine, reaching a logical conclusion from various brilliant deductions."

Like the rest of us, Jim figured that that Jag would be a lot too hot to hang on to. He didn't think they would be stupid enough to try and get a quick paint job and he doubted if they would have the time or the means to forge new papers.

He went one step further. They wouldn't just abandon it. They had a lot of dough tied up in it and they would try to salvage some of it.

I would probably have tried the Baltimore places first, but he outthought me. The Oasis Motel was on the road to Washington, and Washington is a center of sports car fans. So Jim made up a list of twenty-two places down there, and found it at the fourteenth stop.

She had sold it at nine fifteen, just a few hours after we discovered Alice Compton's body. She hadn't tried to disguise herself—the description matched perfectly that given me by her ex-landlady— and she had used her own name, Gale Everts. Probably because the papers were made out that way.

She'd been smart about it. She hadn't tried to give it away, but had bargained like hell. She hadn't wanted to raise any suspicions. As a result, she had picked up $4,100 for the car. While one of his salesmen was going over to the bank to get a certified check, the dealer had called the Motor Vehicle Bureau, and everything cleared through. The clerk at the Motor Vehicle Bureau had no idea at that time that we were looking for a woman named Gale Everts.

The check had been taken to the bank and turned into cash within twenty minutes of the time she signed the bill of sale.

It suggested one thing: she was no longer using her real name. That's why she hadn't minded borrowing it back for her brief transaction. She had another cover all ready to fall back on. Jim had gone one step further. He figured it was just possible, now that she was without wheels, she might make a fast buy of another car under whatever name she might be using. So he called every dealer in Washington, used and new cars, to find out if they had made a quick sale for cash to a rather pretty girl customer within the last few hours.

No one had. In fact, the car business in the nation's capital must be a bit lousy, because they hadn't made a quick sale to anyone for cash.

But it was a good try.

Jim left the report in my office along with a message saying he was on his way up to New York to follow another lead. He'd be in touch.

While Jim was flying up to New York, I was in an apartment on Franklin Avenue in Baltimore. It was a furnished apartment, two rooms and bath with a small kitchenette. Marguerite Crimshaw had signed a six months' lease and had moved in a few of her things, and we were trying out the kitchenette with a pot of coffee when the bell rang.

It was the delivery man from the warehouse with the trunk containing her husband's possessions.

I said to her, "Darling, if going through this stuff is going to make you feel bad, why don't you go out for a while? I can handle it alone all right."

She came over to me then and, standing in front of me, put her arms around me and looked up into my face. Her eyes were very wide, and her voice was low and soft when she spoke.

"Dick," she said, "Dick, I think I told you last night that I love you. Do you remember?"

"I remember," I said.

"I want to tell you something else so that you will understand. I didn't stop loving Harry when I fell in love with you. I stopped loving Harry a long, long time ago. I think I told you that before. When we first talked together."

"Yes, darling, you told me," I said.

"I want to marry you," she said. "If Harry is really dead, I want to marry you. If he is alive, I still want to marry you. I'll get a divorce and . . ."

"If he's still alive, Marguerite," I said, "you won't have to get a divorce. If he's alive we're going to arrest him and he's going to hang."

She shuddered slightly and turned her face away for a moment.

I held her close then and lifted her and carried her into the other room, and we lay down together and didn't get back to opening the trunk for a long time.

It's amazing the junk that a man will collect over the years and hang onto, moving it around, paying storage bills, letting it take up space. Old love letters, photographs of girls whose names he has probably forgotten years ago, theater programs, advertisements cut out of newspapers and never answered, unpaid traffic tickets. You name it. Harry had it.

It was, all in all, a rather sad collection of the furniture of his life, those souvenirs of long-dead petty triumphs, clippings from smalltown newspapers that had reviewed some bit part he had had on a radio show, announcements of club dates he would be playing, bills from a tailor who had made him a cowboy vest and trousers, and God only knows what else.

I went through it all, and the only thing I obtained after about five hours of diligent research was the knowledge that Harry Crimshaw had been at one time a third-class entertainer, a second-rate lover, and probably a first-class heel.

It wasn't until I got to the very bottom of the trunk that I found anything that even began to interest me. I found a small packet of letters, and in the upper left-hand corner was a return address in a fine Spencerian script. The name on the return address was Marguerite Braintree.

She was looking over my shoulder as I picked up the letters, and she saw me read her name. She spoke in a small voice.

"It's all right, Dick. You can read them."

I hesitated for just a moment and then I handed them to her.

"Take them out and burn them, honey," I said. She looked her thanks as I handed them to her. The only thing left in the trunk was a roll of recording tape. I slipped it into my pocket.

We went out shortly afterward and had dinner together and then I walked her back to the apartment and left her. I had to get back to the office.

There was no message yet from Jim, but I hadn't been expecting one. Lloyd Wilson had left word he wanted me to call him; I tried his office, but it was closed. I tried his house, and no one answered there either. I was about to fold up the shop and head for my apartment when I remembered the tape I had picked up. I took it over to the recorder, but it didn't fit, so I carefully rewound it by hand on one of the empty spools from my own machine. I let the machine warm up for a minute or so and then I turned it to PLAY.

They must have cut it in the middle of a program. It started out:

"... will hear the signature song of that newest star in the South's world of entertainment, the Singing Cowboy, Harry Crimshaw."

A guitar solo started in the background, and then a moment later a deep baritone faded slowly in with the words of "Tumbling Tumble Weed." He went through the chorus twice and then took time out for a commercial in which he made a pitch for a used-furniture dealer. It was a fifteen-minute program, all Harry and just about all bad. It wasn't so much that he had a really bad voice, although I am certainly no critic; it was just the way he projected the song, dragging out the consonants and ending his *ing's* with a "kah" sound. You could almost see him put the bear grease on his hair.

I went through that tape twice. He never changed his style in the slightest. He'd had enough sense to stick to the old standards for the most part, but at one point he sang a song for which he announced that he had written both words and music. It was a little number called "God Will Make Me Happy if I'm a Good Cowboy."

Well, God might make him happy, but if I'd have been his sponsor I'd have shot him out of hand. When I was through with the tape I took it off the machine and locked it up and sat down to do some thinking. He must indeed be a man of amazing, and quite blind, vanity.

2.

Sergeant Barnes was waiting for me when I got in the office on Monday morning. He was looking pretty smug.

"What are you looking so giddy about?" I asked a little sourly. "What have you been up to?"

"I have been researching a little gal named Gale Everts," Jim said.

"You look more like you've been sleeping with her," I said.

"Well, I don't think I could have learned more about her if I had been. Sit down. I'll give you an earful."

I sat down.

He had done a good job in New York. He'd tried Actors Equity first—no luck. Then *Billboard* and *Variety*. At *Billboard* he'd run into a reporter who had known Gale Everts several years ago. At *Variety* he learned the name of a man who had been her agent, and later he'd looked up and found the agent.

He had learned just about everything there was to know about Gale Everts until she had come to Baltimore some six months ago to do a strip act at a cheap nightclub down on the block. The strip single was a temporary job because she was broke and had just got through having a little trouble. She'd finished off a three-months' cold-turkey cure in a private sanatorium where she had had herself committed in an effort to get off the needle.

Her legitimate name actually was Gale Everts. She was twenty-nine years old, was born in Buffalo, New York, had been married for two years to a sailor who had been killed in a bar fight. Her second marriage had been to a dress salesman who had committed suicide.

At one time she had been fairly well known, under the name of Jean Jingles, and had her own TV show on a local station in upstate New York. She'd had several fairly good radio shows, one of which she owned and was very successful. The thing had blown up when she'd gone back on the junk.

She played a number of pretty good club dates under her own and half a dozen other names. But it seemed one of two things always happened when she'd start getting successful. She'd either go on junk because of a love affair or she would break up over some complete heel, give him all her money, cut him in on the act, and screw up the whole parade.

The trade papers had always given her good reviews, and both her agent and the *Variety* reporter believed she had a lot of talent. They also said she had good business sense and knew how to promote either a show or a radio or television program.

But she had a weakness that wrecked her every time. She was constantly attaching herself to some no-talent character whom she let take over her act or her show, as well as her money and her personal life.

She had no criminal record. She had just missed it once when an out-of-work bookmaker she was living with had been arrested on a robbery-and-assault charge, but fortunately she had been able to prove to the satisfaction of the district attorney that she had no part in his activities.

Her mother was still living in Buffalo, and Gale sent her money regularly.

Jim had the mother's address.

"You learned quite a lot," I said. "Maybe we should contact the police in Buff—"

"Did better than that," Jim said. "I flew up Sunday and talked to the mother."

"The hell you did," I said. "Did you ask for an expense voucher before you decided—"

"Took a chance that I'd learn enough so the expense wouldn't be questioned," he said.

"So what did you learn?"

"It took a little time and a lot of talk, but I saw the last letter her mother had from her. I can quote it to you verbatim, although I have a copy I'll attach to my report. It said: 'Dear Ma: I'm just writing a quick note and am enclosing a money order for fifty dollars. Don't laugh, but I have a new guy and he is really great. He doesn't have a lot of money right at present so we will have to wait awhile to get married, but he's got a very important deal going and is going to come into some real money. Big money. But that isn't the reason I love him. I'm going to be traveling around for a while, so don't expect too many letters, but I will send along some more dough within the next two months. Love, Gale.'"

"Very, very nice," I said. "Where was the letter sent from?"

"It was mailed in Baltimore. Exactly ten days ago. But that isn't the interesting part. The money order was what interested me. The mother still hadn't cashed it. The money order was made out at a post office in Philadelphia. The way I figure it is this. She is probably living and working in Philly, because I have a hunch that as soon as she got some money, probably a paycheck, she went right to the post office to make sure the old lady got her money order before the dough got blown. And then later she happened to be back in Baltimore and mailed it from here. What do you think?"

"I think you've done a damned good job," I said. "I also think that you will be spending the next few days in Philly. Okay?"

"Okay. I'll write up the report and be on my way."

3.

I was pretty busy with detail work for the rest of the morning, and it wasn't until after I returned from lunch that I remembered Lloyd Wilson had left several messages asking me to get in touch with him. The last message said it was important. I called his office, but he was out and I left word for him. Then I called Marguerite at the Franklin Avenue address.

She asked if we could have dinner together. She wanted me to drive her to the cottage on the Shore so she could pick up the last of her things. I told her I thought we might, and I was about to say goodbye when she suddenly said: "Darn it, you just missed Lloyd Wilson. He stopped by and said he's been trying to get in touch with you. He seemed awfully excited about something."

"How did he happen to drop by?" I asked.

"I don't really know. I guess he just wanted to see if I was all settled and comfortable. After all, he is an old friend, you know. He seems pretty involved with this business about Harry, and I guess he's just sort of keeping track of me. Anyway, try and make it this evening."

I told her I would.

Loring Compton came in shortly afterward. He had certainly made a fast recovery. His wife had been buried the day before, and he'd lost no time in regaining his old arrogant attitude. He wanted to know what the hell the police were doing, why we hadn't made an arrest, whether we just didn't give a damn if a man's wife was murdered. You'd never know it was the same guy who was sobbing his heart out a few days ago. It took quite a while to get him calmed down and convince him it wouldn't do much good to write the papers or call the Governor.

He left at four o'clock, and at four fifteen Lloyd Wilson finally telephoned and reached me. He said that he was on his way home but that he wanted to see me as soon as possible. It was important, very important.

Well, I wanted to get the hell out of the office before anything else happened, so I told him I would drive out to his place and meet him.

The Wilson mansion looked as forlorn and unappealing as ever, and as I parked the car I could hear the radio blasting away through the open front window.

I went up to the door and rang the bell, and Lloyd himself answered. He waved me inside.

The music was coming from the next room, but he didn't bother to close the door. We just sat down, and he offered to get me a drink, which I refused. He seemed very nervous.

Lloyd said he wanted a drink and would be right back. Some damned woman was on the air screaming a commercial. The commercial went off, and the woman introduced someone she referred to as the newest singing sensation, The Golden Voice of the Western Plains, Jerry Something or Other, and the Golden Voice came on accompanied by a guitar, and began to bellow about his lonesome cow pony.

I got up and went into the dining room to shut it off. Lloyd was standing in front of it, apparently spellbound. He looked up as I came in. Then his hand quickly reached for the switch, and he amputated the Golden Voice in the middle of a baritone bray.

"Damned kid always goes out and forgets to turn it off," he said. He came back to the living room but he didn't have his drink; I guess he forgot it.

He sat down and for several moments just stared at me unwaveringly, as though he were trying to analyze me or my mind or something. Finally he spoke.

"Lieutenant," he said, "I think I know where Harry Crimshaw is hiding out."

I looked at him sharply.

"You do? Well, for God's sake don't keep it a secret. Where?"

He sort of half shook his head.

"Let me explain something first," he said. "To begin with, I'm in a lot of trouble personally. The company is holding me to blame for selling that insurance policy, although God knows they okayed it. That wasn't bad enough, but when I reported that I was sure Crimshaw died in a legitimate accident, that just about cut it. As a result, I'm all washed up."

"I'm sorry," I said. "But what about Crimshaw? You said . . ."

"That's part of it. You see, I want to make a deal. I want to cooperate with you, but I also want you to cooperate with me. I want you to give me a break. I want you to let me make the arrest."

I sighed.

"For God's sake, Lloyd," I said, "be sensible. You don't even have a license to carry a gun. Why, this guy is probably a murderer. You wouldn't stand—"

He interrupted me.

"Please listen. Just listen," he said. "Don't you see? The only way I can keep my job, get back in the good graces of the firm, is by solving this thing myself. Now, if I were to make the—"

"You can solve it and get full credit," I said. "But when it comes to picking up murderers—that's police work."

"But you could see that I was deputized. Let me have a gun."

"Don't be a complete damned fool," I said. "Sure, and we could help you commit suicide if you wanted to. But let that go for a second. What makes you think you know where Crimshaw is?"

For a moment his face took on a crafty look; then he shrugged.

"I got a tip. That's all I'm going to tell you. I got a tip. It was anonymous, let's say, but I've checked and I'm dead sure it's right. But you have to play it my way. Now, if I were to approach Harry and I had a gun, he wouldn't suspect anything, and you could be nearby somewhere and—"

"You're out of your mind, Wilson," I said. "You approach that guy, with or without a gun, and you're going to be killed. Understand? Killed. Now, stop horsing around and tell me what you know."

His face took on that stubborn look I had noticed once or twice before, and we started arguing. I got exactly nowhere. I threatened, I pleaded, and I tried to use reason. But he was bound and determined that he was going to be some kind of goddamned hero. Finally I stood up in complete disgust.

"Listen, Wilson," I said. "Maybe you know something and maybe you don't. But I warn you. Don't withhold information from the police. Not unless you want to be charged with being an accessory after the fact, interfering with the—oh, the hell with it! Come to your senses, man. Now, I'm going to leave here, and I'll be at Marguerite's apartment during the rest of the evening. You think it over, and if you regain your sanity call me there."

I started for the door, and discovered I was so mad I was leaving my hat. I went back for it and noticed that I had tossed it on his kid's snare drum.

"By the way," I said, "where's your family? You're a family man, remember, and you shouldn't be planning on making orphans of your children. Not even to save your job."

He glowered at me.

"The wife and children are over at the beach. Been there for a week, but they'll be back in time for school."

I stalked out of the house.

4.

It didn't hit me until I was halfway back to town.

Lloyd Wilson had said that his family had been at the beach for a week. And yet when he shut off the radio, he said that the kid had gone out and left it on. The kid wouldn't have left it on for a week.

He must have turned it on himself.

He'd gone in for a drink, but when I followed him he wasn't getting a drink. He was standing frozen in front of the radio. Listening to it.

And then the whole picture suddenly fell into place. It hit me so hard that I ran a stop light.

I suddenly remembered when I had heard that baritone before that had been coming over the radio when Lloyd abruptly cut the program off the air. I had heard that voice only a couple of days ago in my own office. On my own tape recorder. Except it hadn't been The Golden Voice of the Western Plains, Jerry Something or Other. It had been the Singing Cowboy, Harry Crimshaw!

There could be absolutely no mistake about it. No two men could sing so corny.

I knew then where Lloyd Wilson had gotten his tip. At sometime or other he had heard Harry sing. Or maybe he had heard the very tape that was now locked up in my desk.

I rammed my foot on the accelerator and said goddamn it. I hadn't looked to see what station was being broadcast and I had let him cut the program before it was announced over the air.

For a moment I hesitated. I could return and confront Lloyd with what I knew, and maybe he'd break down. But maybe he wouldn't.

The hell with Wilson. I could find out what I wanted to know fast enough once I returned to my office. I knew the approximate time the program was on the air, and that would be enough. That and the line about The Golden Voice of the Western Plains. It would take a little time, a little telephoning, but I could get it.

I was so excited when I got back to my office that I damned near forgot to call Marguerite. I probably would have forgotten if I hadn't snagged a cuff link on my jacket as I was stripping it off to get down to work. She'd given me the cuff links as a birthday present two days before.

I decided to call her first and get it out of the way.

When I told her that I was suddenly tied up with something very important, she gave a little cry and said, "Oh, Dick, how could you? You promised that you'd—"

"Look, honey," I said. "You're just not used to having a cop for a fiancé. Work has to come first. Anyway, this is going to be very important to you. To both of us."

"But, Dick—"

"Baby," I said, "please try to understand. I can't really tell you anything, but I will say this: I have a lead, and a damned important one. I think I know where your husband is. As a matter of fact, honey, I am damned well sure I do. But it's going to take some time to make absolutely certain."

She gasped then and was quiet for several seconds, and when she spoke again there was no longer any resentment in her voice.

"Oh, I hope you're right. I do hope so much you are, darling. When will you know? When will you know for sure?"

"Well, I can't be absolutely positive, but I'd be willing to make a small bet that Harry Crimshaw will be behind bars by this time tomorrow night. Now, I don't want you to say one word—"

"I don't know anything to say," she said. "And you know I wouldn't anyway." She hesitated a moment and then asked, "Do you think you will be working all night?"

I said I probably would. I told her she should go out and have dinner somewhere and then go to a show or something.

She hesitated again for a moment or so and then said that, no, as long as I would be tied up, she would take the car and make a quick run over to the place on Benoni Point and pick up her things.

I made her promise to call and see if Horace Fletcher was going to be home first, and she said she would. We exchanged a kiss over the phone and hung up.

And then I went to work. I started with the radio columns of the local papers, which I had one of the boys bring me, and while he was getting them I began calling the local radio stations. The networks would come next, and if necessary the Federal Communications Commission. It was just going to be a case of time.

If Harry Crimshaw actually was The Golden Voice of the Western Plains, he would certainly be hurt to realize how few persons had ever heard of him. I drew an absolute blank with both the newspapers and the local stations. I drew another blank with the networks. I called six different radio and TV columnists in Baltimore, Washington, and New York, and I still drew a blank.

It was around then, when I was really getting discouraged, that I had an inspiration. I remembered that Jim Barnes was up in Philly checking on Gale Everts. So I tried a radio and TV columnist in Philadelphia. It was a woman, and I had to trace her down at her apartment and at first she wasn't any help at all. But after I gave her the time I had heard the program, she asked me to hold the wire for a minute or two and then came back and said: "I don't know anything about any Golden Voice of the Western Plains, thank God, but I have an idea that might help. There's a small local station over in Wilmington, Delaware, that carries a program between six and seven called Sally's Magic Hour. It's a fairly new program, and this girl Sally mostly plays records between commercials. But she seems to be a sucker for Western and Country music and usually introduces live some singer or other who nobody ever heard of. You might call the station and check with them directly. It's Station WXWC. That's about the only station in this area on at that time that might have your Golden Voice."

I thanked her and hung up.

I didn't call the station. I was afraid, if my hunch was right, that it just possibly could tip off either Harry or Gale Everts if they were hanging around. And Gale Everts looked like a setup for Sally and her Magic Hour.

I called a detective I knew up in Wilmington and asked him to make discreet inquiries and to call me back just as soon as possible. I told him it was important, urgent, and damned confidential and that under no conditions were the people I was interested in to be alarmed or made suspicious.

Then I sat down to sweat it out.

5.

By one o'clock I had been pacing the floor for better than an hour and a half. I was beginning to wonder if my pal up in Wilmington was letting me down or whether he was merely incompetent. I decided to run across the street and get a sandwich and some coffee, and was putting on my jacket when the telephone rang. It was my old buddy, Detective Claude Morrow, in Wilmington.

"Dick," he said, "I think I have what you want. The program you are interested in, Sally's Magic Hour, did have a singer called The Golden Voice of the Western Plains on this evening at six fifteen. Sally is actually Sally Harris, and she came to Wilmington about six or seven weeks ago and sold the station the program as a package. She pays for the time and sells commercials and supplies the talent, what there is of it. Sally Harris is a redhead, in her early thirties, five foot seven. She leased a small house out on Circle Drive. The people at WXWC think a lot of her. That's all I have on her. I didn't have to ask too many questions.

"Now about The Golden Voice of the Western Plains. He's a guy named Carlton Jones and he's been on the Magic Hour program some ten or twelve times in the last three weeks. Don't have his address yet but we can get it. He's around six foot tall, very blond hair but a slightly swarthy complexion. In his late thirties or early forties. Plays a guitar. That's all I know about him at the moment, except the manager of the radio station told me that Jones and Sally Harris seem to be a little more than merely friends. He hinted that they may be living together. Is this what you wanted?"

I said it was exactly what I wanted.

"Listen, Claude," I said. "I want you to get a man out to that Harris woman's house and keep it under surveillance. Be very careful to do nothing to arouse anyone's suspicions. Try to get a line on Jones, and if you find out where he is staying put a tail on him. These people can be dangerous. I have a feeling that they are the two I'm looking for on a murder charge. On the other hand, I want to be sure before we make a pickup. I'll be up in the morning and I'll bring along a witness who can make an identification, but until then don't do anything to warn them. But keep a tail on them. Okay?"

"Right, Dick, we'll take care of it. What time can I expect you tomorrow?"

"I'll leave here fairly early," I said. "It's about a two-hour drive, so I should be in your office around ten thirty. That all right with you?"

"Fine. Look forward to seeing you."

We hung up and I checked my watch. I hated to wake Marguerite up so late, but if I was going to take her with me in the morning I wanted her to have a chance to prepare herself. So I put in the call to the apartment on Franklin Avenue.

The phone rang for a long time, and I was beginning to wonder if something was wrong, when a sleepy voice answered. It took a minute or two before she understood who was calling and until she was fully awake.

"Tomorrow morning," I said. "Eight o'clock. I'll pick you up and we can have breakfast on the road. It's important, honey, or I wouldn't ask you."

"But can't you tell me what it's all about?" she asked.

"Just trust me," I said. "I'll explain on the way up to Wilmington. You just be ready when I get there. All right?"

She said all right, sleepily, and then hung up.

I left for my apartment to get a couple of hours' sleep. I had a feeling I would be needing them.

6.

The telephone was ringing when I keyed my way in. I tossed my hat on the couch, swore under my breath, and picked up the receiver. I was beginning to wonder if I was ever going to see a bed.

It was Headquarters, and they told me I had an urgent call from a Detective Morrow in Wilmington.

So I called Claude back once more. I didn't get him at police headquarters, but they gave me a number where I could reach him. I figured he'd gone home to get some sleep too.

I called the number they gave me, and a man's voice answered. "Yes?"

I asked for Detective Morrow, and I had to give my name before Claude came on.

"Dick?" he said.

"Yeah. What the hell is—"

"Boy, you must be psychic or something. You got to get up here as fast as you can."

"Why? What's—"

"I sent a man to the house on Circle Drive like you asked me to," Claude said. "I'm out here now myself. Anyway, when my man got out here the first thing he noticed was that the front door was open and the lights were on. He thought it was funny, so he poked his head in. It's lucky he did. We have a dead man on our hands, shot in the guts with a .38-caliber bullet. We have the gun. We have another man who's been shot in the heart and may or may not be dead. The ambulance is taking him to the hospital right now. He's been identified as Carlton Jones."

It took me a second or two to digest it. I said, "The dead man, who is he?"

"We have only a partial identification," Claude said. "Lloyd Wilson from Baltimore, down your way, according to the papers in his pockets. There's a Maryland car parked outside."

I said, "Oh, goddamn it."

"What, Dick?"

"Nothing, nothing, Claude. But how about the woman? Sally Harris."

"She wasn't anywhere around. We have a pickup out on her right now. But you better get up here as fast as you can. If you like, I'll have a trooper meet you at the state line."

"I'm leaving right now," I said. "But make it the airport. I'll have one of our planes drop me there within an hour."

Chapter 9

1.

I could have called Marguerite and broken the news to her, but I didn't. I wanted her to get as much rest as she could because I knew that she was going to need it before very long. What I did do was arrange to have a trooper pick her up at her apartment at eight o'clock in the morning. Knowing that there was the possibility she would get news of the tragedy over the radio or possibly see a morning newspaper, I gave him careful instructions. I told him to let her know what had happened, that Wilson was dead. That the man we were sure was Harry Crimshaw had been shot and might or might not still be alive. I told him to break it as gently as he could while he was driving her to Wilmington.

After that, I called and arranged for the State Police plane to be waiting for me at Friendship Airport on the other side of Baltimore.

We had a set of Crimshaw's fingerprints on file, which we had obtained from the time when he'd been in the service. I took them along with me. We had copies of a number of fingerprints that had been lifted from the red Jaguar, and I took them along. Some of them may have belonged to Gale Everts.

I got Captain Rhinelander out of bed and gave him a rundown on the latest developments and then I drove out to the airport and climbed aboard the plane. I was able to get in a catnap during the flight.

The Delaware State Police car took me directly to headquarters. The house out on Circle Drive was within the city limits, and the local Homicide Division was in charge of the case. Detective Claude Morrow was in his office when I arrived. He looked dead beat, sitting at his desk in his shirtsleeves and sipping from a container of coffee.

He motioned to a chair when I came in and then got up and closed the door.

"Boy, am I glad to see you," he said.

"How is Jones?" I asked. "Or Crimshaw, if that's who he is."

"We haven't made a definite identification yet," Morrow said, "but I'm pretty sure he's your man. The hair was dyed, by the way. He's still alive. I just had a report from the hospital. He's unconscious and under an oxygen tent. They're afraid to operate. I don't quite understand the technicalities, but apparently the bullet lodged in the center of his heart—it showed up in the X ray. It's one of those freak things. He lost a lot of blood, and they're afraid if they go in for the slug he won't make it. They think there is a chance that he'll pull through. He has been conscious off and on, but no one has gotten a word out of him."

I flipped the copy of Harry Crimshaw's fingerprints across the desk and suggested Morrow have them checked out while he gave me the details. He put it in the works and then came back and brought a couple more containers of coffee with him.

"No pickup on the Harris woman yet," he said. "We have an all-state alarm out for her."

"Do you figure she did it?"

Morrow shook his head.

"Let me give you the picture," he said. "When Klotsky—that's the cop I sent out to case the house last night—walked in and found them, Jones, or Crimshaw, still had a .38-caliber revolver in his hands. Three shots had been fired, and those three shots were found in the body of Wilson. The coroner figures Wilson was killed sometime between nine o'clock and midnight. It's a calculated guess.

"Jones, or Crimshaw, was across the room, unconscious. There was blood all over him and he had been shot in the left breast. One bullet, and it must have been from a fairly small-bore gun or it would have gone right through him. We found no other weapon in the place.

"The woman was gone. Her car was gone. It's a late-model Buick convertible, and she had purchased it from a local dealer less than a week ago. There are no really close neighbors and no one heard the shots. We went through the house, and from the evidence the two of them, Jones and the woman, were living together. We don't know whether the woman took any clothes or possessions with her or not. We did find one neighbor who remembers seeing her car in the driveway earlier in the evening.

"We found Wilson's car parked outside. Jones apparently had no car."

I took out the rest of the fingerprints. "You might check these with the prints picked up in the house. The woman who called herself Sally Harris is, I believe, Gale Everts."

His telephone rang and he picked it up.

He listened for several moments, nodded, and grunted a Yes now and then. He put the receiver back.

"The lab," he said. "The prints check out. Carlton Jones is Harry Crimshaw all right."

I reached for my briefcase and took out a sheaf of notes.

"You're looking for Gale Everts, then," I said. "I have her mother's address here. And other information which may or may not help you. Crimshaw's wife will be here in the morning. Now I think I had better start giving you the background. Then I want you to take me to see Wilson. I don't want to have to get in touch with his family until I am absolutely sure. They are someplace at the shore on a vacation, but I have people working at our end trying to locate them. As far as Harry Crimshaw is concerned, he'll be lucky if he doesn't pull through. We have a fairly good case against him for one murder already, although the Everts woman could have done it alone. But it would seem you have him absolutely cold on Wilson."

"Absolutely cold," Morrow said. "The murder weapon was in his hand; he'd fired it. His prints were the only ones on it, and there were powder marks on the hand holding the gun."

"I feel like hell about Wilson," I said. "I could probably have saved his life if I hadn't gotten impatient with him and lost my temper. The poor little bastard, he wanted to be a hero. I'll tell you about it."

So for the next twenty-five minutes I brought Claude Morrow up to date. It did me good to talk. I was feeling goddamned guilty about Lloyd Wilson and I couldn't kid myself about him. I knew that I should have returned to his house when I had finally understood that he had solved the problem of Harry Crimshaw's disappearance. But who would ever believe he could have found him so fast?

When I finished telling Morrow the background of the case, he thought for several moments and then looked up at me.

"Your telling me about Wilson explains something that has baffled us," he said. "I forgot to mention that we found powder marks on his right hand. It is just possible that he did have a gun, that he got a shot in at Crimshaw. What I can't understand is why the Everts woman would have taken the gun if it happened that way. On the other hand, the woman herself would hardly have had any reason to shoot Crimshaw."

"She probably panicked," I said. "God only knows why women ever do anything they do. But if the gun is missing, she would have had to have taken it, whether she shot Crimshaw or Wilson shot him. I just hope he lives so we can find out."

"Well, if he doesn't pull through, we're bound to pick her up sooner or later. We'll find out what happened before we're through with it," Morrow said.

2.

Morrow was wrong. Gale Everts wasn't picked up and still hasn't been picked up. And Harry Crimshaw did pull through. But he didn't talk. He never talked—not during the weeks while he was recovering, not later while the lawyers were preparing his defense, not even during the trial.

I guess he knew it wouldn't have made any difference. Nothing could have saved him.

The thing is over now, finished and completed, and the case is closed and I am finishing up this final memorandum on the Crimshaw Case. There is very little left.

Marguerite arrived in Wilmington, and when she was taken to the prison ward in the hospital she identified her husband without hesitancy. He was still unconscious under the oxygen tent.

I sent her back alone, several hours later, after talking to her only briefly. She was pale and very tired; she had only just fallen asleep when I had called her to tell her she had to come to Wilmington with me. After that she had stayed awake and worried, and was still awake when the trooper picked her up the following morning.

I stayed on in Wilmington for three days, hoping Crimshaw would recover enough so that he could be questioned. He regained consciousness the second day, and the doctors let me talk to him for a few minutes, but he merely looked at me blankly and refused to say a word. We told him he was being indicted for the murder of Lloyd Wilson as well as the murder of Alice Compton, but he still didn't talk.

I accompanied the body of Wilson back to Baltimore. I felt it was the least I could do. I was still blaming myself for his death.

His wife and the two children met the train at the station. They were dry eyed and without words. There were a couple of men from the insurance company present and they took charge of things, and I left after making a feeble effort to express my regrets to the widow. Her only comment was to say that she knew Lloyd would get in trouble, running around with all sorts of strange people.

We finally traced the knife that had been found buried in Alice Compton's breast. It had been purchased from a sporting-goods store in Easton a couple of months before, and the clerk who had sold it identified a picture of Crimshaw as purchaser.

For a while it was a toss-up whether he would be tried in Maryland or Delaware first, but after going over all the evidence we decided Delaware had the stronger case, and so he was charged with first-degree murder and the trial was set for late in the fall. Delaware wastes no time in these matters.

The state appointed attorneys to represent Crimshaw, who still refused to say a word. And he was still carrying that slug around in the center of his heart. The doctors told him that they would operate if he insisted, but they didn't think he would survive the operation. In the meantime, he could drop dead at any moment. I guess, knowing that, he really didn't care a great deal.

Captain Rhinelander and I both attended Lloyd Wilson's funeral, and I was rather surprised to see that Loring Compton showed up. But he didn't speak to us and ignored me when I greeted him.

Marguerite and I debated whether she should attend or not. She felt that it was her duty to, but I discouraged it. The papers were giving the story a big play, making a real sensation out of it, and I didn't want her exposed to what might have been a certain amount of unpleasantness. She finally agreed with me, but she sent flowers. Lloyd's fellow employees took up a collection to start a trust fund to see his children through school, and his firm contributed handsomely. I contributed a lot more than I could afford myself, not because of the children, because of Lloyd.

Marguerite and I had a quiet dinner in a restaurant several miles outside Baltimore ten days after Lloyd Wilson's body was cremated. I had seen her only once since then, and that was in a purely official capacity.

But we finally made arrangements to have dinner, and afterward we had a long talk. We both reluctantly decided that in view of all the publicity that was bound to follow, it would be best if we saw very little of each other until after the trial was over.

The trial came up on November twenty-first, and they had to bring

Crimshaw into court in a wheelchair. He still had that lead slug in his heart.

Neither our people nor the Delaware police had been able to find Gale Everts, but the prosecution didn't need her. It was one of the fastest trials on record.

Harry Crimshaw, indicted for first-degree murder in the death of Lloyd Wilson, was convicted in the record time of two days. The only time he showed the slightest interest or expression was when the judge sentenced him to death, the event to take place sometime between July first and July tenth, the following summer.

He smiled.

3.

We had thought once the trial was over and done with that things would be different. We had thought that the public would forget the Crimshaw Case and go on to something else. They probably would have if it hadn't been for the vicious curiosity and poisonous pen of a certain female crime writer for one of the biggest chains of newspapers in the country.

This woman, assigned to cover the Crimshaw trial, had tried without success to interview Marguerite. It would have been far better if she had seen her. Defeated in that attempt, the reporter had begun digging into everything in her past and eventually had gone to the Eastern Shore in search of some facet on which to hang a story. Some evil fate led her to Horace Fletcher.

The story hit about every major newspaper in the country during the last day of the trial. I don't suppose that Fletcher was even aware of the damage he caused. But he had talked about the Crimshaws and their living on his place. He'd told about Marguerite returning to stay at the cottage after Harry Crimshaw had ostensibly been drowned.

Somehow or other this woman had wormed the information out of him that I had spent time over there with Marguerite, and she at once smelled blood. Poor old Fletcher, probably in a misguided effort to protect Marguerite, had then told what she had said to him on that night he had found the two of us in each other's arms. He told her that Marguerite had told him that she and I were in love with each other and planning on getting married.

It was just ghoulish enough for the lady reporter to see the sensational possibilities. She knew of course about the insurance policy and she checked up and realized at once that if Harry Crimshaw was hanged for murder, Marguerite would collect the money on the insurance. And now she was planning to marry the very man who had made it possible for her to collect that insurance. Planning to marry the man who was directly responsible for the arrest and conviction of her husband.

At best it looked as though the two of us had been in a conspiracy to see that Harry Crimshaw died so that we could mutually benefit from his insurance.

That story damned near cost me my career. And it made it absolutely impossible to continue seeing Marguerite Crimshaw.

We talked it over after I came back, and reached the decision that she should leave Baltimore and more or less go into seclusion. We also decided that under no conditions would we give each other up. And finally, after agonizing over it for hours, we reached a decision. Marguerite would go up to New York and take a job. I would see her secretly once or twice a month. And when Harry Crimshaw was finally hanged, we would be married. If, by then, the scandal had not died down, I'd give up my job and we'd go out to California or somewhere else where neither of us was known, and start over.

We lived up to the agreement. Marguerite took a small two-room apartment on the Upper East Side of New York and had no difficulty getting a job as a secretary with a toy manufacturer. I got away two or three times a month and went up to spend a night with her.

We planned to meet in St. Michaels, in a little church that Marguerite had gone to at one time, and be married, the week after Harry Crimshaw paid his debt to society.

4.

This is the day that I am due to meet Marguerite at that small church in St. Michaels on the Eastern Shore of Maryland. It is Saturday, and I must be there within the next couple of hours. I want to finish this memorandum of the Crimshaw Case before I leave.

I was delayed over in Delaware. I had to wait for the autopsy following Harry Crimshaw's hanging.

I attended it. Oddly enough, I did not attend because of my involvement in the case. I attended it at the specific request of Harry

Crimshaw himself.

He made two requests. He not only wanted me to attend; he asked me to see him on the night he was hanged. It was the only time since his conviction that he had wanted to see anyone or even permitted anyone to see him.

I granted that request.

And that's why I shall be a little late in keeping my rendezvous with Marguerite Crimshaw at the church in St. Michaels.

It is also the reason that instead of bringing our marriage license, I am bringing a different set of papers. I had to make those papers out and I also had to notify the police in Delaware that we are no longer seeking Gale Everts.

The papers I am taking with me are warrants for the arrest of Marguerite Crimshaw, charging her with conspiracy to commit fraud against an insurance company and with being the accessory to murder.

I shall close this memorandum now with the transcription of the taped conversation I had with Harry Crimshaw on the night of his execution. It follows:

Taped transcription of conversation between Lieutenant Richard Martingale of the Maryland State Police and Harry Crimshaw, convicted murderer, made in the death house of the Delaware State Prison at eleven fifteen, July ninth, and witnessed by George Dellis Murphy, Assistant Warden:

Det. Martingale: Hello, Crimshaw. I understand you asked to see me.

Crimshaw: Right, Lieutenant, I did. I want to talk to you. You see, I read that story in the papers about you and Marguerite planning to get married. I wanted to talk to you.

Martingale: I can't see why, but go ahead and talk.

Crimshaw: Don't misunderstand me, Lieutenant. I didn't want to congratulate you. As a matter of fact, I think you're a son of a bitch. I think you are probably as bad as Marguerite. All I want to do is spoil it for you. I'll feel a lot better when I walk through that door in a few minutes if I know I have really spoiled it. Spoil your plans to share the dough that I am paying for with my life.

Martingale: I am not marrying your wife because of the money. I am marrying her in spite of it. Because I happen to love her.

Crimshaw: You know, I almost believe you. I believe you because I loved her also. But let me tell you something, Lieutenant. Marguerite loves no one. Me, you, or anyone else. I think that is one reason I am no longer jealous. She is incapable of loving anyone but herself. And I will tell you something else, just to spoil it for her, in case by some wild accident she does happen to love you. She is more of a murderer than I am. She may not have pulled the trigger, but she murdered Lloyd Wilson. She deliberately sent him to his death. She murdered him, and just so that you have the record straight, she is murdering me. She tipped Lloyd off, told him where I could be found, sent him up after me. And then she telephoned me to tell me he was on his way up. She told me he had a gun, but she didn't tell me that she was the one who gave him the gun. Wilson was another one who believed in her. Was crazy about her. She could talk him into anything, and he thought he was coming up here and take me and be a hero.

Martingale: You're insane, Crimshaw. I feel sorry for you. How could she have known where you were? Why would she have sent—

Crimshaw: You really are stupid, Lieutenant. Don't you understand that Marguerite was in on the thing from the very beginning? That it was a conspiracy between the two of us? Oh, it started out simply enough. The policy on my life and then after the suicide clause expired, I would pull the phony drowning act. It went across perfectly. But then things started going wrong. Lloyd was smarter than we figured, and once he began realizing I might still be alive he began putting the pieces together. He was smart, but he wasn't smart enough to guess that she was in on it. When he began to get warm, when he figured out where I was and what I was doing—

Martingale: Your story doesn't add up, Crimshaw. If what you say is true, why would she have given him the address of the house you were staying in? Why would she have given him the gun so he could bring you in? It makes no sense. The last thing in the world she would have wanted would have been for him to have found you.

Crimshaw: You still don't see it. Sure she gave him the gun, gave him the address. She knew he was on the verge of finding me, and so he had to be eliminated. I haven't mentioned that she also knew that I had a gun. And she warned me he was coming. She had it figured she couldn't lose either way. If I got rid of him, got the first shot in, I'd still be safe. If he got me first, I'd be dead and that's all she needed to collect the insurance. To have me dead. She wins either way.

Martingale: You're a bad loser, Crimshaw. Nothing you say makes sense.

Crimshaw: She's collecting the insurance, isn't she? All of it, not just half. But hear me out. You remember the robbery at the house in Severna Park? Well I was the one who did it. The way we planned. Why do you suppose I didn't just take the stuff when I disappeared, or have her send it to me afterward?

Martingale: Because she wasn't in on it.

Crimshaw: Wrong. Because of the jewels. Remember? Two thousand dollars' worth of jewels. She collected the insurance on them. I gave the jewels to Gale Everts and she was going to hock them, but she never got the chance.

Martingale: Your story gets more and more ridiculous. Are you trying to tell me that Marguerite was in on a conspiracy to have you disappear and didn't care if you took off with another woman?

Crimshaw: That's what I'm telling you. I didn't say she was in love with me; I only said I was in love with her. She was only interested in the money. She didn't give a damn about me. I tell you she only loves herself; you'll find out one of these days. Gale was just another dame who fell for me. I used her. I needed a cover when I disappeared, someone who had a place where I could hide out.

Martingale: How about Alice Compton? You did kill her, didn't you? Or are you going to tell me that Marguerite did that too?

Crimshaw: I put the knife in her; Marguerite made sure I did. Alice was a lush and a nymphomaniac, but she was a great deal smarter than people gave her credit for being. She and I had been intimate at one time and she knew me very well. All along she figured that the disappearance was a fake, but she didn't figure the angle. It was because of Alice that the thing began to fall apart. A piece of bad luck. You probably remember that Alice Compton was at the Severna Park house the night I went to work on Lloyd Wilson. I had been hanging around the place, waiting for everyone to leave, and by accident she spotted me when she herself was leaving. I knew she saw me, and I got in touch with her and swore her to secrecy. I should have known better. Alice got tight and she couldn't resist confiding in Marguerite. Told her that I was still alive. She never dreamed that Marguerite was a part of the conspiracy. Alice was my one mistake. I tried to frighten her into keeping quiet, and she panicked. It was the night that you were both at the place on the Eastern Shore that Alice told Marguerite about seeing me. And then she left for the tourist camp on Route 1. Marguerite called me at once. Told me that Alice had gone and said I would have to do something about it before she told someone else. If she talked, the whole scheme would fall apart. Well, I had the Jag and I followed her out there and killed her. I had picked up her car on Route 1 as she was heading for the place, and I think that she spotted me. I had to act fast. How the hell do you suppose I would have known where she was planning to check in if Marguerite hadn't told me? Outside of Marguerite, no one knew where she was going but Alice herself.

Martingale: You said that you were the one who beat Wilson up. Why?

Crimshaw: I should have killed him. If I had, I wouldn't be in this cell right now. I always knew that Wilson was the one weak spot. The one guy who might figure the angle. Lloyd Wilson was supposed to be a mutual friend, but the truth is he was merely a lecherous old bastard with a yen for my wife. He never had the guts to come out in the open with it, but the fact is, he was a man who was disappointed in his own family, couldn't stand his own wife. He hung around for years, working that paternal interest line with Marguerite, but he never fooled me in the slightest. While I was around, he never had the courage to come out in the open. But he went for the drowning story all the way, and once I was gone he figured the coast was clear. Oh, I knew what was in his mind. And when I saw him come to the house after midnight, it made me see red. I beat him up because I wanted him to stay away. I wanted him to leave her alone. I would have beaten anyone up who I thought was trying to make the grade with her.

Martingale: Is that why you laid that pool stick over my head?

Crimshaw: I knew that you had spent the night with her. She told me herself that you did. It was the sort of thing she liked to do. She knew I was jealous of her and she couldn't resist needling me because she figured there was nothing I could do about it. Yes, I'm sorry I didn't do a complete job on Wilson at that time. And I am sorry I didn't break your skull in as well.

Martingale: You know, Crimshaw, there's only one thing wrong with your story. If you and Marguerite had this thing set up together from the beginning, if she was a part of it, why didn't it work? Explain that, can you?

Crimshaw: It's easy to explain. It did work. She's collecting, isn't she? And if she hadn't become greedy, it would have worked for both of us. Everything was going fine until Marguerite began to realize that the insurance people might get tough about paying off unless they had a body. I tried to tell her that they would have to, but she was impatient. She didn't want to wait. She wanted the whole thing for herself. That's when she began to decide that if I were found, if there really was a body, she'd collect without any trouble and have the whole thing for herself.

Martingale: Are you trying to tell me that she was clever enough to arrange it so that you would be executed for murder? She couldn't have known that you would kill Wilson.

Crimshaw: I am merely telling you that once Wilson got a lead to where I was hiding out, she took advantage of the situation, to bring things to a head. I think when she talked me into killing Alice Compton, she was already planning to tip the police off so that I would be picked up and convicted of that murder. But she wasn't satisfied to leave it at that. She had to tie it up good. And that's when she overplayed her hand. If it weren't for Lloyd Wilson, I still couldn't prove anything.

Martingale: You still haven't.

Crimshaw: I will. Beyond any doubt. As I told you, she knew Wilson would find me. She told him where I was. She was the only one who knew. And when she sent him up to find me, she gave him a gun. She didn't care which way it happened. If he shot me, she'd have her dead husband. If I shot him—well, she'd still eventually have her dead body. The fact is, we shot each other. He came in holding this little automatic in his hand. I knew the minute he pulled it that she'd double-crossed me. So I took out the .38. I got off three shots and killed him, but he got off one shot before he fell and I'm still carrying it around.

Martingale: Why did Gale Everts take the gun when she left? Would you like to explain that, Crimshaw?

Crimshaw: She didn't take it. Marguerite took it. Gale had already left. She left when Wilson first showed up. The second I saw Wilson pull up in his car, I knew that the thing had blown sky-high. I told Gale to leave. To scram. To disappear. I didn't want her involved. But after the shots were fired, while I sat there in the chair bleeding and unable to move, Marguerite walked in and took the little automatic out of Lloyd Wilson's dead hand and put it in her bag.

She didn't even look at me. Just turned and left. Check her alibi for that night. It would only have taken her about four hours to get up and back. See if she can account for those four hours.

Martingale: It's a good theory, Crimshaw. It all sounds logical as hell. There is only one fault and it's a big one. Where's the proof?

Crimshaw: The proof is in my heart. A little lead slug in my heart. You're a detective, Lieutenant. In a few hours, after I'm dead, have them perform an autopsy. Get this lead bullet I've been carrying around. Then find that gun. The gun that Marguerite took out of Lloyd Wilson's dead hand. Make a ballistics check. She'll still have the gun. Marguerite never gave up anything of value in her whole life.

Martingale: Tell me just one thing, will you, Crimshaw? Tell me why you've been quiet all this time? Why you haven't said something before? Why you have protected her until now and suddenly decided to talk?

Crimshaw: I didn't talk for one reason. I wanted to do to her what she did to me. I wanted her to think she was winning. I wanted her to think she had it made. Was going to collect all that dough. Going to get married and live happily ever after. And then at the last minute, when she really thought she was in, I wanted to bring the world down on her head.

Martingale: I'm afraid that perhaps you have, Crimshaw.

Crimshaw: There's one other thing. I needed, as you say, evidence to prove my point. I didn't want some damned doctor probing round in my heart getting the evidence and risking my life. Not until I had to. Do you understand?

Martingale: Yes, yes, I am afraid that at last I understand.

There is only one more thing to say as I close this memorandum.

I didn't have to find the .25 automatic that I had given Marguerite so she could feel secure and protect herself. I had already used it for target shooting down at the pistol range and I had kept some of the slugs.

The piece of lead taken from Harry Crimshaw's heart matched those slugs perfectly when I made the ballistics tests earlier this morning.

THE END

HIJACK

Lionel White

Chapter 1

It wasn't the weather. The heavy ground fog blanketed Southern California, extending north from San Diego along the coast to San Francisco. Turbulent and unsettled conditions east of the San Bernardino Mountains reached northeast beyond the Sierra Nevada Range and into the very heart of the Rockies. But neither was responsible for the delayed takeoff.

It was a small mechanical failure in the number one jet engine which showed up when Kenny Savo, the flight engineer, was making a final routine check.

The problem was not serious and very likely it could have been straightened out during the short layover in Denver without causing any real trouble. Traffic Control, however, frowned on taking even a minimal risk and so the matter was taken care of by the ground crew at International and Flight Sixty-four out of Los Angeles to Chicago, with one brief stopover at Denver, was an hour and three quarters late in departure.

Fourteen passengers, members of a tourist group making a circuit of National Monuments, cancelled their reservations and arranged to stay over in Southern California an extra twenty-four hours.

Because of earlier weather reports—all ominous—at least another dozen cancellations had been made earlier in the evening. And because of the time of the year, the first week in November, and the scheduled time of departure, one-fifteen A.M., the great four-engined Boeing 707 left with a mere handful of passengers rather than the more than one hundred she was equipped to carry.

Executives of Consolidated Airlines, for economic reasons, would have preferred to cancel the entire flight had they been able to do so. You don't make money flying a six and a half million dollar plane a couple of thousand miles with less than two dozen paying passengers, even if she is hauling her usual load of high priority freight and air mail.

But regularly scheduled airline flights are not cancelled in order to save a few dollars and so Flight Sixty-four, in the competent hands of her crew, pilot, co-pilot and flight engineer, but minus two of her four stewardesses, responded to the 17,500-pound thrust of each of her four engines and took off an hour and forty-five minutes late.

The two missing stewardesses, on learning of the aborted passenger list, pleaded illness, quite independently of each other.

Airline officials had not thought it really necessary to replace them with substitutes. Not for a mere eighteen paying customers.

It was no more than an hour or so later, however, when those same officials had a sudden change of heart and were as happy as possible under the circumstances about that sparse passenger list. They were even relieved that the two stewardesses had ducked out, although it didn't stop them from summarily firing the one who was seen half stoned in an all-night Hollywood after-hours joint by a company official sometime before dawn on that fatal morning.

Despite certain minor personality flaws—he was overfond of his booze and rather lacking in imagination—Captain Arch Winter had two characteristics which made him a thoroughly competent pilot. He had a single-track mind and he was conscientious.

The moment he released the air brakes which held the 707 rooted to the fog-bound earth after the initial blast of her jets, and the plane began to move turgently forward to begin its mile and a half run and become airborne, the captain ceased to concentrate on the girl in seat 29. All thoughts of her blonde sensual loveliness, and the plans he had for seducing her into spending the thirty-six-hour layover with him in a Chicago hotel, evaporated from his mind and he concentrated on the complex instrument panels in front of him and above his head.

For the next few minutes, until the wing flaps were flattened and the landing gear retracted, until the plane was fully airborne and he would be able to relax and put the flying of the ship under the control of AUTOMATIC, he was a pilot and nothing but a pilot. A superb flyer, he was, in a sense, almost a continuation of and an integral part of the very airplane itself.

Stewart MacPherson, who at thirty-five was some seven years the captain's junior, sat in the co-pilot's seat. He neither liked nor approved of his senior officer, but he had to admire the icy concentration as Arch Winter tooled the huge airliner down the runway. A dour perfectionist, MacPherson never could understand how a man whom he considered a mental lightweight, as well as a damned lecher and boozer, was able to draw on so superb a talent the moment he assumed control of the complicated mechanism which would carry them at some six hundred miles an hour to their ultimate destination. What irked him more than anything else was the ease and lack of obvious effort with which Arch Winter functioned.

MacPherson himself was a damned good flyer. But he did it the hard way. He agonized; nothing ever came easy.

Captain Winter had spent the hour and three quarters delay while they were waiting for the plane to be checked out, kidding with the stewardesses, making overt passes at a couple of the more attractive female passengers. MacPherson had studied the weather charts, checking back on the plane and the work being done on its number one port engine.

He'd worried. He always worried.

There was a strong possibility they would encounter wet snow at some point before they reached the altitude where they would finally level off to cross over the San Bernardino Range where they would no longer be operating under the Traffic Ground Facility at International, but they would be picking up the Enroute Traffic Control. If they hit the wet snow it would very likely interfere with radio reception. There was a better than even chance that they would go completely off the Ground Radar Scope.

MacPherson's intelligence told him that neither of these possibilities would be particularly unusual at this time of year and under these weather conditions. There would be no real danger. It can happen and it does happen. But it wasn't the usual routine and anything out of the ordinary was bound to disturb and upset him.

Arch Winter, as Senior Captain, should be equally concerned. But Captain Winter, looking like a damned college boy in his perfectly tailored blue uniform and wearing his peaked cap on the side of his blond head as though he were being cast in some Hollywood war picture, had spent his time sipping cokes out of paper cups (which MacPherson could have sworn were spiked with illegal whiskey) and making passes at all available females.

With another man, MacPherson would have been tempted to suggest that the takeoff be entrusted to the co-pilot. MacPherson, however, was thoroughly confident that his senior would handle the situation with complete dexterity. And this is what irritated him and made him squirm in his seat and turn slightly and look over at young Savo, the flight engineer.

MacPherson disliked Captain Winter, but he positively hated Kenny Savo. Hated him for his youth—Savo was in his mid-twenties— hated him for his ugly, open faced attractiveness which women seemed to find so enchanting. Hated him for his breezy, carefree exuberance, his cynical failure to take anything or anyone seriously.

Winter, once airborne, was at least a conscientious and dedicated flyer. Savo, on the other hand, remained a perennial adolescent, irresponsible and indifferent.

The Flight Engineer had an infuriating way of saying, "What the hell, let the fuckin' bucket fall apart. You can only die once."

It was the sort of remark that made MacPherson want to strike him dead on the spot. The worst part about it was that Stewart MacPherson knew Savo meant it. Knew that Savo really didn't give a good goddamn.

How Winter, a senior captain and a real airman, could tolerate Savo was more than the co-pilot could understand. And yet, everyone liked young Savo. Even Mary Mills, whose tenure as the oldest stewardess with Consolidated was indicated by her fading good looks and who was considered the most reliable and responsible girl in the service.

Mary had been quick enough to get Arch Winter's number. How could she be so stupidly blind when it came to young Savo?

MacPherson's small dark face went surly and he sniffed disdainfully. All women, even the seemingly most steadfast and sensible, were shallow and stupid, when they were not downright frivolous and immoral. The less you had to do with them the better. The damned trouble was that it was hard for a normal, healthy man to go through life completely ignoring women. Especially women like Jill Grunsky, the other stewardess on duty in the passenger cabin.

It wasn't that MacPherson didn't understand Jill, didn't know just who and what she was. A damned little bitch, strictly on the make. Ambitious, greedy, utterly amoral.

Thinking of Jill had its usual effect upon MacPherson. He felt the erection coming on and shifted uncomfortably in his upholstered pilot's seat.

There were times when the Scotsman hated his own uncontrollable body almost as much as he hated the women who made it uncontrollable. The Grunsky girl was certainly such a woman.

Jill, at twenty-three, with her young voluptuous body and her blonde Slavic beauty, with the wide blue eyes and that perfect child's face which was only just beginning to really mature, would intrigue any man and usually did. She managed it quite consciously and made no bones over the fact that the only reason she had become an airline stewardess was so that she could find an open field for hunting wealthy husband material. In the meantime, while she was looking around, she flirted outrageously with any male and MacPherson was sure that she would sleep with anyone who would put out for a meal and a few drinks.

He knew that she had had an affair with Winter, and was quite sure that when no one else was available, she was sleeping with young Savo.

Despite his Presbyterian puritanism, MacPherson would have given his right arm to bed her down himself. He simply didn't know how to go about doing it.

Once more the co-pilot frowned, forcing his mind back to his job. This was no time to agonize over his failure as a Don Juan, no time to fight the schizophrenic battle between his libido and his Scotch conscience. His job was co-piloting a four-engine jet plane under adverse weather conditions.

Leave the sexual ruminations to young Savo, who was probably quite capable of fornicating with one part of his mind while he checked his instruments with another.

Kenny Savo was neither fornicating Jill Grunsky with one part of his mind nor was he tending his job. He was, however, thinking of Jill and he was concentrating on just what technique he would be able to use in order to avoid actual fornication once they had grounded in Chicago, where the two of them had planned to shack up in a motel for several hours.

It wasn't that Kenny had changed his attitude toward the stewardess or had suddenly found her any less attractive. It was merely that he had found someone else who struck him as more attractive, someone who would also be available.

Sissy should have told him she was going to make the flight. If Sissy had told him, warned him, he would never have made the date with Jill.

Damn it, you could have knocked him over with a feather, so to speak, when, making his usual casual check of the passenger list, he had run across her name. What the hell was she up to, not letting him know in advance?

It was no part of his duties as Flight Engineer, but Kenny always checked the passenger list. It was a sort of game. A game that Jill Grunsky played also, but played for other reasons. She ran through the passenger list like a Dun and Bradstreet accountant. She checked for unmarried, wealthy men. Kenny checked for women only and he didn't care about their financial status. He had a fatal weakness for celebrities—young female celebrities—and it wasn't potential marriage partners he was looking for. Marriage was the last thing in his mind.

The list had been, on this flight, meager, but it had also been promising. There was that famous French movie star, who, though a bit long in the tooth, was still one damned sexy broad and was certainly an international celebrity of stage, screen and TV, as they say.

There was the spoiled little heiress, the one the Sunday Supplements and the columnists referred to as "The Girl With Everything." Dianne Rhinhardt, darling of the International Jet Set.

And then he had come across the name of Celeste Carr, whom he had met only a month or six weeks ago and whom he knew as Sissy. Sissy Carr, an ex-airline hostess on TWA, the girl he knew Captain Winter would have given his right testicle to sleep with, and the girl Savo had been trying to make from the very first time he had met her at Jill's Santa Monica apartment.

It was going to take a little doing. He didn't have a lot of time to figure it out because they would be coming down in Denver in just a little under an hour and fifty minutes from the takeoff at International and he knew that during that brief layover, he would somehow or other have to get things straightened around with Jill. Have to set it up so he could dump her at the airport in Chicago and keep the date with Sissy that he had managed to arrange during that few minutes he'd talked with her while she was waiting for the delayed departure of Flight Sixty-four.

Time. That was the trouble. There just wasn't enough of it. Between stalling Jill off and making out with Sissy, there certainly wouldn't be any chance to develop those other two. The French enchantress or the heiress.

Savo was a fast worker, but even he had certain limitations.

Kenny Savo smiled, shrugged and, without thinking about it, checked the instrument panel in front of him, automatically noting that all seemed well with the functions of the four jets. The hell with it anyway. The French broad was getting old and the young "girl who had everything" probably wouldn't give a Flight Engineer on a domestic airline the time of day in any case.

His problem was Jill. Dumping Jill so he could take advantage of his lucky break to shack up with Sissy, who for some unbelievable reason had finally agreed to spend a night with him after turning him down consistently for over a month now. It was too damned bad the girls were friends.

A difficult situation, but not insurmountable. Perhaps the best way would be to precipitate a fight with Jill during the layover in Denver. Break the relationship off once and for all.

At least it would make old Mills happy. Mary Mills, who had that sort of maternal interest in him. Mills was a good old soul, but she was as narrow-minded and bigoted as old MacPherson.

The man in Seat Number 34 was drunk.

After ten years as an airline stewardess, Mary Mills could spot trouble a mile and a half away. The minute he had climbed aboard the plane and passed her in the doorway to walk down the center aisle of the plane, holding an attaché case in each hand as though he were carrying twin cartons of eggs, she had known something was wrong. Of course she had smelled the acrid stale aroma of whiskey, but that was not unusual. Even Captain Winter, whom she admired more than any other captain on Consolidated, frequently had liquor on his breath. It was something else, something about the oddly vacant expression in his eyes and about the exceedingly careful, over-cautious way he walked, that tipped her off.

She checked her passenger invoice again. Weems. That was the name, Herbert Weems.

He'd been the last passenger aboard and she knew he had only been able to make the plane because it had been delayed. He had not been on the scheduled list of early passengers and had apparently purchased his ticket minutes before the flight time.

Destination—Chicago. No luggage aside from those attaché cases, which he had point-blank refused to surrender when she'd offered to stow them away.

And, of course, the brief conversation. She had helped him adjust his seat belt and although she knew full well he was booked all the way through, in order to make pleasant conversation, she'd asked, smiling, "You are going all the way through to Chicago?"

He'd looked up at her blankly and then smiled in the most peculiar way. "Why?"

It had taken her a bit aback. But she was an experienced girl and had dealt with some oddballs in her time. She'd broadened the smile.

She had a sense of humor, of whimsy. She'd play along. "Why?"

He must have misunderstood.

"To see Harry," he said.

"Harry?"

"He's my favorite bartender. I always go to see my favorite bartender," Mr. Weems said. He spoke in a very clear voice, over-pronouncing his words, and then, as she stood back, wondering just what to say next, he carefully opened one of the attaché cases and took out a brandy bottle, which oddly enough was uncorked, and lifted it to his lips.

"I love Harry," Mr. Weems said.

The plane was not even airborne before Mr. Weems had twice more lifted the brandy bottle. Mary, over the years, had had a good deal of experience with drunks and although so far Weems had done nothing wrong, she worried. The ones who were a little boisterous, obviously in their cups and feeling gay and talkative, never worried her. She knew that more often than not they merely passed out and went to sleep. But these quiet, fey ones.

Thank the Lord the passenger load was unusually light. As a matter of fact, she couldn't remember when they had taken off with fewer seats occupied. What was even more unusual was the high percentage of celebrities and important people among these few passengers.

Again Mary Mills quickly ran her eye down the list, now and then lifting her head as she checked it against the occupied seats.

It was like a page out of Who's Who.

Walthar Bruno. World famous nuclear scientist and key figure in the nation's space program.

Across the aisle and two seats forward was Gary Gibbons, the great American Evangelist and right-winger, a man whom she had been reading about for years, although he still looked young enough to be her kid brother. She had always admired him, although she prided herself on her liberalism, both in religion and politics. She only hoped that if Weems decided to inflict himself on any of the other passengers, he would spare Dr. Gibbons.

Then there was that Russian who had been so much on the front pages of the press lately. He had boarded the plane with the man who had flashed the card from the folds in his wallet which she hadn't really read, but which she was positive identified him as a member of some branch of the government, probably the FBI or CIA. His name was Brandon Mitchell, but it really meant nothing to her.

And there was the notorious but fabulously wealthy business tycoon who had growled at her as she offered to help him to his seat. Internationally famous for his financial deals, there had even been rumors that he owned the controlling interest in Consolidated Airlines itself. It certainly wouldn't do to have any casual drunk interfering or annoying him.

The nation's outstanding criminal lawyer was aboard, but Mary Mills paid him little heed. She considered criminal lawyers little better than their clients, so far as real prestige was concerned.

Of course there were the two women, the really important ones among the five women passengers. The Rhinhardt girl, who had inherited millions and was the social talk of two continents; and that famous Francine, who was so important and well known as an entertainer that she didn't even have to use a second name.

There were the others on board also, and Mary was quite confident each of them in his or her own way was important and renowned. Some of the names had been vaguely familiar, but the names by themselves hadn't meant too much.

A small passenger list certainly, but an important one. Flight Sixty-four out of Los Angeles for Chicago, always carried important people. Important people and an important cargo. Of course she wasn't supposed to know exactly what the cargo was, but Mary Mills, like a couple other members of the plane's crew, had a long time ago learned that buried deep in the baggage compartment of the great ship, once each month, were some canvas bags which contained a tremendous fortune in government currency.

It was no secret that the currency consisted of old and worn bills, collected over the weeks by the various banks in the Greater Los Angeles area and ultimately gathered together to be returned to the United States Mint in Denver, where they would be systematically and completely destroyed, to be replaced with new bills.

Of course, compared to the combined wealth of the various passengers on almost any given flight, and certainly compared to the human importance of those combined passengers, the money was of small significance. On the other hand, there is something about the knowledge that a given flight is carrying several million dollars in cold cash which lends that cargo a certain romantic aura and Mary Mills was far from being immune to it.

As a member of the crew of the 707, it gave her a vicarious sense of importance.

Looking down the aisle she noticed the only other stewardess aboard, the Grunksy girl, leaning over and talking with the man in Seat Number 21.

Mary Mills lifted her finely chiseled face and sniffed through her patrician nose.

It was typical of Grunsky to seek out the handsomest man among the passengers upon whom to devote her attention.

Mary's eyes went back to the passenger list but the name was meaningless to her.

She started walking slowly down the aisle, unable to explain to herself the sudden curiosity which overcame her. Certainly there was nothing unusual about Jill Grunsky hovering over an attractive male. This one was a rather slight man, who in spite of his gray hair appeared to be in his early or mid-thirties. His eyes were concealed by lightly tinted glasses, as though he had spent long hours under a hot tropical sun. He was immaculately dressed, but somehow gave the impression of a man who spent plenty of time out of doors. He had the look of an athlete and as Mary Mills approached, she was aware of his voice which was low and pleasant.

". . . a sort of silly name," he was saying. "My friends call me Dude. I'll take you up on the drink, but I think I'll wait just a few minutes."

Miss Mills was about to stop, to say something pleasant, but then she saw that the girl sitting on the opposite side of the aisle, a couple of seats forward, was beckoning to her. She knew, instinctively, that she was going to be asked directions to the ladies' room.

The plane canted slightly, still rising at a sharp angle and she knew they were circling to make sufficient altitude to clear the San Bernardino Mountains before straightening out on their northeast heading. They would be doing about three hundred miles an hour and they had been airborne for better than twenty minutes.

Jill Grunsky was thinking, Damn it, I know he's not a live one. Probably a field engineer for an oil company or something. And probably married with a half dozen kids. But he is damned attractive.

She said, "You must have been a pilot or at least have done an awful lot of flying. It is so rare that we get really intelligent questions." She smiled down at him. "The alternate landing would be Omaha, Nebraska, but I don't think you will have to worry. Denver is closed in but we expect things to improve once we get over the Rockies. It won't make a great deal of difference in any case, if you're scheduled all the way through to Chicago. It takes an additional thirty thousand pounds of fuel to go from Denver to Omaha, but we always carry a sufficient amount. And Omaha is on a direct line. How did you pick up the nickname Dude?"

"Just one of those things. By the way, would you mind a great deal if I changed seats? I like to ride as far forward as possible and there seems to be plenty of vacancies. Maybe you could come up forward with me. And bring a drink for each of us?"

She smiled and started to shake her head and then laughed.

"No objections at all if you want to sit forward," she said. "But it is against policy for the stewardesses to sit with the passengers. Especially to have a drink with them."

"I like to do things which are against policy."

Jill rested her hand on his shoulder and leaned forward.

"I do myself," she said. "You go on forward and I will be with you in a few minutes. I have to check some of the others. I won't be long."

She moved out of the way as he stood up. When he slumped into the seat opposite the locked door which led into the flight deck, he carefully checked his wristwatch.

They had been in the air just over thirty minutes and he knew that the plane had gathered speed and leveled off at its normal cruising speed of approximately six hundred miles an hour. They would be passing somewhere over the ridge of the mountains which separated the metropolises of Southern California from the deserts to the west and north.

When Jill Grunsky dropped into the seat next to him some five minutes later, carrying the two glasses of bourbon and soda neatly balanced on the tray, he again checked his watch.

It read 3:35.

He had exactly five minutes to go.

The tall, emaciated man with the freshly shaven bald head, the flushed cheeks which looked so red that Miss Mills could have sworn he was wearing rouge (he was), and who had refused to give up the violin case he'd carried aboard under his arm, leaned forward in Seat Number 44 and held his wrist so that he could see the face of the platinum watch in the dim light.

His liquid black eyes glowed feverishly and he half smothered a hacking cough. He moved the violin case so that it lay across his lap and noiselessly unsnapped the two latches which secured the cover.

Directly across the aisle from him, the short, truncated man with the almost freakishly barrel chest and the ugly, scarred face, took the fifth of whiskey from his side pocket and quickly uncorked it. He hesitated for several moments before lifting it to his thick sensuous lips. Then, taking a long slug, he shuddered and coughed as he recorked the bottle.

It was his first drink in over a year. He had faithfully followed the dictates of Alcoholics Anonymous for thirteen months and the straight, hundred proof alcohol went down his throat like a searing flame.

He didn't bother to look at his watch. Instead he swore under his breath and his right hand went up and pulled off the blond wig he was wearing when he'd boarded the plane.

He said, in a muffled whisper, "A lot of shit—screw it!"

He considered taking a second drink, but then decided against it. He had an uncanny sense of passing time and time was running out. There wasn't enough of it left to accommodate the second drink.

Back in the ladies' room, the girl whom Mary Mills was sure was going to be airsick, sat on the upholstered couch, her face pale as she looked up at the stewardess.

"... can't imagine what came over me," she said. "After all the time I spent with TWA, to think that I ..."

"It can happen to anyone," Mary Mills interrupted. "I'm sure you will be all right in a moment. Now, if you will just sit back and relax for a few minutes, I'll just check the other passengers and then I'll be right back ..."

The girl reached for her hand.

"Please," she said. "Please, just a couple of minutes more. I don't want to be alone. If I can just sit here for another two or three minutes ..."

"Well ..." Mary Mills looked at her own wristwatch and realized that they had been airborne for exactly forty minutes. "Well," she said hesitantly, "I daresay Miss Grunsky can manage a little longer by herself. It is odd," she went on a moment later, "that you should know her. I am surprised she didn't say anything to me when she saw you board the plane in L.A."

At this precise moment, Jill Grunsky thrust the key which she had taken from her leather flight bag, into the door lock of the pilot's compartment.

Neither Arch Winter nor Stewart MacPherson, both of whom were facing forward, were aware of the door being opened by the stewardess.

Kenny Savo, seeing the girl entering the compartment, quickly turned his eyes away, pretending to study his instrument panel.

He didn't want to get involved in a discussion with Jill until he had planned his strategy.

As a result, he failed to see the man who followed Jill into the cabin, so close behind her that the .45 caliber automatic in his hand was completely concealed.

Of the three passengers who were aware of the door of the pilot's compartment opening to admit the pretty stewardess and the gray-haired man, only one was even mildly surprised.

Dianne Rhinhardt, however, didn't waste time speculating on why a passenger should be following the girl into the cockpit where passengers obviously were prohibited. Her mind was preoccupied with her own problems and a decision she had to make. The decision as to whether she would take the handful of sleeping pills which she carried in her small overnight case and swallow them at once, or whether she would wait until she was checked into the hotel in Chicago, and then swallow them.

Chapter 2

The first indication that anything might be amiss with Consolidated Airlines Flight Sixty-four out of Los Angeles came at exactly 3:42 when a man named MacNamara, who was monitoring the flight on his radar scope at Airways Ground Control, suddenly missed the blip which represented the great four-engined airline.

It could have been the weather, very likely was. MacNamara was well aware that Flight Sixty-four had probably encountered wet snow. Pilots of other planes in the general area had reported running into snow, and Flight Sixty-four wasn't the only one he'd been having difficulty keeping track of.

It was a lousy night, weather conditions were all but impossible.

On the other hand, it was more than likely that Enroute Traffic Control had picked up Sixty-four from its station high up in the Rockies near Ft. Smith, Arizona.

MacNamara made a quick routine check with Enroute Control and learned at once that Sixty-four had not been picked up.

Nothing too unusual. The thing was to check the radio contact, just to be on the safe side. The last radio message from the plane, received less than seven minutes ago, had indicated everything was fine and that Sixty-four was on course, where she should be both from the standpoint of altitude, latitude and longitude.

The static was something fierce and Radio swore under his breath after several minutes of fruitlessly attempting to get through. It was quite possible of course that the unusual atmospheric conditions could temporarily be interrupting contact.

The Traffic Control facility at Los Angeles was not unduly alarmed. Not yet, at least.

It would, in any case, be necessary to alert the airline that one of its planes was temporarily out of contact; there was no immediate reason to take other steps. Airline officials were pretty unhappy about anyone starting rumors of possible trouble. Such rumors, or alarms, had a way of getting out of hand in no time at all and the first thing you knew the newspapers or radio or TV people would get on to them and then all hell could break loose.

It was bad for the airlines, bad for flying in general.

The company dispatch office took the news in stride and was, foreseeably, not overly upset. Not for at least another fifteen minutes during which Radio still failed to make contact with the plane and during which Enroute Traffic Control also failed to pick up any signal on its powerful receiving scope.

Damned unusual, in spite of the foul weather.

Along about this time someone in GTC remembered that Flight Sixty-four had been delayed that hour and three quarters in departure as a result of a small mechanical failure, which had, subsequently been taken care of.

Air Traffic Control in Los Angeles didn't like it. Didn't like it at all.

"Greedy bastards," ATC said, completely ignoring the fact that Flight Sixty-four had taken off more than eighty percent empty. "Those guys will let them blast off with a missing wing if it's a case of making a fast buck."

ATC wasn't a man to rest on optimism and he didn't want to take any chances in being considered derelict in his duties. He at once made contact with his superiors in Washington. By the time he reached the proper people, reached someone who had any real authority, he had to report that Flight Sixty-four had been out of contact for approximately forty minutes, that Flight Sixty-four had been airborne for a total of eighty minutes and that she would, normally, be due in Denver in another thirty minutes. The flight should have been picked up by any one of four Enroute Control stations, as well as the scope in Denver.

It was not logical that all of them could have missed. And unless there had been a mechanical failure with the plane's own radio system, neither was it logical that radio contact would have been cancelled out. Weather or no weather.

Flight Sixty-four carried some sixty thousand pounds of fuel and still had better than two hours' time left on her engines. Two hours before she had to come down—somewhere.

But Flight Sixty-four was undoubtedly in trouble.

Washington agreed.

The Air Defense Command was alerted to the situation within the time it took to make a direct telephone call and although it would seem utterly senseless, Air Defense, under the command of the Air Force itself, at once ordered an interceptor, a Century Supersonic Fighter, aloft.

The incredibly swift military plane, backed by the powerful thrust of a jet engine capable of driving her at speeds exceeding two thousand miles an hour, took off from a field in central California within three minutes of being alerted and at once headed for a course which would intercept the supposed course of the missing plane, assuming she was still on that course.

At approximately the time Flight Sixty-four was due to zero in at the airport in Denver, several high officials of Consolidated Airlines, including the vice president in charge of advertising and public relations, were already nervously pacing the dispatch offices at International Airport.

No one was quite prepared to admit it yet, but there was not only the question of whether the plane was lost, but also there was an excellent chance that the Boeing 707 might have crashed somewhere in the bleak mountain stretches between Los Angeles and the city in Colorado which had been her first scheduled stopover.

The vice president in charge of public relations, an affable Irishman, decided it was time to check over the passenger list and possibly the bills of lading on the cargo. No point certainly in letting the press in on it or alarming the public, but it was just as well to be prepared. The supersensitive and highly sophisticated electronic devices currently in use are certainly subject to failure; the weather really was lousy, and the plane had better than an hour's fuel left in her tanks, assuming she was still airborne. It was damned unlikely she could have made a landing, either forced or otherwise—which meant of course a crash—without someone's knowing about it.

It was wholly possible she was somewhere far off her course. But an hour is a damned short period of time and the company executive believed in being prepared.

The vice president in charge of public relations was a man who rarely lost his cool, but when he glanced down that sparse passenger list, his face grew very serious and he whistled thinly through the slit between his two upper front teeth as he shook his head.

"Goddamn," he said. He beckoned to one of his fellow directors on the board of governors of Consolidated.

"Bruno—Walthar Bruno," he said, pointing to the name. "If anything happens to him, our space program will be set back five years. The brass in Washington will castrate us. What the hell is *he* doing on Sixty-four?"

Parker of Company Dispatch spoke up apologetically, as though he personally were responsible for having booked the famous scientist.

"Heard or read he was attending a scientist's convention at UCLA. Probably returning to the University of Chicago, where he lectures on occasion. You are right, of course. His loss could prove critical to the Defense Department. We should never let men of his caliber travel . . ."

"This one," the vice president in charge of public relations interrupted, stabbing his finger at a name further down the list. "Serge Krinsky. Isn't he the Russian military attaché who it was rumored has defected and who has offered to show up in Washington and spill his guts? My God, if he's lost Moscow will say the whole thing was a conspiracy to kill him or some such hogwash."

"No one is lost yet," a third executive, the vice president in charge of traffic, said shortly. "I don't worry too much about some damned Russian or a long-haired scientist. But if the papers learn that people like that Rhinhardt girl are on the plane . . . All she has to do is be seen frugging in a night spot to make the first page on every paper in the country. And . . ."

He hesitated a moment and his face paled.

"Gene Farris," he said. "Oh God, don't let anything happen to that plane! If there's an accident and old Farris comes through alive, there won't be an official here at Consolidated who will have a job tomorrow morning."

The vice president in charge of public relations had turned away to lean toward a uniformed girl who whispered for a moment into his ear and when he turned back to the others his face was pale.

"Associated Press on the telephone," he said. "Someone, probably in Washington, spilled their guts. They say they understand the plane has been lost and they want an immediate statement."

"Stall them! The hell with them. There will be no statement of any kind until—" the Traffic man hesitated, his eyes going to the large clock on the wall—"until, well for another thirty-eight minutes. Not until the pilot of that plane has used up the last cup of his fuel and we know for sure the plane is down somewhere."

The vice president in charge of public relations shook his head.

"Can't handle the press that way," he said. "Not now that the cat's out of the bag. The Air Defense people have without doubt notified the Civil Air Patrol which means that the airwaves are being monitored by the communications people. We are going to have every damned reporter in Southern California on our necks within minutes. We have to tell them something."

"All right. Tell them the plane is out of contact for the time being. But nothing else. Above all, no publicity on the passengers. Let's try and keep it as far from being sensational as we can. God only knows, once they get that passenger list . . ."

The man from Air Traffic Control interrupted.

"Gentlemen," he said coldly, "I hardly think this is a time to be worrying about your company image. Worrying over the possible effects of the publicity which you are bound to get in any case. I think we should be concentrating on an all-out effort to find that plane. If it is down somewhere, and it is my frank opinion that it is, there's a fair chance some of the crew and passengers may still be alive. In that case, the sooner we find them, the better."

"You are right, of course." The vice president in charge of public relations turned to the others. "Let us be sure Civil Air has been alerted. I want to get every plane and helicopter available aloft and starting a search. All pilots on our line as well as competing lines who might be passing any part of the perimeter where she could have gone down, should be notified to be on the lookout. Forest rangers, the military, state police, local law enforcement agencies. Any and all persons who might be of possible aid in the search. Let's get them on the job. A general alarm to fire spotting towers, to . . ."

The general manager of the southwestern division put down the telephone he'd picked up while the others were talking.

"I think we'd better go out to the lobby," he said. "We are being overrun by the press. The story seems to have been released by a local radio station a couple of minutes ago and the place is being mobbed. And one of you gentlemen had better call back the local offices of the FBI. They just got in touch here and it seems they have been informed by some other federal agency that Flight Sixty-four was carrying a cargo of more than twelve million dollars in currency to be delivered to the mint in Denver. They are concerned."

By the time the final editions of the morning newspapers were rolling off the presses—editions which had been replated several times to keep pace with the latest news, or rather lack of news—it was established that Flight Sixty-four could no longer conceivably be airborne.

Last heard from and pinpointed forty minutes out of International Airport, several thousand feet above the desert country beyond the San Bernardino Range, the plane had not been picked up by Enroute Control, had neither been located by Ground Radar at Denver, nor Omaha, her alternate landing location. No radio contact had been made. She had landed at no recognized airfield and there was no official report of anyone's having seen her.

Flight Sixty-four, it could be assumed, was lost. It could also be assumed the plane had crashed, almost certainly carrying to their deaths all passengers and crew. The grim task of notifying relatives and nearest of kin must begin. Insurance companies must start their macabre bookkeeping. Government and airline officials must alert their investigative teams. The public at large must be prepared to accept a disaster involving the lives of a dozen or more famous persons.

The story would be dropped from the front pages of the national press as soon as the scene of the tragedy was discovered and the salvage troops began their unpleasant tasks. In case the fragments of the presumably shattered airliner were not found immediately, the story would linger on for a few more days, but must sooner or later be replaced with some fresh and equally chilling event. In the meantime, life must go on.

Six hours after the time that it was determined that Flight Sixty-four could no longer be airborne, the offices of Consolidated Airlines, at International Airport in Los Angeles, were a scene of utter and complete chaos.

The vice president in charge of public relations was bearing the brunt of it. He had lost, for once and for all, that good-natured and optimistic appearance which had been so helpful in enhancing his career. It hadn't helped when Gene Farris' only son had personally telephoned him from Paris to coldly remind him that his father was the principal stockholder in Consolidated Airlines and that if his father were to be proved lost on the missing plane, he, the son, would cause a shakeup in the executive staff which would make the Russian revolution look like child's play by comparison.

It was, of course, only one of many such calls. The State Department had kept the line from Washington hot, concerned not only about the missing nuclear scientist whose presence was so vital to the national defense, but also concerned about a certain Russian military attaché, who, accompanied by a man from the CIA, the government had entrusted to the care of the airline.

There were other calls.

A member of the John Birch Society, a national nuisance but also an important political figure, had forthrightly accused the vice president and Consolidated Airlines of a conspiracy against the life of the famous Evangelist, Gary Gibbons.

A woman who had identified herself as a Mrs. Griswald, maintained her husband had been on the plane under an assumed name. His real name she said was Horace, and further, that Horace was responsible for the tragedy because she was sure God had struck him dead—obviously taking the plane and others along with him because he was leaving her for another woman.

The French Consulate seemed to feel the whole thing was some sort of publicity stunt arranged by Hollywood to discredit someone they kept referring to as "Our fabulous Francine."

A federal judge from Chicago had checked to make sure the reason the famous criminal lawyer, Marlo Phillips, had failed to show up in his court was because he was actually a passenger aboard the ill-fated ship and not pulling one of his notorious legal bits of deception and trickery.

At least a half dozen nationally known and reputable attorneys involved in the complicated affairs of the international jet setter and socialite, Dianne Rhinhardt, had been in touch with the airline.

The relatives of the two school teachers, a Miss Arthur and a Miss Salmon, who had boarded the plane to begin a Sabbatical, sought information.

Someone from a motion picture trade paper had called to verify that Ned Gaines, the well-known movie publicist, had actually been aboard. They couldn't believe that anything could ever really have happened to Ned baby.

There were some six other passengers listed as having boarded the plane and the odd thing was that no one had showed up to ask about them.

What made it even stranger was, when the company itself attempted to contact the nearest of kin, using the addresses which they had given when they purchased their tickets, four of the names and addresses proved to be false. The fifth, a young woman named Celeste Carr, apparently lived alone in an apartment which she had subleased three weeks before the date of the tragedy.

The sixth person, a man named Weems, had given the right name and address, but his wife swore he couldn't have been on the plane. She said he was off somewhere on a drunk but that he hated planes and wouldn't be caught dead taking one.

The public relations man thought that he very likely was dead, assuming his wife were to be wrong and he had made the flight. However, he made no comment, except to say that he certainly hoped she was right and that her husband had not been on the plane when it took off.

The crew—well, the crew was a little easier. At least the relatives and nearest of kin of airplane crews understand that there is a certain occupational risk involved in their jobs. Newspapers, of course, were clamoring for photos of the crew members, and especially of the two stewardesses who had been aboard. But the public relations man was damned if he would release them, certainly not until it was firmly established that the plane had really crashed and that there were no survivors.

During those first few hours, no one gave much thought to the cargo carried in the hold of the ill-fated airliner. Human life, at least for the present, was of far more interest.

Except, that is, to certain federal government officials, who were quite aware that twelve million dollars in currency aboard the plane was in the form of old and worn bills. Unlisted bills of comparatively small denomination. Bills which, in the wrong hands, could easily be disposed of for their full face value and with virtually no risk at to whoever might come into possession of them.

It is probably unfair to say so, but it is quite possible that the federal people involved would be just as pleased to learn that, if the plane had gone down in a fatal crash, at least the currency might have been burned or destroyed along with the corpses of those persons it was already assumed had been lost.

Chapter 3

Until the voice came over the public address system carefully pronouncing those terse words which were to create that quick, sudden fear, to send the blood rushing through their veins, quicken their pulses and react on their adrenalin glands—until those few fatal words, only she, Dianne Rhinhardt, had suspected anything was wrong.

"All passengers please fasten your seat belts and put out your cigarettes. We are preparing to make an emergency landing. There is no danger. I repeat, there is no danger. Remain calm, extinguish all cigarettes, cigars or pipes. Fasten your seat belts. Prepare for an emergency landing."

She had always been extremely sensitive to her surroundings, to other people, to what was going on around her. That had been her trouble. Perhaps it may even have been the very basis of all that was wrong with her. Her supersensitivity. Her unfortunate ability to get at the truth, to see the reality, to pick out the flaws.

Dianne smiled wryly. God only knows she had been able to pick out her own flaws. And God only knows there were plenty of them to pick out.

When she had first seen the stewardess going forward, into the flight deck, followed by the passenger, it had bothered her. Oh not that there was anything too unusual about a stewardess, or for that matter, a passenger, entering the flight deck. The passenger could have been an airline official or some very special person. But it was a bit unusual, and in her casual, disinterested way, she noticed.

Yes, she had watched and made a sort of mental note of it. A moment or so later, when that tall, emaciated man with the ruined face who carried the violin case but who she could have sworn was no musician, also got up and went forward and let himself through that same door leading to the flight deck, she also made a note.

She was conscious of the other man as well. The one with the scar.

The one who looked and walked like an ape. The one who also got up from his seat and started for the rear of the plane.

It really was strange. The way the newspaper people, the gossip columnists and society and fashion editors, always hinted that she was completely selfish, interested in no one in the world but herself. Well, perhaps they were right at that. The fact that she was completely and utterly aware of everyone and everything, didn't mean that she was interested.

But she had suspected something was not quite normal, something was just a little off, a little wrong. Not of course that she had been expecting the words which informed her that the plane was about to come down for an emergency landing. Just that something was slightly off key.

Of those who heard the words, she was one of the few to react with no possible sense of fear. Only curiosity. A sort of routine, indifferent curiosity.

The gossip columnists probably were right about her at that. In reporting her escapades, those times when she had raced cars and speedboats, climbed mountains, ridden surfboards in the brow of forty-foot combers, they had said she hadn't a nerve in her body, that she didn't know what fear or caution meant.

One particular newspaper savant had gone so far as to suggest that Dianne Rhinhardt, "The Girl Who Has Everything", also had a subconscious death wish.

It had been a long, pseudo erudite article, loaded with facts, mostly correct, and conclusions, mostly wrong. The writer had referred to her as the darling of the jet set, the poor little rich girl who had tried everything, been everywhere and done everything. Beautiful, rich and spoiled. Cold and selfish. These were the words he had used.

Her friends had been indignant but she had merely been amused. She was always amused at the sensational press reports of her activities, real or imagined. But he had been right about the death wish. Except it was no longer subconscious.

True, those words coming over the plane's public address system, brought no sense of fear to her. They merely gave her a small secret sense of self-satisfaction. She had suspected something was wrong, something slightly amiss.

It is strange how the same simple words and phrases can affect different people in so many different ways. If the only reaction Dianne Rhinhardt had was one of satisfaction blended with a vague curiosity, the reaction of Serge Krinsky was exactly the opposite. Even as his trembling hands reached for the seat belt, his face became white with fear. Fear and the utter conviction that fate had at last caught up with him.

It wasn't, however, fear that the plane was about to crash

Krinsky had also observed the two passengers as they had individually gone forward and entered the flight deck. He had watched as the short, scar-faced man had gone to the rear of the plane. When the words had come over the public address system warning them of the impending emergency landing, the Russian had been the only one to suspect the real truth. The truth about what was taking place up forward in the pilot's quarters.

He was only wrong about one thing. He was wrong in assuming that it was the first stage in some secret plot to land so that he would either be immediately assassinated or held while they questioned him and tortured him and then assassinated him.

He couldn't help but look over at his companion, the tall, square jawed youthful man sitting next to him on the aisle. The sudden grim look on that old-young face did anything but reassure him. Nor was he in the slightest reassured when he observed that his companion, before fastening his seat belt, reached up with his right hand and shifted the position of the shoulder holster which he was so obviously wearing.

God, the naïveté of these Americans! Didn't they ever learn? And he had warned them. Told them that there would be an attempt to stop him before he could talk and tell what he knew.

They had been quick enough to reassure him. Tell him he would have every possible protection. That they would see no one would reach him. And so they had assigned this callow boy—well not really a boy but hardly more than a boy—to protect him while they brought him East where he would give his testimony, or "spill his guts" as the Americans would say.

Once more looking over at his companion he was tempted to say something, but then decided to stay quiet. He could understand English without too much difficulty but it was hard for him to speak it. Hard to make himself understood.

An emergency landing? Where? Good God, he knew more about the United States than the people of the country itself. He was a diplomat, or at least that's what his passport said. But he was really a lot more than that. For the last ten years, in as many countries, he had served in various embassies and consulates. But he had served as an undercover agent along with his other purely surface duties. It was one reason he had so much to tell, now that he had decided to at last defect.

He knew what apparently the man beside him did not know. He knew there was no emergency landing field anywhere within a reasonable distance. It was fascinating how little knowledge these naive Americans had of their own country.

Emergency landing? Hogwash. His intelligence told him better. It was odd, but from the very moment he had been informed they were to fly east on a regular common carrier, he'd had a premonition. And then the delay at the airport. More than one hour. Right then the premonition had firmed up in his mind and he'd felt for sure that something would happen. And now it was happening.

America was a rich, a prosperous and fantastic country. The Americans he had met were kind and friendly and simple people. But essentially simple. They meant well, or at least most of them did. But they were incredibly naïve. He'd been a fool to assume that he could trust them to protect him.

Krinsky, who knew something of jet planes as well as geography and a great many other subjects, sensed the turning of the plane, sensed the cutting of speed. There was no doubt the pilot was changing course and no doubt also that he was preparing for a landing. It was no surprise. He had not believed for a moment that this was merely a case of taking over the great transport and stealing it and kidnapping those aboard. The Russian knew full well that such a plan would be all but impossible. It might happen off Cuba or in Central or South America, but the controls and counter controls in the United States would make any such bizarre plan completely impractical.

No, the plane would land all right, airfield or no airfield. The plane would land and this simple fool next to him would probably be dead before he could so much as draw that revolver he was so obviously wearing. And he, Serge Krinsky....

The Russian gave a typical Oriental shrug. What would happen, would happen. Quite unconsciously his right hand reached toward his naval where the small, lethal pill was concealed in the folds of flesh.

Eugene Farris was very much inclined to get out of his seat and go forward to the flight deck. What the hell kind of a way was this to run a goddamned airline? Especially *his* airline? And where in the hell were the stewardesses? Why didn't that damned fool pilot get back on that public address system and let them know what was happening? What it was all about?

Well, he had purposely taken a seat on a regular run instead of coming east on his private twin engined jet because he'd wanted to make one of these spot checks of his. Wanted to find out . . .

What the hell had he wanted to find out? What utter damned foolishness. Was he kidding himself?

Farris was not a man to kid himself for long and he didn't this time.

He'd taken Flight Sixty-four because like a damned senile idiot, he'd loaned his private plane to Kitty because Kitty had wanted to fly down to Acapulco for the week to get a little sun and fun before she went back on location. Selfish little sexpot. Why couldn't she be the one to . . . But the hell with Kitty. If he spoiled the hell out of her it was worth it. They say there's no fool like an old fool, but at least he had walked into it with his eyes wide open. He was used to paying for what he got and getting what he wanted.

The point was, didn't this goddamned pilot realize that he was on board? Didn't those fools in the crew know?

But of course they didn't. Very few people, outside of a couple of the directors and certain gentlemen on Wall Street realized that Eugene Farris owned Consolidated Airlines, lock, stock and barrel. Or at least controlled the majority of the voting stock.

If this goddamned thing was going to crack up in making some sort of stupid emergency landing, if this was to be his fate after going to all the trouble and conniving he'd gone through to gain control . . .

What a stupid, ironic way . . .

He started to unfasten his seat belt. Something was very wrong. His ears had subconsciously told him that none of the four engines had cut out. There had been nothing unusual about the flight pattern. No sudden drops in altitude or anything like that. Why the hell was an emergency landing suddenly necessary? A fire? He doubted it. If one of the jets were afire, the first thing the pilot would have done would have been to cut the power.

Something peculiar was going on and damned if he wasn't going to see about it.

He was half out of his seat, turning into the aisle, when he first became aware of the man standing next to him. A short, truncated man with a nasty, newly healed scar extending from his right eye down the side of his face. A man who was pressing a very hard, blunt object into his flabby rib cage.

Marto Phillips was frightened and he would be the first to admit as much. The fact is, he was frightened much of the time and certainly he sensed fear even in the process of a normal landing or takeoff. He was used to fear. The thought of physical violence of any sort, in relation to himself, had always bothered him.

No one, however, watching as the dapper criminal lawyer carefully adjusted his seat belt with iron steady fingers, would have dreamed that he was disturbed in the slightest. He even managed a slight yawn as the buckle snapped into place. It is quite possible that Phillips' famous poker face was his greatest asset as an attorney.

Even as the fear mounted in him and his active and acute imagination began to conjure up all sorts of horrible and grisly pictures of scattered wreckage and torn and bloody corpses, a separate and completely isolated part of his brain was reviewing his will, was speculating on who might possibly replace him as the defense counsel in the murder trial he was about to embark on out in Chicago.

His keen intelligence told him that certainly all emergency landings did not end in disasters. But it also informed him that many did. And even as he suppressed the involuntary shudder that went through his lean frame, he began figuring the odds, began figuring exactly how he would make book on his chances of survival—were he lucky enough to be on the ground rather than exactly where he was at the moment.

For one flashing moment he almost lost his cool as his desperate eyes darted around seeking some possible way of improving the odds. He wondered if perhaps one of the forward seats, or perhaps a position at the rear of the plane, or maybe kneeling down . . .

But it was beyond his control and again his intelligence came to his aid and he knew there was nothing he could really do but sit it out and wait for what was to happen to take place.

Jesus, but it would be a mean and bitter way to go out. He only hoped that if they did crash, it would be sudden. Be over with quickly. The thought of his shattered, still breathing body lying on some lost mountainside . . .

But they were over the mountains now.

If they did crash, if the plane did falter and smash as she landed, if it took hours or perhaps even days to find the wreckage—well, that judge out in Chicago would be certain it was another one of his, Marlo Phillips', famous ploys to avoid bringing the case to trial.

Phillips smiled wryly, but it didn't alleviate the physical fear. Didn't erase those gaudy pictures of fragmented bodies.

Carefully he closed the attaché case and pushed it as far under the seat as he was able to. It had hard, sharp corners. He removed his heavy framed glasses, put them in a leather case and returned them to his breast pocket. For a moment he thought of taking the pillow from behind his head and holding it over his face. God, he hated to think of his face being smashed into a bloody pulp. He did take the pillow from behind him but at the last moment was embarrassed to publicly show his fear by burying his face in it. He held it against the seat in front of him instead so that if they were to land with a crashing jolt his face would fall forward on it.

He'd sworn each time he had flown that he would never fly again and by God if he lived through this one, he never would. The trouble was, time was so precious. He never did have enough of it.

The sweat was beginning to pour down his body and his mouth twisted in distaste. Fear is a terrible thing. A dirty, filthy, embarrassing thing. Christ knows he'd seen enough of it. Seen it in the eyes of a hundred men he'd defended as they'd waited jury verdicts.

But my fate, he thought, is not in the hands of a jury. My fate is in the hands of God. The trouble was, he didn't believe in God.

His eyes went to the darkened window almost as though he were looking for some sign that he might be wrong. That out there, somewhere, there actually was a God.

How often in a fraudulent effort to comfort some unfortunate client he had used these very words. "Your fate is now in the hands of God." What utter shit. Their fate had been in the hands of twelve simpleminded idiots whom he, the defense attorney, had attempted to sway and influence.

His fate was in the hands of the pilot of this plane and although he fully realized that this pilot was undoubtedly a competent and experienced man, the thought gave him little comfort. He would much have preferred to have his fate in the hands of someone whom he personally could have twisted and turned and controlled.

Thank God for one thing at least. His destiny and the pilot's destiny were bound to each other. At least he could be sure that whatever talent, whatever genius the pilot had, would be exerted to its limit.

For a moment Marlo Phillips wondered if perhaps during one of those times in the past when only he and his own brand of genius stood between a criminal and justice, had he himself been involved as well as the client, perhaps by some little extra effort....

The hell with that. They were making an emergency landing. In a moment the plane would be down. Was there any possible thing he might do to give himself a break? Any possible way . . .

His beautifully manicured hand went to the breast pocket of his coat and he took out the fine Irish linen handkerchief with the hand embroidered initials, M.P., and wiped his high, pale forehead.

Of all the stupid, lousy luck!

The trouble was, he didn't believe in luck any more than he believed in God. For a brief second he wondered if he believed in anything.

His teeth began to chatter and he closed his mouth grimly. He thought of Alice. Oh, Alice would probably have hysterics—but actually she would enjoy every second of it—if anything did happen to him. And then for a moment his agile mind again began its little game of bookkeeping. He tried to count the people who would really be happy to read about his death. And those who might feel sad.

There would be that client out in Chicago who was counting on him to get him off the murder rap. He'd be more than sad because he knew, as well as Phillips himself knew, that Marlo Phillips was probably the only lawyer in the country who would be able to keep him out of the chair.

But who else? Who else would feel anything even akin to sadness? Who else, after sixty-four years, would care one way or the other?

This time when he put the handkerchief to his forehead it came away wringing wet.

His mouth opened and a small whisper of a groan escaped between his lips.

Good God, he was urinating in his trousers!

Ned Gaines, known to his Hollywood contemporaries—he was a man who had contemporaries rather than friends—as Ned baby, was a man of imagination. He dreamed in technicolor and he thought in terms of headlines. At the moment they were anything but modest headlines. They were front page, eight column streamers.

The headlines which were passing through his fertile and

imaginative mind involved the woman seated next to him, a woman who paid him a great deal of money to obtain headlines concerning her activities. Under normal circumstances Ned should have been delighted to visualize headlines concerning his client, the internationally renowned Francine, but at the moment the thought of those possible headlines was not only distasteful, it was frightening. Paralyzingly frightening.

The headline passing before his wide open, thyroid eyes read:

FAMOUS FRENCH ACTRESS
KILLED IN PLANE CRASH

Yes, Ned Gaines had imagination, but it was a somewhat limited imagination. It never occurred to him that should the plane crash and the press of several continents carry the story, there might be anyone aboard more important than his own client.

Once more his bloodshot eyes moved as he looked at the face of the woman in the next seat. His heavy sensuous lips moved as he mouthed the words silently. "Bitch!" he said. "If it wasn't for you and your stubbornness, I wouldn't be here."

Damn her anyway. Why had she insisted on leaving at midnight? Why, in fact, had she wanted to leave at all? Violating her contract, quitting right in the middle of the picture. Blowing everything sky-high. Walking out on the entire company. It was because of that stupid little item in the gossip columns! God if she ever found out that it was Ned himself who had planted it . . .

But didn't she have enough sense to pay no attention to a Hollywood gossip column? An American actress would have had the brains to have realized that it was meaningless. An American actress . . .

And even if it was true, so what? What could she expect? Any forty-eight-year-old woman, no matter how beautiful or glamorous, who was stupid enough to marry a boy twenty-five years her junior should know what to expect. Not, God knows, that Francine was beautiful. Her public should see her now, see her without the advantage of a fifty thousand dollar a year makeup man, without the tricky lights. Should see her as she sat there, her face like parchment and the hundreds of tiny wrinkles showing all too clearly beneath the powder and rouge. Maybe the story was right after all. Maybe her young husband was seeing that belly dancer in London. Certainly no one could blame him.

But it didn't give her the right to walk out on the picture. Didn't give her the right to take off in the middle of the night on this particular plane which was going to have to make a forced landing in some godforsaken spot.

Stupid. The whole thing was stupid.

What was it she had just said to him? Tell the pilot not to stop. She had no time to waste if they were to make the connection in Chicago.

Good God! The vain, selfish old hag. Did she think the pilot was about to make a forced landing because he wanted to? Did she think he was doing it merely to inconvenience her? Didn't the fool have enough sense to be frightened?

Probably not. In her condition, doped to the gills with cocaine, it was a wonder that she'd even been able to understand the announcement.

He hated planes. Had always hated them. They knew about it at the studio, knew how he felt. The thoughtless bastards. He was a public relations man, not a goddamned babysitter. Why couldn't they have given someone else the assignment? Why him?

He felt her clawlike hand clutching at the fabric of his tweed sports jacket.

"Imposeeble!" she said in her high, scratchy voice. "We haf no time to waste. You mus tell the pileet—"

He shook her hand off and turned toward her, his voice furious, but a fury inspired by sheer fright rather than anger.

"If we are landing it is because the pilot cannot avoid it," he said. "In America we don't tell pilots . . ."

"In America everything is stupid," she said. "The pileet is stupid, you are stupid. In my country the planes do not stop. The planes . . ."

"In your country you are lucky if the planes even start," he mumbled, turning away from her. Goddamn it, why was he even listening to her? Here they were, possibly on the verge of death, perhaps within minutes or seconds of disaster, and this foolish, vain old woman wanted to discuss the comparative merits of French and American pilots!

Gaines started to reach for a cigarette with a nervous, shaking hand and then remembered they had been instructed not to smoke. Oh Christ, they must be expecting to crash. Must be expecting....

Once more the voice came over the public speaking system and it interrupted his thoughts. It was a different voice this time, a man's voice, but he failed to make the distinction. Failed to notice the unusual introduction to the words which were to follow. In fact, the only one on the plane who did notice those rather odd phrases was Brandon Mitchell, the CIA man, and although the peculiarly military phrase registered with him, it merely registered in his mind as being unusual and he drew no conclusions.

"All passengers aboard this ship—all passengers. Now hear this. We are making a forced landing on the desert. There is no danger. I repeat. There is absolutely no danger. Keep your seats. Keep your seat belts fastened. Do not panic. Do not smoke and keep all seat belts fastened until we are told to release them. We will be on land within four minutes. Again. There is no danger so long as you do exactly as you are told."

Gaines heard the words but didn't believe it. He knew damned well there was danger. There is always danger in a forced landing. His eyes darted across the aisle and for one mad insane moment he felt an almost irresistible desire to throw off his seat belt and get up and reach over and rub the hump on the man's back who sat crouched down opposite him.

Gaines, like a good many Hollywood people, believed very strongly in luck and in omens. Touching a hunchback was supposed to bring luck. It was one of the superstitions in which he had a good deal of faith. He still liked to tell people about the time he'd rubbed the hump on the back of an extra that day he'd gone out to Santa Anita and put down a hundred on a fifty to one horse and the horse had come in and paid off.

The hunchback on the lot had been in no position to object and anyway, he'd given the man a twenty dollar bill the next day after telling him all about it. But the man sitting opposite didn't exactly look as though he would take it that way and Gaines quickly dismissed the idea. In any case, he was feeling so weak in the knees that he doubted if he would be able to make it across the aisle.

The man with the oversized head, the child's body and the hump between his narrow shoulder blades, repeated the words under his breath.

"Fasten your seat belts."

Out loud he said, "Bah!"

A shoulder harness might at least do some good. But seat belts? At best the seat belt was guaranteed to rupture the bladder or crush the kidneys. A stupid, inefficient gadget, designed obviously by some demented shoemaker; rather than an engineer or scientist. If this plane were to crash during its forced emergency landing, if it were to explode or to catch afire, the very last thing Dr. Walthar Bruno wanted was a seat belt trapping him in his chair.

Good God, it had taken him a good five minutes to release that stupid buckle after they had become airborne over Southern California. He had no intention of going through that charade again!

Dr. Bruno, a man who held both actual and honorary degrees from a dozen universities on three continents and a member of every important scientific and engineering society in both America and Europe, had a theory about almost everything which crossed his mind. Most of his theories were correct. Until the moment he learned that the plane was about to make a forced landing, he had not held any particular theory about methods of safety in case of a crash, but he was quick to formulate one.

He at once dismissed the seat belt as impractical. Assuming there would be a crash landing, he immediately concluded that his frail body would be propelled forward with terrific force. He didn't fancy the idea of its being propelled against a relatively narrow seat belt, which, assuming it didn't break from its moorings, would at best injure him internally. If it were to break he would be thrown violently against whatever he would encounter in his flight through space.

Dr. Bruno's scientific mind followed somewhat the same pattern as had Marlo Phillips' logistically legal mind. He thought of the pillow supplied by the hostess—in his case, two pillows, one for his back and one to sit on. But unlike the attorney, the doctor never failed to implement a plan on the grounds of possibly losing dignity, a characteristic for which he had small tolerance.

Jerking the pillows from beneath his small frame, he dropped to the floor between his own seat and the one immediately in front of it. He placed one pillow in front of him and one behind and as the pillows were each almost as large as he was himself, he was immediately neatly nestled in a feathery cocoon between the stanchions of the chair in front of him and his own. With his knees bent in the fetal position he reflected for a moment that he was probably as safe as he had been in his mother's womb. Very possibly even safer; it was because of his mother's falling down a flight of stairs during her third month of pregnancy that he was believed to have acquired the twisted spin which had forced him to go through life as a hunchback. He had never forgiven his mother for the accident which had been responsible for his affliction, and now as he neared the end of a full and fruitful life, loaded with degrees and honors and more material awards from a grateful society, he never forgave the members of that society nor ceased to resent them for their straight spines and their normal bodies.

Considered one of the world's outstanding nuclear experts, Dr. Bruno had the questionable distinction of being perhaps the only top man in his field who was completely indifferent concerning the ultimate uses of the lethal devices which he had done so much to develop. Cold, taciturn, cynical, he despised all men and was utterly indifferent to their particular fates. His sole interest was in his work and his own comfort, so long as he was alive. He had no fear of death and no particular desire to postpone it. He merely wanted to be sure that when it came it would be painless and swift.

A forced landing could well be a crash landing and in crash landings, people were more often than not injured and crippled. He had gone through life as a cripple and he was not anxious to compound the indignity.

Never once during the forty-three years of his life had Gary Gibbons ever doubted but what God was on his side; that God would protect him and take care of him. It was only just and reasonable that he should feel this way. After all, since the time that he had first felt the call, when he was not yet in his teens, he had been on God's side.

When the Reverend Dr. Gibbons—more familiarly known to his myriad followers as Brother Gary—heard that the plane was about to make a forced landing, he experienced but a momentary tinge of fear, a temporary anxiety. The thought did cross his mind that there would be a delay in reaching Chicago and that he might well be late for the great revival rally at which he was to preside within a few hours. But he felt no annoyance. If he was to be late it was God's will and there was nothing to be done about it. After all, God worked in mysterious ways and it was hardly up to one of God's servants to question those ways, even though that servant might stand at the very right hand of God, which Brother Gary was sure he did.

The handsome, virile profile broke into the slightest of wry smiles and his chiseled lips moved ever so slightly as he put his thoughts into words.

Brother Gary—in his mind as well as in reality he invariably referred to himself in the third person—Brother Gary, if this forced landing will make me miss my appointments, it will be an inconvenience, but I must not think of it as bad luck.

He had no belief in luck, good or bad. The very word fate was not in his lexicon. All things were preordained. Should things turn out well, should life be a rich and rewarding adventure, then one must thank God. But one must on no account complain. Pray, yes. Because prayer after all was in a sense only a form of thanking God in advance for that which was about to happen and that which would happen.

It is true that Brother Gary had many things for which to thank God. He had been endowed with a superb body, a fine sensitive mind, a beautiful voice, a fantastic and never flagging energy which had permitted him for years to toil in the vineyards of the Lord.

He had no need for that reassurance which the pilot of this plane had just given him that there was no danger involved in this forced landing. At once the words came to his lips: Yea though I walk through the valley of the shadow of death, I shall fear no evil.

Evil of course was everywhere. Evil and sin and corruption. But evil was the product of man and had nothing to do with the preordained plans of God. Evil was something which had started back in the Garden of Eden. Oh yes, there was evil all right and man, that weak vessel, would always know it. But evil was nothing to fear. Evil was something to fight. Evil was an invention of the Devil, and man, all too often the Devil's surrogate, went on endlessly practicing evil.

Again his lips moved soundlessly and he said: The Lord is my shepherd, I shall not want.

With a characteristic gesture, he shook his head slightly tossing the blond cowlick out of his eyes, the cowlick which was to a great extent responsible for giving him that oddly boyish look, and as he did he saw that the girl across the aisle was watching him with cold, brazen eyes.

For a brief moment he held her gaze and then his own eyes dropped, unconsciously taking in the delicate childlike features of her face which could not be concealed by the heavy makeup. Dropped to the slender column of her neck, the too tight bodice of her dress which emphasized rather than concealed the swelling mounds of her twin breasts.

He blushed in spite of himself and quickly turned his head away. He said, again under his breath, "Shameless."

He had first observed her when she had followed him aboard the plane and taken the seat opposite him. He had recognized her at once. He had seen her face staring back at him from a hundred newspaper columns. An international celebrity himself, he knew who she was and was immediately aware of the fact that she in her notoriety was well known to the American public in her own way as he was in his.

It was strange but as she had turned toward him, looking blindly past him as she'd seated herself, he had at once sensed something peculiarly tragic in her young beautiful face. Some odd quality of dissatisfaction and bitterness and frustration. Yes, he had recognized her at once and believing but only a tenth of what he had read about her, he had not been surprised. For one quick second he had been tempted to say something to her. Perhaps to offer her comfort, to seek her confidence so that she might relieve her mind and her heart with confession.

He had, however, resisted the impulse. It was of course his duty to extend the helping hand of the Lord to all who needed salvation. But there was a time and place for everything. During those first few minutes after he had seated himself on the plane, other duties called. He must review the sermon he would be delivering in Chicago the following day. Must hone and improve, must edit and revise, must . . .

But he determined to speak to Dianne Rhinhardt sometime before they reached Chicago. It was his duty and Brother Gary was not the man to shirk his duty in the service of God.

Hattie Arthur's pudgy right hand moved and she grabbed at her companion's wrist which was angled on the armrest separating their seats.

Her eyes popped wide open so that the whites completely circled the blue irises and her cupid lips formed a perfect O as she expelled a quick breath of air. Her soft, chubby childlike face took on a mixed expression of surprise and delight and for a moment she looked as excited as a child with a new doll.

"Melody," she said. "Melody, did you hear that? A forced landing! What fun. I told you this trip would be filled with adventure, and, you can't say it isn't starting right. Whatever do you suppose . . ."

Melody Salmon's cold grey eyes stared at the other woman for a moment and her thin, astringent mouth tightened as she jerked her arm away at the same time reaching for the seat belt.

"Don't be a perfect ass, Hattie," she said, in a cold voice which somehow or other held a subtle note of affection, making her sound just a little like a loving mother speaking to an adored but slightly delinquent youngster. "Do as you are told and fasten your seat belt. Save your delight until we are safely on the ground. And try to realize that a forced landing can well be a dangerous landing. Sometimes, Hattie, you act as irresponsible and silly as one of your own fourth grade pupils. The only adventure I want is to get safely to Chicago and . . ."

For a moment Hattie Arthur's moonlike face suddenly seemed to dissolve and collapse as it took on an expression of wild fright, mock or real it would be hard to say, and she looked every bit of her fifty-eight years. But quickly she shook her head and again assumed a mask of childlike delight.

"Now Melody," she said in a small, girlish voice, "don't you try spoiling it. It is an adventure. Can you imagine. We haven't even really got started yet and already the unexpected is happening to us. Now I wonder where . . ."

"Hattie, fasten that seat belt. And put out your cigarette. I have told you a hundred times that those cigarettes will be the death of you yet. I should think a woman of your age, knowing what you do about lung cancer and the dangers of tobacco . . ."

"I thought it was the forced landing I had to worry about," Hattie Arthur said, a little slyly. But she took the cigarette and crunched it in the ashtray and reached for the seat belt, struggling to stretch it across her more than ample stomach.

"That man," she said, nodding to where Mr. Weems was sitting on the opposite side and up ahead of them, "that man is drinking again. I don't know what is keeping him upright. I must say, I could use a little . . ."

"You could use a little plain common sense," Melody Salmon said. "Something told me when this plane was an hour and a half late in taking off that things were bound to go wrong. I just knew . . ."

She suddenly stopped speaking and her thin eyebrows angled upward as she stared at her companion.

"Now what is the matter with you?" she said. "You're as pale as a . . ."

"I think—I think I am going to be sick," Hattie Arthur said.

If the announcement of the unexpected forced landing had any effect on Horace Griswald, no one looking at his thin, nervous face could have told it. He had arrived at the airport in Los Angeles wearing a neatly pressed, conservative grey suit, black shoes and black silk socks, a white shirt, a grey tie and a pale grey complexion to match the tie and suit. His eyes were grey behind the gold rimmed frames of his glasses and his expression was harassed and worried, an expression somewhat enhanced by a perpetual tic in his right eyelid.

Horace Griswald's countenance was not fraudulent; it perfectly conveyed his emotional condition.

Like Mr. Weems, who had refused to relinquish the attaché cases which held his priceless supply of brandy, Mr. Griswald had also adamantly refused to free himself of the airplane overnight bag which he carried aboard with him when the airline hostess had offered to relieve him of the burden.

Unlike Mr. Weems' attaché cases, however, Mr. Griswald's luggage didn't contain brandy. It contained something of far greater value. It contained, to be exact, seventy thousand dollars in cash and negotiable securities.

It was the possession of this money which was responsible for the worried and harassed look in Mr. Griswald's myopic eyes. Even the final realization as he climbed aboard the jet liner that for the first time in thirty miserable domestic years he was at last taking the initial step into freedom, was insufficient to free Griswald of that worried, harassed look.

The money and securities in that briefcase were his, but only if one were to accept the premise that possession is nine-tenths of the law. Otherwise it must be admitted that the rightful owner of the loot in the briefcase was the Coastwise National Savings and Loan Company, a firm from which Mr. Griswald was even now in the process of leaving after thirty-five years in its employment, the last ten as assistant head teller. Mr. Griswald had not resigned his position in the formal sense of the word. He was merely leaving—and taking with him what he hoped would be enough money to safely get him to some far away sanctuary where he would never again have to hear the sound of that whining, nagging voice of the woman, who, in an insane adolescent moment he had promised to love, honor and obey. The promise had been made thirty years ago and it had taken him less than a year to violate its first part. Within three years he had ceased to carry out the honor provision and now, for the first time in all thirty years he was violating the final condition of the contract.

This last violation, Horace realized, would be a far greater crime in the eyes of Martha Griswald, than would be the fact that her husband was a thief and had absconded with seventy thousand dollars of the bank's funds, when this ultimate knowledge finally reached her, which it was bound to do in short order.

And so if it is quite true that anyone observing Horace Griswald when those unexpected words reached his ears—the information that the great transcontinental jet plane was about to make a forced landing some forty minutes out of Los Angeles—would have seen no change of expression, it is anything but true that they failed to react emotionally on him.

But it was not fear which they brought to Griswald. It was something far greater and more significant than fear. The sudden knowledge of the unexpected landing brought to him a sense of complete and utter disaster.

It had nothing at all to do with whether it would be a crash landing or a thoroughly safe and normal landing.

Krinsky, the Russian, may have been correct in his analysis of the geographic intelligence of most Americans, but he was wrong so far as Horace Griswald was concerned. Griswald knew very well that if the plane was making a forced landing, that landing would take place at no regular airport. That the landing must of necessity be made somewhere in the desert country north of the San Bernardino Mountains.

Even as he fastened his seat belt, his mind was racing and he knew that so far as he was concerned, it little mattered whether it was a safe landing or a crash landing. He was doomed either way and perhaps even a crash landing and the total wreckage of the plane and the death of its crew and passengers might be best in the long run.

His plans were totally and irretrievably destroyed. The plane might, with luck, land safely. But it would never, within the time limit he had allowed himself, be able to take off again in time for him to get to Denver within the safety margin he had allowed himself. One way or the other, there would be the disastrous delay. One way or the other he was trapped.

Horace Griswald could feel the tears coming to his eyes as the sense of total frustration overwhelmed him.

It wasn't just the loss of the money and securities. It wasn't even the thought of the disgrace or the idea that he might well end up in jail.

The fact is, he probably wouldn't end up in jail at all. He had covered that possibility. The bank would have its money back and there were those thirty loyal years. His cover story in case of a sudden disaster was thin, but it would hold up.

No, the thing which brought the sense of utter defeat was not the loss of the money or the loss of his position with the bank or the disgrace or even prison. It was the realization that he had again lost and that Martha had again won.

He should have known from the very beginning that there had been no chance of ever escaping her.

Horace Griswald was the sole person aboard Flight Sixty-four who, learning of the forced landing, was indifferent as to whether it was to be a safe landing or a grisly tragedy. In fact, he almost hoped for the latter.

Mr. Weems was very drunk. When the first announcement reached him, it went in one ear and out the other. He heard the words all right, realized in a dim way their meaning. But he closed one eye tightly and focused on his wristwatch with the other and by a gigantic effort read the time and realized they were not due in Denver for at least several drinks.

He assumed he had heard wrong.

When the second message came through from the cockpit of the plane, it penetrated. He understood.

Reaching over to the vacant seat next to him, he carefully settled his twin attaché cases and then secured them firmly with the seat belt.

Drunk or not, he was no fool. He was taking no chances. He had, in fact, even managed to find a cork and plug the half empty bottle from which he was currently taking his refreshment.

And then he secured his own seat belt, closed his eyes and within less than two minutes was softly snoring.

Chapter 4

In spite of everything, the word had slipped out.

Handle could have bitten his tongue off. It was exactly as the Captain had warned them. Damn it, here he was, doing it again. Even if he hadn't said the word this time, he'd thought it.

Exactly as Dude had said. Habits are the hardest thing in the world to break.

Thank God none of the four of them had heard him use that word when Dude had put the forty-five in his belt and slipped into the pilot's seat, preparing to switch off the automatic and take over the controls.

He must watch himself from now on. Dude had caught it, even if the others hadn't. Dude had given him that warning look, had known.

With the others of course it was easier. Easier to remember. They had not known him the way he had known Dude. It was just so hard to remember that Dude was no longer Captain. Especially then when he had seen him going through that old routine, slipping into a pilot's seat behind the instrument panel.

Yes, Dude had been smart. Very smart about it. Insisting on the phony use of the nicknames. He had foreseen the danger, realized how easy it was to make a slip. That is why he had insisted, right from the very beginning, that they use the phony names, even when no one was around.

Dude was a perfectionist.

It was going exactly as Dude had predicted it would go. Right down to the last little detail.

Handle's eyes went to the four of them, sitting in a small circle on the floor, back-to-back, each one's hands cuffed to the wrist of the person next to him.

No one had offered the slightest resistance. For a moment he'd thought that the co-pilot was going to be difficult but he had been wrong. Well, it wasn't too surprising. After all, only the damnedest kind of a fool is going to argue with a submachine gun, especially when it is backed up by a second man with a forty-five. At least not a few thousand feet up in the air in a plane travelling at almost the speed of sound.

The girl, and she was a pretty young piece, had looked as though she was about to faint, but she hadn't and now she seemed to be coming around all right. The co-pilot sat there, grim and furious. He looked stubborn and Handle expected they might have trouble with him before they were through.

The flight engineer, well, he'd taken the whole thing as though he thought it was some sort of practical joke. Sort of just laughed it off, but he behaved. It isn't everyone who can laugh off a submachine gun.

The Captain had been the unpredictable one. Hadn't actually given them any trouble, but he'd looked as though he were facing a firing squad. It was only after Dude had taken his seat, cut off the auto pilot and assumed control of the plane that the real pilot had seemed to relax. Handle assumed that he knew a good man when he saw one in charge. Handle guessed the pilot didn't mind being relieved of his command but that he probably objected to risking his skin with an inexperienced captain.

Well, he didn't have to worry. A man like Dude, a man with his record in Vietnam, could certainly handle this bucket with no sweat.

Looking down again at the four people handcuffed in a sort of reverse daisy chain on the floor, Handle felt a sudden sense of complete unreality. God, he thought, what a place to find myself. Less than six months ago I was in an Army hospital, not expected to live. Six months from now, give or take a little, I will very likely be dead, whether we pull this thing off successfully or not. So I suppose I might just as well be here as any place else.

His eyes travelled to Dude where he sat in the pilot's seat and he shook his head slowly.

But him? What in the name of God is he doing here? Why is he risking it? What is he trying to prove?

He'd thought about it a hundred times since they had first talked it over and formulated the plans.

Young, handsome, a legitimate war hero. Not only was Dude risking his freedom and very possibly his life but he was putting up better than twenty-five thousand in cash as well. It wasn't as though Dude couldn't make a buck. Hell, he could have gotten in with any of the major airlines. Good for at least twenty-six to thirty thousand a year. So what was he doing in this plane? A million dollars, several million perhaps—well, it was something all right. But as Handle saw it, the odds weren't worth it. For himself, yes. Dude, no.

Again Handle shook his head. It must have started a long time ago. Must have started when Dude had learned about his wife. His ex-wife now.

Odd what bitterness can do to a man's perspective.

Of course the others were easy to understand. Red and Scar especially. Neither of them certainly had anything to lose. Nothing at all. And Sis? She had something to lose, but then again, Handle figured she was just young and a little stupid and a maybe she was in it for kicks. Kids today, well you never knew quite what they would do for kicks.

Of course in a way, Sis almost had to be involved. It had been Sis who knew, because of her own past as an airline stewardess and the connections she had made, about the money. Sis who had had the essential knowledge, or at least the original knowledge which had made the entire thing possible.

Not of course that it had been Sis' plan. It had been Dude's from the beginning to the end. All the way through. His brain which had plotted it, his connections and friendships which had brought them all together, his money which had paid for the rental of the ranch, purchased the second-hand helicopter, paid the advance expenses.

He, Handle, had brought the two of them together. Dude and Sis. He was beginning to wonder if he didn't regret it.

He became aware then that Dude was changing course, throwing the aircraft into a long circle and they were rapidly beginning to lose altitude. The sounds of the jet engines changed and he realized that the air speed was slowly diminishing.

Dude looked at him over his shoulder, nodding slightly to where the others were huddled on the floor of the flight deck. Handle held up a thumb and forefinger in a circle and Dude gestured with a thumb over his shoulder.

It was time for Handle to return to the main cabin. Dude would be throwing the switch for the inside lights shortly, if all went well and he could pick up the beacon light.

There was no doubt about it. The turbulence was rapidly decreasing, the weather clearing, the ceiling improving. It helped to verify his calculations. They were over the desert now, if he was right, and there was every reason he should be. For the hundredth time in his flying career, Dude thanked God that he had had the foresight to take that extracurricular course in advanced navigation while he'd been operating as a fighting pilot.

He only prayed that nothing had gone wrong on the ground. That Red had had no unforeseen difficulties with the four giant spotlights. Each powered by its own diesel generator, they had cost a small fortune and he himself had been at the ranch only a week before to check them out.

Red, of course, would be worried sick. There had been no way to inform him of the hour and a half delay in taking off from Los Angeles. But Red wouldn't panic. Red would stand by until the last possible moment.

There was the one danger which couldn't be helped. The remote possibility that some private plane may have spotted the tall reaching beams of those lights and the pilot, realizing the unusualness of the phenomena, may have reported it. It was a chance however that had to be taken. Fortunately he had been able to find the ranch in a location which was well away from any scheduled airline route. That was at least one break in their favor.

No, Red would not panic. He was a violent man, emotional, temperamental and unpredictable. But he was a superb mechanic and he operated best under pressure. Red would be there all right and he would keep those beams piercing the night sky until the very crack of dawn if necessary.

Thinking of Red, he began to think of the other members of the group. It was odd how his mind was capable of dividing itself so that with one part of it he could concentrate wholly and with total efficiency on the piloting of the plane and yet, with a completely separate part, review those incidents in the recent past. It was a schizophrenic mental gymnastic which had served him well during those years as a fighting Air Force officer.

They made, the five of them, almost a perfect team. Each had his or her own personal weaknesses and faults, but through the strange alchemy of their relationships with each other, those very personal weaknesses more often than not were converted into a strength. Yes, Red was emotional and unpredictable, a romantic, and in spite of his violence, more or less of a dreamer. But within the framework of what they were going to do, he fitted perfectly.

Handle, despite the frailty of his body and the fact that he was a dying man, was the most valuable and the most reliable. His vast practical knowledge as a demolition and weapons expert was essential, but even beyond this was his keen intelligence and his unquestioned loyalty to Dude himself. He was the only one with whom Dude had any real human rapport, the only one whom Dude ever expected to see again once this was all over and done with.

Scar was the most dangerous and the one who presented the greatest risk, at least during the execution of the deed. It is highly doubtful if anyone but Dude would have trusted him. Scar was a born killer, cold, merciless and totally lacking in imagination. He was also stupid and had an IQ barely above that of a high-grade moron. He had two almost impossible weaknesses. He was an alcoholic and was insane about women. To complicate his sexual mania, he was more often than not frustrated in pursuit of even the saddest female types.

But Scar had a quality which offset every defect.

Dude had first met him when Scar, a corporal in the Air Force, had been a member of his bombing crew. Scar had been on the plane that day it had been shot down in the corridor between North and South Vietnam. He and Scar had been the only ones to survive and Dude had been badly injured. Scar had escaped the crash unscathed.

Both of course had been taken by the Viet Cong. Both had spent the following six months in the same prison camp far north of the border.

They had never liked each other. Above and beyond the natural antipathy between an enlisted man and an officer was a total lack of identity and empathy.

But Dude knew full well that had it not been for the attentions of Scar during the first of those six months while he lingered between life and death, he would have optioned for death.

That was part of it. But a far greater part was Dude's realization that had he personally undergone the torture, the brain washing, which Scar, the uninjured flyer suffered, he would have cracked. Scar didn't crack. Nothing they could do to him would make him crack. The odd, unbelievable part of it was that Scar's fantastic courage was not motivated by any sense of patriotism. Scar cared no more for the man, his captain, with whom he was sharing his starvation diet, than he cared for the very men who were torturing him. He cared no more for the country whose uniform he was wearing than he did for the country which he had been bombing. He was completely and totally anti-social.

But he was stubborn and once he had decided on a course nothing in God's earth could change him.

The Viet Cong, backed by two brilliant Chinese interrogators, one a psychiatrist, had been smart and after a month or so, began to understand their prisoner and they changed their tactics. They quickly discovered his weaknesses and switched from a routine of starvation and torture to the other extreme. They plied him with liquor and with women, gave him his own private room in the prison, hot baths and good food. It was this food which was responsible for Dude's being alive today.

But Scar had never wavered. Drunk and satiated with sex, or starved and tortured, he held firm. Later, when the opportunity of escape had presented itself, he had reduced his chances of success by about seventy-five percent in taking the still convalescing and sick Air Force captain along with him. He did it through neither love or loyalty, affection nor patriotism. He did it because it was the thing to do. An authority, in this case the Air Force, had laid the groundwork for the pattern of his behavior and he mindlessly followed this pattern.

In the present case, Dude represented the authority and he had laid the current pattern of behavior. He would bet his life, in fact was betting his life, that Scar would undeviatingly follow this particular pattern.

But Sis. Sis was something else again.

Half of the time he thought of her as Sis and the other part of the time he thought of her under her real name, Celeste Carr. In her case, of course, the nickname was not really important. She was the only one who was taking no chances on later being identified by those others, the crew of the 707, or her passengers. They would know her only as a fellow victim.

She was the safe one, so far as she herself was concerned. But so far as the group was concerned, she represented the greatest danger.

It was an odd contradiction that it had been Sis who had made the plan possible in the very beginning, but because of Sis that he had been on the verge of abolishing the entire scheme. It was only when he had learned one basic factor of her character that he had decided to go through with it. Only when he had understood her overpowering, psychotic greed for money and ever more money. It had taken him long hours of searching his mind to formulate a plan by which he could turn this characteristic into a strength so far as the ultimate success of the venture was concerned.

What he came up with was so obvious in its simplicity that he was amazed it hadn't struck him at once.

They were going to divide the money at the conclusion of the crime and each go his or her own way. But Sis was not going to receive her share when the others did. She would get hers on a pro rata basis, so much each six months. There was one qualification. She would get it only so long as Dude himself was free of apprehension.

In the beginning she had turned the idea down completely, trusting no one and believing in no one. It had only been after he had made the arrangements for the joint account in a Swiss bank, under two aliases, that she had gone along with the plan. Withdrawals would be made only on vouchers signed by each of them.

Greed would keep her from talking and cupidity would keep her from making some blinding mistake which might later give things away. But she still represented the weakest link in the chain.

It was because Sis herself had made the plan possible that she was the weak link.

Dude remembered when he had first met her.

It had been that hot smog-bound late spring afternoon when he had gone out to the Veteran's Hospital in one of those endless dismal suburbs southwest of Los Angeles. His car, at the time, was being overhauled and so he'd taken a taxi. He had gone to bring a couple of books and an illegal bottle of brandy to his friend, Handle, who was recovering from the removal of his right lung in the same ward from which he himself had been released only a couple of months previously.

Dude had been moved to the kindness because he knew that Handle was without family or friends and he himself knew only too well the bitter loneliness that a man can suffer in the sterile institutional confines of an Army hospital.

Handle was still in a private room, an unusual luxury only afforded the critically ill. Dude had been amazed, on opening the door, to see the girl. She was seated with bare legs crossed under the briefest of miniskirts. She wore a tight sweater over swelling breasts and her blonde hair was cut shoulder length. She was wearing bobby socks above saddle shoes and in spite of the obviously false eyelashes and the overemphasized makeup, she looked like a sixteen-year-old school girl. She had a bright, pert face.

She stood up as he entered the room and he saw that she was a little above medium height. That she had a superb figure. She leaned over the bed and kissed Handle lightly on the forehead. She said, "It has been a pleasure seeing you, Lieutenant. I will try to come again."

Even as she stepped back and he looked over at his friend, he realized that she never would.

Handle must have also realized it.

The sick man looked from one to the other and then he said, a little embarrassed, "This is Miss Carr, Captain." He turned to the girl. "This is my old Captain," he said. "You want to meet a real flyer, a real honest to God legitimate war hero, this is one. The Captain here got his wounds honestly. Gunfire, not malaria in a stinking jungle. He also did his bit in a Cong prison camp. Fact is, he has everything but the Medal of Honor and the only reason he hasn't got that is somebody goofed."

Handle sounded stiff and embarrassed and Dude at once obtained the impression that the two were virtually strangers. Had probably been finding it difficult to find something to say to each other.

The girl turned toward him then and cooly looked him up and down in unabashed appraisal.

She said, "Hi, Hero. You look the part."

Moving, she passed him and when she reached the door she again said, "Yes, I will be seeing you."

Dude watched her leave, closing the door behind her with curiosity but with no interest. He was curious because he had never before seen Handle with a woman and he couldn't imagine who she might be. But he had no real interest in spite of the girl's very obvious attractiveness. He was still suffering the wounds from his disastrous marriage and they were taking a lot longer to heal than the wounds he had brought back from the other side of the Pacific.

Taking the seat which the girl had vacated by the bed, Dude looked at his friend with a raised eyebrow. Handle shrugged under the white sheet which had been drawn up to his chin.

"Celeste Carr," he said. "She was engaged to Major Wilkins, a chap I knew on the other side. He died two weeks ago in a fire raid outside of Saigon."

Dude nodded. "Is that why she came?"

"That, and curiosity."

"Explain."

"Well," Handle said, "you see she got this letter from the Major. You didn't know him, by the way, did you?"

Dude shook his head.

"Anyway, she got this letter. He asked her if she had the chance to stop by and see me. You see, we were good friends. Anyway, the letter reached her a few days after she was notified that he was killed. Maybe it was because of some sort of sentiment that she was moved to come out here. Or, as I say, perhaps just curiosity."

"You are being cynical," Dude said.

"No. You see I knew about Celeste Carr. The Major had told me a good deal about her at one time or another. He didn't take his engagement too seriously."

"No?"

"No. You see, there are all kinds of girls. Some girls made it a practice to hang around racing car drivers. They have a thing about them. Others, well they follow jazz musicians around. They even tell me there is a collection of female kooks who follow around after writers and artists. Anyway, this particular babe seems to get freaked off when she runs into a flyer. Understand she was engaged to a couple before she hooked onto the Major. Fact is, engaged or not, he told me that she had slept with half the Air Force and about eighty percent of the commercial pilots. You see she's an airline stewardess herself."

"Sounds like a break for you, my boy," Dude said smiling.

"Wrong. She wasn't in this room five minutes until she learned I not only wasn't a heroic fighting pilot, I wasn't even a navigator. She makes a distinction between the ground forces and you death defying daredevils of the upper stratosphere. And of course," Handle smiled through pale lips, "when she surveyed my physical equipment, it is hardly the type to make up for her initial disillusionment."

"She sounds like a dull little bitch," Dude said. "The hell with her. Man can live, and probably a lot more happily, without women, but man cannot live without the staff of life itself."

He took the brandy bottle out of the paper bag which had concealed it and pulled the cork.

"I trust this will not interfere in any way with that bottle of glucose which is being fed through the tube in your right arm," he said. "In any case . . ."

"In any case stop talking and pour," Handle said.

Twenty minutes later a male nurse opened the door without warning while they were on their fourth drink. He stared for a moment and then screamed that he was going to report them at once to "Doctor Major" and wanted I know if Dude was trying to kill his patient.

Handle said, "Shut up you silly old fag and get yourself a paper cup."

The male nurse opted for the drink, but then insisted that Dude leave as visiting hours were over.

Outside the hospital, opening the door of the taxi which he had ordered to wait for him, Dude heard the high-pitched sound of the horn impatiently blowing behind him. He turned and the girl in the Karmann Ghia had opened the door and was leaning out, blonde hair in her face.

"This car goes to Los Angeles and all points north," Celeste Carr said. "Pay off your driver, Captain, and fly with the group."

He hesitated a moment and then walked over to the sports car. He looked at her coldly and he was remembering what Handle had told him. There was nothing friendly about his voice when he said, "I never fly with anyone I don't sleep with."

Her mouth twisted and she looked back at him with equal lack of warmth.

"You are not a man to waste time on idly romancing girl, are you Captain? The Lieutenant should have told me you were suffering from shell shock. However, the invitation still goes. Anything for a legitimate war hero. Pay your driver."

He turned, without smiling, and went back to the cab. Taking out his wallet, he extracted a bill and handed it to the cab driver. He more than half expected to hear the Karmann Ghia pull away with a roar as he did.

But she waited.

That was the afternoon Dude first met Celeste Carr and that night he lived up to his word and she lived up to her advance publicity.

Had the meeting occurred at another time or another place, it is highly doubtful if Dude would have given Celeste Carr a second glance or a second thought. The emotional sterility of his life, however, at the moment following on the heels of the disastrous ending of his ten-year-old marriage, served as the catalyst and established the pattern of the relationship which so quickly developed between them.

Later on, when he thought upon it, Dude reflected on how strange it was that a man can be married for more than ten years, be completely in love with his wife, completely intimate and emotionally secure with her, and know absolutely nothing about her. Or, on the other hand, he can spend twenty-four hours with a girl, one night in bed with her, and know every last possible thing there is to know about her.

It had been the first way with his wife.

It was only much later on that he also realized that a man who is in love is both blind and vulnerable, but that a man who is in love with his own wife is completely blind and vulnerable. It was when the shock had begun to wear off and the first stages of emotional convalescence began that Dude understood Caroline, knew what she really was and what made her tick.

There is a very good chance that had it not been for the accidental discovery of her infidelity, he would have gone on blindly for another ten or more years, neither knowing or understanding her.

To a man less in love, there were certain sure signs which might have indicated that all was not as he thought.

There was the semi-frigidity in bed, Caroline's strange hesitancy to fully give herself sexually. Her innate selfishness, her flirtatiousness with other men. Her overriding vanity. But it took a more dramatic and conclusive thing than any of these to wipe the film from his eyes.

The incident occurred when Dude came back to San Francisco on unexpected leave to find Caroline in bed with one of his closest friends. Had it been an isolated incident, the wound might eventually have healed, but Dude, remembering small things out of the past and inflamed by a wild and uncontrollable jealousy, started making an investigation. The "best friend" was not the only one. There had been others. Many others.

It was, as has been said, only then that Dude began to really know her and understand her. The love died slowly and it never turned into hate. It did worse. It turned him numb and almost destroyed him.

And of course he divorced her.

With Celeste Carr it was the exact reverse. He never did love her, had a limited faith in her, but after that first twenty-four hours, he understood her and knew her completely.

Quite possibly it has no significance, but Celeste was also the first woman with whom he found total and complete sexual gratification.

They stopped half way back to Los Angeles, at one of those badly lighted little Italian restaurants which fraudulently pose as having a French cuisine. They had spoken little on the drive and when they entered they found the place almost as sad as their individual moods.

They stopped at the bar, had a double martini apiece and ordered from the menu.

Later, during the meal, the conversation was desultory and uninteresting. She asked him where he lived and he told her he had an apartment in Beverly Hills, living room, bedroom, bath and kitchenette over a garage on a private estate. Swimming pool privileges. She wanted to know what he was doing with himself now that he was detached from the service. He said, casually, "Oh, looking around for a bank to rob."

She shrugged. He obviously didn't want to talk about himself.

She told him that she had a small apartment out in Studio City; that she had just quit a job with TWA.

He was no more interested in her than she was in him.

They left the restaurant after she had rejected the suggestion of a B & B with her coffee.

When they reached Hollywood, she took a right turn up the Canyon road, over the mountains, just south of Beverly Hills. He was aware of it but said nothing. Twenty minutes later she pulled into the parking lot behind a garden apartment complex as routine and dull as a hundred others in the Valley.

Wordlessly he followed her through the courtyard, around the small heated swimming pool. She keyed open the door of a ground floor apartment and he waited for her to turn on the inside light and then he walked into the living room.

It was like a thousand others in California. More than half furnished by the management, the usual Mexican hat on the wall, the fraudulent oriental small tables and doodads, the Indian shawl tossed over the opened baby grand. An exaggerated ten-foot-long couch, a high wing-backed Malaysian wicker chair in violent colors. Parquet floor, standing, oversized lamps.

A comfortable, clean decorator's room, utterly lacking in character.

He took a chance on irretrievably burying himself in the oversized couch and slumped.

She disappeared, still without speaking, behind a screen at the far end of the room and he heard the door of an ice box slam.

The coffee table in front of the couch held a dozen periodicals. An unopened copy of the *Hollywood Reporter*, the *Hollywood Variety*, a two-month-old copy of *Time*, two copies of *Playboy* and and *Esquire*. He reached for the *Esquire*.

She returned from behind the screen and she was carrying a full pitcher of ice cubes, two twelve-ounce glasses, a can of grapefruit juice under her arm. She put them on the coffee table and then went to a sideboard and opened a drawer under it and took out a bottle of tequila. A half-gallon bottle, unopened. She didn't put it on the coffee table but held it out to him.

"Here, you surly son of a bitch," she said. "Get drunk."

He looked up and then, for the first time, he smiled at her. He reached for the bottle.

"I will," he said. "Thanks."

At some time after midnight, after she had turned on the hi-fi and cut it down low so that it only served as background music, she suddenly turned to him and said, "All right, Captain, let's get the show on the road. I think you are still a very sick man and I only practice two types of therapy. Which would you prefer? Shall we screw or shall we talk?"

She was standing in front of him then, her hands on hips, her pert face cocked to one side, smiling slightly.

He didn't have a chance to answer.

She said, "On second thought, as your doctor, I opt for talk. The other can come later. Now why don't you get off your chest? Tell me about your wife. And you don't have to start at the beginning. You can save the lead-in. I know the story by heart. Don't know you, don't know anything about you. But I can recognize a guy who has been kicked in the balls from a hundred yards, blindfolded."

Later on he figured it was the old theory, you can tell a complete stranger those details of your life, the most intimate sentiments, locked away secrets, which you would never dream of divulging to your most intimate friends. He also figured that she hadn't been lying about being a natural-born therapist. And of course, the tequila undoubtedly helped. But whatever it was, before he realized it, he was talking. He was talking about Caroline. Everything, everything he had been thinking and feeling and repressing for the last three years came gushing out. And before he was through, before dawn came creeping like a quiet burglar through the slits of the venetian blinds, he had exhausted himself and they had exhausted the half gallon of tequila and were well into a second bottle. He lay half-conscious in one corner of the oversized couch, the maudlin, drunken tears coursing down his cheeks.

She managed to get him into the bedroom and managed to get his clothes off, but the time for the second step in her therapeutic program had come and was long past. He was snoring deeply as she herself stripped naked and crawled in beside him.

She was sitting on the side of the bed, holding the glass of orange juice in her hand, when he opened his eyes.

She said, "Here, it won't help your breath but it will make your mouth feel better."

She slipped out of the bathrobe and again naked, crawled in beside him and he raised himself and drank the juice.

"You have had ten solid hours sleep," she said. "It is time for my innings."

In spite of the liquor he had awakened as he always did. Completely and fully. With total recall, utterly alert. As she fell half across his body, her lips searching for his mouth through the mass of fine blonde hair, he was aware of the firm pear-shaped breasts pressing into his chest. Aware of the slender long thighs wrapping themselves around his legs. Aware of her soft arms as she reached up to pull is head to her own.

He felt the first surging of an overpowering sex drive with the meeting of their naked flash in preliminary love play and his erotic senses were quick to react to the half sweet, half musky feminine odor of her naked body.

Coming at the end of his three celibate years since the disastrous end of his marriage, years during which on several occasions he had made half-hearted efforts to achieve sexual gratification with casual girls, all without success, the sudden awakening of old longings stunned him with surprise.

His hands moved down to her tightly fleshed buttocks as he rolled her over. There was a moment of feverish activity and then suddenly his body relaxed, his mouth pulled away from hers and he lifted his head and shook it. His words were angry when he spoke.

"No good," he said. "It's no good. It's not you. It's me. I have the equipment and I have the desire, but it just won't work. You have mistaken a zombie for a man and I guess you are entitled to a laugh if you care."

She didn't laugh. She held him close and said, "Have you forgotten? I am the doctor and you must trust your doctor if you want your doctor to help you. Now just lie still. Don't do anything. Don't even think. You have been thinking of that bitch who emasculated you. That wife of yours. Forget her. All women are not alike and especially in bed. I'll show you what I mean."

He'd twisted to his side as she spoke, exhausted in defeat, and he started to say something, but she closed his mouth with her opened lips and then she was holding him like a baby. The mouth moved and her soft lips tongue caressed his neck and his chest and her arms were like willowy snakes as they circled down around his waist, the knowledgeable hands knowing exactly what to do as the progress of her technique developed until finally and ultimately he again felt the urgent and irresistible urge.

She had the skill and the knowledge of a thousand generations of Eve and she was totally without inhibitions. All she wanted was to awaken him and to please him and at last he knew and he muttered as he pulled at her.

"No—no, not that way . . ."

She said, "Yes—yes," drawing her body up and under his own thrashing nakedness and then the bed was groaning under the feverish activity of their pounding sex gymnastics.

He would never love her, never trust her or get to more than half like her, but he would never cease to be grateful for the thing which happened that morning when the evil spell of those last three bitter years was suddenly broken.

They spent most of the afternoon in bed, exhausting themselves time and again. At five o'clock she sent out for some sandwiches and coffee as he dressed and a few minutes later they sat in the living room, having a drink while they awaited the food.

"You know," he said, "I owe you a great deal. A very great deal. You have done something rather wonderful for me. I would like to do something for you. Just about anything for you. Tell me, can't I be the doctor now? What can *your* doctor do for you?"

She looked at him, laughed a little, without humor.

"Well, doctor," she said, "I would like a million dollars. More than anything in the world, I would like a million dollars. Can you give me a million dollars?"

He laughed, without humor.

"If I had it I would," he said. "Fact is, I think I also would like a million dollars more than anything in the world."

She looked at him and her eyebrows raised and she cocked her head.

"I guess you forgot," she said. "When I asked you what you were going to do yesterday, you told me you were looking for a bank to rob. What's the matter, haven't you found one yet? I'm the kind of girl who wouldn't mind a bit if you were to rob a bank."

"I remember," he said. "A figure of speech, unfortunately."

Celeste shook her head with mock sadness.

"Too bad. You didn't by any chance just mean you were looking for money, a lot of money?"

"That's what I meant. A lot of money. A very big lot of money."

"And—and perhaps, perhaps you wouldn't care exactly how you come by it? Like say, 'rob a bank'?"

"I couldn't care less."

For several seconds she leaned back and looked at him speculatively.

"I wonder," she said.

"You wonder what?"

"Well, I just sort of wonder if you are a real, legitimate desperado as well as a real hero. And if by any remote chance you could be serious. About wanting a lot of money and not really caring too much about how you got it."

"The only qualifications are that it be a lot—and I am talking in terms of a million or more—and that I get it fast."

She was silent for several minutes and then said, "You probably won't believe me, but I happen to know where there is a lot of money, and I don't mean just a million. I mean five, ten, maybe even more."

Dude laughed.

"So do I," he said. "Fort Knox."

"I'm serious," she said.

He looked at her almost pityingly. "I'm serious too."

"Then maybe you would like to hear about it," Celeste said. "Millions. They just could be available. Just could be for the right guy. And there is one very nice thing about them. They come in small used bills. Unmarked—unlisted—unidentifiable. Quite negotiable, assuming of course—"

He laughed, shook his head, but she saw that at least he was listening. Curious.

"I lost my belief in miracles along about the time I lost my girlish laughter," he said.

"Stop being a smart ass," she said. "Would you like to at least hear? Not of course that I think you could really do anything about it."

"I'm always willing to listen," Dude said, half serious at last. "After all, you have made a lot of sense to me during this short span of our, shall we say, romance."

"All right, wise guy, listen. I told you I was a stewardess with TWA.

Well, do you know anything about Continental Airlines?"

"A little, not too much."

"A girl friend of mine is a stewardess with them. She's on the run out of International here, to Chicago. Twice a week with a couple of days layover at the end of each run. Nonstop flight except for a stop off in Denver on one flight each month."

"Sounds like a rather unusual schedule," Dude said.

"It is. Now can you tell me why the plane makes that one monthly stop in Denver? Only, by the way, on the easternward flight."

"I wouldn't have the slightest . . ."

"Then I will tell you. There is a Federal Mint in Denver. Transcontinental, like most common carriers, has government contracts to transport mail and certain other items of high priority freight on its regular passenger flights. Item one.

"Item two: The banks in the greater Los Angeles area each day receive thousands and thousands of dollars in worn-out, mutilated and otherwise retireable currency.

"Item three: This currency is replaced with new bills and it must subsequently be listed and systematically destroyed.

"Item four: The place where the exchange is made is the mint in Denver.

"Item five: A very important item. The crews on the Transcontinental Airlines frequently learn certain facts through the grapevine as well as through normal intelligent observance, which are unknown to the general public and which are really none of their business.

"Item six, and the really important item: The monthly flight which stops over in Denver does so in order that a cargo of said damaged and worn currency may be transported from Los Angeles to Denver. And because I am a very good friend of a certain girl, and incidentally know other members of the flight crew, I have this information. Still interested?"

For minutes on end he sat silent and thoughtful. At last he looked up, still skeptical, but no longer merely aroused. "Tell me more. As much more as you know."

"What I know is little and it is mostly scuttlebutt. You see," she smiled thinly, "after all I *wasn't* looking for a bank to rob. I was only hoping I could find someone who was. Anyway, here it is.

"The money is delivered to the airport by armored car. And I mean armored car. Guards, machine guns, police all over the place. Delivery in Denver on arrival, the same, with possibly even more security precaution. It would take a small commando task force to do anything about it at either place and even then the getaway would be impossible. Which leaves it this way. The only possible time that the money could be removed from the sealed in, stainless steel vault in the cargo department of the plane would be some time during the actual in-flight period. A couple of hours take a few minutes one way or the other. Tough?"

He nodded, cautiously.

"Difficult," he said, non-committal.

"I have given it a bit of idle thought, in a purely academic fashion. It would seem to me the only hope would be for someone or several persons to be aboard the plane. To manage in some way to get from the passenger cabin into the cargo department in the belly of the plane. I happen to know that the only entrance is from the outside while the plane is grounded. But assuming it were possible they might then get the money, hole the bottom of the compartment or force the entrance hatch, and jettison the loot to the ground by parachute where confederates would retrieve it. What do you think?"

Again Dude was thoughtful for several minutes and at last he looked up and shook his head.

"Afraid it wouldn't do at all," he said. "To begin with, I don't know too much of the construction details and so forth, but I am confident that you would need a blow torch and other rather cumbersome equipment to gain entrance to that cargo area. Not only would it be virtually impossible to get the equipment aboard, but in the very limited time span available, it is highly doubtful if the job could be accomplished. But assuming I am wrong and it could be, we then have to parachute it overboard. Now with a jet travelling at six hundred miles an hour even if you knew the exact moment when you were going to toss something overboard, to have it land anywhere near a predetermined area, you would have to damned well have a bomb sight. And that, my girl, on a commercial plane, is out of the question. We will take it one step further. How about the man or men who accomplished this impossible feat? They cannot stay on the plane because they would be picked up at the end of the flight."

"So let them parachute overboard as well."

Dude smiled. He shook his head.

"Out of an intercontinental jet doing six hundred? I don't quite think so. It would be absolutely impossible to predict within a hundred miles of where they would land, if by some stroke of luck they landed in one piece. No, it sounds great in theory but it simply wouldn't work. Which I might add, is why it probably hasn't been tried. Thieves, after all, very rarely overlook possible bets."

Celeste nodded. "I know. But that's why I thought you might be interested. You are not a thief. You are a war hero, a very, very experienced flyer and a man of obvious keen intellect. You have the tremendous advantage of not being a thief nor do you have the mentality of a thief. You merely want a lot of money, fast. And have the equipment to get it—I hope."

"Perhaps," Dude said, "just perhaps you may be right. Tell me, are you really serious about all this? Is what you have told me . . ."

"Captain, I am a lot more serious than you will ever know. And everything I have told you is absolutely gospel."

"How many people realize that you have this information? How many people have you discussed this with? How many . . ."

Celeste Carr shook her head.

"Of course the girl who told me, if she were ever to think about it, might remember. The others I don't think were even aware of dropping certain hints. I was very cautious. As to discussing it, well, let me explain something to you. I have talked with no one at all. No one. Not because I didn't want to, but until today, last night to be exact, I hadn't been able to find anyone who might fit the bill."

She smiled then, without humor.

"Let me ask you something and tell me the truth. The honest truth," she said.

"The time has arrived," Dude said, "when I think it might be a little dangerous for either of us to be dishonest with the other."

"Right. Now then, did Handle, out at the hospital, tell you I was one of these nutty broads who was starstruck by flyboys? Slept around with any guy with a set of wings?"

He looked up at her open eyed.

"Now what the hell . . ."

"The truth," she said. "Did he?"

He nodded. "Yes."

"He's right. I have slept around. But buddy, I am not starstruck or anything like it. I was looking for a certain guy for a certain purpose to solve a certain problem. Are you beginning to see the light?"

His mouth twisted unpleasantly.

"And that's why you brought me home and . . ."

"Think what you want," she said quickly. "We are talking about money, a great deal of money. Keep your mind on your work. Be satisfied with what you get in one department and let's move on to the next. We were discussing the problem of removing a certain bit of goods from a fast-moving plane while in flight. Any other ideas? Of course . . ."

"Of course our mythical hijackers could take over the plane, the crew, the passengers, the cargo and all. Being done rather frequently these days on Cuban and South American flights. Yes, the plane could be hijacked, if that is what you are thinking. But I can tell you without giving it a second thought that it wouldn't work. You still have to come down somewhere. We both know that secretively landing a four engined passenger jet is not exactly a simple little problem. There are such factors as radar which follows a flight, there is the additional problem of landing strips—you don't drop those babies down in someone's cow pasture—there is the ultimate getaway after the plane comes down.

"The continental United States seems out of the question. In fact, aside from something like Cuba—and there wouldn't be sufficient fuel to make it anyway—everything is out of the question. And even if Cuba were possible, who wants to hand it over to Castro?"

"Well, I can agree with you there," Celeste said. "Wherever that plane comes down, and as you say there are very limited areas available—it must of necessity be discovered within minutes if not a few short hours."

"There is of course, one further possibility," Dude interrupted. "The plane could come down, the money taken from the cargo department and the plane again sent on its merry way minus both money and those who took the money. At the moment, however, I see almost the same problem. No safe margin of time for a getaway before the discovery of both the crime and the location of the landing position."

For several minutes then Dude was silent, staring down at the coffee table with narrowed thoughtful eyes. At last he looked up to see her staring at him with intense concentration.

"I really think I would like to give this a little serious thought," he said. "It is just remotely possible that you can cease and desist in your search for a suitable candidate to solve your problem. As I see it, the getaway is the key to the entire thing. Time. Time, as they say, is of the essence. In this case, I think a safety factor might be around a week or ten days."

Her eyes suddenly widened and she paled.

"If you are thinking what I think you are," she said, "if you are thinking perhaps that concealing the plane, getting rid of the people aboard, killing . . ."

"And if you think," Dude quickly interrupted, "that I am either a complete idiot or a homicidal psychopath, you shouldn't even be in the same room with me. Don't be an utter damn fool. I have done all the killing I will ever want to do. Far more than I ever wanted. Get that very firmly in your head. I am interested in money, not murder. Now listen to me. I want to think this over. For several days. And while I am doing my thinking, I want you to do something. You will have to be extremely careful and create no overt suspicion. I want to know everything there is to know about that particular flight. The members of the crew, exact times, dates and schedules, average number of passengers. Instrument locations—although on second thought I can probably get technical details of the plane more safely and easily than you can. Concentrate on the crew. Everything about them. I want to even know if the co-pilot eats Wheaties or bacon and eggs for breakfast. Get the idea?"

She looked at him in amazement.

"My God, Captain," she said, "you are serious aren't you?"

"You said five or ten million dollars, didn't you? Perhaps more, I believe you put it. Yes, I am serious, Aren't you? I hope you are."

"Mister, I was never more serious in my life!"

They stood up then and she poured a last drink and as he left, he said, "This is Monday. I will call you on the telephone Wednesday evening at exactly six o'clock."

He hesitated, looked around the room.

"This is the last time I will ever be here, the last time we will ever be seen together very possibly. When I telephone I will not use my name and you are not to use it. I will just say this is Dude. That should be easy to remember."

"I will remember, Captain."

"And never again call me Captain. Dude from now on. I am going now."

"It will be just as you say," Celeste said. "Okay, Dude."

"Okay, Sis. And it will be Sis as well as Dude."

They kissed then, and it was a kiss without sexual implications. Each was preoccupied with a subject far more interesting than sex, at least at that moment.

Chapter 5

He hadn't been able to stay indoors even during that first fifty minutes when he knew there was no chance of hearing the far away whine of the jet engines, and so he'd left the long, low, white adobe ranch house, climbed into the Land Rover, and driven out to the improvised airstrip. Dude had carefully checked the time element with him, told him the earliest moment he might expect to pick up the flight as he came in, but warned that it was impossible to be exact.

Red checked the chronometer on his wrist and, an hour after midnight, cut the engine of the Land Rover and began straining his ears.

The four powerful search lights, placed at each corner of the mile and a half long rectangular airstrip, cut far up into the clear desert sky. He'd parked the car half way down the strip, and now he lighted the first of an interminable series of cigarettes and began his long wait.

Red alone had bulldozed the airstrip and he had done a competent job. The desert floor had been perfect for his purpose. After he'd cleared it and scraped it, careful to check for pot holes and soft spots, he'd again gone over it, distributing hundreds of small cover bushes and tumbleweeds. The camouflage was effective and the only thing which distinguished the area were those four huge lights, each mounted on a trailer with its own diesel-powered generator. The strip was to be used once, on this night. After that the lights would be quickly removed and the crew of a plane flying overhead would never know it was there.

The auburn wig which concealed his completely bald head itched and bothered him, and he was tempted to take it off. But he didn't. He knew that once his alert ears picked up the sound of the plane, he'd have no time for readjusting it. Red had kicked like a steer at the idea of the wig, but Dude had insisted. And of course, Dude had been right.

"No detail, no precaution," he had insisted, "must be overlooked. It isn't going to be enough to get away with this, pull it off successfully. It's what happens afterward. If a person must change his identity, lose his identity, resort to a disguise, it is a lot better to use the disguise in advance, not have to live with one for the rest of his life."

When they had finally firmed up the plans for the job, Dude had ended by explaining that when it was completed, each of them would be on his own. Each must separate and go his own way. It was the one thing they would not do in concert. Each must make his own plans. And he had insisted that each keep his blueprint for disappearance private.

In the beginning, Red had known exactly where he wanted to go and what he wanted to do. He would return to the Orient. Of the thousands of Americans who had been in Vietnam, Red was probably one of the very few who had really loved the country. Someday the war would be over and he would return. In the meantime, there was Cambodia, Indonesia, a hundred places where he could hole up. And then suddenly two things changed his mind.

He met Sis, and he saw the desert ranch on which Dude had taken a year's lease. He fell in love with both.

A city boy, born and reared in a slum section of Brooklyn, Red had managed to get through two years of high school before he dropped out. He bummed around the streets for a year and a half, then joined the Army. He was assigned to the ground division of the Air Force. He did his first four-year hitch mostly in Germany, stationed at a field on the outskirts of Stuttgart. When his time was up he reenlisted, not because he particularly liked the service, but because he didn't have anything better to do. And then he went to Vietnam.

Despite the filth and the dirt, the backbreaking work, the danger and the grinding day to day boredom, he loved it. He would still be there if it hadn't been for the court-martial.

Red had been a good soldier, a valuable member of his ground crew. The court-martial had not been because of any military delinquency. As a matter of fact, it was only because of his military record that he had escaped with a dishonorable discharge rather than a long prison sentence.

It all came about because of the girl in Saigon. The prostitute he'd fallen in love with. He hadn't known that she was a whore when he picked her up in the bar, but it is doubtful that even if he had, it would have made any difference. The fat hipped, listless girl he'd shacked up with in Germany had been a professional, as had been every woman he'd ever had.

It wasn't a matter of choice; Red didn't take his women off the streets because of preference. They were the only kind he'd ever had the opportunity of knowing.

The soft, brown-eyed girl he'd met in Saigon had been different than all the others. She was only sixteen when he first met her; she was delicate, almost frail, but very beautiful. He called her Toy, but her name was actually Joy. She'd mispronounced her name in her broken, pidgin English and he'd misunderstood her.

A more sophisticated man than Red would have understood. Would have realized that the little bar girl, in spite of her gentleness, her softness, her childishness, was like a thousand other girl-children of the country. She accepted her particular fate in typical oriental fashion, without complaint, and without feeling immoral. She went from one soldier to another, accepting what they had to give her and giving them what they requested in return.

But Red was a romanticist. He not only fell in love with Toy from the first moment he saw her, but he assumed that because of her compliance, her willingness, her practiced affection, she was in love with him.

He took her out of the bar within an hour of their meeting, and they spent that first night in the broken-down hotel room she shared with three other bar girls. Neither then nor later were they able to really communicate or say much to each other. But they understood each other in the important things. In his own rude way, he was gentle and kind with her and he treated her more like a child than a woman. After that first night, he found her another room, and because at the time he was able to get away from his base almost every night, they began living together.

He would have married her had regulations permitted, but it was impossible. However, he talked to her about getting married later on and she would smile at him and nod, not really understanding or quite believing him. Many men had talked to her about getting married at some dim time in their future.

Toy didn't go back to the bar for more than four months, and Red gave her whatever money he had. He spent every free hour with her. They lived as man and wife, and it might have gone on indefinitely if his unit hadn't been transferred to an airfield a hundred and fifty miles north of the city.

Before he left he paid several months rent in advance and gave her almost a thousand dollars he'd saved up in war bonds. He promised that he would return. She nodded and smiled, "Yes, yes, I wait for you."

If there was a misunderstanding, it was probably a matter of communication. Toy had heard the same words from a number of soldiers. They all told her they loved her and that they would come back. But they never did. She had always nodded, smiled, said she "would wait". Red, to her, was actually little different. Perhaps a little kinder, a little more gentle, more considerate in his demands. But also, like the others, a stranger and a foreigner. A man she had met and spent some time with, who had given her what he had to give, and taken from her what she was willing to offer in return. She liked him; perhaps, in her own inscrutable fashion, may have loved him. But he was a soldier and he would go like all the others.

Two days after Red left, Toy was back working as a bar girl. Orphaned and on her own from the time she was twelve, it was the only life she had ever really known. Within a week she was living with a colored corporal who was attached to a local US artillery unit. They kept the furnished room Red had rented.

Under normal circumstances, Red would not have returned to Saigon for at least a year or so. By that time he would very likely have gotten over his infatuation with Toy, have met some other girl in some other town and formed a new attachment.

But the unforeseen happened. He received a minor injury when a land mine exploded while he and four other men were clearing a landing strip. Three of the men were killed, and Red received painful injuries when fragments of steel shrapnel penetrated the left side of his head. He was shipped to a base hospital in Saigon.

A week after he returned, he got a pass and went at once into town to the place where he had left Toy. She was in the tiny kitchen making breakfast when he entered through the unlocked door. The colored corporal was in bed.

The soldier, naked and still half asleep when Red dragged him from the bed, kept saying as fists beat into his face, "Now you just stop this—I don' want no trouble from you. Jus' stop."

But the insane little man with the bald head didn't stop, and finally the corporal, who outweighed Red by fifty pounds, and stood a good six inches taller, lost his temper. He picked him up with one huge hand and held him against the wall. He beat him unconscious, then threw him out of the door and down a flight of stairs.

The MPs found him on the street and returned him to the hospital.

Two days later Red again left the ward, without a pass this time. When he reached the furnished room, he was carrying a loaded forty-five automatic. This time the door was locked and he kicked it open. This time the girl was in the bed and the corporal was stripped to the waist, washing at the tin sink in the corner of the room.

Red shot him six times. He didn't touch the girl, didn't say one word to her.

An hour later, he turned himself over to the military police.

They court-martialed him, of course, but he was lucky. He could have drawn twenty years hard labor. But because of his record, because of the head wound, because he had good friends among both the men and officers of his company, friends who came to his aid, he got off with a dishonorable discharge.

He'd been back in the States for about six months, working as a mechanic in a custom sports car garage out in Encino, when he'd run into Dude. Dude had stopped by the place to have a four-barrel carburetor adjusted, and Red had recognized him at once as one of the flying captains whom he'd known in Vietnam. They'd not been intimate friends or anything like that, but he'd had a great deal of respect for Dude as a flyer, and Dude in turn had admired him as an excellent mechanic. Dude had also been one of those who had gone to bat for him when he'd faced the court-martial.

He used the flashlight to again check his watch and saw that it was already a good hour and a half past the time when he expected to hear the sound of the jet.

"Where the hell are you, Cap'n?" he said, half under his breath. "Where are you, boy?"

Red was worried. Something must have gone wrong, fouled up somewhere. It was inconceivable to him the Dude could have become lost, failed to locate the ranch and the landing strip. Dude was far too competent a navigator and flyer to miss on that sort of thing. No, something must have happened.

Red pulled the collar up on his jacket and opened the door, stepping to the ground. He shivered in the thin, cold night air of the desert and hunched his shoulders. His eyes went to the sky as he futilely searched it. He knew, however, that he would hear the sound of the engines long before he would be able to see the lights of the plane.

Any of several things may have happened. For Dude could have postponed his plans at the last minute. There may have been too many passengers. If this had happened, it wouldn't be fatal.

There was, of course, that odd chance that because of the weather,

Dude could have become lost. Red had been getting reports over the portable transistor radio all evening, and he was aware of the snow over the mountains. If it were the weather, however, Red doubted that Dude would be late because he was lost. He may well have had to go out of his way to avoid certain turbulent areas. It was possible, but not likely.

There was another possibility and this one, Red didn't even like to think about. Could something have gone wrong on the plane itself? Could they have fouled up someway when they were taking over? Could Sis' information have been wrong? Was it possible there were armed guards aboard the plane because of the cargo? Could the pilot and co-pilot have been carrying guns? Could . . .

The hell with it. There was no point in even thinking about it; nothing he could do but sit here and wait.

Climbing back into the Land Rover, he found the pint flask of whiskey he'd put in the glove compartment. He uncorked it and took a cautious slug. He needed it to keep himself warm, but he was going to be very careful not to take too much. One thing was for sure, he wanted to be cold sober when and if that plane hit the runway.

He lighted a cigarette and in order to stop worrying, to get his mind off it, he began thinking about the ranch. By God, he'd really put in some work these last few weeks. The airstrip itself hadn't been too tough. He had the four-wheel drive Land Rover, with the bulldozer blade out front, to help; and the desert floor itself had been smooth and hard to begin with. No, that part had been easy. It was the work on the ranch house which had taken time.

"Could be as many as fifty-five people," Dude had said. "More than that, well, we just won't do it. We'll wait. But figure for at least fifty. They got to eat and they got sleep. For at least a week, maybe two. There's got to be maximum security. There aren't enough of us to stand twenty-four-hour guard and we won't have the time in any case. So they have to be secure. And I don't want them crowded in like animals. I want them to be as comfortable as we can reasonably make them."

It had been decided that the best way was to set it up so that the women were in one area and the men in another

"The living room will do for the women," Dude said. "If it isn't quite big enough, we can open the door into the dining room and put some extra cots up there. The men will go out to the old stables. We'll knock down the walls and make it into one large open area. We're all going to have to improvise a couple of toilets because I don't want anyone wandering around. Get the steel bars up in the windows, reinforce the doors. A couple of space heaters can handle the chill in the stables at night and they'll have to be satisfied with electric fans in the daytime. They'll eat in shifts. Once we get them inside, we keep them there. No one is to get out unless they get sick or it's some sort of emergency."

Dude had laid out the plans, but Red had done the work. He was a good amateur carpenter as well as an excellent mechanic; and he had enjoyed it. It was when he was outside, working on the runway, that he had really started falling in love with the place. He liked the cool clear desert nights as much as he enjoyed the infinite space of cerulean sky and the dry hot air of the daytime. He liked the loneliness and the sense of total possession it gave him. He could stand by the hour looking off to the mountains to the north and the west, barely distinguishable on the far horizon past the shimmering mirages of the endless wastes of the mesa.

Gradually the secret plan began to form in his mind. Why shouldn't he return? Come back in a year or two, when it was all over and forgotten, when the heat had died down. Why shouldn't he return and buy the place? It would be safe enough. Until now, no one had ever seen him there. Dude had done all of the buying of materials and supplies and trucked them in. The only people who would ever see him would be those on the plane. The chance of any of them ever coming back was too remote to even consider. And of course, by then, when it was over and done, he would have his new identity.

The more he thought about it, the more feasible it seemed. Of course the ranch would never support anything, would never be able to sustain livestock or a crop. The lack of water insured that. But the place wouldn't have to be self-sustaining. Once he had cut out from the others and had taken his share, money would never again be a problem.

He had considered at one time discussing it with Dude, but then, remembering those long sessions when all of them had been together discussing details and plans, he quickly realized that it would be best to keep his own council.

Most of the time there had been only the four of them, the four men. Dude had been extremely cautious about those meetings, cautious to see that no one ever saw them together, cautious that no one should know they had any contact with each other other than those contacts which had taken place before the forming of the plot.

They were equally involved, but it was Dude who had made the plans, figured out the angles. Red and Scar had had nothing to contribute except a willingness to go along. Handle had made a suggestion or two, asked questions, but it was Dude's blueprint from beginning to end.

He had spent as much time and energy in planning what would happen after the takeover of the plane, planning the escape and getaway, as he had the crime itself. He had not only predicated his plans on a complete success, but he had also taken into consideration the possibility of failure. No detail had been too small or insignificant for his consideration.

"The one really important thing," he stressed, "is that no one be killed. No one even be injured or misused. And don't misunderstand me. I don't say this on moral or ethical grounds. I have no moral objections on being responsible for someone else's death. When you have dropped napalm on innocent women and children, which we all did in Vietnam, you lose your sense of moral responsibility about the death of strangers.

"No, it isn't because I am thinking of the victims. I am thinking of us. If by any chance this thing falls apart, and there is always the chance of failure, if we fail and are picked up, at least we have some chance of beating the chair so long as no one is hurt or killed. Of course they will have a technical kidnapping rap, but you can be sure a judge and jury will be more lenient if no one has been murdered.

"More important than that, however, is what will happen if we do pull it off successfully. They will never stop looking for us, never close the case. But they won't look one tenth as hard if only money is involved. There won't be the vicious element of personal vengeance which is always there when it is a case of murder. There is one other big factor. If one of us is picked up, the people on that plane are going to have to make an identification. They will never be absolutely sure. But one thing is certain, they will be more inclined to entertain doubt if they personally didn't suffer. So unless it is absolutely unavoidable, no one is to be touched while we are holding them.

"Another thing. We take the money and nothing else. The money is the only thing which will not be able to be identified and which is safely negotiable. We certainly take no chances on taking any personal possessions from either the passengers or the crew. And whatever money they might have, no matter how much, will be insignificant compared to the main prize.

"Holding these people, at least for the first few hours while we are all going to be there, will not be too great a problem. But then, after the three of you have left and are on your way to the border and while I am here alone with them, alone with them for at least a week to ten days, there will be problems. That's why they must be as comfortable and as secure as we can make them."

It was at this point that Scar had interrupted, wanting to know why they all couldn't leave together. Why Dude should stay on for that extra span of time. Why they couldn't just pack the money in the Land Rover and all take off simultaneously.

Dude had patiently explained.

"You must understand what will be going on once that plane has been reported missing," he said. "Once that plane is known definitely to be down somewhere and missing, the three of you will be crossing the Mexican border, separately and at the three places we have already determined on. You will be able to do it safely because there will be no reason on earth to tie any of you in with a missing plane. You will be carrying nothing which will incriminate you.

"But the money cannot leave. The money must stay at the ranch with me. For the first week or ten days, there will be an extensive search for the remains of the plane. It had to come down somewhere. But then, when it hasn't been found, when a thorough and complete search has been made, things are bound to die down. They will not be going over the same territory time after time. It will be a mystery, certainly, but there will be only one thing for them believe. That the plane is down in some obscure mountain canyon, possibly covered by snow or an avalanche set up by the wreck of the plane itself. That sooner or later it will come to light.

"In any case, by the end of that week or ten days, I can safely leave. With the money. And there is only one safe way to get that money across the border and that's by air. By air and at night. I can fly the helicopter at a sufficiently low altitude so that it will not be picked up on any radar screen. I have made my arrangements once I am across the border, but there is no point in going into the details as none of you will be involved. Let me just say that I have the spot picked out where I will land. I have seen to it that the helicopter will not be discovered for a long time, if not forever. A car will be there waiting and available. A safe car with the proper registration. The car which will take me to the rendezvous with the rest of you in Mexico City."

"And the people left at the ranch?" Handle asked.

"That is another reason I decided on the copter," Dude said. "The letter will be mailed from the airport at Phoenix. It should reach the state police sometime within thirty-six hours of the time I will have left the ranch. I'll have plenty of time to get across the border between the time I drop it into the box and the police receive it."

They had gone on talking, discussing every detail until Dude had finally stood up and said, "Well, this will be the last but one meeting. It is about as foolproof as we can make it. The way I look at it, there is only one ultimate danger. A danger which involves all of us. The danger of our individual personalities. The possibility that through carelessness or stupidity one of us may sometime later on give himself away, be picked up. It won't necessarily mean that the others will be caught, but it will complicate things and add a certain perpetual risk. However, I know you three fairly well. I am not too worried."

Handle said, "If you aren't worried, Dude, then I'm not. But it does seem to me, speaking of this last thing, that the girl is the one who really represents the danger. The authorities, once they have understood what took place, are going to have to suspect that it might have been an inside job. That some member of the crew might be involved. They will never give up on that angle. And if they suspect the crew, they'll proceed to the next logical step in deduction. They'll suspect anyone who might be a friend of any member of the crew. And of course Sis . . ."

"You're right," Dude said. "Sis along with a hundred other people will be investigated. Thoroughly and completely. And they will never close the file on her."

"It would seem to me," Scar said, "that if this girl were to sort of disappear once we have got the money and made our getaway . . ."

Dude looked at him pityingly.

"If you are thinking what I think you are," he said, "forget it. The girl will, without doubt, disappear at the proper time and in the proper way. It has been arranged. But aside from the fact that we don't go into something like this without complete honesty and faith in each other, you want to look at it from a practical point of view. If anything were suddenly to happen to the girl, suspicion would automatically and immediately attach itself to her. And then they really would make an investigation. They would find out about every last single person she has as much as spoken to or seen in the last five years. They would discover that she'd visited Handle in the hospital, would probably learn that she had met me there. The next step would be to discover we have both disappeared. It would be the direct line of contact with all of us. No, the one thing which can't happen, which we can't let happen, is for anything to happen to Sis. So long as she is safe, we are."

"Well, if they are going to be watching her like that, never giving up, how is she ever going to be able to use any of the money she gets? How will she account for the dough?" Red asked. It was the only time he had ever questioned anything about the caper.

Dude smiled.

"You'll be meeting her at our next rendezvous," Dude said, "and then maybe you'll understand my confidence in her. In the meantime, just trust me. I have told you that arrangements have been made. She, like all of us, will simply disappear, cease to exist, at the proper time. And it will be done so as not to raise suspicions. I am not going to give you any details of the plan for the same reason that I am taking no one into my confidence concerning my own plans, once we each have our cut and split out. For the same reason I don't want to know what your individual plans are. The less we know, the safer we will all be—in case, of, say, that accident I mentioned of us being picked up. Okay?"

The next meeting was the last one and it was then that Red met Sis. From the very minute he'd walked into the room of the motel down in Tijuana and seen her sitting cross-legged on the couch, sipping the Scotch and soda, he'd been entranced. He spent the whole time staring at her mindlessly, hearing nothing that was being said and only watching her every move with wide, enchanted eyes.

Sis was the kind of girl whom he'd always dreamed about but had never really known. Smooth, beautiful, sexy and sophisticated, she came out of a different world.

Under normal circumstances Red knew that she was the sort of woman he might dream about, but that he would never have the opportunity of knowing or being with. He automatically mistook her sophistry and wit for intelligence, her style and manner for true culture. He found her blonde youthful beauty as glamorous, and very likely as unattainable, as the average soda jerk might the picture of his favorite movie star in a fan magazine. The fact that the two of them were now partners, in a manner of speaking, were about to share a very dramatic and vital experience, almost overwhelmed him.

In spite of himself, he couldn't help resenting Dude's easy familiarity with her. And when he saw Scar virtually undressing her with his protuberant, obscene and lecherous eyes, he burned with a secret fury.

Although they never once spoke directly to each other, although she treated him with the same casual friendly good will that she treated all the others, by the time the meeting was over, Red was already hopelessly in love with her, or at least the myth of her.

Later on, some two weeks before the night of the flight of the Boeing 707, Dude had brought her out to the ranch for a brief visit. They had arrived together in the helicopter. Dude had at first objected to her coming along, feeling that it was pointless and there was always an added risk on them being together. But Sis had insisted that she wanted to see the ranch, go over it in person.

"I am going to be stuck with the others there," she'd explained, "and I think it is important I know everything about it. The layout of the rooms, the security measures, the possible places where there might be trouble."

"There are two times when I can expect trouble," Dude said. "When we take over the control of the plane and after we land, while we are transferring the passengers and the crew to the ranch house. There is always the possibility that one of the passengers may have a concealed weapon which we won't find at once. But aside from that, I expect no trouble once they are locked up. It will be tough, of course, once the boys have left and I am alone. But I have both the men's and women's quarters bugged and I will hear everything which goes on."

"How about when you are sleeping?" she asked.

"They'll be securely locked in. However, there is a fair chance they'll make some attempt to break out. I'm going to arrange that you and one of the airline stewardesses will be handling the food in the kitchen. You'll have access to the men's quarters as well as the women's. There is a good chance that if there's a conspiracy to make a break, you'll learn about it. I've devised a method by which you can warn me. But I don't really expect any serious trouble. I'm just hoping no one panics."

"Well, I'll be there if they do," Sis said. "Anyway, I'll feel better about it if I see the actual layout beforehand."

She'd won her point and Dude brought her out to the ranch. He used every precaution. She drove to Las Vegas and checked into a motel. The following day she drove forty miles northwest into the desert and left her car concealed in an abandoned mine shed. Dude dropped down in the helicopter and picked her up. They took the long trip back to the ranch, spent that afternoon and night, and he returned her the following day.

Red had been expecting only Dude and when the girl stepped from the helicopter, he blushed and stammered with a mixture of surprise and pleasure.

At the time, he half-suspected that Dude and Sis were having an affair, and he felt an odd sense of jealousy and resentment. The three of them spent an hour or more going over the place and inspecting his work, and Dude was silent and preoccupied most of the time, asking incessant questions, carefully checking out every possible detail. Sis was gay and enthusiastic and she treated Red in a casual, friendly manner, as though he were an old and trusted friend.

Later on they had dinner together, a huge tenderloin steak which Red cooked over charcoal. When they finished eating, Dude said he was tired, and he went into one of the bedrooms and lay down. Sis asked Red if he played gin and he nodded. They opened a bottle of Scotch and broke out a deck of cards; for the next four hours they played and drank and she won seventy-four dollars from him. They didn't get particularly tight, but she told him a few slightly off-color jokes, which he failed to completely understand, but which he laughed at uproariously.

Her easy intimacy, her immediate acceptance of him as a bosom companion, completely disarmed him. She was the most glamorous and enchanting woman he had ever met, and by the time Sis and Dude climbed aboard the helicopter the following morning to return her to her hidden car in the desert north of Las Vegas, Red was hopelessly head over heels in love with her.

It wasn't long after Red got the idea of returning sometime and buying the ranch, that he began to dream of the possibility of getting Sis to come back with him. After all, she did seem to like him, they got on fine together. And whereas he had thought in the beginning that she was Dude's "girl," he no longer believed this to be true.

After all, what could be more logical? She was going to have to disappear eventually. She was going to need sanctuary. There was a very good chance she would need a loyal and strong protector as well.

There was, of course, one major difficulty. She had no way of knowing how he felt about it, about her. And there was going to be a very slender opportunity of letting her know.

She would be arriving on the plane—assuming it ever did arrive—any moment now. She would be at the ranch and Red would be there, but he would be there for only another twenty-four hours. And there would be almost no chance that they could find a minute together in privacy. Certainly, even if he were to have the entire day at his disposal, he doubted if that would be sufficient time for him to make a successful courtship.

But, sooner or later, she'd leave the ranch and she'd be returning to Los Angeles. She would at least be where he could find her, some day when the heat was off enough that he might take a chance on making a contact.

The one thing he could do, in that twenty-four hours, was to see that that contact was possible. To arrange somewhere, sometime to get in touch with her.

He would have to be exceedingly careful about it. Neither Dude nor any of the others must suspect anything. There was little doubt in Red's mind that Dude, Scar or Handle, if they thought he'd jeopardize them by contacting her afterward, would shoot him down on the spot.

The whole idea of course was impossible, or so far-fetched as to be almost impossible; and this Red realized. But Red was a romanticist and a dreamer. He was in love with the ranch and he was in love with Sis; and for a romanticist, when you are in love, nothing is impossible.

He was butting out his cigarette with one hand, reaching for the whiskey flask with the other, still lost in thoughts of Sis and his impossible dream, when he first became aware of the sound of the engines.

He dropped the still uncorked flask to the floor of the car as he jerked the door open, and a second later was standing beside the Land Rover, scanning the night sky.

The roar increased, coming in from the northeast. The sound became rapidly deafening, and he knew that the great plane was circling far overhead long before his eyes finally spotted the wing lights.

Red reached for the remote-control switch and the great twin beams at the far north end of the runway blinked several times. He climbed back in the car, started the engines and began moving in low gear toward the south end of the long desert strip he'd cleared for the landing of the 707.

He felt a vast surging of blood coursing through his veins. His heart seemed to be almost bursting under the sudden tension. He himself couldn't have told you whether it was because of the sudden relief at the sight of the plane, or the thought that within minutes now he would be seeing the girl again.

Chapter 6

Seconds after the wheels gently touched solid earth, Dude began to softly apply the air brakes. Far ahead he could see the flood lights outlining the ranch house go on and he again reached for the switch which activated the public address system in the cabin. At the same moment he pulled a second switch which brilliantly lighted its interior. His voice was cool and precise when he spoke.

"All passengers," he said, "will keep their seats. This plane is now safely down and in a moment will come to a full stop. This is an emergency and I want your attention. I repeat, I want your attention. Your safety depends on it."

His eyes checked the ground speed instrument and he again touched the brakes as he stopped speaking for a full half minute. He began again when the plane was still several hundred yards from the place where the temporary runway ended and as the great airliner gradually came to a full stop.

"Keep your seats and give me your attention. This airplane has been commandeered and is no longer under the control of its crew. I repeat. This plane has been commandeered. There is a man at either end of the passenger compartment and these men are armed with automatic weapons. Follow instructions and no one will be hurt."

Once again he ceased speaking, waiting for the passengers to adjust to the obvious shock his words must have created. He cut the power then, turned off the landing lights.

Again he flicked the switch on the mike and spoke.

"Follow instructions and no one will be hurt. This emergency landing in no way involves any passenger or member of the crew. There is no reason for anyone to panic or be frightened. Do as you are told and you will be safe. Arrangements have been made to care for you until you can be safely removed from this landing area. A landing ladder is now being brought to the exit and when you are told to unfasten your seat belts you will do so. You will then file to the exit door and climb to the ground. You are to carry no luggage with you. Your personal possessions will be turned over to you once you are where you will be held temporarily. No one is to be molested and this is not a robbery or kidnapping. Please do as you are instructed.

"Once you have left the plane, you will proceed in single file to the house. You will follow the instructions of your guides. Any person in any way attempting to disobey these instructions will not only be jeopardizing his own life, he will be endangering every other person on this airplane. Now unfasten your seat belts and proceed slowly to the exit at the rear."

For a moment, as he stopped speaking, there was a dead silence in the pilot house and then Kenny Savo whistled and said, "Well, I will be goddamned. If this ain't somethin'!"

Captain Arch Winter looked up at Dude and slowly shook his head.

"Fellow," he said, "I must say you gave me a few bad moments there. I still don't see how you got us down but I must admit it was a great job. I don't know what the hell you are up to, but I can tell you one thing. You'll never get away with it."

Dude looked down at him, half smiled and winked. "We are getting away with it," he said.

MacPherson, the co-pilot, was neither grateful for the safe landing nor was he amused.

"If this isn't a kidnapping or a robbery," he growled, "I would certainly like to know just what the hell it is."

Dude turned and stared at him. His voice was icy when he spoke.

"What I told the passengers goes for the crew," he said. "Give us no trouble, do as you're told, and you won't get hurt. What we're up to is our business. But for the next few days, you people are going to be held. We are going to make you as comfortable as possible, but we want no trouble. You in the crew are the lucky ones. At least you'll probably draw full flight pay for the time we do have to hold you. But just take it easy and give us no trouble. Understand?"

"It's a ball," Savo said. "A ball. You won't get any trouble from me, brother."

Arch Winter shrugged. He wasn't planning to give anyone any trouble.

MacPherson merely looked more surly.

"We'll wait for the others to get to the house and then we'll follow them," Dude said.

"How about the plane?" Captain Winter asked. "Don't tell me you're doing this just to get a plane. Hell man, you may have been lucky and managed to land it, but you couldn't get her up again in a . . . "

Jill Grunsky interrupted, speaking for the first time.

"Wow," she said, "I thought you spoke like you knew something about flying. Would you mind telling me just where we are?"

"You are in the middle of a dry lake, in the middle of the desert and in . . . "

"You may be able to hide us," Captain Winter cut "but believe me, fellow, you can't hide a four-engined Boeing 707. Once this ship is reported missing, every disaster facility west of the Mississippi River is going to be out searching. You guys must be crazy if you think you can get away with whatever you are trying to do. I just hope when the shooting starts that the rest of us are out of the line of gunfire."

"The only shooting which will start will happen if one of you gets out of line," Dude said shortly. "Keep that in mind. And now, let's get on our feet. It will be a little clumsy but we won't remove the handcuffs until we get you on the ground and over to the house. You'll just have to make it down the ladder the best way you can."

Red was back waiting at the foot of the landing ladder when they climbed down. Dude sidled over to him, asked, "Everything okay?"

"There were so few of them," Red said, "we kept 'em together for the time being in the main room. Most of them went peacefully."

"Most of them?"

"Well, for a minute we thought we might have a little trouble. Two of the guys insisted on hanging onto their hand luggage."

"And?"

"One was a drunk. So stoned he could hardly stand. Handle took his two briefcases and checked them. Both filled with booze. We let him keep them."

"And the other?"

"A weird little creep. Was hanging on to his airline bag like grim death, and looked like he was ready to go down fighting for it. Scar made him open it. And by God, it was filled with money. Bills. Must have been thousands. Maybe eighty or a hundred grand in it."

"So what happened?"

"So we just let him keep it. Didn't want anything happen or any trouble and he may have been a little runt, but he was hysterical and . . . "

"You did right," Dude said. "We don't want his money. And we sure as hell don't want anyone panicking. How about the others? You frisk them?"

"They're doing it now," Red said. "Want me to drive these four to the house or shall they walk like the others?"

"Let 'em walk," Dude said. "Here is the key to the cuffs. Take them off once they are inside. I'll be along in a few minutes."

At no time had he been tempted to use the gun. Brandon Mitchell never forgot that very important lesson which his superiors in the CIA had drilled into his mind again and again. Your brain will always be your most important weapon. And right now there was no doubt that his brain was a lot more important than his muscle, the muscle being represented by the thirty-eight police special he had taken from its shoulder holster and tucked into the his trousers.

From the very moment when he had heard that announcement over the public address system, the announcement that the plane was being commandeered and he had looked up and seen the man standing in the door leading to the flight deck, the man with the submachine gun cradled in his arms, then turned in his seat and seen the second man at the rear of the plane, he knew that his weapon would be useless. He might get one of them, but not both.

His job was solely to ensure the safety of the man whom they had put in his protective custody. Protect him, not subject him to a hail of submachine gun bullets.

Now, standing against the white wall of the large square room in the ranch house he heard the words of the thin, consumptive looking man who had stood by the door of the flight deck, and he had to make a second decision.

"If any of you are carrying firearms, I want you to carefully take them and lay them on the floor. You will all be searched and it will be a lot better for you if you drop any weapons, guns or knives, before we make the search."

Like the others, Mitchell had no way of knowing what was happening or why it was happening. The man on the public address system had informed them that it involved none of the passengers and perhaps he was telling the truth. On the other hand, the CIA man, with the private knowledge of the importance of the man he was protecting, could well suspect that the hijacking of the plane and her crew and passengers might well be aimed at the security of his protégé. It was his job to ensure that security.

Because he knew in real life it doesn't happen the way it does on TV or in the movies, and that a lone man with a single revolver cannot overcome two men with automatic weapons, he had realized the futility, the suicidal hopelessness of trying to do anything. Perhaps the gun would remain futile and hopeless. But on the other hand, he hated to give up his weapon unless he was forced to do so. There was the remote possibility he would need it and might use it with effectiveness.

Out of the corner of his eye he could see that the one with the scarred face was starting to search those who stood facing the wall on the opposite side of the room. The tall man was in the center of the room, the gun still in his cradled arms as he watched all of them.

He was still thinking about it, still trying to figure a way of retaining his gun, when his eyes moved and noticed the half-opened attaché case where the man next to him had dropped it to the floor a few inches from his own right foot.

Mitchell knew what was in the attaché case. He had been standing next to Mr. Weems when the man had checked his two pieces of luggage. At the moment, Mr. Weems was still holding his other case and he was weaving slightly, a broad, vacuous smile on his face.

Moving slowly Mitchell reached into his left-hand trouser pocket and took out a thin bladed folding knife. And then he slowly squatted, holding the knife openly his hand.

As his coattails swept the floor, his right hand quickly darted to his belt and he jerked out the thirty-eight. Simultaneously as he dropped the pen knife, his other hand reached over to the half-opened bag, concealed by his jacket, and he laid the gun on top of the brandy bottles. Without rising, he looked up at Mr. Weems. He smiled ingratiatingly.

"Could you spare a drink?" he asked.

Mr. Weems turned slowly, smiling a benign smile.

"I should love to have one," he said. "I never refuse."

Mitchell took a bottle from the attaché case, at the same time burying the gun as best he could. He jerked the case closed as he got to his feet. He uncorked the bottle and handed it to Mr. Weems.

Scar was perfunctory as he quickly ran his hands over the Reverend Gary Gibbons' torso and then patted down each trouser leg. He was pretty damned sure the Reverend wouldn't be toting a gun, but as he started to rise from a kneeling position, he purposely felt his crotch with his opened palmed hand and laughed when the Evangelist twitched self-consciously and blushed.

He moved to the girl next to the Reverend Gibbons and stared at her for a moment.

"If you dare lay your filthy hands on that child," Brother Gary said, "you shall have me and God to answer to."

Scar slowly turned his bloodshot eyes from the cleavage of Dianne Rhinhardt's low-cut dress and looked up at the minister.

"What's the matter, Rev? You got a dirty mind?"

Scar started to turn back, his eyes again going to the girl's swelling bosom. Handle spoke from the center of the room.

"Get on with it," he said. "You don't have to worry about the women. We'll just check their pocketbooks and luggage."

Scar glowered at him and moved to Marlo Phillips.

"I can assure you, sir," the attorney began, but Scar quickly interrupted him.

"Just raise your arms," he said in a bored voice.

When Gene Farris' turn came, the industrialist spoke quickly.

"You will find no weapon on me," he said. "But if you will be good enough to look into my wallet, you will see that I am carrying something over fifteen hundred dollars. You are more than welcome to it. Now if you could see that I have private quarters while we are . . . "

Dude was entering the door, followed by the members of the plane's crew and Red, and he spoke in a low, neutral voice.

"You will be properly taken care of," he said. "For the time being, an hour or so, you must remain here in this room. Later on, separate quarters will be provided for the men and the women and you'll be able to go to bed. But for right now you must remain here. There's a coffee urn in the corner over there. Some wrapped-up sandwiches. In the morning you'll have a regular breakfast. You are going to be locked in and please don't try to break out. The windows and doors are barred. If you should try and make noise there is no one within fifty miles to hear you. There will be a guard outside."

As several voices started to speak out, to ask questions, the four of them left the room and Dude carefully shot the steel bars across the reinforced door. A couple of minutes later, they entered the garage at the side of the building where the flatbed trailer stood. It was loaded with the equipment which Red had been readying for the past several days.

"You think they will be all right?" Handle asked Dude in a low voice. "They won't be trying to break down the walls or something. Maybe one of us . . . "

"I am going to need all of you," Dude said. "Anyway, the bugs are all turned on and I can pick anything up off the tape with the walkie-talkie. We'll keep a constant check on them but I don't expect any trouble." He turned to Red.

"Get the Land Rover," he said, "and let's get hooked up. I want to be through well before daybreak. By sunup I want to be damned sure our bird is deep sixing somewhere in the Bay of California."

Crossing the room to where Captain Arch Winter sat in a canvas backed deck chair sipping a cup of black coffee from a paper cup, Brandon Mitchell took the wallet from his inside breast pocket and held it open to expose the CIA identification card.

"I'd like to have a word with you if I may, Captain," he said. "I don't know what this is all about, but because of the mission I am currently on, it may be very important that I learn as much as I can. Could you tell me if there happens to be anything of unusual value on your plane? This could, of course, be a kidnapping on a grand scale. It may just be that these men are trying to steal the plane itself for some reason or other. But neither theory seems to make a great deal of sense to me. What are your own ideas?"

For several seconds the airlines captain looked up at the federal man with raised eyebrows. And then he spoke in a low voice, so that the others were unable to overhear him.

"Well," he said, "your guess is probably as good as mine, or in fact, anyone's. I can't quite see them pulling this sort of thing in order to get the plane. What the hell would they do with it if they did get away with it, which I think is pretty impossible in any case. But there is a good chance they might want the cargo the plane is carrying."

"The cargo? What kind of cargo?"

Arch Winter hesitated several seconds and then shrugged.

"I can't tell you anything officially, because, officially I am not supposed to know anything. But I can give you an idea based on the scuttlebutt that goes on around an airline, and my own observation.

As you know, this plane was scheduled to make a stopover in Denver. I have noticed when we make that stop-off—it happens about once every month or six weeks—that an armored truck always arrives at the airport in Los Angeles. Several canvas bags are transferred to a special safety deposit compartment on the plane and are removed in Denver, to be placed in a second heavily armed and guarded armored car. It is only logical to assume the canvas bags contain money. And probably quite a lot of money."

The CIA man was thoughtful for several moments and then he nodded and said, "I think you are probably right. If you were carrying a cargo of currency, that's what they would be after. And if you are right, they will probably be unloading that plane right now."

"If they are," Arch Winter said, "they have a job on their hands. The compartment is stainless steel and damned near impregnable. But let's say that's what they are after and they get it. What do you suppose they plan to do with us?"

"It all depends. Have you any idea of where we are?"

Again Winter shrugged. "Somewhere in the desert very likely," he said. "Could be New Mexico, could be Nevada or even Arizona. Hard to say,"

"Well, if you are right and it is the money, I don't see how they can hope to get away with it. If we are out somewhere in the desert, that plane is going to be spotted and damned soon. I would say sometime shortly after daybreak. Another thing. These men have been seen by all of us. There are a couple of dozen witnesses at least and . . ."

"We have seen them, it is true," Winter interrupted, "but I suppose you noticed that they aren't exactly what they seem. I could swear one of them is wearing a wig, couple of them look as though they had some sort of weird makeup on. The leader, or at least the one who took over the controls of the plane, has on those heavy rimmed dark glasses. Identifying them might be a little tough."

Brandon Mitchell nodded. "I agree," he said. "But at least it is a good sign so far as we are concerned. If they are trying to conceal their identities, at least it means they expect to keep us alive."

Arch Winter looked up sharply. "Good God, man," he said, "you don't think for a minute that they would plan to murder us or something like that do you?"

Mitchell shook his head. "Hardly," he said. "But it is always a possibility. Only a psychopathic case would go in for mass murder of that sort. And I don't think for a second that we are dealing with a bunch of nuts. No nut could have arranged the takeover of the plane as cleverly as these boys have managed it. I wonder if they are planning to just leave us here? The idea of being marooned in the middle of a desert . . ."

"As you say, the plane is bound to be spotted," Winter said. "And at least for the time being, we seem safe enough. They must have made their plans well in advance, stocked food and that sort of thing."

"It might be a good idea to sort of reassure some of your passengers," Mitchell said. "That French actress and the Hollywood type who is with her seem to be on the verge of hysteria. My own guy, he's a pretty important person, a Russian VIP, is also a little panicky. Thinks this whole thing is some sort of plot against him personally. Which reminds me, I better get back and try and calm him down. Don't want him blowing his stack."

Arch stood up.

"Right," he said. "We don't want anyone blowing their stack. As long as no one panics, no one tries to get heroic, I think we will all be safe. These guys seem to be real professionals, whatever else they are. They probably don't want trouble any more than we want it. I'll talk to some of the others."

"Talk to that preacher," the CIA man said. "He strikes me as the sort who couldn't resist a grandstand play. That sort of thing could be fatal. If they had to kill one of us, they'd be in for murder and you can't tell where it might end up. We don't want any dead heroes."

"Glad you feel that way about it," Winter said. "Being a CIA man, I thought maybe you . . ."

"I'm CIA, not FBI," Mitchell said. "My job is seeing to the safety of my Russian VIP."

"Mine's protecting all of my passengers, and my crew," Winter said. "I'll be talking to you again."

"We'll start with the acetylene torch," Dude said. "Work around the combination lock, Red; that would be the most vulnerable place. I want you to be damned careful because we don't know how close the money will be and a good deal of heat will be generated inside. If you think it will be getting too hot, then we'll just have to take a chance and use the high-speed drill and give it a crack with a touch of nitro."

"I should think the nitro would be a lot safer anyway," Handle said.

Dude shook his head.

"It would be if the tanks in this bird were not still holding some thirty-five to forty-five thousand pounds of highly volatile airplane fuel," he said. "Nitroglycerine is always tricky, no matter how careful you are. We'll use it if we have to but for the time being, we'll just leave it in the Land Rover and hold it as a last resort. Now you two get started and Handle will help me. I want to make very sure to deactivate the transponder so there will be no unnecessary amplification of radar return when we release this baby. They may pick up a blip or two but the signal will be so light that they can't be sure of what they are seeing."

Scar waited until Dude was out of earshot and then turned to Red who was setting up the equipment he would use to break into the safe deposit vault.

"I just hope he knows what he's doing," he said. "I still think it would be a better idea to just blow this tub up, let her burn. Getting her into the air again under autopilot seems to me a sort of crazy way of doing it. This whole thing is too complicated. Hell, if it were up to me, I'd wipe out all the evidence. No plane, no witnesses."

Red looked at him, startled.

"You weren't talking this way before," he said. "What the hell's the matter with you anyway? You must be drunk or crazy or something."

"I probably wouldn't be here right now if I wasn't crazy," Scar said. "By the way, did you catch that little chick who got off with the others? The one with the red hair and all the jewels. I could certainly take a crack at that."

"You would take a crack at anything that moves," Red said. "Come on, let's get this box open. And you better lay off the juice, fellow. If Dude . . . "

"Dude!" Scar said. "The hell with Dude. He makes the rules for the rest of us and why should he give a damn. He'll be in the sack with that Sis broad before the night's over so what does he care?"

Red glared at him and then turned away quickly.

"You got a big mouth," he said. "Come on, let's get going. The quicker we get the money the better. And when you get your cut you can stop dreaming about rape. You'll be able to buy it."

When Dude finished working on the transponder, he said to Handle, "We'll have to wait until I can get the plane turned around and set on the runway for the takeoff before we do the rest of it. You got the chocks and everything in the car?"

"Everything is set," Handle said. "I checked it out with Red. But Dude, you sure this thing is going to work? Those landing flaps are going to have to stay half down after the takeoff. There's no way to retract the wheel trucks. It doesn't seem possible."

"It's possible and it will work," Dude said. "We just have to be damned sure of our timing. Have to be sure that we pull out the chocks at the same instant that we cut the hydraulic line loops to the brakes. The air speed will never get over three hundred an hour, but that will be enough. And the autopilot will do the rest. You can count on it."

"If you say so," Handle said. He shook his head, a little sadly. "Seems sort of a shame though. Sending six and a half million dollars' worth of aircraft all to hell. She will sure make some splash."

"It will be a splash all right," Dude said. "I don't like to see that kind of loss either. But it is the only safe way. If this plane should be found, minus the money, before we've had the chance to make a clean getaway, there'd be just too much heat. We want them looking for a missing airplane, not looking for us."

"And you are sure . . ."

"I am sure that if we get that money out within the next half hour, get this plane on its way within the next forty-five minutes, it will be crossing the coastline and heading south over the Bay of California, somewhere between the mainland of Mexico and the peninsula, before daybreak. That it will be under a hundred fathoms of water before anyone will have the faintest idea of what has happened to it. So let's get back and see how the boys are coming along."

Red was shutting off the acetylene torch when they returned. He said to Dude, "We got a break. It cut like cheesecake. Get me a crowbar and some asbestos gloves. We're goin' in."

Fifteen minutes later the two large canvas sacks were stowed in the back of the Land Rover. Handle was in the front seat, coughing violently. When he stopped at last and took the handkerchief from his white-lipped mouth, it was stained red and he cursed and wiped the sweat from his pale forehead.

"Damned night air," he muttered. "Gets to me."

"You shouldn't have tried helping with those bags and suitcases," Dude said, looking over to where they had stacked the passengers' luggage next to the car.

"None of us should have bothered with that junk," Scar grunted. "What the hell do we care . . ."

Dude swung toward him, his voice cold.

"Your job is to do what you're told," he said. "Goddamn it, haven't I explained it to you clearly enough? I said we want to give them every possible break. The better we treat them, the less trouble there will be. Now and maybe later, in case anything should go wrong."

"They wouldn't be no trouble at all if . . ."

Dude's hand shot out and he grabbed Scar by the shoulder, pulling him around so that his face was only inches from his own.

"Just what have you got in mind, boy?"

"Hell, he didn't mean anything," Red quickly cut in. "He's just had a couple of drinks, Dude, and . . ."

Dude stepped back and he slowly took the forty-five out of the holster under his left armpit.

"Now Captain," Scar said quickly, "Now Captain, for God's sake. I just had a couple, to kind of pull me together. You know I'm okay. You know I'm with you all the way. Hell . . ."

"I know you told me you'd lay off the booze until we were all through with this. Until we were ready to cut out," Dude said. "We might as well get this straightened out right now. You just called me captain. It's Dude, understand? Dude. And I'm running this show. Right straight through. So make up your mind and make it quick. No drinking. Not another goddamned drop. No drinking and no more lip. We are doing this thing my way."

"Of course we're doing it your way, Dude," Scar said, at the same time stepping back a pace. "Of course we are. Hell, I didn't mean anything. Just excited and all. And don't worry, I'll lay off the booze. You can count on me. I'm one guy you could always count on."

"I can count on you if you stay sober," Dude said. He slowly returned the gun to its holster.

"I can stay sober," Scar said. "Hell, didn't I go for a year without taking a drop? Didn't I . . ."

"Go for another couple of weeks," Dude said. "And I mean it. We've been through a lot together and maybe I owe you a lot, but I am not going to let anything crap up this deal. Anything at all. Remember that if you are tempted to take one more goddamned hooker. Just one. And I mean it."

He turned toward the car and looked at Handle for a moment, a worried expression on his face.

"Stay in the car and go back to the house with Red," he said. "When you get the dough unloaded, Red can come back, but you take it easy and stay there."

Handle shook his head.

"I'm okay," he said. "Just a little weak. You'll be needing all of us when . . ."

"The three of us can handle it," Dude said. "You stay at the house. You can open those bags and start counting the money. It will make you feel better."

He nodded at Red.

"Drive him back," he said. "While you are gone I'm going to fire up and get this plane turned around and in position at the far end of the runway. Bring the car back there and be sure you have everything in it we will need. Okay?"

"Okay." Red climbed into the driver's seat as Dude and Scar returned to the Boeing 707.

Three minutes later the night air of the desert was suddenly shattered as Dude successively activated the four jet engines of the great airship.

The Reverend Gary Gibbons rapped his knuckles sharply on the table in front of him as he stood up. He looked slowly around the room and then rapped again.

"Please, people," he said in his stentorian voice, "please. I would like everyone's attention." He waited for silence, his clear blue eyes slowly going from one face to the other around the room.

Hattie Arthur turned to Melody Salmon and said, "He has such a beautiful voice, don't you think?"

"Be quiet and listen to him," Melody said sharply.

"Now what is eet?" Francine asked Ned Gaines petulantly. "Who iss he? Iss he also one of the gangsters?"

"For God's sake," Ned said, "he's a minister. He's one of us."

Walthar Bruno, who had been whispering to Gene Farris, looked up angrily. "Damned fool," he said. "Never knew a preacher yet who wasn't a damned fool. What does he want?"

Brother Gary's eyes lingered for a moment on Dianne Rhinhardt, lingered a bit longer on Sis. He raised his hands and lifted his square chin slightly looking toward heaven. He waited until the last mumbling and rustling stopped. Until he was sure he had their undivided attention.

"We are here together in this perilous position," Brother Gary said in his deep, resonant voice, "and in a moment I am going to ask you all to kneel with me in prayer. But first I would like to say a few words."

"Well say them and get it over with," Marlo Phillips muttered under his breath. He would listen but he would be damned if he would kneel in prayer. He was safely on ground and he felt no need of prayer, even if he had believed in God. The lawyer was used to dealing with criminals and he had no fear of his captors now that the plane was on the ground and he was out of it.

Serge Krinsky, who shared the criminal attorney's atheistic viewpoint, took one look at Gibbons' clerical collar and didn't even bother to listen. He was still convinced that the whole thing was a part of some devious plot to kidnap him before he could defect, and he put what slender hope he had in the CIA man at his side and not in any mythical deity.

Mary Mills who had been talking with Jill Grunsky, the other airline stewardess, at once made the sign of the cross as she always did at any mention of prayer, God, or anything even remotely connected with religion. She was a good Catholic, but she had infinite respect for any man of the cloth, no matter what his faith, so long as he wasn't Jewish or Mohammedan.

"We are obviously in the hands of a gang of desperadoes," Brother Gary said. "I do not know what this is all about or what may happen to us, but I do know that we must put our trust in God. That our fate rests only in the hands of God."

He paused dramatically, again looked from one to the other of the people in the room.

"God," he said, "helps those who help themselves and if God is to help us, we must help Him."

Mr. Weems smiled and clapped his hands.

"Hurrah for God," he said in a very clear voice.

Brother Gary frowned at him but overlooked the interruption.

"The first thing we must do," Brother Gary said, "is to make every effort to see that the women among us are protected." Again he looked around the room, his eyes stern and only softening slightly when they came to Dianne Rhinhardt.

"We have been told that they plan to put us men in separate quarters for sleeping," he said. "This we must try and avoid. We cannot leave the women alone and at their mercy. I am sure every man in this room feels as I do. That every one of you is prepared to lay down your life to protect the honor of the helpless women among us."

"I am not prepared to lay down my life to protect anyone's honor,"

Ned Gaines said. "My experience has been that no woman's honor is infringed upon unless she invites the infringement."

Brother Gary looked at him coldly.

"We are not dealing with normal people here," he said. "We are dealing with desperate men, with hardened criminals. We cannot leave these helpless women open to rape and assault."

Arch Winter slowly got to his feet.

"I know your intentions are good, Reverend," he said, "but I think you are off on the wrong tack. In any case, I am the captain of the plane and the safety of all the passengers is my responsibility. There is no reason to believe that because the men and women among us sleep in separate quarters, that the women will either be assaulted or raped."

Savo looked at the captain and leered.

"In fact," he said in a low voice, "perhaps there would be less chance."

Winter ignored him and continued speaking.

"I think the most dangerous thing we could do would be to try and argue with them, try and disobey their orders. I feel responsible and I . . ."

"Captain," Brother Gary said, his voice cold and hard, "I believe when you permitted these people to take over the command of your ship, you relinquished your responsibilities as its captain. God alone is now our captain and it is in Him that we must have our faith and confidence."

"It doesn't matter a damn who our captain is," Marlo Phillips said. "But I agree with our pilot. It is certainly best to go along with their plans and not antagonize them. Furthermore, we might as well be rational about this thing. I don't believe for a minute they have plans for misusing these ladies. I can't believe that a gang of hijackers would go to the trouble of stealing a plane and a plane load of people for the simple purpose of committing a few casual rapes."

"Rape is not simple, sir," Gary Gibbons said sternly. "It is a crime against God and man."

"I thought it was a crime against women," Kenny Savo said.

Arch Winter turned to him angrily. He said, "Shut up, Savo. You aren't helping things." He looked back at Brother Gary.

"Make a damned fool of yourself if you want to," he said. "But don't involve the rest of us. Our situation is bad enough and there is no point in making it worse. Trying to make something out of nothing . . ."

Dr. Gary Gibbons had had years of experience in coping with hecklers and dissenters and he knew how to handle the situation.

"Hear me," he said in a loud, commanding voice. "Hear me! I beg you, I plead with you. Listen. We are together in this and our situation is one of gravity and peril. Why are we here? Who are these men? I do not know. You do not know. But one thing we all know. They are desperate criminals. This is not the first airplane to be commandeered by gangsters. By communists and fellow conspirators."

Krinsky grabbed Brandon Mitchell by the arm and shook him.

"What did he say? Communists? Did he say they are communists? I told you, I warned you . . ."

The CIA man shook off his hand.

"For Christ's sake," he said, "will you relax? That fool doesn't know what he's talking about. He's just another rabblerouser, who happens to be wearing a turned around collar, and can't resist shooting his mouth off when he has a captured audience. There is nothing for you to worry about just so long as you take it easy and keep calm."

"Nothing to worry about," Krinsky said. He threw up his hands. "My God, you Americans!"

"Someone should shut the mouth of that horse's ass," Gene Farris grumbled to himself. "He's going to talk us all into trouble."

He suddenly remembered then that sometime around a year ago he had made a very large donation to Dr. Gary Gibbons' Protestant Fellowship when he had learned through the press that Dr. Gibbons was a member of the John Birch Society, a Republican and an unabashed right-wing Conservative. He began to feel that perhaps it had been a mistake.

". . . and you men," Brother Gibbons said, "who are not afraid to stand up for American womanhood, for what is decent and right and virtuous, will stand behind me. You others, well, all I can say is that I shall pray for you. And now I suggest that all of us bow our heads. It is time for us to turn to the Lord God in our hour of stress and danger."

He bowed his own massive head.

"Dear God, You in whom . . ."

The sudden deafening roar of the first of the four jet engines being brought to life by Dude, some four hundred yards outside of the ranch house, drowned out the rest of his sentence.

Stewart MacPherson, the co-pilot, who had dropped to his knees when Brother Gary began to pray, quickly looked up at Captain

Winter.

"The plane!" he said. "They have started the engines. You don't think they would dare try and take off from here?"

Winter shrugged.

"That guy didn't seem to have any trouble bringing it in here," he said. "I don't see why he should have any trouble taking off from here."

"But Captain, a Boeing 707. Out of some cow pasture?"

"You saw him land it," Winter said. He listened for several seconds and again shrugged. "Sounds like he's making a turn. I guess they really are going to leave." He got to his feet and went over to where Brandon Mitchell was standing with Serge Krinsky.

"Well," he said, "looks like the boyfriends are getting ready to leave."

"You think all of them will be going?" Mitchell asked.

Winter shrugged. "Can't say," he said, "but I would imagine so. Can't see much sense in them leaving anybody behind. Except us, of course."

"If they are leaving in that plane," the CIA man said, "they are a lot more stupid than I would have guessed they were. Where in the hell do you suppose they could land it? Don't suppose they'd have enough gas to make Cuba, would they?"

Arch Winter shook his head.

"No. But they could make Mexico all right. Can't see why they would want to, however. Radar is bound to pick them up before they get across the border and even if they were extremely lucky and weren't intercepted, where the hell could they land? There are less than half a dozen fields in the whole country large enough, with long enough runways. They'd be under arrest before they could step to the ground."

"Canada perhaps?"

"They wouldn't have a ghost of a chance," Winter said. "Why by now every radar station, every listening post, every airport on the continent will have been alerted. There will be literally hundreds of police, military and private planes in the area searching. It will be daylight in an hour or so and the chances of that plane being able to land without being spotted are so remote as not to exist."

"Well, they landed here without apparently being observed," Mitchell said.

"Sure," Winter said, "but this spot, this desert country is about the only place on the North American continent that they could have done it. And remember, from the time they took over the plane until they landed, there hadn't been a long enough lapse for the alarm to really get out. The situation is different now. No, I tell you if they are going to try and use the plane for a getaway, they're dead ducks."

"Then I guess they are dead ducks," Mitchell said. "Listen, what's it sound like to you?"

"It sounds . . ." Winter hesitated, held his cupped hand to his ear although there was no need for the gesture as the roar of the revved-up jets almost deafened him. ". . . sounds like you are right," he finished. "They are taking off, by God!"

Dude made one final check of the charts and then made a tiny adjustment on the autopilot. He looked quickly over the instrument panel and checked to see that the rudder flaps were set at the proper angle. The last thing he did before leaving the flight deck was to advance and coordinate the throttles of the four jet engines so that each would have the necessary 17,000 pound thrust for the takeoff.

He could feel the great body of the plane throb under him like some wild animal held down by fragile ropes.

He wasted no time leaving the cabin, opening the escape hatch and swinging down the rope hand over hand until his feet touched the ground.

Scar and Red were standing under the huge belly of the plane, between the great trucks which supported the landing wheels. Each held a sledge hammer. He had to shout above the sound of the jets to make them hear.

"Wait," he said. "Wait until I am in the car and you see it start to move. Then hit those chocks with the sledges and be damned sure they are free and clear. After that you'll have to move fast."

He himself moved quickly, then made doubly sure the slender strong wire cables were firmly attached to the twin airline loops which went down to the landing wheels.

When he reached the Land Rover, he checked the back where the cables were attached to the bumper hitch. He climbed in the driver's seat and cut on the headlights and the rear light.

He blinked the lights, several times and then he gunned the engine and threw the car into gear. He kept it in low and pushed the gas pedal to the floor.

It took the car less than ten seconds to take up the slack in the twin cables. He could feel the sudden jerk and shock as the cables reached the limit of their tension and then suddenly came clear, severing the hydraulic brake lines.

Quickly he swung and circled the Land Rover and he was in time to see the great plane as it slowly gathered momentum. The roar of her four jet engines was deafening.

She moved like some sullen dark giant into the blackness of the desert night and would have soon been swallowed up in the stygian blackness had he not been able to follow her path by the quadruple glow of the jets which drove her on. Time seemed to stand still then and he wondered if his calculations had been right after all. Wondered if the 707 would lift and be airborne.

It seemed like minutes, almost hours, before he saw the reflections of the afterglow which had blended into a single light, slowly lift and he knew that the plane was airborne.

Red and Scar reached the Land Rover as he was wiping the perspiration from his forehead. The night air was freezing, but he could feel the sweat as it ran down his body.

Chapter 7

As the sound of the plane diminished into final silence, Captain Arch Winter went to the door of the room and rattled the handle. He grunted and turned back to the others in the room.

"Perhaps, Reverend," he said, "you have been worrying about nothing. It seems that our hosts have left but we're still locked in."

Kenny Savo had crossed the room and was talking with Jill Grunsky. He reached for the heavy curtain covering the window at his side and pulling it back, looked through the barred window.

"Not all of them," he said. "There are lights across the way and I think I hear the sounds of a radio. Someone still seems to be around."

Dianne Rhinhardt looked up from the couch where she sat chain-smoking. She spoke for the first time.

"I think this whole discussion has been utterly stupid," she said in a bored voice. "If you men would start figuring on how we are going to get out of here, it might be a little more practical than worrying about our virginity. To begin with, I don't need anyone to protect my honor. I never have and I never will. It also seems to me that the matter of where we sleep, or if the women are separated from the men, is a matter of sheer nonsense. If these men who are keeping us here want to rape us, they will do it and it wouldn't matter where we happened to be. I can't see anyone in this room who could do much about it, even if they wanted to. Those *were* submachine guns they were carrying, I believe."

She laughed sarcastically. "So far as I am concerned, a little rape couldn't be any more boring than this conversation has been."

Mary Mills looked at the girl with sheer hatred.

"You might find it boring," she said. "I wouldn't. And I for one am grateful for Brother Gary's thoughtfulness, whether he would be able to do anything or not. However, I do feel that we women should be consulted about it."

"Why?" Dianne asked. "It seems obvious to me that we will sleep where they tell us to. They will be making the decisions."

"There is strength in togetherness," Brother Gary said. "The Lord . . ."

"The Lord my ass," Ned Gaines interrupted. "The girl is right. We are completely helpless and they will do whatever they want to do. You don't fight submachine guns with your bare hands. There is no point in taking additional risks trying something which is bound to fail."

"Speaking for my companion and myself," Melody Salmon burst out, "I can assure you we will stay here with the rest of you. The Reverend Gibbons is absolutely right. You men should be ashamed of yourselves. Here we are, defenseless women at the mercy of these monsters . . ."

"You two have all the defense in the world," Dianne said, half under her breath, and smiled slightly. "I for one," she went on, aloud, "shall do exactly as I am told to do. The rest of you can do as you wish."

Sis so far had stayed as much in the background as possible. She had been tempted to try and reassure them and she wished she could have let them know that they were in no personal danger. But there had been no way she could do so. She decided it was time she said something. It would be only natural that she, like the others, would talk.

"Miss Rhinhardt—it is Miss Rhinhardt, isn't it—is absolutely right," she said. "I don't think anything is going to happen to any of us so long as we do what they tell us to do. And I feel quite sure that if we all want to stay together, they probably couldn't care less. I don't believe they care what we do just so long as we give them no trouble."

"You are right, Miss," Marlo Phillips said. He had been talking with Brandon Mitchell and learned about the money which was believed to be on the plane. "These men appear to me to have been interested in the plane and what the plane might have had aboard. A considerable sum of money I have been led to believe. I don't feel that they have any interest in us at all. Except as possible hostages. As an attorney, and as a man who has had considerable experience with the criminal mentality, I strongly advise you to just sit tight and take it easy. Do as you are told. I believe this whole thing is some sort of robbery plan and that we, all of us, are merely innocent bystanders. These men who are holding us do not strike me as ordinary criminals by any means. Their modus operandi is far too intelligent, this thing was far too carefully planned. They have nothing to gain by harming us, but possibly a great deal to lose when and if they are captured. I think our only real danger would be in interfering in whatever plan they have. And, believe me, Miss Rhinhardt is quite right. They will do whatever they want to do in any case."

"Quitting in the face of enemy fire," Brother Gary began in a loud voice, but the criminal attorney quickly cut him off.

"Oh for God's sake shut up," he said. "You've had the floor long enough. If you want to make a damned fool of yourself, go ahead and do it, but don't try and involve the rest of us. In any case," he turned backs to the others, "in any case, I just want to say one more thing and I'll shut up also. None of us really knows what is happening and what might happen. The best rule to follow when you don't understand what you might be up against is to keep quiet and play it by ear. Wait until the opposition shows its hand and then look for the weaknesses and form your strategy."

"Most sensible damn thing that's been said yet," Gene Farris growled.

Kenny Savo turned again from the window he had been staring out of.

"Car's turning into the yard," he said.

Dude slowed down as he pulled into the compound, turned the wheel of the Land Rover, made a half circle and came to a stop next to where the two-seater helicopter was staked to the ground. The compound itself was a large open square formed by the three sides of the sprawling ranch house. The main house faced the opening of the compound and the two sides were formed by the old stables which had been made over into a prison to hold the male passengers and crew, the other side by the garage and a storage room and kitchen which joined the main structure.

The storage room contained a small office and it was here that they had installed the powerful AM-FM radio which would monitor the news of the missing plane and the search procedures. It was here that Handle had taken the money sacks for safe keeping while they stayed at the ranch.

Dude climbed to the ground.

"Red," he said, "you and Scar go out and pick up those four trailers with the lights. I want them off that runway and well out of sight before the sun comes up. Pick up that luggage we left out there. Be sure there is nothing which can be seen by a passing plane to cause suspicion or awaken any curiosity. Check the airstrip itself for wheel marks. If you have to, when you get the light in and put away, attach the dozer blade and go over the runway."

He entered the office next to the storeroom as the Land Rover again pulled out of the compound.

Handle sat in front of the radio, listening to a broadcast. He flipped the switch as Dude entered. Dude noticed the two canvas money bags still intact on the floor.

He nodded at them.

"Didn't you open them, kid?" he said.

"They'll keep," Handle said. His face was colorless and he looked sick.

"Boy! You're sure cool about several million bucks! I should have thought . . ." He stopped speaking suddenly and looked hard at Handle. "What's the matter?" he said, his voice concerned. "Are you okay?"

"Feeling a little rocky," Handle said. "Damned malaria seems to be coming back. But I'll be all right, don't worry. If the dough is there it'll keep. I been interested in checking the air. Christ, everyone is going nuts. They simply can't understand how that plane could have just disappeared into thin air. By the way, I heard the engines. It get off all right?"

"Right on schedule," Dude said, smiling.

Handle shook his head, worried.

"With the extent of the search that's going on, I don't see how it will ever get out of the country before some trace . . ."

"You're forgetting one thing," Dude said. "Sure, they'll be searching for it. Making an all-out effort. But that plane is heading south to southwest. They are making the search to the north and the east of us. It won't occur to them in a million years that it could be going in the opposite direction. There is another thing. They won't be looking for it in the skies. Not much longer in any case. They'll be looking for the wrecked remains on the land."

"I hope you're right," Handle said. "I just hope you're right. Anyway, we may have another little problem. Nothing serious. I been listening in on the bug. Those people inside are getting all stirred up. Seems we got us some sort of preacher in there and he's getting the women all up in the air because he's sure we're about to gangbang the whole bunch of them. Afraid if we split them up from the men we'll move in and rape . . ."

Dude laughed.

"From what I saw of that collection the rape would be the other way around," he said. "I think they'd be safer with us than they are right now."

"Just thought I'd tell you," Handle said. "The preacher wants them to all stay together."

"It just doesn't sound decent," Dude said and laughed again. "What the hell, I couldn't care less. There are only eighteen of them anyway, so if they want to stay together it's their own business. I'll just go over and calm them down."

"They got it figured out it was the money we were after," Handle said.

"Not surprised," Dude said. He took a six-inch switchblade knife out of his pocket and tossed it to Handle.

"Go on, split 'em open," he said. "I'll be back in a couple of minutes and we can start counting."

The thing which had always defeated Horace Griswald was life itself. A small, mild, even meek man, he had lived with defeat so long that accepting it was almost second nature. It wasn't fear, it wasn't that he was a coward. Of course he hated violence, but this hatred was more of a technical thing than anything real. He had, actually, known very little of violence. There had been no actual violence in his relationship with his wife, Martha, except in the sense that succumbing to a stronger personality always contains an element of violence.

To say that over the thirty-year period of their life together he had grown to hate her would be wrong. He was incapable of so strong an emotion. But he had grown to dislike her intensely, the same way he had grown to dislike his work at the bank. To dislike the very routine of his life.

In many ways Martha reminded Horace of the bank. Martha had the unyielding strength of righteousness. She was a bulwark of respectability. She was a "good woman," in the same way that the Coastwise Savings and Loan Company was a "good bank."

The trouble was that there were actually two Horace Griswalds. In real life, Horace was a mild little man, a conformist and a conservative. He bent uncomplainingly to the winds of reality and the reality of his life dictated that he spend his days as a loyal and faithful servant of the financial institution where he used his time adding up meaningless columns of figures, making small notations in passbooks, pushing carefully counted bills through the grillwork of his cage to countless faceless people. That he spent most of his spare time acting as a sounding board to a large, overweight and unattractive woman whose only interest was in her garden club, her church work and the mindless television serials which she followed each day and reviewed each night for his benefit.

That had been the real life of Horace Griswald, but he also had a second life. A secret life. The life of a dreamer and a rebel.

He had always been a great reader, although in recent years, he'd had to do most of his reading secretly after Martha had gone to bed as she'd taken to resenting any time that her sole captured audience escaped her endless monologues. He had found his own escape in the romances and adventure novels he pursued. At first he had been reasonably satisfied with his schizophrenic existence, stealing for a few hours a day from the monotony of his actual life to live vicariously in the endless novels and adventure books which carried him off into a world of faraway places and wild and dangerous missions. Of beautiful, slender dark-skinned girls on lonely Pacific Islands, of evil and sinister bars in Singapore and Hong Kong, of gay Parisian night clubs.

Gradually as he had grown older, he found less and less satisfaction in reading of the lives of other men, men who had fascinating adventures and did wild and unimaginable things in far-off places. Instead of his Walter Mitty dreams making his own dull existence more bearable, they began to make him increasingly dissatisfied with his existence. A stronger man, a more positive man, would probably have reevaluated his life and done something about it.

Would have quit his job at the bank and struck out on his own in some field he might have found more challenging. Would have deserted the woman whom he had married and grown to detest.

But Horace Griswald was a man who hated unpleasantness, hated to make decisions, especially when the decision was bound to lead not only to unpleasantness but very likely to really ghastly scenes.

Habit was his jailer and habit kept him working at his job at the bank. Habit kept him married to a woman who not only bored him to death but a woman whom he had come to thoroughly dislike. A woman with whom he had ceased having a sexual relationship within two years of their wedding.

Martha, from the very beginning had let him know that she considered sex a dirty and disgusting thing, and when she discovered that she would be unable to bear children, she'd seen no further reason for succumbing or tolerating the indignity.

Under normal circumstances, Horace would probably have gone on to follow the same orderly, disappointed and unhappy pattern of his days until he eventually died of a combination of old age, discontent and ennui. But suddenly, a year ago, an incident occurred which changed everything. The incident involved a bottle of whiskey.

Horace had been brought up in an ultra-conservative, middle class, non-drinking home, and aside from a few casual beers while in college, had never drank himself. He had known Martha's attitude toward drinking even before the marriage, having first met her at a temperance meeting of the local Epworth League at the First Baptist Church which they both attended. Soon after their marriage, Martha had become an ardent prohibitionist and there had never been any question of having alcoholic beverages in their home.

It is ironic that it had been Martha who had brought the fifth of cheap rye whiskey into the house. She had purchased the bottle not to be used for drinking purposes but as a prop to bolster up a slide lecture she was giving to a neighborhood group of the Women's Christian Temperance Union which she headed.

Martha Griswald had a sense of drama and the idea had been one of her best. She would show a typical slide, perhaps the photograph of a man lying in the gutter dead drunk, perhaps a woebegone woman with half a dozen starving children in a tenement, a scene in divorce court, an auto accident with bodies scattered around. After each slide she would turn on the lights and dramatically point to the bottle of cheap rye she had purchased, saying in her deep, masculine voice, "And there, dear people, is the criminal!" It was quite effective.

When the meeting ended, Martha saw her guests to the door and when she returned to the living room she said, pointing to the bottle of whiskey, "Horace, pour that down the sink, and then come to bed."

Her husband nodded.

"On second thought," she said, "you had better not. It could rot out the pipes. Just put it in the garbage pail before you come up."

"I thought I might read for a while," Horace said.

She looked at him coldly for a moment, then said, "As you wish." She turned and went upstairs.

Horace took the bottle to the kitchen and put it in the garbage pail under the sink. When he returned to the living room, he began looking for the paperback copy of Somerset Maugham's *Moon and Sixpence* he'd bought on his way home and started reading before the meeting. It wasn't where he'd thought he'd left it and he spent a futile fifteen minutes searching for it.

Not finding the book, he went upstairs and knocked on his wife's bedroom door. She asked what he wanted and he asked her if she'd seen the book.

"I don't want that sort of trash around my house, especially when I am having my meeting," Martha said.

He was silent for a moment and then said, "Well, what did you do with it?"

"I put it in the garbage where it belongs. You had better go to bed and get your sleep."

He heard her light switch click as she turned it off.

Horace went back downstairs, hesitated a moment or so in the living room and then went out to the kitchen. He opened the cupboard under the sink and dragged out the plastic garbage pail. He reached into it, pushing the bottle of whiskey to one side and when he found the book, he discovered that she had thrown the coffee grounds and other assorted leftovers on top of it. He saw at once that the book was unreadable and for several seconds he knelt, holding the soggy pages in his hand and then slowly dropped the book back in the garbage can.

He said, "Darn. Darn it, Martha, you shouldn't . . ." He continued to kneel and then he said, "Goddamn you, Martha!"

When he stood up, he had the whiskey bottle in his hand. He held it for a moment under the faucet in the kitchen sink and then carefully dried it off. Carefully he twisted the thin metal cap off and then raised the neck of the bottle to his face and smelled it. He grimaced and shook his head, screwing up his eyes as he said, "Ugh!"

His eyes went back to the garbage pail and then raised to the ceiling of the kitchen.

He said, "The hell with you Martha."

Two minutes later he'd filled the water glass half up with whiskey and poured water on top of it. The first swallow almost gagged him.

A half hour later when he staggered upstairs, the bottle was half empty.

Martha opened her eyes the second he turned on the light. For a full minute she stared at him as he stood by the doorway, weaving slowly back and forth, her own eyes wide with bewilderment. She asked, "Are you sick?"

"You threw my book away," Horace said, slurring the words.

Martha sat up in bed.

"Now Horace," she began when he interrupted her.

"You're a bitch, Martha," he said. "A damned bitch, I hate you. I hate you, I hate the bank, I hate everybody. I want my book. I want a divorce. I ..."

He took two steps forward and fell flat on his face at the foot of the bed, out like a light.

Martha reached for the telephone at the side of the bed and called her doctor. It never occurred to her that he was drunk. She assumed that he was sick and that very possibly he had lost his mind.

Later, in spite of what the doctor told her, in spite of the half-empty whiskey bottle, she still couldn't believe that Horace had drunk the liquor.

Had Martha Griswald reacted the way she might have been expected to, it is very possible nothing would have changed and Horace would have gone on the same as he had always gone on. Had she bawled him out, nagged him, accused him, things probably would have quickly returned to normal. But she didn't. The next day, after he had partly recovered, she had talked to him, kindly if patronizingly. She assured him that he was a very sick man. That he was suffering from at least temporary mental derangement. When he was fully recovered, she insisted he see a psychiatrist.

Griswald had no memory of what had taken place in the bedroom, no memory of what he'd said to his wife. But the psychiatrist, who had been briefed by Martha, was quick to review the details for him and it was then for the first time that Horace Griswald seriously began to consider the possibility of sometime, sooner or later, actually leaving Martha and leaving his job.

The germ of the idea for emancipation, planted by that bottle of cheap rye whiskey, had been quick to grow and thrive and now, one year later, Horace Griswald found himself after but a few hours of freedom, sitting in an isolated desert ranch house with seventy thousand dollars of his bank's money, facing the dismal prospect of being rescued within the next week or ten days. Rescued and thrown back to Martha if not in jail as well.

Standing with his back to the door and facing them, Dude raised his hands and waited for the clamor to die down.

"All right," he said, "all right. Just be quiet for a moment and listen to me. I know that some of you have important appointments. I know that you have people who are worrying about you. I know that you want to know what is happening and what is going to happen. Just let me explain a few things again. You are not going to be hurt in any way. You are safe as long as you do what you are told. But you are here and you are going to have to stay here for at least a week or ten days. There is no way you can telephone, or radio, or communicate with the outside world. The best thing you can do is take it easy and relax. The plane is gone now. And you are here and there isn't a thing you can do about it."

He hesitated a moment and then continued.

"For the time being you must stay in this room. In a couple of hours or so, after daybreak, the men can be taken to separate quarters and we will make you all as comfortable as possible."

"We will not be separated," Brother Gary said, stepping forward. "We have decided . . ."

Dude shrugged.

"Any way you want it," he said. "It doesn't matter to us. If the women prefer not to be separated, that's up to them. But we have arranged separate sleeping quarters if you wish. We will be serving breakfast around eight o'clock. I am going to ask two of the women to volunteer to help with the cooking. Perhaps a couple of you airline stewardesses . . ."

Sis stepped forward and spoke quickly.

"I'd be glad to help out," she said. "I have had some experience."

"Good," Dude said. "Just find someone to help you and . . ."

"If you men are holding us for ransom," Gene Farris interrupted, "I can assure you . . ."

Dude looked at him and sighed.

"I have already told you this is not a kidnapping," he said. "We are not holding you for ransom, we are not going to rob you or in any way injure you. We . . ."

"Keeping us here against our wishes," Melody Salmon said. "Don't you consider that injuring us? Don't you think . . ."

"I can open this door and let you out right now," Dude said coldly. "If you think you would like to start out walking a hundred miles or so in the desert, without food or water . . ."

Horace Griswald had edged across the room and stood a few feet from Dude. He spoke in a low voice.

"Could I, could I speak to you alone for just one moment?" he asked.

Dude looked at him and shook his head.

"You're the guy with all the money in his bag, right? I've already told you that we don't want your money."

"It isn't that. It isn't that at all," Griswald said. "Please, please let me talk to you alone for a minute. It's a matter of life and death."

Dude looked down at the little man for several seconds and then shrugged.

"Oh, all right," he said. "Come on."

He opened the door and slipped out and Horace followed him. Dude closed the door but didn't bother to bar it.

"Okay," he said, "what's on your mind?"

"I can't say here," Griswald said. "Please, I simply can't stay. I . . ."

"You have to stay."

"But don't you see, I can't. I will give you half . . ."

Dude sighed.

"I told you we don't want your money, fellow," he said. "If I wanted it, I'd take it all. Now why don't you just take it easy and . . ."

"You don't understand," Griswald said, speaking so fast that the words all but ran together. "You don't understand. It isn't my money. It's the bank's money. I—I am stealing it." He looked at Dude with pleading in his eyes. "Stealing it."

Dude took a step back and suddenly he began to laugh. He banged his leg with his open hand and cocked his head.

"Well I'll be damned," he said. "I might have guessed it. So you are lamming with the bank's dough. Don't tell me. You were the teller and you . . ."

"How did you know?" Griswald said, wide-eyed. "Assistant teller actually. Now can you understand? If I stay here and they find us, and you told us they would sooner or later, then . . ."

"I think I understand your problem," Dude said. "You realize that when they do come for you . . ."

"That's it. Yes, that's it. So you see, I must get away. I can't just stay here and wait . . ."

Dude shook his head, stepped back a pace.

"I'm sorry," he said. "Believe me, I really am. I'd like to help you if I could. The trouble is, there's nothing I can do. Even if I could trust you, there is still nothing I can do. We have exactly one car here and that will be gone within a few hours. If I just let you go, you wouldn't get fifteen miles. Once the sun comes up on the desert, why you wouldn't have a chance. Anyway, I couldn't take the chance of having you wandering around loose."

"But you say there's a car and it's going to leave. Couldn't they take me with them?"

Again Dude shook his head.

"Not a chance," he said. "I might be foolish enough to trust you to keep your mouth shut, but believe me, an amateur like you would be bound to be picked up within hours. And the second they got you . . ."

"But I tell you, I wouldn't say anything. I promise, as God is my witness . . ."

"You wouldn't have to say anything," Dude said shortly. "All they'd have to do is find you and identify you . . . No, no I'm sorry, fellow, but there isn't a thing I can do for you."

"But . . ."

"No buts about it. Now go on back in there and just take it easy."

"Please," Griswald said, "please . . ."

"Listen," Dude said, his voice changing and his face suddenly hard, "you took your chances the same as we are taking ours. Except maybe you face five years. If we get caught we face life or maybe the chair. So stop whining. I'm sorry, but you will just have to face it. There's nothing we can do for you. Now let's get back inside."

The round ball of fire that was the morning sun had already cleared the horizon far off to the southeast when Red was finally satisfied that he had removed the last traces of the jet liner's great wheels from the temporary runway.

"Looks like another scorcher today," he said. "Damndest funny weather I ever saw. Freezing cold at night and then a day like a furnace. They tell me a blizzard comes in every now and then and we really get it. Can be in the eighties one day and then maybe below zero the next."

Scar grunted.

"Well, if we are through here let's be getting back. We still got a lot to do. Get this dozer blade off, get the car ready for the trip. And I want to see a count on that dough before we leave."

"Countin' it don't mean anything. It's spending it I want." Red swung the wheel and let out the clutch, heading back for the compound. "It's a funny thing," he said, "but you know I'm going to kind of hate leaving this place. It grows on you."

Scar stared at him. "You must be nuts," he said. "I'd rather be in jail. Who needs this? What I want is Mexico. Acapulco. A suite in a big hotel, food, drinks, broads."

"Well, every man to his own taste," Red said as he pulled in and parked next to the helicopter. He left the engine running. "You get the dozer blade off," he said, "and clear those tools out of the back. Be careful of that ammo box. That's the one with the nitroglycerine. We should have taken it out before. I don't want to be riding around with that stuff in the car."

He reached past Scar and opened the glove compartment, feeling for the pint flask of whiskey he'd stashed. It was empty and he swore.

"You could have at least left me a slug," he said. "And you know what Dude . . ."

"The hell with Dude," Scar said. "What does he think I am? Some punk who can't handle booze? Anyway, there's plenty more in the house so don't worry about that jug."

"I don't worry about nothing," Red growled, "except getting away from here and into Mexico." He added, under his breath, "And getting away from guys like you, you ugly sonofabitch."

Walking over to the office next to the storeroom, he lifted his eyes to the main wing and saw that someone was staring at him through the barred window. A minute later he was in the office where Dude and Handle were squatting on the floor surrounded by stacks of neatly wrapped bills. Dude looked up.

"All clear?"

"All clear," Red said. "My God, it looks like millions. How much . . ."

"It is millions," Dude said. "We've just made a rough check, but I would say ten, maybe even twelve." He began shoving the money back into the canvas bags. "Sis and one of the other women are going to make some food for everyone. You go on in and get them and stay with them in the kitchen while they are working. When the grub is ready, have Sis bring me something in here." He turned to Handle, "Boy, you better go in and lie down for a while. It's going to be a long trip and you gotta get some rest. We can't have you getting sick and . . ."

"I'm sick already," Handle said. "But don't worry. I'll be all right. I'll just try and get a little sleep though. You sure you won't need me now when we take that food into them?"

Dude shook his head. "Red and I can take care of it. Those people aren't going to give us any trouble. No trouble at all."

He looked thoughtful for a minute and then said to Red, "Tell you what, Red. There is one guy who might make things difficult. Get them all stirred up. A little mousey guy named Griswald. The guy with the airline bag with all that dough in it. Seems he is some sort of bank official taking it on the lam with his bank's cash. He's beginning to panic because he knows that once they get out of here, he's bound to be picked up. I don't want any trouble from him so I think, maybe after you got the girls started on the breakfast, you better go back and cut him out from the others. Take him over to the stables and keep him separate for the time being. I don't want him blowing his top."

"Right," Red said. He started to leave the room and he felt a sudden quickening of the blood in his veins. It was the opportunity he had been waiting for. Sis would be in the kitchen alone except for the other woman who would be helping her. It would be his one chance to talk with her before they left. His one chance to try and make a meeting with her later on. It would be tricky and he would have to somehow or other get her alone for a few minutes. Separate her from the other one.

Propositioning Sis would be tough but Red knew that he had one thing going for him. One very important thing. Of the five of them, Sis was the only one who was going to have to wait a long time before she would be able to get her hands on her cut of money. She would be rescued when the others were, and she would be, along with the rest of them, an ostensible victim. But they would be watching her and checking up on her for a long time. Red knew about the plans for her share being placed in the Swiss bank and knew that it would be months and possibly years before she would be free to get her hands on it.

But he would have his share. What he must do was to convince her that if she would agree to secretly meet him after they made their getaway, he would be able to help her. He would have money to spend on her. She would be suspected, of course, but he would be in the clear, living under a new identity with the proper cover story to explain his wealth.

In one sense it would be double crossing Dude. But Red was convinced Dude had no interest in the girl himself. Red knew that once they had split up the money and gone their separate ways, Dude had no intention of ever seeing any of them again. So why should it really matter to him if he and the girl were to get together?

Unlocking the door and taking down the bars which secured it, he stepped into the room. He was wearing a gun in his shoulder holster but he didn't bother to take it out. He didn't expect any trouble.

"You two women who are doing the cooking," he said, "come with me. The rest of you just take it easy." He hesitated and then said, "Mr. Griswald?"

Horace Griswald, standing at the window and sunk in pessimism, looked up.

"Get your stuff together," Red said. "We're putting you in a separate room. I'll be back for you in a few minutes."

Brandon Mitchell had set up a pair of cots and he and his charge, Serge Krinsky, lay on them at one side of the room. He'd been dozing but he quickly came alert when Red entered the room. As the two women followed him out, he again closed his eyes.

Several of the others had also set up cots and lay on them, some dozing, some in deep sleep.

Arch Winter stood over at the end of the room, talking with Dianne Rhinhardt. She was half listening to him, yawning and wishing he would go away. She'd taken several sleeping pills, and they were beginning to work.

"And the minute I saw you board the plane," Captain Winter was saying, "I was really touched. It isn't often we have a really beautiful girl . . ."

She turned away from him, again yawning and not bothering to cover her mouth. She said, listlessly, "Perhaps, Captain, you would like to set up one of those cots for me. I think I can get along without breakfast. I'm tired. I just want to get some sleep."

Mr. Weems was occupying a couch by himself. He lay stretched out, his mouth open as he gently snored, a beatific smile on his face. His two brandy laden attaché cases were on the floor at his side and he held an empty bottle in one hand.

Horace Griswald had been standing at the window, looking out into the compound when the Land Rover returned. He'd watched Red leave the car and then continued to watch as Scar wheeled near one of the open sheds to take off the dozer blade. He left the engine running as he began to unload tools and equipment from the back of the vehicle.

Griswald noticed that each time Scar, loaded down with equipment, left the Land Rover, he stayed longer and longer between trips. Scar was beginning to stagger. He'd stumbled and almost fallen twice.

He suspected, and rightfully, that Scar was nipping at a secret bottle every time he went into the storeroom.

It was infuriating to think of the Land Rover, out there unattended, its motor running. If he were only outside, if he could only get to the car. The car was escape and freedom.

But between him and the car was a barred window and locked doors. And men, desperate men with guns.

It was when he thought of guns that he suddenly remembered.

When Brandon Mitchell had surreptitiously hidden his own revolver in Mr. Weems' brandy filled attaché case, he'd been sure he had not been observed. But he had been wrong. One pair of eyes had seen, one pair of eyes had followed his action. And the eyes belonged to Horace Griswald. At the time, Griswald had not been particularly interested. He had his own problems and he didn't care what any of the others might do. If someone wanted to take a chance and hide a gun, it was his business.

Griswald was anything but a man of violence. The fact is, he doubted very much if he would even know how to use a gun if he had one. The only gun he'd ever fired had been a single shot .22 which he'd owned as a boy.

It was hopeless. The whole thing was impossible.

It was only when Red entered the room and spoke, telling him that they were going to put him in a separate room, that the two facts came together and suddenly took on meaning. The car waiting outside with its engine running and the hidden gun in the attaché case.

For the first time he felt hope. He was, as has been said, not a man of violence. He had not been cast in a heroic mold. But he was also not a coward; and he was a desperate man. He was a man who no longer had any options. If a straw was the only thing available, then he must grasp at straws.

Griswald looked over at Mitchell and saw that the CIA man was again dozing. His eyes then found Mr. Weems, who lay stretched out on the couch, snoring.

Leaving the window, he went to the couch where Mr. Weems lay. Weems, earlier, had asked him if he wanted a drink. He'd shaken his head at the time. Drinking made him sick.

Now, squatting at the side of the couch where Mr. Weems lay, he said in a too loud voice, "I do think I will accept your offer and have a drink."

Mr. Weems continued to snore and none of the others paid him the slightest attention.

Griswald snapped the latch on the attaché case and he reached in. Taking out a bottle, he struggled to open it and then raised it to his lips. It almost gagged him and for a moment as the liquid burned his throat like acid, he didn't think he was going to be able to swallow it. But he managed to get it down and then recorked the bottle. He had to hesitate for a moment as he gasped for breath.

Once more his eyes searched the room. No one was watching as he replaced the bottle. A moment later his searching hand found the gun. When he stood up, he was holding it under his coat. Walking back to the window, he managed to tuck it into his waistband and carefully buttoned his jacket so as to conceal it. He was very conscious of the bulge it made.

Scar had again disappeared into the storeroom.

It would work out perfectly. Dude was in the office and he wanted his breakfast there. Red could send the other girl, the airline stewardess, in with Dude's breakfast on a tray. And while she was gone, he would have the chance to talk to Sis. He wouldn't have but a minute or so, but it would be long enough. He'd explain that he had things to tell her in private and they could arrange some way to get together for a few minutes later. He would go back now and cut that guy Griswald out from the others and by the time he returned, they would have started with the breakfast.

He showed them where the food was, lighted the stove for them. Then he said he'd be right back and left.

He was a little surprised when he opened the door to see Griswald standing there, his airline bag firmly clutched in his left hand.

"Okay," he said, "let's go." He was glad that the little man was not going to resist, not going to make any trouble. Red wondered why Dude had been worried about him.

"We'll cross over to the other wing," Red said. "You'll be comfortable there. I'll see you get something to eat as soon as it's ready. Just follow me."

Griswald nodded dumbly as Red re-barred the door. He didn't trust himself to speak. The brandy was burning in his stomach and he was feeling strangely light, almost dizzy. He wasn't sure whether it was the liquor or the tension.

Red led the way as they walked down the hallway, turned the corner and then entered the kitchen. He saw Sis at the stove, dropping eggs into a frying pan and surreptitiously he winked one eye at her. The other girl was putting toast in the oven.

Red went to the door leading into the courtyard and opened it.

"This way," he said. "Close the door after you."

Griswald stumbled slightly as he stepped to the ground. He suddenly felt so weak that for a moment he doubted if he would be able to go on at all. And then his eye took in the Rover at the side of the compound. Scar was not in sight.

For one wild moment he thought of taking the gun out and putting it against the other man's back. Ordering him into the car.

But he knew it wouldn't work. He wouldn't even know how to pull the trigger if he had to. He couldn't even trust his voice to give the necessary order.

As Red took a step out into the courtyard, Griswald dropped his airline bag. Simultaneously, trying not to even think, he jerked the gun from his waistband. He was holding it by the barrel.

Red, hearing the sound of the bag falling to the ground, hesitated, started to turn.

The butt of the gun caught him just over the right ear as Griswald brought it down with all the force he had. For a fraction of a second he was staring directly into Red's startled eyes and then Red slowly dropped to the ground.

Griswald grabbed for his airline bag and ran to the car. Climbing behind the wheel, he didn't bother to close the door. His foot found the clutch and he gunned the motor. The gears clashed torturously as he slammed the car into second. The tires spun, screaming for a moment, and then took hold.

Chapter 8

When the sound of the gunned motor and the squeal of the tires reached his ears, Dude was just turning off the powerful shortwave radio set. He was smiling with satisfaction. For the last five minutes he'd been monitoring the airwaves and he knew he had gotten away with it.

There had been no reports of the plane being sighted, no reports of any mysterious plane crossing the border. And by now, the great Boeing 707 was well beyond the border, well beyond the mainland itself. Was down and gone forever. Deep under a hundred or more fathoms, off the Mexican coast, carried to her doom by the dictates of her own auto pilot.

The futile search, of course, would go on, but they were safe. Safe at least for the time being. Safe until their hostages were ultimately released, after they'd had time to make a clean getaway.

For a second, after he heard the engine of the Land Rover being raced, he didn't think anything about it. Merely that Scar should be a little more careful. The car was essential to their plans and nothing must happen to it.

He started to get up and then he heard the screech of the tires as they fought to take hold. At once he knew something was wrong. He started for the door and was opening it when he heard the quick, staccato of the submachine gun.

Scar had the bottle to his lips when he heard the Land Rover take off with a roar. He acted without thinking, out of sheer instinct. The submachine gun was standing against the wall and be grabbed it up as he ran for the door.

He was drunk but he was in that in between state where he was almost overly sensitive.

Even as he stepped to the ground of the compound, his eye took in the figure of Red sprawled out on the ground. He saw the big safari wagon tearing out of the compound. He raised the gun without even aiming and pressed the trigger. He saw the pattern of the bullets where they hit the earth behind the car and he raised the jumping barrel.

But it was too late. The clip held thirty-eight shots and by the time he had the proper range, it was empty.

Dude didn't know how it had happened, but one glance told him just what had happened. Somehow or other, the little man with the bank's stolen money had managed to slug Red and had made off with the car. Scar must have left it unattended, with the key in the lock. With the engine running. Even as he walked toward Red be thought, damn it, no matter how carefully you plan, there is always the human factor. Always the possibility of human weakness or human stupidity screwing things up.

He was leaning over Red then, beckoning to Scar. Red began to open his eyes and Dude looked up to see Sis in the kitchen doorway. He said, "You! Come here and take care of this man."

He got up and met Scar halfway across the yard. His eyes were on the Land Rover, disappearing into the desert.

"He isn't going anywhere," Dude said. "Nowhere at all. Come on, we've got to stop him. We'll take the helicopter."

He squatted down to release the ropes which held it to the stakes in the ground.

"Reload your gun," he said to Scar. "We'll catch up to him. But be careful. Damned careful. I don't want him hit and I don't want that car wrecked. I'll come up behind him and you try for one of the rear tires. Try not to get the gas tank."

Scar said, "We get that sonofabitch, I'll kill him."

"We aren't going to kill anyone," Dude said. "Understand? We are just going to stop him."

"Which one was it?" Scar asked. "How . . ."

"Never mind," Dude said. "Just reload and climb aboard."

Dude didn't rush it. He gave the engine of the helicopter plenty of time to warm up. He knew that there was no hurry.

Griswald had taken off to the north following the twin wheel tracks into the desert. Dude knew that they would soon peter out. That they led nowhere. Sooner or later the Land Rover would be bound to bog down in the soft sand and stall out. But he wanted to stop it before then. There was always a chance one of the search planes could fly overhead, become curious.

Seven minutes after the Land Rover left the ranch the helicopter was in the air. Dude was going a little faster now. Scar had told him that he'd left the car in regular gear and not four-wheel drive and Dude realized that Griswald, probably unfamiliar with the vehicle, could very well burn up the engine in his anxiety to get away.

As they quickly overtook the fleeing car, Dude dropped down so that he was only a few feet off the ground. He yelled at Scar over the sound of the motor.

"The tires. Try only for the tires."

They were less than fifty feet behind and slightly above the careening vehicle when Scar began to fire.

"Got him!" Scar yelled as Dude began to lift the helicopter.

Even as he spoke, the flame shot out from the back of the Land Rover and Dude cursed.

"You got the gas tank, you damned fool," he yelled. "We're landing. Get that extinguisher!"

He knew that Scar's bullets had penetrated the tank and that the gas had spurted out and fallen on the hot muffler.

He thought that there might be some chance of saving the car if he could get to it in time, get the flames out before the explosion. Griswald would stop the car when he realized it was on fire.

But Griswald didn't stop.

He'd seen the helicopter in the rear-vision mirror even before he'd heard the sound of its motor over the roar of his own racing engine.

He heard the harsh explosion of the machine gun and when the Land Rover suddenly jounced and slowed he knew that the back tires had been hit. But he wasn't going to stop. They'd have to kill him to stop him.

The car continued on but it covered less than an eighth of a mile when the flames in the rear suddenly opened up like a giant blossoming flower and then the explosion came. The repercussion rocked the helicopter and Dude fought to control it, turning away.

Less than five seconds later, the second explosion came and this time the terrific roar made the first explosion when the gas tank went sound like a cap pistol by comparison.

Again the 'copter lurched wildly and Dude fought to control the machine. He said, under his breath, "The nitro! You must have left the nitro in her."

They circled the car for several minutes and then be landed and climbed to the ground. Scar stood beside him, still speechless with shock.

Slowly turning his head, Dude wordlessly looked around in wonder. Then he said, "My God, nothing! A few pieces of scrap metal. A hole in the ground."

He reached into the helicopter and found the folding trench shovel. Handing it to Scar, he said, "All right. Get started. Bury anything that might look suspicious. We can't do anything about that hole, but get rid of any stray pieces of metal. Anything you find."

Scar looked at him and shook his head.

"What happens now?" he asked. "What do we do without the car? I guess this is one you didn't figure out."

Dude looked at him coldly.

"I didn't figure you'd start drinking and get careless," he said. "But the hell with that. We got other problems now, real problems. Try to get this mess cleaned up a little. There isn't much left to clean up so it won't take too long. I'm going back to the ranch. I'll return later and pick you up. You'll have a chance to work the booze out of your system."

"It wasn't me let that guy out so he could get to the car," Scar growled. "Instead of worrying about booze, maybe you better start thinking about where to get another car so we can get out of here."

Disgusted, Dude turned and climbed back into the helicopter. But Scar was right. He'd better start doing some thinking.

Handle was standing in the compound when Dude brought the 'copter in for a landing. He walked over and said, as Dude stepped to the ground, "What in hell was that explosion?"

"Land Rover," Dude said. "We stopped it all right. Scar got the gas tank."

"Sounded to me more like an H-bomb than a gas tank," Handle said. "Where's Scar?"

"It wasn't only the gas tank," Dude said. "You guys left the nitro in the car. Scar's out there picking up the pieces and getting rid of them."

"And the guy who took the car?"

Dude shrugged. "There isn't enough of him left to pick up," he said. "Where is Red? How is he? Could he tell you what happened?"

"Red's all right. Got a pretty sore head. He says the man who got the car had a gun. Bashed him over the head. Maybe the guy was lucky he got blown up. Red would have killed him if you'd brought him back here."

"The guy isn't lucky and neither are we," Dude said. "Up to now, we've played it smart. No one killed, no one even hurt. The trouble with killing is, it usually doesn't just stop with one. It gets to be a habit. This is just not a simple robbery anymore. Now it's murder."

"Yeah," Handle said. "Murder. And we got other problems. When

Sis was bandaging Red . . ."

He stopped suddenly, interrupted by a fit of coughing. When he took his hand away from his mouth, there were traces of blood on it and he stood pale and shaken for several moments.

"You better get back inside and take it easy," Dude said. "You're sick and . . ."

"I'm all right," Handle said, but his voice was a weak whisper and his face was bloodless. "I'm okay. Got to tell you about Red. Sis was bandaging his head. In the kitchen. He seemed to be groggy and maybe a little off his rocker. He was talking to her, sort of half mumbling. Telling her he'd been nuts about her ever since he first met her. That he wanted to see her again."

"The damned fool," Dude said.

"That isn't the trouble," Handle said. "It was the other girl. That airline hostess. She was there, taking it all in. I still got her there in the kitchen. Didn't want her going back and talking to the others."

Dude shook his head. "That goddamned fool," he said. "You know what this mean? We're going to have to change the plans. Sis won't be able to go back now. She's cooked if she goes back."

"Either that," Handle said, "or the airline girl has to be taken care of. It's one or the other of them."

"No," Dude said. "Not one or the other. Goddamn it anyway. I should have known that if Scar gets around booze or Red gets around broads . . ."

"And I have to get sick on you," Handle said. "But Red, I don't think he knows what he was saying. He was still half out."

"It doesn't matter, he said it. And don't worry about your getting sick on me. You're the only one of the whole bunch I can really count on. Scar would just as soon slaughter the whole lot of those people in there. Especially if he's been drinking. Red is usually all right. But if he's gone and flipped for that gal, you can't tell what he's capable of doing. Women have always screwed him up. Well, I am going to have to do something. Go in and get Sis. I want to talk to her. Tell her to see me in the office. And keep that other girl away from the others until we decide what to do about her."

Walking over to the office next to the storeroom, Dude thought maybe Scar was right. Maybe life doesn't mean anything. What the hell, Dude himself had dropped bombs on civilian centers when he knew they were next to military targets. Dozens, perhaps hundreds of people had been killed. Old men, women and children. People he'd never seen or heard of. Innocent people. People without political convictions who had never harmed him in any way. Yes, he'd left plenty of maimed and crippled people and dead behind him. Why should he now make such an issue out of taking human life?

But he did. That was the trouble. He did care. Perhaps the fact that he had been responsible for those deaths in the past was one of the reasons he now cared. Now that his own personal safety was at stake.

He felt bad about that little absconding bank teller, Griswald. But he hadn't tried to kill him. He'd only tried to get the car back.

The car. That was another problem and an immediate one. He had to get another car. The trouble was, he was the only one who could fly the 'copter. The only one who could go outside and pick up a car and drive it back. And if he went he would have to leave these dozen and a half innocent people to the questionable mercy of the others.

Handle he could trust, but Handle was a sick man. A dying man. He could trust Sis also. But Sis in a way was in more danger than any of them. Sis was the weak spot and now that Red had tipped his hand, let one of them know that Sis was involved, it wouldn't take Scar long to realize she would always be a danger.

Red? No one could tell which way he might go. Red's judgment was never too good and if he had really flipped for Sis, there was no telling what he might do to get her.

For one brief moment he thought, God, all I really have to do is grab that money and take off alone. Leave them to whatever fate has in store for them. All of them.

But he knew he would never be able to do it.

Brother Gary, again holding the floor, turned to Sis and asked, "The other girl. What have they done with her? You left with Miss Grunsky and only you have returned. Did you learn what that explosion was?"

Sis hesitated for a moment and then said, "She's all right. The explosion? A car blew up. That little man, Griswald, I think his name was, tried to get away and he was killed when the car blew up."

Brother Gary bowed his head for a moment and then looked up, slowly moving his eyes around the room.

"They have murdered him," he said dramatically. "He tried to escape and they murdered him. It has started, as I knew it would. They have killed one of us and they have taken one of the women for their own evil purposes. They . . ."

Sis cut in, interrupting him.

"They didn't kill one of us," she said. "He was escaping, but not from them. You see, he was a thief himself. He was a bank teller in Los Angeles and he had robbed his bank of a great deal of money. He tried to steal their car and make his escape and he was killed accidentally when they attempted to stop him. I am sure if we just don't panic and do as they ask us . . ."

Ned Gaines said, "Sure—sure, do what they ask. That's all right for you. You broads can always do what they ask. Make your private little deals. That's probably what that other dame is doing right now. What they ask, and I guess I don't have to spell that out. But how about the rest of us? How about . . ."

"Why don't you shut up, mister," Captain Winter said. "You have a dirty little mind and no one wants to hear you. I agree with Miss Carr. If we just play it cool, take it in our stride . . ."

"You're not on the plane anymore, Captain," MacPherson said. "We are all equal here and all entitled to our opinion. Maybe the Reverend is right. Maybe we should try and see what we can do to protect ourselves. After all, so far as I can see, there are only four of them. There are, let's see, there are eleven of us men still here. We are unarmed, but we are not exactly powerless. And it is up to us to see that the women are protected."

"You're all talking like damned fools," Marlo Phillips said. "So far no one has threatened any of the women or any of us. That man who got killed was asking for it. None of the rest of us has been as much as threatened. So far as I am concerned, I am doing exactly what they ask me to do."

Walthar Bruno, the nuclear scientist, nodded his head in quick agreement. "Of course," he said. "Of course. We have no choice."

Mr. Weems suddenly opened his eyes and stared blearily around.

"These waiting rooms," he said. "They get more and more crowded. Where's my bottles?"

Handle opened the door and beckoned to Sis.

"You," he said. "Come on."

Brother Gary glared at him.

"If you dare misuse this young girl," he began, but Sis herself cut him short.

"Can't you ever shut up," she said. She followed Handle out of the room.

They walked outside and stood next to the helicopter and Dude said, "What's this with Red? What did he say to you in front of the Grunsky girl?"

"He was still half out of his mind from the bump on his head," Sis said.

"I didn't ask you that. I asked you what he said."

Sis shrugged. "Oh, just a lot of nonsense. Some crap about falling in love with me the first time he met me. And then when we played cards out here that day . . ."

"Damn," Dude said. "What the hell has gotten into him anyway? What have you done to the poor sucker?"

"Me?" Sis said. "Don't be silly, Dude. Do you think I encouraged the little monkey? He's nice enough I guess, but I don't have any interest in him. You should know me well enough by now to know what I want. The money, Dude. Just the money."

"That's the trouble," Dude said. "You are making it hard to get the money now. You can't go back, you know. They are bound to know that you are in on it."

"Only Jill Grunsky knows," Sis said.

Dude stared at her.

"You too?" he said. "What are you suggesting, that we knock her off?"

"Well . . ."

"Forget it," Dude took a step away from her. "I told you we are not going to ask for extra trouble. My plans . . ."

"You're plans seem a little screwed up," Sis said.

"And so are yours now. You're going to have to duck out with the rest of us. Take your chances that way."

"It's all right with me," Sis said. "I'm not anxious to see any more killing."

"Well stay clear of Red," Dude said. "I don't want any more trouble."

"I'm not interested in him, you should know that. But Dude, how about us? If I have to disappear with the rest of you, how about you and me? Just the two of us. We get along all right. At least we do in bed. And maybe . . ."

"No," Dude said. "No, Sis. I play it alone from now on out. You'll just have to take your chances alone. And you are going to have to be doubly careful. They'll know about you. Be looking for you. There's another thing. I trust you because I know you. I know if you get picked up you won't talk. But Scar and Red? Maybe they aren't so sure."

"Just see that I get away clear and free," Sis said. "I can take care of myself. I always have. But what are you going to do? We have to have another car."

"There's only one thing to do," Dude said. "I'll take one of the boys with me tomorrow and we'll fly into Phoenix and I'll pick up another car. He can drive it back and I'll fly back."

"Who will you take?"

"Handle's sick. Too sick to try the drive back alone. I'd take Scar but I'm afraid to trust him. He's been hitting the bottle and if he gets drunk you can't tell what he might do. He'll be safer left here. Which means that with Handle sick, I should leave Red here in charge. I guess maybe I'd better plan on taking you in with me."

"It's okay with me," Sis said. "I'd be glad to get away from here, if it's only for a day."

"All right, we'll talk about it later. I'll get the Grunsky girl now and stick her back in with the others. Maybe you could go in and stay with Handle. I've got him in bed in the office and he's a pretty sick guy. Someone should be with him."

Sis shook her head.

"God, Dude, I'm awful with sick people," she said. "I never could stand to be around anyone who is ill. Why not ask one of the other women to stay with him? The airline girls know all about taking care of sick people. That was the one part of the job I hated."

"Okay, Sis. You go on in and start getting ready for dinner. I'll have someone come in and give you a hand. It will be better if I don't use the Grunsky girl again, now that she knows what the story is. While you are getting some grub ready, I'll go back and pick up Scar. He's probably getting a little lonely out there by now. At least he should be dried out."

Following Jill Grunsky into the room, Dude waited a moment for the voices to die down.

"I have a very sick man in the other part of the house," he said. "I would like one of you ladies who may have had nursing experience to come in and stay with him for a while." He looked over at Mary Mills sitting very straight in a chair in her airline stewardess uniform. "How about you, Miss?"

She stared at him coldly.

"I would not move one inch to help any of you gangsters," she said.

Dude looked at her for a moment or two and then shrugged.

"Anyone else?" he asked.

Dianne Rhinhardt slowly stood up and yawned.

"Well, I guess I would do about anything to get out of here," she said. "Anyway, he probably can't be any sicker than a lot of the people in this room. I once took a nursing course, in a misguided moment. I'll come if you like."

"Thanks," Dude said. "And how about one more volunteer? To help the girl in the kitchen who is going to get your dinner."

Brother Gary stepped forward.

"If I can be of any assistance to the young lady," he began.

"I thought maybe one of the ladies would offer," Dude said, "but then I guess you will do just as well. Come on."

He stopped in the kitchen and said to Sis, "The Reverend here has offered to give you a hand."

Sis looked up at Brother Gary and smiled. Red, sitting in a rocking chair in the corner of the room, glared at him. He had a bandage on one side of his head.

"How the head?" Dude asked.

"It's all right," Red said.

"Good. I'm taking this girl in to stay with Handle. He's feeling pretty bad. Then I'm going out after Scar."

Leaving the kitchen he asked, "What's your name, Miss?"

"Dianne. Dianne Rhinhardt. Didn't you know?"

He stopped and turned, looking at her.

"Am I supposed to?" He looked at her closely and then said, "Yes, I guess I know. I've seen the picture in the papers."

"Don't believe anything you see in the papers," Dianne said, almost flippantly. "What's your name?"

"You can call me Dude."

They entered the office and Handle was stretched out on the bed against the wall. His forehead was dripping with sweat and his eyes were open and staring at the ceiling.

"Handle, Miss Rhinhardt here is going to stay with you for a while," Dude said.

The girl crossed the room and put a hand on his forehead.

"He's burning up with fever," she said. "I'll get his clothes off and get him under some blankets. Do you have any alcohol? Quinine? I think if I can rub him down, get some pills into him . . ."

"Anything you say," Dude said. "We got alcohol, quinine maybe. I'll see that you get them."

Stopping back in the kitchen for a minute, he spoke to Sis and then went out to the helicopter.

He was remembering some of the stories he'd read about the girl in Sunday feature stories. Well, maybe she was right. Maybe he shouldn't believe everything he read in the papers.

The four of them sat together off to one side of the room. Jill was between Arch Winter and Kenny Savo and Kenny had his arm thrown carelessly around her shoulder. MacPherson sat opposite them in a straight-backed chair.

Arch Winter was thinking what a damned fool he'd been to turn the girl over to his flight engineer. With her high cheek bones, the large blue eyes in the dark-skinned face, she was a pretty little thing; and she had a superb body. Large firm breasts, a slender waist and hips perhaps a trifle too full. But good, very good. The trouble was, she hadn't quite lived up to her appearance. She really wasn't very good in bed. No enthusiasm, very little technique.

The captain liked girls who were familiar with the more subtle sexual variations. He didn't want them just laying there like a corpse. She had the equipment all right; she'd just never learned how to use it.

MacPherson, like Arch Winter, was thinking more what she was than what she was saying. He knew damned well that the little airline stewardess had layed both the captain and the flight engineer and the thought made him furious. She'd probably sleep with anyone. So why not him? He simply didn't know.

It never occurred to him that Jill Grunsky, like most women, merely needed to be properly pursued. MacPherson was not the pursuing type.

"And I am sure," Jill was saying, "that she is in with them. That she was the one who tipped them off about the money on the plane. She had known that one called Red before. She as much as admitted it while he was talking to her. I couldn't have been more surprised. Sissy Carr—who would ever have believed it!"

"How did she know about the money?" Winter asked.

"Well, I might have mentioned it," Jill said. "We see quite a lot of each other. I have known her for a long time, since we worked together for TWA. Or maybe it was Kenny here. He's met her several times up at my place."

"Neither of you are even supposed to know about the money,"

Winter said.

"Oh Arch! Everybody knows. You know you can't keep a thing like that secret."

"Well, I guess so," he said. "So you think she deliberately pumped you. Has been working with these hijackers all along?"

"I do," Jill said. "I do—and I'm scared stiff."

"Nothing to be scared of," MacPherson said. He wished he could keep his eyes off her breasts, particularly as he saw Kenny Savo watching him with a knowing, amused expression on his cynical face.

"Nothing at all to be scared of. You didn't know how she would use the information. No one can accuse you of being involved."

"It isn't that," Jill said. "Don't you understand? I know she's in with them and she knows I know it now. So does that one called Red. He knows. When I tell the police and they find her, then she'll tell about all the others. You know the police can always make people talk. And these men, they will know that."

"You still don't have anything to be afraid of," Winter said. "So you know about her. But shutting you up won't help them. We all know now."

"And suppose they shut us all up?" Jill asked.

"Don't be a fool, girl. Do you think they are going to kill eighteen people?" MacPherson shook his head. "Impossible," he said.

"It would be better if they just killed Sis," Savo said.

"What the hell, she's the one who can tell who they are. We can't. It would be better for them to just kill one than all of us."

"They won't touch her," Jill said. "I told you, that Red is in love with her. I heard him tell her so."

"They're not going to kill anyone," Winter said. "Do you think they would have gone to all this trouble if they planned to knock us off? They are just going to hold us until things quiet down and then they'll blow. Make their getaway. No, if they had planned to kill us, they would have done it before this."

Jill snuggled closer to Savo and he reached over with his right hand and caressed her thigh. "I want to leave," she said. "I just want to get out of here."

"Not me," Winter said. "Hell, I like it here. Makes a nice vacation spot."

"You just want time to try and make that Rhinhardt broad," Kenny Savo said.

"You couldn't be more right," Winter said, and laughed. "Trouble is I am afraid it would take too much time. She's an icicle. Won't even give me a tumble."

Savo's hand moved up Jill's thigh to her breast and MacPherson suddenly stood up, his face red with fury. He stalked off and Kenny looked after him and laughed.

"What's the matter with him?" Jill asked naively.

"You," Winter said. "He wants to screw you so bad he's aching."

He stood up himself.

"Behave yourself, boy," he smiled at Kenny. "You don't want to shock these peasants, at least until after dark. I'm kind of sorry now I didn't sign up for that kitchen detail instead of the preacher. Our Sis may be a mobster's girl, but she has something. Yes indeed, she has something."

"There's always Mother Mills," Savo said.

"What she has I don't want," Winter said. "I am afraid I'll have to leave her for our friend MacPherson. Those two would make a great little team." He yawned, started to walk away. "Wish that grub would come," he said. "I'm famished."

Red couldn't take his eyes off of her.

She was over by the stove, preparing the chickens for the broiler. They had brought the luggage in and she'd changed her clothes and she was wearing a very short miniskirt, a thin cashmere sweater, without a brassiere so that the nipples of her breasts each formed its own tiny pyramid. Her long slender legs were bare and she'd pushed her feet into a pair of low-heeled slippers. She had wound a silk scarf around her head to keep the blonde hair out of her eyes and face as she worked.

Red watched her with greedy half-closed eyes and he cursed Dude under his breath. Why had Dude brought that damned preacher in to help her? Red was sure it was because he didn't trust him and Sis alone together while he went out to pick up Scar. That must have been it.

He wished he could remember exactly what he'd said to her when she'd been taking care of him. Dressing the wound and putting the bandage on his head. Of course he knew that he'd said too much and said it in front of the other girl. Dude had told him about that.

He'd blown her cover all right. Really messed it up. There would be no going back for her now. But what had he said? Yes, he dimly remembered that he'd told her he was crazy about her. That he could remember. Apparently it hadn't surprised her, hadn't bothered her. Even now she kept looking over at him and when the preacher wasn't watching, would wink provocatively. If that goddamned preacher wasn't there, he'd get up and go over and do what he'd wanted to do to her the very first minute he'd laid eyes on her.

They wouldn't be leaving now, as they planned, and Sis wouldn't be going back into the room with the others. Not after they'd sent the other girl back to tip them off about his spilling his guts and implicating her. There would still be time for him to get her alone. The only trouble was, Dude would be returning and Dude very obviously didn't want them to get together.

Red doubted if it was jealousy. He was sure that Dude had been sleeping with her, but he was equally sure that Dude was not going to entangle himself with any woman once they were free and clear and had the money. What Dude was afraid of was that the two of them would get together after it was all over. Dude was the one who had always insisted that none of them must ever see each other again.

If Dude was afraid of them getting together, it must be because he mistrusted Sis. Must be that he suspected she could go for him, Red. That must be it. Red looked at his wristwatch and saw that Dude had been gone for about five minutes.

He stood up. He simply had to talk with her alone for a few minutes. He had to be with her. The desire to touch her, to caress her, was more than he could stand.

Crossing the room, he reached out and gave her a light slap on the rump as she leaned over the open oven.

"Come on," he said, "I want to see you alone for a few minutes."

Brother Gary swung around from the sink. He had left the others before Jill Grunsky had returned to tell them about Sis's involvement and had no idea that she was in any way connected with the hijackers.

For a second he stared hard at Red.

"Leave the child alone," he said. "Keep your filthy hands to yourself."

Red swung around and stared at him, his chin dropping and his mouth agape.

"What did you say?"

"Leave the girl alone!"

Red slowly shook his head and looked as though didn't quite believe his ears.

"What are you, some kind of a nut?" he asked at last.

"Don't lay another hand on that girl," Brother Gary repeated. He stood tall and firm and his voice was like the voice of doom.

Red said, "Well, I'll be goddamned!" He turned again to Sis, giving her another quick pat on her behind. "Come on kid, let's get away from this creep. We can go into the other bedroom down the hall."

"If you try to take this child by force, I shall call down the very wrath of God," Brother Gary said. He took a step forward and Red quickly stepped back, reaching for the gun in his holster.

"She's not a child, she's a woman, Preacher," Red said. "I think you've got a dirty mind. Now get the hell out of my way."

Sis spoke up quickly.

"Look," she said. "He's not going to hurt me. He just wants to talk to me. Please!" She swung to Red, "He means all right," she said. "He just doesn't understand."

"Tell him to start understanding and right now," Red said, his voice ugly. "Get back to peeling those spuds, Preacher. One more word out of you and I'll put lead right between your eyes."

The Reverend Gary Gibbons stood his ground. He looked at Sis. She was watching him, her face beseeching.

"I'm all right," she said.

Red took her by the arm and half dragged her out of the room. "Come on, we haven't too much time," he said.

They went past the barred door of the room where the others were and Red pushed her, not ungently, into the bedroom at the end of the hallway. He closed the door and she turned around facing him, her eyes angry.

"What's the matter with you, anyway?" she asked. "For God's sake, can't you . . ."

"Look," Red said. "I told you. I told you before. I'm nuts about you."

"Yeah, I know. You sure did tell me before. And I heard you, loud and clear. So what?"

"I'll tell you what. You come into the kitchen, dressed like this, about half naked. You drive me nuts. Goddamn it, I been out here alone in this desert now for weeks. I need a woman, and you are the woman. Come here."

Sis dropped her shoulders and sighed.

"Oh for Christ's sake, Red," she said. "All right. So you want me. But do you have to want me right now? Right this minute? Can't you wait?"

"No, I can't wait. I'm not going to wait."

His arms went out and circled her waist and he pulled her to himself, bending her backward. His lips found her neck and then he moved and pushed her against the bed and when she fell, he fell on top of her, his mouth smothering hers.

After a minute or two she managed to pull her face away. She was breathing heavily and she said, "God, for a little man you are certainly impetuous. You could at least take the gun off. It's making a hole in me."

He half lifted off of her then and quickly took off his shoulder holster.

He had no words as his hand went between her legs and he jerked away the fragile fabric of the shorts she was wearing under the mini skirt. It was Sis herself who managed to zip open his fly as he was fumbling for it.

His knees straightened and he thrust forward, deep into her and she cried out.

"Oh God! Wait! Wait. Please wait."

She was groaning, moving under him and with him in a wild ecstasy of unison when the door opened. Her arms were around him and her fingers clawed through the fabric of his shirt into his back and her eyes were closed. Their opened mouths were glued together. His own hands had found her breasts under the sweater and he was rising to again thrust deep into her when the Reverend Gibbons' hand reached out and clawed into his belt.

With one mighty heave Brother Gary lifted him bodily off of her, throwing him halfway across the bed.

The Reverand's voice was an outraged bellow as he cried, "Animal! Animal! Animal!"

Sis's eyes opened wide to stare into the wild blazing eyes of the man of God as he leaned over the bed. She couldn't stand to look at his livid face and she dropped her eyes and it was then she saw the butcher knife in his left hand.

She screamed.

"Red! Red, he's got a knife!"

Brother Gary wasn't looking at Red. He was staring down at her naked breasts below the sweater which had been pushed up around her neck. He raised the knife high in the air.

"Woman of evil!" he said. "Woman of evil, God will strike you . . ."

He never finished the sentence. The shot from Red's revolver struck him full in the mouth.

For a full half minute he stood there frozen and then slowly the insane expression left his eyes and they went blank. His hand opened and the knife dropped to the bed, nicking Sis's naked thigh. And then he crumpled and fell to the floor.

Sis began to scream.

Red dropped the gun and slapped her hard on each cheek and she stopped screaming and then began to cry.

Red slowly crawled off the bed and stood up. He reached down to pull up his trousers which were around his ankles. His belt buckle had broken and he stood for a few seconds holding up his pants. And then he said, in a whisper, "What a hell of a way to come."

Sis stopped crying and wiped her eyes with the edge of the sheet.

"He must have been crazy," she said. "Yes, he must have been crazy. Is he dead?"

Red nodded. "He's dead all right. He's dead—and anybody else who ever tries to interfere with us is also going to be dead."

Sis looked up at him wide-eyed.

"Yes," she said, "yes, for a little man you certainly are impetuous. Dude isn't going to like this."

"The hell with Dude," Red said. "From now on it's what we want. You and me. That's what's going to be important." He looked down at the body and said, "He asked for it. One more second and that knife would have been buried in your guts. The guy was nuts."

He walked around the bed and pulled Sis's sweater down.

"Pull yourself together," he said. "I hear the helicopter coming in."

Chapter 9

When things finally quieted down, when they were together in the bedroom where Brother Gibbons had been shot, it was Scar who first spoke.

"Where's Handle?" he asked.

"He's sleeping," Dude said. "He's a very sick man. We gave him some pills and he's sleeping. We won't need him tonight. I can speak for him."

"I think it's time we all spoke for ourselves," Scar said. "Things have changed."

"Yes, things have changed," Dude said. He looked over to where

Red and Sis sat side by side on the bed. "They certainly have changed. Sis, well Sis can't go back. She's going to have to disappear along with the rest of us. We don't have a getaway car anymore. And we've got two dead men. We're in for murder now as well as kidnapping and robbery."

"It wasn't murder," Red said. "They asked for it. Both of them. We didn't murder them."

"Try and tell that to a jury," Dude said. "But it doesn't matter. The thing that is important now is what we are going to do about it. The first thing we have to do is get another car. We have to have some way for all of us to leave."

"As long as we are in for two murders," Scar said, "maybe the next thing to do would be to see we don't leave a lot of witnesses behind."

Dude stared at him coldly.

"I just hope you're kidding," he said. "I told you in the beginning and I'll say it again. We are not going to hurt these people. We have nothing to gain and everything to lose if we do."

"I wasn't really serious," Scar said. "Just a crazy idea was all."

"It's crazy, all right," Dude said. "Now here's the way it stacks up. The only tough part is that now the police will know Sis is involved and will start tracing her back. Every move she's made in months and maybe even years. But that can't be helped. Red tells me he and Sis want to stay together once we all split out. Personally I think they are foolish if they do, but it's their business. The dead men can't be helped and there is no use crying over spilt milk. The car is unfortunate, but we can get another one. It is going to tie us up for a couple of days extra, but that is all right. We're still safe and we still have about twelve million dollars to cut up. Tomorrow we will see about the car. In the meantime, I think we can all get some sleep. I'm dead on my feet and I should think that the rest of you are too."

"If you'd been burying garbage out on the desert all afternoon, you'd really be dead," Scar said.

"Right. All right, Sis, you can't very well go back with the others. Where do you want to stay tonight?"

"I'll stay with Red, wherever he stays," Sis said, reaching for his hand.

"Okay. That's good enough for me. I suggest you two go over to the quarters we fixed up for the men and that we haven't used. Scar, I wish you would set up a cot in the storage room and stay with Handle. Somebody . . ."

"How about that little broad you got with him?" Scar said.

"She's had it long enough," Dude said. "Anyway, I don't want any more of the passengers wandering around and getting into trouble. We've had too much trouble with them already." He got up and stretched. "I'm going to hit the deck right here," he said. "I'll go in now and get that girl and take her back with the rest of them."

"We going to leave that preacher out in the garage all night?" Red asked.

"Unless you feel like digging a grave now," Dude said. "He's all yours, Red. Take care of him now or in the morning, whichever you want."

"He'll keep," Red said. "Come on, Sis."

"I'm going to the kitchen and get something more to eat," Scar said. "Need some coffee. I'll be in with Handle in a few minutes."

Dude followed them down the hallway and entered the office. Handle was lying under a couple of blankets, on his back, and he was breathing noisily. Dianne Rhinhardt sat near the bed in a deck chair. She'd taken off her shoes. She looked up sleepily when Dude entered the room.

"How's the patient?" he asked.

"Sleeping. I gave him another pill, maybe it was the wrong thing to do, but he got all excited when he heard that shot earlier and couldn't seem to get back to sleep. He needs rest. I'm no doctor, not even a nurse, but you've got a sick man on your hands. He's running a very high fever."

"He's had malaria," Dude said. "We'll let him sleep. And I think you better get back and get some rest yourself. "

"I can stay here tonight if you want."

Dude shook his head. "One of the boys will stay with him," he said.

For a second or so Dianne Rhinehardt looked at him curiously.

"The movies and TV must be wrong," she said. "You don't look, talk, or even act like a gangster."

"You don't act like a rich little playgirl," Dude said. "Come on, I think you better . . ."

"Do I have to go back with the others?" Dianne asked, standing up and yawning. "You can't imagine what a prize collection of old fogies and classic bores they are."

"I don't exactly know where else you can go," Dude said.

"Well, how about a drink first anyway. I could do with a Scotch and soda if you happened to have one around."

"Okay. Come along then."

They stopped in the kitchen and the girl stood by, holding her shoes in her hand as Dude reached up and took a bottle of Scotch from one of the shelves. He found a pewter water pitcher and filled it with ice. He put both on a tray, with two glasses and a couple of quart bottles of club soda.

Scar sat at the table and stared at the girl.

Dude said, "See you in the morning."

Scar grunted. As they left the room his eyes stopped following the girl and went to the cupboard which Dude had opened to get the Scotch.

Ten minutes later, when he left the kitchen, he was also carrying a tray. There were no bottles of soda but there were two bottles of Scotch, a single glass and no ice cubes.

"You people listen to me," Ned Gaines said. "I tell you I saw it with my own eyes. They were carrying his body across the courtyard. They killed him, the same as they killed Griswald."

Hattie Arthur turned to her companion and said, "What's he saying? They killed someone? Who did they kill?"

"Do be quiet and listen," Melody Salmon said. "He's talking about Dr. Gibbons, Brother Gary. He says those men killed him. It was the shot we heard earlier."

Hattie's good-natured face was stubborn.

"I don't believe it," she said. "I just don't believe anyone would hurt him. A good man like Dr. Gibbons."

"Oh, do be quiet, Hattie. Good men are always getting killed. But Brother Gibbons . . ."

"What they are doing," Gaines said, his voice almost hysterical, "is getting us one by one. First Griswald, now the preacher. They've got Miss Carr and the Rhinhardt girl and God only knows what they are doing with them."

"Miss Carr is one of them," Gene Farris growled. "I wouldn't worry about that little lady."

"She may be and she may not," Marlo Phillips said. "The fact that Miss Grunsky knew her is no real evidence any more than is the fact that she may have known one of the hijackers. I know a lot of criminals but that doesn't make me a confederate of any of them."

"Well, I for one don't believe for a minute that she is mixed up with them," Mary Mills said. "We only have Miss Grunsky's word . . ."

"It doesn't matter," Gaines said. "All I am telling you is that they are taking us out of here, one by one, and . . ."

"They aren't taking us out," Phillips said. "There is no point in getting hysterical and leaping to conclusions. Dr. Gibbons left this room on his own accord. So did both of the girls."

"Well, I tell you they murdered him," Gaines almost screamed the words. "I saw his body."

"Maybe they did," Phillips said coldly. "Maybe he asked for it. He's been grandstanding, playing a little tin hero, ever since we have been here. But that doesn't mean they intend to kill the rest of us."

"Well how about those two girls?" Mary Mills asked. "How about us women here? Even now they could be assaulting and raping the two they have with them."

The criminal lawyer spread his hands and sighed.

"Miss Grunsky," he said, "you were out there in the kitchen with them. Did anyone try and assault you? Were you raped?"

Jill shook her head.

"No. No one touched me."

"Well if they didn't touch you," Phillips said, "I am sure the rest of you women here will be safe."

Brandon Mitchell whispered something to Serge Krinsky and stood up.

"Mr. Phillips is right," he said. "If they had wanted to rape anyone, molest anyone, they would have done it before this. Griswald was killed, it is true. But Griswald was responsible for his own death. I can tell you this now. He had taken a revolver which I had purposely hidden. He was undoubtedly trying to escape and that was why he was killed. Don't misunderstand me. These men are desperate and extremely dangerous. I believe they would shoot any one of us down if given the slightest provocation. But I believe their only interest is the money. That they are holing up here only until it is safe for them to make a break. So long as we don't interfere with them, cause them any trouble, I don't believe they have any interest in us. But get in their way and you will probably be killed. They have killed at least twice already and I warn you that murder is a progressive thing. It becomes increasingly easy. So I advise you all just don't panic, don't cause them any trouble or inconvenience. Do what they ask you. We just have to remain calm and wait it out."

"But they still have those two girls," Mary Mills said, her voice indignant, "I don't know what you men intend to do . . ."

Arch Winter interrupted, glaring at her.

"We intend to do absolutely nothing," he said. "If Miss Carr is actually involved with them she won't come back here and we can stop worrying about her. So far as the Rhinhardt girl is concerned, she volunteered on her own hook to help take care of one of them who is supposed to be sick. I don't think we have to worry too much about her. From everything I have read in the papers, she's quite capable of taking care of herself. The fact is she's probably getting some new kind of thrill. As the captain of your plane, I feel responsibility for all of you, but if any of you leave this room and volunteer to help them, then you are on your own. Miss Rhinhardt obviously preferred their company to ours."

He sat down and Kenny Savo looked at him and smiled cynically.

"What's the matter, Captain," he said. "You sound a little bitter. Did the lady turn you down?"

"Your humor, Savo, gets a little stale," Arch Winter said. "I don't exactly see you making any time with her."

"Who needs her, Captain, who needs her?" He reached over and patted Jill on the side of the face and then his hand dropped down to her lap.

"I think I'll see our friend Mr. Weems again," Winter said. "I could use a drink."

"Good. You stick to your vices and I'll stick to mine," Kenny said. He lifted his feet and stretched out on couch, his head in the girl's lap. "Isn't it about time they turned off the lights in this place?"

"My God, Kenny," Winter said, "Don't you have any sense of decency at all."

"None."

Jill slipped out from under him and stood up. "I'll go with you Arch," she said. "I could use a drink myself."

Crossing the room, her eyes went to Gene Farris. "They say he's worth fifty million dollars," she said. "Can you imagine."

"They also say he's married, that he's got a mistress and that he's the tightest bastard who ever lived," Winters said. "You better stick to Kenny, kid. Unless, of course, you want to come home to Daddy again."

"No thanks, Arch. I don't like playing 'the only girl in town' every time you can't make the grade with somebody else. We've gone through that routine too often."

Arch shrugged.

"Come on, let's get that drink. If our pal, the friendly drunk, hasn't emptied his supply. Then you can go back to your boyfriend and start giving old MacPherson another attack of high blood pressure. One of these days he'll break a blood vessel when he sees Kenny put a hand on you. His fine old Scotch Presbyterian morality . . ."

"Presbyterian morality my ass," Jill said. "He has a mind like a sewer."

"You phrase it so elegantly," Arch laughed. "But you are right. He has."

She sat on the bed, two pillows behind her back and her knees doubled up with her arms around them. She held the half-filled glass in one hand, a cigarette in the other. Her hair had been done up in twin pigtails, but she had removed the rubber bands and shaken it free so that it made a golden amber halo around her small face. It was her third drink and she was beginning to feel it.

"I don't understand you," she said. "I don't understand you at all. What are you doing here with these thugs."

"They are not thugs, Miss Rhinhardt," Dude said. "Put a uniform back on them and you could call them patriots and heroes."

"I think it's time you stopped calling me Miss Rhinhardt," she said. "And don't call me Dianne. You can call me Ann. That's what my friends, or at least the people I know call me."

"All right then, Ann. Just what is it you don't understand?"

"I don't understand you. You're not at all what you pretend to be. I am not as naïve as you might think. I've known gangsters and racketeers. You'd be surprised, but they follow around the set I go with like leeches. In fact it is quite the thing to develop them. Like pet poodles. You'd be surprised at some of the people you can meet in the best places. They are not only tolerated, they are even courted. But you don't fit the pattern at all."

"What pattern do I fit?" Dude asked. He smiled thinly, raised his glass to his mouth.

"I don't know. But I can guess a couple of things. You must be a very good pilot. The Captain on the plane said you brought the jet in like a real expert. He couldn't get over the way you handled it. You speak well and I would bet ten to one you picked up a college degree somewhere along the line. The accent is Ivy League. You dress well and you are presentable, I might even say handsome. I would guess you were a flyer in the army so that means you must have been an officer. So what are you doing here? What made you decide to be a thief? I can't believe it was just the money."

"You're a romanticist," Dude said. "What's wrong with money? Everybody wants it."

"Everything's wrong with money."

"You say so because you have it."

"That's right. Because I have it. That's just why I know." She cocked her head, looked up at him.

"You know something. Almost everyone I know or have ever known, has money. A great deal of money. And I don't know one single solitary person with a great deal of money who is happy. I know a good many who are completely miserable. They are the ones who inherited it or who get it quickly and suddenly, legally or illegally, without working for it. The ones who are still working for it are neither happy or unhappy. They are too preoccupied in trying to get money for either. So what good is money?"

"It's easy for you to say," Dude said. "Having money, you can despise it. Look at you; you go from place to place, do all the things you want to do . . ."

"I go to new places because I am bored with the place I am at. I have gone from man to man for the same reason. They are all cut out of the same dull, aimless pattern. They have their yachts, their favorite planes, their polo ponies—their toys. None of them enjoy them, none of them . . ."

"I would enjoy them," Dude said.

She shook her head, sipped the last of her drink and handed him her glass.

"Will you make me another, please?"

He stood up.

"I'll make us both one."

"That's just the point, what you have said," she said. "You would enjoy them because you look forward to them. It's like if you eat hamburger every day, you look forward with pleasure to the thought of a filet mignon. But suppose you eat filet mignon every day? Do you think you would look forward to a hamburger? No, you would merely be bored with the filet."

Dude handed her the whiskey and soda. He said, "Mind if I kick my shoes off and be comfortable?"

She laughed.

"Of course I don't mind. My own are off. You know, you are very polite for a hardened criminal, if that's what you prefer to consider yourself. It isn't in character at all. If you are going around being a thief, you are going to have to learn the social mores of your profession."

Dude stretched out on the chair and loosened his necktie.

"God, I'm tired," he said.

"Do you want me to go now?"

"No. I like talking to you. I'm tired, not sleepy. It's been a long time since I've talked to anyone who has really interested me."

"And I interest you?"

"Yes, yes you interest me. So instead of talking about me, let's talk about you for a while. I think you are kidding yourself. That you are very young, probably spoiled as hell, going through a stage . . ."

"Would you really, honestly like to know about me?"

"I really, honestly would. You are a new experience."

"All right. I am young, but I am a lot older than you would ever dream. I started getting old when I was fourteen and I have never stopped. Spoiled? Yes, I am spoiled. And in other ways than you mean. And of course I am going through a stage. Everyone is, all the time. Would you like to know something?"

Dude nodded. "Yes, I would like to know something."

"You'll believe me? You won't laugh at me?"

"I'll believe you."

"All right. When I got on that plane in Los Angeles I had a full bottle of sleeping bills in my bag. Enough to kill half a dozen persons. I was making up my mind whether I should take them, the entire bottleful, before I got to Chicago or whether I would wait until I was checked into a hotel there, when you and your friends hijacked the plane."

Dude suddenly straightened up in his chair and stared at her.

"You're kidding me," he said.

"I am not kidding. I never kid about anything serious. Death, to me, or at least my death, is serious."

He shook his head.

"Why?" he asked. "Why? Have you tried something like this before?"

"If I had tried it I would have been successful and wouldn't be here telling you about it," Dianne Rhinhardt said. "I have a lot of faults, but failing isn't one of them."

For several minutes he was silent, looking at her. He reached for the cigarette pack and took two out, lighting them and giving her one. Then he spoke.

"You asked me why I wanted to become a criminal and I told you. I said money. Twelve million dollars to be exact. Split several ways, of course. It may be stupid and pointless and perhaps as you say the money is really valueless. But I gave you an honest answer. Now you give me one. Just why do you want to kill yourself?"

She drew on the cigarette and very slowly expelled the smoke. Her eyes were looking sightlessly at the foot of the bed when she spoke.

"I don't know. I honest to God don't know. Perhaps it is what I have always been doing. Looking for something new. Some new place. Some new experience. Maybe I am just mortally sick of everything I have done and everything I am. I don't really know. All I know is that I had decided to die."

"Is that why you decided to come into this room with me? To sit here and drink with me? Because you don't care what happens to you?"

"I didn't say that. I didn't say I didn't care what happens to me. I just said that I wanted to die."

"If you wanted to die, then why didn't you take those pills? They must still be in your bag. You could have taken them in that other room. You didn't have to offer to sit up with a sick man. Didn't have to come in here."

"I offered to sit with a sick man because I wanted to. Maybe it was just a subconscious desire to postpone my decision. I don't really know. But I did it for the same reason I have always done everything. I wanted to do it at the time. I came in here with you for the same reason. I wanted to."

"But why? Why would you want to?"

"You interested me," she said, "and it's a long time since I have met anyone who has. Somehow or other you seemed to remind me of myself. You seemed to me to be a man who was not really at all what you appeared to be. Doing a pointless, bizarre and rather ridiculous thing for no apparent reason. The sort of thing, only different, that I have been doing most of my life. I read stories about myself in the paper and although the facts may be more or less correct, I know very well that it isn't really me at all they are talking about. I am a completely different person. What I have done has little or no actual relationship to me as I feel and see myself. I had somewhat this same feeling about you. You are not what you appear to be. You are doing something which is totally and completely inconsistent with your actual self."

Dude stood up and paced the room for a minute or two and then reached for his glass and emptied it.

"You know," he said, "I believe you really were going to take those pills. I have half a mind not to let you go back to that room tonight."

"I don't want to go back," Dianne said. "I would just as soon stay here with you. But why do you care? What does my life mean to you? Two people have already lost their lives because of you and what you are doing."

He looked at her sharply, almost in anger.

"A lot of people have lost their lives because of me," he said. "Let me explain something to you."

He refilled his glass and went back to the chair.

"You were right about my being in the service. I was a captain in the Air Force. It cost the government something like three hundred thousand dollars to make me one. Do you know why?"

"Why?"

"Yes, why? They made me one for a very particular reason. So they could put me in a plane with a load of bombs and send me somewhere to kill other people. At an even higher price. I think they have figured it out that for every enemy we kill it cost about a half million dollars, But that only applies to the enemy soldiers. They haven't figured out the ones that come for free. The innocent civilians who are killed, both the ones on our side of the lines and the other side. They haven't figured out the costs in property and broken lives.

"I was trained to kill. I was trained to create vast untold misery and destruction. So if two men have died here today, if we have grabbed off a mere little twelve million dollars of the taxpayers' funds, I just can't be too shocked or impressed with the moral wrong of it."

"But you would be concerned about my going back into that other room and taking those sleeping pills?"

"Yes, I would. Don't ask me why, but I would. I am afraid I would be concerned about anything happening to any of those people in there also."

"You see," Dianne said, "you're not as cynical as you think you are. You're bitter, but you are not cynical. You do care about something. I am afraid you will never make it as a real professional in the criminal line. We are alike. Both failures. I couldn't quite make it as the image of an international little rich girl. The 'darling of the Jet Set', I believe they call me in the newspapers."

She stopped talking and tossed the hair out of her eyes.

"I think I am getting a little drunk," she said.

"We both are."

He looked at her for several minutes. "Are you sure you don't want to go back with the others? I can take those pills away from you, you know? In case you might be tempted, Ann."

"I want to stay here," she said. "Fill my glass and then come here on the bed with me."

She saw the sudden surprised look on his face and again she shook her head.

"Oh, don't misunderstand," she said. "I'm not some cheap little spoiled sexpot looking for new thrills. It isn't what you might think at all. I just wanted someone warm and close. Someone I can lean against for a while."

"I don't think there's anything cheap about you at all," Dude said. "And I don't misunderstand you. I know very well what it means to want someone. To need someone. I'll get you a drink."

She watched him as he poured the whiskey in the two glasses. She said, "What is your name? Your real name?"

She saw the sudden guarded look on his face and quickly said, "Never mind. It doesn't matter. It doesn't matter at all. Let's just sit here and have our drinks. I like you being with me."

He handed her the glass and then he walked to the door.

"If you don't mind," he said, turning the key, "I don't want anyone barging in. The last time it happened, this afternoon—I told you about it—it wasn't very pleasant."

"And is it going to be like this afternoon?"

"I don't know," he said. "I really don't know."

He moved to the bed and lay down beside her, hunching himself up so that he shared the pillows.

She took his arm and put it around her shoulders and moved close to him.

"I'm glad I didn't take those pills on the plane," she said.

"I'm glad too."

Red lay naked on the single bed, his arms around her and his head buried between her breasts, sleeping the sleep of utter physical exhaustion. Sis had her arms around him, holding him close and she was wide awake and had been for hours. She couldn't stop thinking.

I can't get over it. I simply can't. I've had some of the handsomest guys, some of the very greatest sex athletes around. And this funny little bald-headed man reaches me as no one else ever has been able to. Every time he touches me—and God knows he's inexhaustible— every time, it starts all over again. I can't seem to get enough of him. It makes no sense at all. There's nothing extraordinary about him physically and certainly his technique is not unusual. Completely normal and routine in fact. No fancy gimmicks, no unusual positions. Maybe it's just his insatiable appetite. Well, thank God he's asleep at last. I'm a wreck and I am going to be so sore in the morning I won't be able to go to the can.

She thought it, but she knew that if he awakened and rolled over on her again it would start all over and she wouldn't be able to resist him.

She wondered if she loved him. It didn't seem possible. She'd always thought she was through with love. In any case, what the hell did sex and love have to do with each other?

But he loved her and that she didn't doubt. My God, he was just like a schoolboy. Mumbling sentimental and romantic phrases, treating her with a strange gentleness, even when he was in the throes of an impassioned sexual attack on her.

Sis had been loved by many men but she was not used to being idolized. She found it hard to understand how Red could be so carried away, but she accepted it as a fact and didn't question his obvious sincerity, adolescent as it might seem.

She didn't know if she loved him in return. She wasn't sure exactly what love really was. But she knew one thing. He was great in bed. The best. And he loved her and that was important. He loved her and he would look after her and protect her.

She had a feeling that she might very well need protection.

It wouldn't be one sided. Red was tough, very tough, in a physical way, for a little man. But he really was a bit stupid and childish. The idea of them returning to the ranch! It was insane to even think of it. Once they made their getaway, they must put as much distance between themselves and the ranch as they could. Get away from the ranch, from the United States, from the whole North and South American continents. Their safety would lie in distance.

Yes, they would help each other. They would be good for each other. He had the physical courage and he could be the muscle. She would be the brain.

She was glad that it turned out the way it had. Dude had been wrong, wanting her to return with the others. To lay low and wait until it might be safe to get her end of the money. God, she could have waited forever.

It was better this way. She'd have her money and she'd be free to spend it. Of course they would be looking for her and they would never stop looking. But she could disappear. Disappearing wasn't nearly as difficult as it was made out to be. Didn't thousands of people simply disappear every year?

The world was a big place and if you had money, a great deal of money, you could call your shots. They would have a great deal of money between them.

She began doing a little mental arithmetic and then she thought of Handle. Handle was dying. There was no doubt about it. She had seen the signs of death in his eyes as long ago as that first time she'd visited him in the hospital. The time she'd met Dude.

She had looked at him closely this evening and she wondered if he would live long enough to get away from the ranch. So long as he had to die anyway, it was a shame that he didn't die now. What would he need his cut of the twelve million for? He'd never live long enough to use it.

It was funny, but dead people never created any problems. It was the live ones who did. Those people locked up in the main part of the house. They were the problem. The danger. The two who had been killed, Griswald and the preacher. They were no longer a problem. There was no danger either of them might run into her in some strange city ten years from now and recognize her.

Of course it was insane thinking of destroying them. You can't just kill off a dozen or more persons in cold blood. On the other hand, dozens, hundreds, thousands of people were being killed all over the world at this very moment. Did it really matter so much which ones were to die and which were to live?

Maybe that ape Scar was right after all. Maybe they should be thinking a little more of their own safety and less about what happened to strangers who really meant nothing to all of them.

She sighed, pushed herself away from Red and turned on her back. He moaned softly in his sleep.

She thought, Scar thinks this way. He said as much.

Red will think any way I tell him to think. And, if this is what I think?

It makes three of us to one.

She didn't consider Handle at all. He was, so far as she was concerned, already dead.

It was the collected phlegm in his throat and the resultant paroxysm of violent coughing which finally awakened him. For a long while, as the violent fit of continued hacking coughs racked his thin body, he thought he was back in the army hospital and he wondered if now at last he was dying. He was on fire and he speculated whether it was a recurring attack of malaria or his diseased lung which was killing him.

The paroxysm finally subsided and he became aware of the mumbled cursing from somewhere across the room.

And then he heard the sound of the electric generator and he identified it and he remembered where he was.

Slowly Handle opened his eyes and moved his head and saw Scar sprawled out in the chair opposite the bed, an empty whiskey bottle in his hand. He thought, the animal has been drinking again. He's drunk. I should get up and find Dude.

He started to rise but fell back on the bed. He was weak, weaker than he'd ever been. The blinding dizziness came over him the moment he tried to move.

He managed to open his eyes again and he saw Scar drop the bottle and reach for the other one on the floor at his feet. Scar held the opened bottle to his mouth until the liquid came gushing out of the corners and then he dropped this bottle also on the floor where it spilled its amber contents across the rug. He rose apelike out of the chair, pushing his great thick arms down straight against the bottom sides of the seat. He staggered for a moment, still muttering a string of obscenities.

When he left the room by the door which opened into the courtyard, Handle again tried to rise from his bed. But again his body failed his will power and he fell back and closed his eyes in a half faint.

It would have to wait; he could warn Dude in the morning. In the meantime, there probably wasn't anything to worry about. The animal had probably gone outside to relieve himself.

The full moon streamed down across the compound and Scar softly closed the door behind himself. He knelt down and untied his shoe laces and kicked off his shoes. There was a cunning, crafty look in his bloodshot eyes.

He crossed the compound moving like a ghost. Subconsciously he realized that there were no lights in any of the rooms of the ranch house except the dim forty-watt bulb he'd left burning in the office where he'd left Handle. His voice became quiet as he stealthily approached the door of the wing which housed the stables they had converted into the stockade where he knew that Red had taken the girl. His hand reached out for the door knob and he twisted it but the door failed to give, and he put his ear to the door. He heard movement in the room somewhere, a small rhythmic movement.

Backing away from the door he looked along the wall and he saw that the second window down had been opened. Bending low, he moved toward it making no sound at all. When he was under the window he straightened up slightly and listened. This time there was no mistaking the sound he had heard. It was the steady pounding of bed springs and he could feel the excitement surging through him as the blood raced in his veins.

He lifted his head above the window ledge then and the moon, flooding into the room, showed him the pair of them, lying naked on the bed and locked together as they moved up and down in a frantic sexual dance.

He could hear the torturous breathing above the sounds of the straining bed springs and then the girl gave a small, thin sounding scream and there was sudden silence.

Scar sobbed deep in his throat, ducked under the window and he seemed to be crawling on all fours as he scurried crabwise back across the compound.

When he reentered the office he saw the spilled bottle on the floor and he picked it up and drained the few ounces which still remained in it.

He wiped his sleeve across his eyes and shook his head and then again moved out of the room. He went through the kitchen and down the long hallway, again walking as noiselessly as a ghost. Outside of the door to the bedroom where he knew that Dude was sleeping, he again put his ear to the door and listened.

He heard the voices but he couldn't understand the words. They were whispered voices, barely distinguishable, but he recognized one as Dude's. The other was a girl's voice.

When he turned away again his face was red with fury.

He stopped back in the kitchen and quickly found another bottle.

He was speaking in a harsh whisper as he opened it.

"I'm the one! I'm the one who needs it. They get it but I need it. Why should I be the only one who never gets the girl? Why, goddamn it, why?"

When he reentered the office he went over to Handle's bed and dropped down on it heavily. His hand reached out and he shook the sleeping man and Handle weakly opened his eyes.

"You know what they're doing?" Scar half roared at him. "Do you know? While you and I stay in here like goddamned fools, they're out there with those women. Both of 'em. Screwin' 'em. Screwing, all of them. Anyone they want. And what the hell are we doing? We're in here like a couple of dummies. Hear me? Like a couple of dummies!"

Handle opened his eyes and looked at him half blindly.

"Go away," he said, his voice barely above a whisper. "Go away. Leave me alone. I'm sick."

Scar again shook him by the arm.

"I'm sick too," he said. "Sick of being the only one who doesn't get any ass. What am I supposed to be anyway, some kind of orphan? What's wrong with me?"

Handle's eyes opened again and suddenly cleared. He said, "Get away from me. Don't bother me with your problems. Take 'em to the chaplain."

Scar threw his arm away from him and stood up. "The hell with you," he said.

He finished the bottle he had taken on his way through the kitchen two hours later. He had fallen asleep and dozed a number of times between drinks. When he finally again staggered to his feet he was as drunk as a man can be and still remain conscious.

Going to the sink in the corner he turned on the cold water and then leaned down and forced his head under the faucet. He stayed there for minutes, letting the cold stream flood over his head and bull-like neck. He used both hands to splash the water over his shoulders and chest. Finally he stood back and again moved to the door, not bothering to turn off the faucet.

The cold desert night air burned in his lungs and for a long time he just stood outside the door breathing deeply. Gradually his eyes began to focus and slowly the cunning, crafty animal look came back. He looked across the compound and then moved. But he didn't cross over. Instead he went to the first of the windows of the room which held the people from the plane.

The moon had shifted and it was almost as bright as day in the compound. The window had been opened slightly from the bottom and the curtains pulled back and when he raised his head he had no trouble seeing into the room.

They had set the cots up in two rows on opposite sides. The five women slept on the south side, each in a single cot, and although he couldn't make out their individual faces, he was able to tell they were women by their hair. The men were sleeping on cots which lined the opposite wall.

For long minutes he stared into the room. There nothing but the sound of breathing, an occasional snore.

When he passed through the office again, he stopped for a moment and his hand found the coat pocket of the trench jacket he'd thrown over the back of the chair he'd been sitting in while he drank. He took out the razor-sharp jackknife and shoved it in his trouser pocket and then looked over at the bed. Handle lay on his side, eyes closed, breathing torturously and the air made a grating, hollow sound as he expelled it from his lungs and through his constricted throat.

The light from the half-opened kitchen door cast an ape-like shadow against the floor as he moved down the long hallway and stopped before the door of the room. He made no sound at all as he carefully removed the bar which made the room a prison.

They had all been tired and exhausted and finally, when the lights were turned out, those who were able to sleep at all, slept like the dead. Mr. Weems of course had no problem at all. He'd consumed enough straight brandy in the last thirty-six hours to permanently embalm a half-dozen lesser men. Arch Winter who had said earlier that he needed a drink, discovered that one drink was hardly enough and so he had kept on until he too passed out cold.

Serge Krinsky, the Russian, had something better than liquor. Neurotic and tense to the point of almost being psychopathic, he'd depended for years on the more potent drugs and he was never without a good supply. He had been generous and had offered a couple of his pills to his companion, Mitchell, the CIA man, and they were both now dead to the world.

Ned Gaines, like most Hollywood types, had for years alternated between pep pills and sleeping pills and he took them as regularly as most people took food and drink. He'd swallowed his Nembutals early in the evening, taking a double dosage just to make sure.

Walthar Bruno, the nuclear scientist, needed neither pills nor liquor. He might have a weak and twisted body, a deformed spine, but he had a will of iron. When he decided it was time to sleep, he slept. He never permitted anything to interfere with what he wanted to do. He could have slept through one of his own nuclear explosions once he'd made up his mind not to be disturbed.

Kenny Savo had no trouble at all in falling asleep. He had earned his exhaustion honestly and it was this fact which had made it impossible for Stewart MacPherson to sleep at all. Kenny had waited until the lights were off and things had quieted down and then he had quietly gotten out of bed and gone into the community bathroom at the north end of the room and closed the door after himself. Five minutes later Jill Grunsky had also gotten out of bed. She too went to the bathroom and the door opened for her and closed and MacPherson could plainly hear the click of the lock. There had been sounds of giggling and it infuriated him. After a few minutes he heard the shower when they turned it on.

He timed them on the florescent dial of his wristwatch. They were in the shower for an hour and fifteen minutes. He assumed they must be doing it under the shower. It would have been the only way possible in the small, tile-floored room.

He was livid with anger by the time they finally came out, brazenly together. Kenny walked her over to her bed and kissed her and then returned to his own bed and dropped into it like a log. Within two minutes he was snoring.

MacPherson could have killed him without a qualm. He would have given twenty years off the end of his life to have been naked under that shower with Jill, himself. If it had not been for the others in the room he would have relieved himself the way he always did, but he was ashamed that someone might guess what he was doing.

Two other men besides the dour Scotsman were not asleep when that door slowly opened and the hunched over, truncated figure slid into the room; Marlo Phillips, the criminal lawyer, and Gene Farris, the financial wizard.

Phillips was amusing himself by planning a theoretical defense of the hijackers, assuming they were to be arrested later on and should he be the attorney selected to defend them. It was a fascinating idea.

Farris was thinking of his little movie starlet down in Acapulco. He was figuring out how much it would cost him to get rid of her. He was also thinking about Jill Grunsky. Damned funny, but he'd never realized before they had cute little tricks like that working for his own airline. She would certainly be a damned sight less expensive than Kitty.

Four of the five women in the room had had no trouble at all in falling asleep. Jill Grunsky, having shared Kenny Savo's therapy, had, like him, dropped off almost the moment her head hit the pillow.

Mary Mills had been another one who had watched the two of them go into the bathroom, but unlike MacPherson, it didn't keep her awake. It disgusted her and she had no illusions as to what they would be doing in there. Unlike the Scotsman, she was unable to actually visualize them doing it under a running shower, but she was sure about what was happening. It disgusted her but it didn't infuriate her or even make her angry. And she certainly had no desire to imagine herself taking the girl's position in what she was sure was some obscene and perverted sexual rite.

She merely shrugged, mentally at least, and turned on her side and closed both her eyes and lips firmly and was asleep in minutes.

School teachers on sabbaticals never have trouble with insomnia, even under the most trying conditions. At least that is a theory and it is probably true because Hattie Arthur and Melody Salmon were dead to the world twenty minutes after the lights were turned off. Hattie had wanted to talk for a while, as she always wanted to talk, but Melody had been firm.

"We don't know what tomorrow will bring," she had said firmly, "and we shall need all of our wits and strength. Now please be quiet and let me get my rest. And you get your sleep too. A rested body makes an alert mind and we will need all the intelligence we have before we are out of this."

Francine, the French entertainer, however, did not fall asleep. She didn't want to fall asleep. The events of the last thirty-six hours had not only shocked and frightened her, they had completely confused her. She simply couldn't understand what it was all about. Certainly that idiot the Hollywood people had sent along with her had been no help.

It was neither the shock nor the fright, or even the confusion that was keeping her awake, however. They had merely served to make her really think for one of the few times in her life.

She started thinking about her young husband, who without doubt was playing around with other women. She ended up thinking solely about herself.

She was getting old. There was no point in any longer fooling herself about it. It is true that she still had a fabulous figure. Small, of course, but her breasts were young and firm, like a schoolgirl's. Her legs? Her legs were her best feature. They were beautiful and they hadn't changed in forty years.

She could still squeeze into a size eight dress and a size ten often had to be altered to fit her snugly enough. She had her posture and her stomach was flat and unwrinkled. Of course her buttocks—but then who actually sees one's buttocks?

Her face? Well, there was no point in lying to herself. No double chin, or perhaps just the sign of one, but her face was old. Her eyes had lost that sparkle and her mouth and lips, well, they were not what they had been. Everyone's lips become thin, colorless in time. Of course the makeup people, especially out in Hollywood, did wonders and she could still fool the cameras. Television of course was a lot tougher. She could still dance, and although her voice had lost a lot of its strength and vitality, it was amazing what the new electronic devices could do for one.

The big trouble wasn't her appearance or even her fading talent. The big thing was the way she herself felt. Each year she lost a little more self-confidence, a little more self-assurance.

Was that why she had to keep marrying younger and younger men? Good God, a boy of twenty-five! Why, she could remember when she couldn't stand a man under forty. When she'd been a girl, she'd liked them even older.

Did she marry youths half her age to reassure herself of her own youth—which of course was long gone—and attractiveness? Or did she marry them because the older ones were smart enough to know her for what she was and the younger ones didn't care, just so long as she supported them.

Maybe this crazy thing with the airplane—this hijack that fool Gaines had called it—maybe it was the best thing which could have happened after all. It was giving her a chance to think.

She really had been a fool walking out on that Hollywood contract. Contracts had not been quite so easy to come by in recent years. And God knows, she needed money. She always needed money.

Going to London, chasing after that young idiot she'd married was probably even more foolish. All she could possibly do was humiliate herself even further. The thing to do was face the realities, accept the truth no matter how painful.

She would return to the coast and finish out the contract. And she would get a divorce. Both would certainly help as far as the money problems were concerned.

She was still deep in thought, lying flat on her back with her eyes wide open and staring at the ceiling, when she heard the soft shuffling sound at the side of her bed.

Marlo Phillips was the first of the three of the men to see him as he stood there in the half-opened doorway. He didn't immediately recognize him, but when the short, truncated figure moved and started slowly across the room, a patch of moonlight struck him and the lawyer recognized him as the one they called Scar.

The sudden shock of fear disappeared almost as soon as he sensed it. His mind was quick and logical and he made the obvious deduction at once. If one of their hijackers was sneaking into the room, it could only be for a single reason. It wouldn't be Marlo Phillips who interested him. It would be one of the women.

For a fleeting moment, but only very fleeting, a vague sense of long lost and buried chivalry flashed across his brain. He was a man and men defended women.

He dismissed the idea at once as both hopelessly romantic and utterly impractical.

Any action, no matter how romantic and chivalrous, which would be futile and bound to fail, was sheer stupidity. And any action which was bound to fail and also put one's own life in jeopardy, was worse. It was criminal stupidity.

He watched, completely fascinated and staying breathlessly still as Scar crossed over and stepped between the two beds which Phillips knew were occupied by the little airline hostess, the girl they called Jill, and that French motion picture actress.

He had no doubt at all as to the man's intentions. He only wondered in a vaguely technical way if the man intended to actually rape one of the women right there in the open in front of them all. It didn't really seem possible. But then, what else could the fellow have in mind?

The attorney was absolutely sure he was about to witness an act of violence. Rape most likely and possibly even murder. In all fairness to him, if he'd actually thought he could have done anything effectively to stop it, he would have made a move. He might just possibly have taken a certain personal risk if he'd believed for a second it might have a chance of success in preventing a crime from taking place.

But he was quite sure nothing he could do would prevent it. It might very well turn a simple rape into a regular carnage.

So he did nothing. He watched and speculated, intellectually curious but not really emotionally aroused. He wondered which of the women would be selected.

Almost subconsciously he laid odds of three to one it would be the airline hostess.

Gene Farris' eyes had been failing in recent years and he had trouble seeing at night. But there was nothing wrong with his ears. He heard the sound of Scar's soft footsteps the moment he entered the room, but he didn't see him for several seconds.

Farris' mind in its own way was as sharp and alert as the criminal attorney's, but the first thought he had when he became aware of the man sneaking across the room had nothing to do with possible rape. Had nothing to do with the women at all.

He was sure that one of them, one of their captors, had come in to rob them. He wasn't of course thinking too clearly or he would have realized that if any of them wanted to commit a robbery of their personal effects, they wouldn't have to come sneaking in after everyone was asleep.

Almost without thinking, he moved his hand and found the wallet he always placed under his pillow when he slept in strange beds. He moved cautiously and carefully tucked it in between his bare legs under his crotch. Then he closed his eyes tight and feigned a deep sleep. Even if he had known what was going to happen, even if he might have prevented it, he would have done nothing. He didn't believe it paid to interfere in other people's troubles. The innocent bystanders were the ones who always got clipped and he hadn't gotten where he was by being an innocent bystander.

MacPherson had kept his bitter, furious eyes glued to Jill Grunsky's bed from the moment she had climbed into it after kissing Kenny Savo goodnight. He only saw Scar when the hunched over, broad shouldered figure stopped next to her bed.

MacPherson didn't know who it was but he was sure it was one of their captors. Like Phillips, he automatically sensed why the man was there.

There was no question at all in his mind. It was one of them and he'd come in for Jill Grunsky. He watched, his eyes wide with suppressed excitement, as he saw the man hesitate, then step forward and peer down at the sleeping girl.

Goddamn her, it was going to serve her right! He wouldn't make a move to help her if someone paid him for it and gave him the Medal of Honor. The little slut had been asking for it all along. She was as bad as those other two. The Carr girl and that society broad who had both voluntarily gone over to their captors.

All women were sluts at heart and anything that happened to them they deserved.

MacPherson was absolutely sure that the girl was about to be attacked and raped. The odd thing was that when he'd known she was voluntarily giving herself to a man, it had driven him crazy with fury, but now that he believed she was to be taken by force, he was pleased. MacPherson considered himself a decent man and a moral man and it would never occur to him there could be anything wrong with his thinking. At least it didn't occur to him until the following morning.

Phillips saw it all, every move.

Scar stood there for moments on end, staring down at the sleeping girl. And then he moved.

The sudden startled cry came from the next bed. He saw the slender figure of the French actress as she sat suddenly bolt up-right.

The man whirled like lightning and before she could open her mouth to release the full scream which was building up in her throat, one huge hand was over her face. He lifted her small body out of the bed with a single movement and he turned and fled to the open door, carrying her under one arm like a child, or a small sack of potatoes.

He still held her under his arm, his hand hard over her mouth, as he stopped to put the bat back over the door. Then he moved down the hall to the kitchen, closing that door after him.

He lifted her and turned her, so that she was facing him, her feet not quite touching the floor and her body pressed hard against his own. He started to take his hand from her mouth and then in a second he gave an animal roar.

She had sunk her teeth deep into the inside of his palm. He dropped her, at the same time jerking his hand away. At the same instant his doubled right fist smashed into her face.

Her neck snapped back and she slowly dropped to the floor.

He reached down and with one jerk stripped off her nightdress and she lay naked as he loosened his belt.

He fell on her like a wild beast and his mouth found her breast and he sank his teeth into the soft yielding flesh. He had her, again and again, and it was a full hour before he finally rolled away from her, panting with exhaustion.

He hadn't realized that she'd died a second after he'd struck her, as her spinal column had snapped from the force of the blow from his fist.

Chapter 10

Fleeing under the driving force of a strong southeast wind, the heavily water laden cumulous clouds began moving northwestward across the states and the barometer rapidly dropped. Simultaneously, freezing cold air from the far north of the Arctic Circle crossed the Canadian Border, creating an unusual high as it moved south to where, sometime just before dawn, it met with its counterpart which had originated in the Gulf of Mexico.

At five o'clock in the morning the cold azure sky above the desert was a clear frozen crystal dome and the full moon, slowly sinking over the Pacific far to the west, threw an eerie and unreal light over the vast mesa. There was no movement of air and the sterile stillness had the quality of an uninhabited and dead and forgotten planet.

For one small space in time, a matter of minutes, as the moon slowly disappeared over the edge of the world and the reflections of the rising sun illuminated the eastern sky, the air stirred and a secretive whispering wind rustled the tumbleweeds and blew stray grains of sand across the desert floor. The eerie early morning light changed in quality and there was a promise of daylight. But the promise faded like the memory of the kisses of yesterday and by seven-thirty in the early morning, the world was suddenly darker than midnight.

The wind which had started as a small caress, making tiny ripples in the sand, was a howling dervish as it roared unimpeded over the rolling dunes.

A typical, seasonal blizzard was beginning to rage in full force.

At first it was only the sand which was picked up as though by some gigantic vacuum cleaner from the desert and tossed wildly into the churning air to form blinding, formless scuds that obliterated the landscape. The very pattern of the desert floor shifted and changed and new arroyos and valleys were formed and reformed. Later, shortly before noon, snow crystals, as sharp and ruthless as broken razor blades, fell into the maelstrom and the blizzard began to develop its true muscle and maturity.

Unprotected and unsheltered, life could no longer exist while it lasted.

He was the first one to awaken.

It was the shattering crash of the slatted metal awning outside of the bedroom window, torn loose by the first true gust of the oncoming storm, which brought him out of unconsciousness and for several moments he lay still, listening. He knew at once what was happening. His eyes remained closed but his thoughts quickly went to the helicopter staked to the earth outside in the compound.

He knew all about desert storms, had made it a point to check on them. Knew how suddenly they might come up and that one might be expected at any time during the winter months.

The 'copter would be safe. It was firmly staked to the ground and it was protected by the three wings of the ranch house which enclosed it.

He didn't have to check the weather reports or go to the window and look out to realize that there would be no flying this day, and that he would very likely be grounded for several more days.

The winds must have suddenly shifted and for one brief moment there was silence. It was then he became aware of the soft sound of breathing at his side. He opened his eyes.

They lay there, next to each other, fully clothed. She was facing him, her head in the hollow of his outstretched arm. She was breathing quietly, her mouth slightly opened and her lipstick a little smeared. There were dark smudges under her eyes and her hair was spread in a halo around her head. She looked like a little girl and he half sat up, watching her for long moments. Then he leaned over and very softly brushed her lips with his own.

Her eyes opened and she looked at him without expression. Finally her lips moved in a trace of a smile. "What a nice way to wake up," she said.

He leaned over and kissed her again.

"I think my arm must be broken," he said, and smiled at her. She lifted her head and he moved his arm away and up in the bed, swinging his feet to the floor.

She kept her eyes on him as he stood up and stretched. Then she looked down at herself and straightened her skirt. She smiled again at him, almost mischievously.

"So this is the way we went to bed together," she said. "Some gangster, some playgirl."

"Nobody would ever believe it," Dude said. "I'm afraid your reputation is shot."

"My reputation has been shot for years," she said. "I wish I could tell you that it has always been shot for so little reason."

A small frown crossed his face.

"I'm afraid it may be just a little embarrassing for you when you go in there with the others. I'm sorry."

"You haven't anything to be sorry about. Nothing at all. And even, well even if anything had happened, you'd still have nothing to be sorry about. I am with you because want to be with you."

"Well, it may be a little embarrassing," he began, but she leaned over and reached up, putting her fingers across his lips.

"I won't be embarrassed at all," she said. "Anyway, I don't want to go back with the others. I want to stay with you."

He stepped back and stared at her. "You want to stay with me? Ann, you're crazy. You can't stay with me. You don't know what you're saying."

"But I do know what I'm saying. Don't you understand? I do know. You see, in a crazy sort of way, I am really yours now. You gave me my life back."

He shook his head, bewildered.

"Gave you your life back? What are you talking about, baby? I haven't given you your life. Your life is your own, to do with as you wish."

"That's just the point. Yesterday, the day before, I wanted to die. I planned to die. If you hadn't hijacked that plane, if we weren't here right this minute, I would be dead. So in a way you see, my life belongs to you. It's like the Chinese, you know. If you save a Chinaman's life, then you are morally obligated to take care of him as long as he lives."

"Damn it, we aren't Chinese," Dude said. "Anyway, you know you still have those pills. Nothing has really changed, nothing really happened. After all, it's just two lonely people coming together by accident and spending a few hours talking with each other."

"I still have the pills, but you are wrong about the rest of it. Something has happened. I don't want to die anymore. I can't tell you why and maybe you are right and it is just a case of two lonely people finding a few hours of peace and contentment. But I no longer want to die. I won't die."

"I'm glad," Dude said. "Very, very glad. I don't want you to die. Now or ever. But Ann, be sensible. You can't stay with me. Don't you understand how impossible that is? Why we don't even know each other. We have only just . . ."

"But I do know you," she said. "I do know you. Time isn't the important thing. Time is meaningless."

He was thoughtful for several moments and then looked up at her curiously.

"You know, you may be right," he said. "Maybe you do know me. It's a funny thing, but I was married to a woman for ten years. I lived with her and slept with her and I guess in a way I loved her, for at least seven of those ten years. And yet I really never knew her at all. I've known you for less than a full day—and well, of course I haven't slept with you. But I do feel that I know you. Know you better than I ever knew her."

She smiled at him wickedly and said, "If you haven't slept with me, that can very easily be arranged at your convenience, sir."

"You know something, I think I'm being propositioned," Dude said.

"Not at all, my good man. I am merely bribing you not to send me back to stay with those dismal characters in your private prison ward."

She laughed then and jumped off the bed and flung herself at him, standing on her toes and putting her arms around his neck, drawing his face down to her own upturned one. Her eyes glistened as they looked fully into his.

"I'm staying with you as long as you will let me stay," she said. "And I will seduce you any way that I can."

"You won't have to seduce me," Dude said. "You'll never have to seduce me."

He leaned down and kissed her and this time her parted lips pressed hard against his own and she moved close to him, tightening her arms around his neck.

His arms circled her waist as he pulled her even closer.

There was the sound of a crash somewhere out in the compound and he quickly dropped his arms and stepped back. He went to the window and pulled back the curtain.

Another metal awning had torn away and was a twisted sculpture as it rattled in the corner of the two wings where they came together.

He strained his eyes and saw that 'copter was all right.

She was standing at his side and she said, "Is that what you will be leaving in—the helicopter?"

He nodded.

"Yes. Yes, if this storm doesn't . . ."

"I want to go with you," she said.

He turned to her and held her arms with his hands.

"Ann," he said, "you're acting like a child. Don't you understand what you are saying?"

His voice was suddenly angry. "You're making a game of it. It isn't me that you want. You have some romantic idea that I am some kind of Robin Hood or something. I'm not. I'm a common thief. A criminal."

"It doesn't matter . . ."

"It does matter," he said, his voice suddenly furious. "It does matter! What am I? Some sort of new toy? Some new thrill for the 'Girl Who Has Everything'?" He shook her and continued, "Goddamn it, don't try to take me up the way you would buy a new yacht or a prize race horse. What am I supposed to be? Another escape? A new sort of thrill? What's the matter," he ended bitterly, "haven't you slept with a real mobster yet?"

She put her hand to her mouth and looked at him as though he had struck her across the face, her eyes stricken. And then she turned away as the tears formed and began falling like tiny glass beads down her cheeks.

The anger left him as suddenly as it had come and he moved quickly and again took her close to him and held her very tight.

"I'm sorry," he said. "Oh God, I'm sorry. I don't want to hurt you. I wouldn't hurt you for anything in the world. I know it isn't that. I know you mean what you say. But don't you see, you are dreaming an impossible dream. It isn't me that you want. I am merely a symbol. You are looking for something. We are all looking for something. Most of us never find it. But what you are looking for might be found. You want it so bad that you are blinding yourself. It isn't something outside of yourself, someone else you must look for. You must look inside of yourself."

She looked up at him and shook her head wiping the tears away with the back of her hand.

"I looked inside myself last night—while we were talking," she said. "I looked inside myself and I found I wanted to live. But it was because of you. Oh, can't you understand? I am not seeking new thrills, trying to buy you. But because of you, because of the things you said to me, I suddenly changed. I don't know why, but I did. Maybe it is because I found I was in love with you."

"People don't fall in love just like that."

"Nobody really knows why anyone falls in love," she said. "But they do. And they fall in love 'just like that.' All I know is that you changed me. And I want to be with you."

He walked her over to the bed and carefully sat her down on the edge of it and then he went to the chair and fell into it, putting his elbows on his knees and bowing his head into his cupped hands. His voice was almost a whisper when he spoke in an emotionless monotone.

"I don't know what love is," he said. "I could be in love with you. Maybe I am. But there is one thing I do know. I'm in this thing, deeply and irretrievably. I am responsible for stealing and wrecking a plane worth millions of dollars. I am responsible for kidnapping and holding almost two dozen people. I am indirectly responsible for the deaths of two of these people. That's murder. Kidnapping, robbery and murder. Do you understand?"

He looked up at her and she stared back and then nodded.

"Yes. I understand."

"You are a girl who has everything. Money, youth, beauty, social position, security. Me? Well, for the rest of my life I will be running. Now . . ."

"That's what I've been doing," Dianne interrupted. "Running. All my life, running. Don't you see, that is just the point. You say money. Let me tell you, money has been a curse. It hasn't been anything I have enjoyed. It's been a jailer. Social position? Only the money bought the social position and the social position is valueless. Like most of the things my money has bought. You did two things for me last night, Dude. You made me want to live. And somewhere along the line I became convinced that the best thing I could do was get rid of those totally useless and surplus millions I inherited. I've probably got it all mixed up, but money is like power. A little bit of it may be all right but a great deal of it is evil."

He looked at her and smiled in spite of himself.

"You've got it all mixed up all right," he said. "You know something?" He laughed. "This is almost hilarious, us two sitting here. You wanting to give away several million dollars and me, well me departing from a completely honest and I guess you would say honorable life in order to become a criminal and steal several million dollars."

"Maybe," Dianne said, "maybe if you just didn't steal it . . ."

He stood up and stretched.

"It's a little too late for that, I'm afraid," he said. "There are, well there are other people involved."

"I'm involved," Dianne said. "I'm going to involve myself, even if you don't want me to."

"You're going to have a cup of coffee and some orange juice," Dude said. "Right now. Go in and wash up. Bathroom is over there." He nodded toward the door next to the closet. "I'll be back in a jiffy."

Sis had been awake for a long time; lying there, listening to the howling wind and the rattling of the windows. Listening and thinking, but not thinking about the storm outside. Thinking about the money.

God, how she had wanted money. Wanted it all her life. And now they had it. Now, less than a couple of hundred yards away, there were the canvas bags which spelled the culmination of a dream. A dream that had become a complete and total obsession.

She would have liked nothing better than to climb out of the bed and cross the courtyard, go into the office and just sit there running her hands over the stacks of bills.

In her mind she conjured up the classic picture of a lean-faced bearded miser with mad eyes, running bony fingers through mounds of gold coins and she laughed aloud. She knew exactly how he must have felt. She felt the same way.

She moved and turned and took Red by the arm and shook him. There was no reason why they shouldn't go over and look at it. Count it. Figure exactly how much they would have.

He groaned, pushed her hand away and she poked him hard in the ribs.

"Come on," she said, "wake up. Time we got up, Red."

He groaned again, turned on his back and his bloodshot eyes opened and blinked several times.

He said, "Wha', wha'sa matter? Wha's happening?"

"Time to get up," she said.

He slowly came fully awake and lifted his head and looked around the large room as though he'd never seen it before.

"Christ," he said. "I'm pooped. Say, what's goin' on, anyway? Close that goddamned window. It's freezing in here."

Sis got out of bed shivering and quickly closed the window. She hurried back, saying, "There's a regular blizzard outside. Don't know where this came from all of a sudden."

He didn't answer her but closed his eyes again. Once more she took his arm and shook him.

"You know, I've been thinking," she said. "Come on, wake up and listen to me. I've been planning just what we're going to do."

"Hum-m-m."

"Listen to me," she said. "When we get the money, when we get out of here, I know just what . . ."

"We'll get a ranch," Red said. "A real spread. Something like this place . . ."

She shook her head.

"Not like this. Not anything like this or anywhere around here. But you can have your ranch. Only in South Africa."

Red opened his eyes. "South Africa? What are you talking about, South Africa?"

"I got it all figured out, Red," Sis said. "It's the one place we will be safe. You see, because of their apartheid policy . . ."

"Their *what?*"

"You know. Colored people. That business with the natives. Separation. Non-integration. Anyway, because of it, they have broken off diplomatic relations with us and almost everyone else. We don't trade with them and they don't trade with us. A sort of international boycott on them. If you follow me."

"I guess I do," Red said.

"So it would be the one place we would be safest. There won't be any American police or FBI men down there nosing around. I doubt if they would even be able to extradite us."

"So?"

"So that's where we'll go. They are anxious to have white people come into the country. Especially white people with a lot of money to spend. And boy, we'll have the money. We have it already, right here."

"I'd still like," Red began, but she cut him short.

"Your ranch? Yes, I know. Well you can get the greatest damned ranch you ever saw. Up there in the back country. As lonely and private and secluded as you could want. We can get a plane or a helicopter and learn to fly it and that way we can each have what we want. We can go into Cape Town or any of the other cities and get good food, nightclubs, the racetracks . . ."

"Sounds fine to me," Red said. "But how do you figure we are getting into the country if they are so . . ."

"Money," Sis said. "Money, that's how. Money does anything, buys anything. It gets you what you want, when you want it, the way you want it. And we have the money. No, don't worry about how we get in. I'll take care of the details. You just be sure when that cash is split up, we each get what is coming to us."

"I'll be sure," Red said. He reached over and pulled her around so they lay facing each other. "You worry about the money," he said. "I got other things on my mind at the moment."

Sis laughed.

"My God," she said, "don't you ever get enough?"

He froze, one foot inside of the room, hand still holding the door. The blood drained from his face, rushing to his heart. His eyes opened wide to reflect the shocked horror which overcame him as he looked down at the nude, blood smeared, ravaged body on the floor.

Swallowing the lump in his throat, he whispered, "Oh my God!"

It took all of his will power to force himself forward and to kneel down; he could feel the muscles in his stomach grow tight. He thought for a moment he was going to vomit.

He couldn't touch her, but he didn't have to in order to know that she was dead.

At last, when he finally stood up, his eyes were dazed and he looked blindly around the kitchen seeing the empty whiskey bottle broken near the door, the blood splashed floor, the handful of twenty- and fifty-dollar bills scattered near the sink. He saw it all but none of it registered.

Again he spoke, "Christ! Good Christ!"

He moved then, circling the body and walking like a zombie, reached the door of the office and opened it.

The sight of Handle lying half off the bed with the submachine gun still grasped tightly in one hand, brought him to. For a moment he thought he also was dead, but as he moved quickly toward the bed, he heard the hard tortured breathing. Handle's eyes were closed and he was unconscious.

Dude pried his finger from the stock of the gun and then gently lifted his body and placed it between the sheets. He took the top blanket from the bed and crossed the room again and entered the kitchen, covering the woman's broken body.

Going to the liquor cupboard, he rummaged among the bottles until he found one containing brandy. He found a glass and then returned to the bedroom. He pulled the cork from the bottle, poured a glass half full and drank it in one gulp. Refilling the glass part way, he leaned over the bed and lifting Handle's head, allowed a small amount to trickle into the partly opened mouth.

Handle coughed violently and the liquor spewed out of his mouth.

Dude found a towel at the end of the bed, soaked it with the rest of the brandy in the glass and wiped Handle's forehead. He returned to the kitchen and filled the glass half full of water and then went back and put brandy on top of the water and mixed them together. Again he held up Handle's head and forced a small amount into the opened mouth.

This time Handle gulped and started to choke and then suddenly swallowed. His whole body stiffened and began to shake and gradually his eyes opened.

"It's all right, boy, it's all right," Dude said.

Slowly the light came back into the eyes and they focused and Handle turned his head and he saw Dude. His lips moved and he tried to talk but at once was overcome with a fit of coughing.

Dude laid him back on the bed and returned to the kitchen, emptying the glass into the sink. He refilled it with water and when he returned, managed to get several ounces down Handle's throat.

Handle's lips moved again but the words didn't come and Dude said quickly, "Don't try to talk. You will be all right. Just take it easy and don't try . . ."

The croaking sound came then and Dude leaned close.

"Scar . . . Scar . . ."

"It's all right, all right, kid," Dude said. "I know. Just lie back. Later you can tell me."

He laid the head gently back on the pillow, pulled the blanket up under his chin and then quickly went to the desk and opened the top drawer.

Strapping on the shoulder holster, he took out the revolver and checked it.

"Just rest," he said, again turning to the bed. "Rest. You can tell me later. I'll get someone to take care of you."

He stopped in the kitchen, hesitated a moment and then walked to the form under the blanket on the floor. Gritting his teeth, he leaned down and, wrapping the edges of the blanket under the body as best he could, he lifted it and went to the door. The door opened inward and almost blew off its hinges when he turned the knob.

He had to fight every inch of the way to reach the shed which they had used to store the Land Rover but he finally made it. He was breathless when he finally got back to the kitchen, but he didn't stop. He walked down the long hallway and a moment later entered the bedroom where he had spent the night.

She was back once more sitting on the edge of the bed, hair combed and tied in pigtails and hanging down over her shoulders to rest against her breasts, face bright and shining and expectant as he opened the door.

The second she looked up and saw him her expression changed and she stood up.

"What's happened? What is it? You look as though . . ."

"No time now," he said. "No time for questions. I need your help. I want you to come with me."

"Is anything wrong? What . . ."

"Please," he said. "Please. Just come. I need you. Just take my hand and follow me."

He reached out to her and turned and he started back down the hallway.

Speaking over his shoulder, he said, "We are going into the office, through the kitchen. Don't look around. Just hold my hand and follow me."

A moment later, as he crossed the kitchen floor he heard a quick gasp and the small hand tightened in his own and he knew she must have seen the blood. Carefully he closed the office door and locked it. He nodded over at the bed.

"I want you to do anything you can for him," he said. "I can't tell you what, but anything that you can. I am going to leave you for a while and I am going to lock the door after myself. Don't open it for anyone. Anyone at all. Not until I return. Do you understand?"

She nodded, looked at Handle on the bed, and then back at Dude.

"I think he is trying to say something," she said.

Dude went to the bed and put his lips close to Handle's mouth. The words were less than a whisper as they whistled thinly through the choked throat, but Dude was able to catch enough of them to understand.

"Scar," Handle gasped. "Scar. Hit me. Tried to stop, but hit. Took money. Canvas bags. Insane."

Dude jerked his face back and stared at him.

"Took the money? Where? Where did he go?"

"Out." Handle lifted his eyes to the kitchen door. "Outside," he whispered. "Heard him outside. Tried to . . ."

"Don't talk," Dude said quickly. "Lie back and don't talk anymore. We'll take care of you."

He stood up and said to Dianne Rhinhardt, "I think he's been hit somewhere in the body. May have internal injuries. I wouldn't try and move him, but do anything you can. And I won't be long. You'll be all right?"

"I'll be all right, Dude."

"And remember, don't open the door for anyone. Lock it after me as soon as I leave."

She nodded.

"Hurry back. And, please God, take care of yourself."

He opened the door and slipped through as the wind blasted through the room tearing a calendar from the wall. Forcing the door from the outside, he held it for a moment, to be sure she had shot the bolt on the inside.

"It's the wind, I tell you," Red said. "God I had no idea it could blow like this out here."

"I tell you it's not the wind," Sis said. "Somebody's banging on that door."

Red groaned, good-naturedly.

"If you think someone's at the door, why don't you get out on that cold floor and open it?"

"I'm not going to go to that door bare-assed naked for anyone," Sis said. "Now be a good guy and haul your lazy butt out of bed and . . ."

"Oh, all right," Red said. "All right."

He slipped out of the covers and his teeth began to chatter as he reached for his trousers and pulled them on.

"Jesus, what a man has to do for a little piece of . . ."

"Sure—sure, it's tough," Sis said, pulling the covers up under her chin. "But just get moving and let 'em in, whoever it is. And you might tell 'em to bring us some coffee."

The gun was in Dude's hand as he pushed past Red and quickly looked around the room.

"Scar," he said. "Has he been here?"

Sis sat up in bed, her mouth open in amazement. Red just stared at him, mouth agape.

"I said has Scar been here? Have you seen him?"

Sis was the first to recover. "What's happened, Dude, what is it?"

Red found his voice as Dude's eyes searched the dark corners of the room.

"He's not here, Dude. Hasn't been here. What's happened?"

"Were you two in here all night?" Dude asked.

"We never left the room," Sis said quickly. "What's it all about?"

Dude turned to Red.

"Get your clothes on," he said. "And bring your gun." He turned again to Sis.

"Scar murdered one of the women last night," he said. "Last night or sometime early this morning."

Sis said, "Oh dear God! Who—who was it? Not Jill?"

"Not Jill," Dude said. "That French singer, Francine."

"How? Why . . ."

"He managed to get her out of the room somehow," Dude said. "Killed her over in the kitchen."

"But why . . ."

"For the obvious reason," Dude said quickly. "You wouldn't want to know the details, Sis, believe me. The man has gone completely berserk. Drunk I guess. He beat Handle and it may be fatal. We have to find him."

"But Dude, why would he . . ."

"That isn't all of it, Sis," Dude said. "He took the money. All of it. Where he is, where he went . . ."

Sis's scream cut his sentence short.

Red dropped the shoe he was holding to the floor and stood up.

"He did what?"

"He's got the money," Dude said. "Handle tried to stop him, but Scar slugged him and knocked him out. Come on now, hurry it up. If he's anywhere around here we want to find him as soon as we can."

Red said, "We'll find the sonofabitch. Find him and shoot him down like a . . ."

"You have to get him," Sis said in a high-pitched scream. "Got to find him and get that money. Oh my God, all that money and he . . ."

"The money isn't the important thing right now," Dude said. "I tell you the man's insane. Completely berserk. We've got to get him before someone else is killed. He can't go anywhere with the money."

"You fool," Sis said, her eyes mad with fury. "You fool, it is the money. The money is the important thing. That's what this is all about. The money. He can't take our . . ."

"Shut up, Sis," Dude said. "You're hysterical. Didn't you hear what I said? I told you he murdered a woman. He may have killed Handle. The man is insane. Do you think he would have taken the money if he wasn't? Where the hell could he go with it? What could he do with it? There's no way out of here. We just have to find him and when we do, we'll find the money also. So calm down. Are you ready, Red?"

Sis threw off the covers and stepped to the floor, stark naked.

"I'll come with you," she said. "I'll help you look. That bastard! Our money . . ."

"For Christ's sake, get back into bed," Dude said. "What do you think you could do if you did find him? Strangle him to death with your pubic hair?"

"You stay here," Red said.

"Stay here and lock that door after us and keep it locked," Dude said. "If he's still here, we'll find him. If he isn't, and he left after this storm started, he can't have gotten far."

She had done everything that she could think to do and it had been pathetically little. Looking down at him as he lay there, his sick eyes staring half blindly at the ceiling, Dianne felt a sense of frustration at her own inadequacy. Her lack of knowledge. If I could only get some food into him, she thought. Some warm broth or almost anything to try and build up his resistance and strength.

Another spasm of hollow coughing came from his throat and it was then she decided to disobey Dude's instructions. She hated the thought of going into the kitchen; she'd seen the blood-spattered floor and knew that some scene of terrible violence had taken place there during the night. But the man had to have something and food was the only thing she could think of which might help.

She said, "Please rest. I'll be back in a few minutes."

It wasn't as bad as she had thought it would be. The trick was just not to look around, keep her eyes on the water boiling on top of the stove.

She'd managed to find the bouillon cubes after a short search and she had the container of them on the tray with the instant coffee she would make for herself. Once, as she waited, the outside door rattled wildly and she thought it was going to burst open. The wind was rising steadily and when she looked over at the window, everything beyond was opaque.

Fifteen minutes later, she was back again with the sick man and she lifted him to a sitting position. He looked at her and he seemed to know what she was trying to do.

She spoon-fed him, like a baby, and it took a long time as he continuously choked and coughed and had a great deal of trouble in swallowing. But she managed at last to get almost a pint of the bouillon into him and when she laid him back in the bed again, he sighed deeply and turned his eyes to her. He said, very weakly, "Thank you."

She looked over at Handle again and got up and adjusted his pillows. She said, "I wish I could do more for you."

He did look slightly better and there was the faint suggestion of color in his face.

"You've done plenty. I'm sorry—sorry to be trouble."

His voice was still weak but she could hear him clearly.

She said, "Please don't talk if it hurts you."

"I'm all right," he said. "It doesn't matter."

She watched his face for several seconds and then she said, "You are his friend, aren't you? Dude."

His head moved and he whispered, "Yes—his friend."

"You're not like those other two," she said. "You're different. You and Dude."

His eyes were speculative as he studied her face and when he again spoke his voice was a little stronger and less of a whisper.

"A mistake," he said. "A bad mistake. He shouldn't be here at all. This is not for him. He's not a killer."

"I don't think either of you are," she said. "I don't think either of you should have been here."

Handle shook his head.

"Me—it doesn't matter. I'm dying anyway. But Dude—I'm sorry for him. It just didn't work out the way we thought it would. I guess nothing ever works out right. No one was supposed to be hurt, to be killed."

His face suddenly congested and he partly raised up in bed as the muscles in his chest and throat contracted and he began again to cough.

She went to him quickly, lifting him up and trying to pat his back.

"Don't talk anymore," she said. "Please, don't talk. Just try and rest."

It took them well over an hour and before they were through; they had covered every possible inch of the ranch house and the grounds. The rooms inside had taken the longest, but it was the outside, the sheds and storeroom and the grounds which had been the worst part of it. The sand blinded their eyes and the bitter wind cut through the fabric of their trench coats and canvas trousers, seeming to penetrate their flesh to the very marrow of their bones.

Twice as they traversed the compound, Dude found currency, once a twenty-dollar bill and once a hundred-dollar bill.

When they were finally through, when he had completely satisfied himself that Scar was nowhere on the place, Dude took Red's sleeve and gestured toward the storeroom. Inside, he shivered and rubbed his hands together.

"Nowhere," Red said. "He isn't here. There's no possible place he could be hiding."

"You mean you think he could have gone?" Dude said. "It's insane, of course, but that is what he must have done. God knows what he could have had in mind. Even without this storm, there is nowhere he could go. No place he could reach."

"Then he must be out there somewhere," Red said, gesturing with one hand toward the desert beyond the compound. "And if he . . ."

"He could be anywhere," Dude said. "Anywhere. But wherever that might be, it can't be far off."

"Well, shall we start looking?"

Dude shook his head.

"Impossible," he said. "Five hundred yards from the house and we would be hopelessly lost in this storm. There's nothing we can do, nothing at all. Just wait. Wait for this thing to blow over, for the wind to die down. You go back there with Sis. I'll be over in a few minutes. I want to see how Handle is doing."

"You're sure, Dude? Sure there is nothing . . ."

"I'm sure," Dude said.

Red left the storeroom, putting his arm up to protect his eyes as he again crossed the compound.

For several minutes Dude stayed where he was, sitting on a packing case, his head bowed.

"It was perfect," he said in a whisper, "perfect. What went wrong? Oh God, how stupid it all is."

For the first time he stopped thinking about the money and began thinking of what had happened. The two men and the woman who had lost their lives. Scar, psychotic, alcoholic, criminally insane, futilely escaping into sure death somewhere out on the mesa. Sis, whose dream had only been money and who had sacrificed everything in the pursuit of it. Handle—but Handle would have died very shortly anyway. The whole thing was such a tragic waste.

He shook his head and again spoke in a whisper, "I've been a fool, a complete fool."

He got up then and pulled his trench coat belt tight and turned the collar up again and went out and fought his way to the door of the kitchen. He knocked on the office door.

He yelled to make his voice heard above the sound of the wind and the storm.

"It's me, Ann. Open up, it's Dude."

She put her finger across her lips and nodded toward the bed when he entered the room.

"He's sleeping," she said. "I disobeyed you and made him some bouillon and I think it helped him."

"Good," he said. "But you shouldn't have gone in the kitchen. I didn't want you to . . ."

"Don't worry about me, Dude," she said.

"All right, I won't. Listen, I have to be busy for a little longer. Do you suppose you could do something?"

"I can do anything you ask me to."

"Give me about five minutes. I want to clean up in there," Dude said, nodding toward the door. "Then go in and make up a couple of big pots of coffee and take it in and give it to those people. They'll be getting up by now. Tell them they will have breakfast later. Think you can manage?"

"I can manage. But suppose, when I open the door . . ."

"I don't think you'll have to worry," Dude said. "If any of them want to come out, it won't matter anyway. There's nowhere they can go, nothing they can do."

She nodded.

"You look strange," she said. "Are you sure you're all right?"

"I'm all right," he said. "Just give me a couple of minutes to clean up, okay?"

"Okay."

They sat next to each other on the bed and he stood facing them, legs apart, his hands on his hips.

"Nothing," he said. "There simply is nothing we can do. Scar is gone and the money is gone. He's out there somewhere in the storm. It would be suicide to try and find him. You might as well face it."

He took the two bills which he had found in the compound from his pocket and tossed them in Sis's lap.

"The money sacks were open where we cut them," he said. "God only knows how much may have spilled out. He may have them with him or he may have dropped them. He could be a thousand yards from the house, a mile or maybe as far as ten miles if he started early enough. There's no way of telling. There is no way of telling in which direction. Only one thing is sure. Until this storm dies down we can't even start looking."

Sis glared at him and her voice was harsh when she spoke.

"You mean you want to just sit here? Let twelve million disappear?"

"I said there is nothing we can do," Dude said. "Red, you were out there with me. Tell her. Tell her what it's like."

"It's bad," Red said looking at the floor. "Bad."

"Bad! My God, what kind of men are you?" Sis screamed. "Are you just going to sit here and let him get away . . ."

"He can get nowhere," Dude said. "Don't you understand? Nowhere. Even if he weren't drunk, even if he weren't weighted down with those canvas sacks, how far do you suppose he could go? And how far could we go if we went out there looking for him?"

"You fool," Sis said, "oh, you fool! You've blown this whole thing. My God, if I were only a man! I wouldn't just sit here. I'd do something."

"Now Sis," Red said. "Now Sis."

"You too," she screamed. "You too! What's the matter with you both, anyway? Doesn't the money mean anything . . ."

Dude sighed and dropped his hands.

"All right," he said, his voice resigned. "All right, whatever you want. But I'll tell you both. Go out into this storm and you'll be committing suicide. As for me, well, I'm going back and get some breakfast. See that those other people are taken care of."

He went to the door and opened it without turning back and without saying anything more.

Sis waited until the door closed and then she took Red's arm and pulled him to his feet.

"Get my coat," she said. "Go on, get it. He can quit if he wants to, but we aren't quitting. I've worked too hard and gone too far, risked too much, to just stop now. There are twelve million dollars out there somewhere and I mean to get my share of it. Come on."

Red slowly shook his head.

"Sis," he said. "For God's sake, Sis, be sensible. Dude's right."

She dropped his arm and pushed him away.

"You too? You? What were all those things you were telling me last night? I was the only one. Anything I wanted, anything, anytime, anywhere. What was that? Just a lot of lies? All right, chicken out if you want to. But give me that gun. If you won't come with me, I'll go alone. I am going to get that money while it is still there to be had. I won't wait for it to blow over. I won't sit back . . ."

Red said, "All right. All right. Just take it easy. We'll try if you insist. But goddamn it, let's not go too far. You don't know what it's like out there, Sis."

"I know the money is out there. He was drunk. He could have fallen within two hundred yards of here. Anywhere. So come on. Let's start moving."

Chapter 11

Lifting his arm and holding his wrist so that he could read the figure in the tiny panel in his watch which showed the date, Kenny Savo said. "Three days! My God, I didn't think that wind was ever going to stop."

Ned Gaines glared at him. "I have to get out of here. I'm going crazy. If I have to spend one more goddamned day . . ."

Mary Mills dropped her bridge hand on the card table face down. "Someone," she said, looking at her partner, Melody Salmon, "should do something about that disgusting man. He can't say a single sentence without swearing."

Hattie Arthur looking up said, "I know how he feels. It's this not knowing. Not knowing what is happening or is going to happen. He's probably still worrying about that actress . . ."

"Let's just finish the hand," Marlo Phillips said. "There's no use speculating. None of us know anything."

"I know one thing," Arch Winter, who'd been watching the game, said. "I know that something must have been happening around here during this storm. The woman disappeared and no one has even seen her. The Rhinhardt girl has left us, but we do know she is still around. I see her in the kitchen when I go in to help with the food but she won't speak with me. The one they call Dude, the pilot, is still with us. But there has been no sign of the other two men or Miss Carr. I think they have gone but I don't understand how they could have left once that storm started."

"If they've gone," Savo said, "it means there is only the one left. Dude, the pilot. He has that helicopter out there. We are," he hesitated, looking around the room, "we are ten, that is ten men, against one. If we could manage to overpower him . . ."

Gene Farris looked up and frowned.

"You're a fool," he said. "If you want to try and tackle a man with a gun, why go ahead. As for me, I'll take my chances in believing him. He told us that forty-eight hours from the time the storm ended, we would be out of here. That someone would be coming for us. I would prefer myself to wait and see if he's telling the truth."

He stood up and walked to the window and looked out and then turned back.

"Sun is beginning to show," he said. "This thing is dying down fast. Be over in another couple of hours."

"Mr. Farris is right," Brandon Mitchell said. "You don't tackle an armed man unless you are very sure you can take him. So far we haven't been harmed . . ."

"Those two girls who are missing," Mary Mills said. "Don't you think they have been harmed? And Dr. Gibbons and that poor little Mr. Griswald?"

Mitchell looked at her coldly and turned away. "We are all in this together," he said, "but we all have our individual problems and responsibilities. I intend to take care of mine and I can only suggest that each of you handle yours as you see fit."

Mr. Weems looked at Walthar Bruno and smiled sweetly.

"Hear, hear," he said. "My problem is where I will get a drink when this bottle is empty. Will you join me, sir?"

Serge Krinsky, the Russian, who had been watching Weems and overheard the remark, looked at the CIA man and said, "You Americans never cease to amaze me. Where in the name of God do you suppose he gets it from? He must have a hidden, a hidden what do you call it—still?"

He put the shovel back in the shed and wiped the sweat from his forehead and turned and went back into the house. He stopped in the office and for several minutes stood there, staring at the floor and seeing nothing. At last he sighed and shook his head and left to go down the long hallway to the bedroom at the end.

She was sitting in the chair, by the window, waiting for him. She looked up and seeing the strained, discouraged expression around his mouth, the sick defeated look in his eyes, she wanted to say something to express her sympathy in some way. But she knew there was nothing she could say.

"I'm sorry, sorry Dude," was the best she could do.

He dropped to the bed and tossed his sweat stained shirt on the floor.

"It's over," he said. "Probably a wasted effort, but I couldn't just let him lie there. I guess they'll dig him up like they will the others when they get here, but maybe they won't. I shouldn't have brought him in on this. He never should have left the hospital in the first place."

"He would have died anyway," Ann said. "You know that. He was with you because he wanted to be."

"I guess so," Dude said. "I guess so. I'm just feeling a little beat. It seemed so perfect in the beginning. And now Handle dead. The others, Sis, Red, Scar, rotting out there somewhere in the desert. Those other three people . . . the money . . ."

He shrugged and looked up at her as she watched him.

"But we're not dead, we're alive," she said. "What's happened has happened and nothing can be done about it. The thing is what are we going to do about it? What happens now?"

He stood up and there was a wry expression on his face as he looked down at her.

"What happens? Well, the helicopter is outside and there's enough gas to get into Phoenix. I have one thing to do before I try and make it across the Mexican border. I want to mail a letter to the police and let them know where these people are and how they get out here for them. After that . . ."

She got to her feet and stood directly in front of him, her eyes on his face.

"I was packing while you were out taking care of Handle," she said. "It didn't take me long. A change of clothes and my jewel case. I'm ready whenever you are."

For several seconds he returned her stare, and then the astonishment leaving his face, he slowly shook his head.

"You don't understand," he said. "I will be running. Today, tomorrow and probably forever. Why within another twenty-four hours, every cop in the country, every cop on the North American continent, will be looking for me. Don't you realize . . ."

"I only realize one thing. I want to be with you. After these last three days together, I want to be with you, always and forever. If you will be running, then we will be running together. So if we are going, I guess we better be getting started."

"But Ann . . ."

"I've been running all of my life," she quickly interrupted. "It will be nice to not be doing it alone. Now—shouldn't we be getting started."

Twenty minutes later Dude strapped her into the seat next to himself and then reached for the switch to start the engine of the helicopter.

For a moment his hand hesitated and he turned to her, eyes filled with a peculiar tenderness.

"Oh, God," he said. "Oh God, I hope we make it!"

She looked back at him, smiled ever so slightly.

"But darling, don't you understand, we have. No matter what happens now, we've made it."

THE END